Adelaide's Gift

Anne Wilson

First paperback edition printed in 2025

A catalogue record for this book is available from the British Library.

ISBN: 978-0-9931390-6-2

Published by Successfactory™ , Chester, United Kingdom

www.thesuccessfactory.co.uk

Illustrations by Martin Teviotdale – tevocreative.com

For my grandchildren:
Hannah, Olivia, Harvey, Alex, and Sophie-Lee

"The beginning of love is to let those we love to be perfectly themselves, and not to twist them to fit our own image – otherwise, we love only the reflection of ourselves we find in them."

Thomas Merton, "No man is an island."

Prologue

Highgate Cemetery, London – March 1914

The ancient trees stood tall, straight and unyielding, like silent sentinels bearing witness to the passage of life. Their dense green canopies offered shelter from the wind and the first droplets of rain as the coffin was carried toward its final resting place.

At the head of the small procession, Reverend Turner pressed onward, his robes billowing in the wind, sail-like, propelling him forward. A tall, skinny boy struggled to hold a large umbrella over his master, wrestling with the gusts. "For heaven's sake, John, put the umbrella down, will you? It's about as useful as a candle without a wick!" The Reverend snapped. Flushing scarlet, John bobbed and fumbled before finally obeying, retreating awkwardly to the rear.

As the mourners entered the graveyard, a curtain of mist unfurled around them, softening the outlines of the ancient gravestones. The worn path led them to the farthest corner, where a solitary grave awaited. The coffin was placed gently on the ground, and the bearers withdrew.

The mourners formed a solemn circle as Reverend Turner began the committal. To one side, a young woman holding a white rose leaned into her companion, drawing comfort from his solid presence. Across from them stood an elderly couple, shifting uneasily. At a respectful distance, three men stood rigid and alert, their gaze sweeping the graveyard with unwavering vigilance.

"Earth to earth, ashes to ashes, dust to dust: in sure and certain hope of the resurrection to eternal life through our Lord Jesus Christ…" Reverend Turner intoned.

As he finished, the bearers carefully lowered the coffin. The young woman stepped forward, casting her rose onto the coffin and whispering something toward the dark depths. Dabbing her eyes with a handkerchief, she stepped aside, allowing the others to approach. One by one, they took handfuls of earth from a small wooden box held out by the Reverend's young assistant and sprinkled it onto the coffin.

As the funeral party began to walk back along the path and towards the church, the young woman hesitated. Shivering, she turned toward a cluster of moss-covered gravestones, ancient and long forgotten. Instantly, her face drained of colour, and before she could react, a dark figure lunged towards her, tackling her to the wet, muddy ground. With terrifying speed, the assailant pinned her down, shoving her head into the sodden grass. "It's all your fault. You killed him, and now you must die too!" the figure howled.

A sharp gasp cut through the mist as the attacker wrenched the woman's head upward, bringing their mouth to her ear. In a chilling whisper that echoed with hatred, they hissed, "Ich verfluche dich für immer!" *I curse you forever.*

Chapter 1

Liverpool, England – Spring 1960

Although the spring sunshine felt warm on Joseph Ellwood's face, he shivered. He had managed to stay strong and determined to give Kitty the perfect send-off she deserved, but now he felt exhausted. The Olde Ship Inn, where they had gathered after the funeral, seemed impersonal, and he could hear Kitty's voice saying, "I don't need a fuss, love. I only need my family." However, their children, Sam and Grace, had other ideas.

Sam had been insistent. "I understand how you feel, Dad, but some people have a long journey home, including me, so we should at least offer them something to eat and drink before they head home."

Grace had agreed. "Perhaps a few sandwiches, and plenty of hot, strong tea! If they want anything stronger, they can buy that themselves."

Eventually, Joseph relented, and they agreed on a simple buffet lunch at the Olde Ship Inn. It was chosen because it was near the Church, and the landlord's wife, Joyce, had been a good friend of Kitty's.

After lots of handshaking and being reminded constantly of the fact that his beloved wife had died, he had finally had enough. As the last of the mourners said their farewells, he faced his children and said, "If you don't mind, I'd like to walk home alone. The fresh air will do me good."

"Dad, are you sure? Sam and I were going to come home with you. I don't think you should be alone right now." Grace took hold of her father's arm as she spoke, tears falling down her cheeks.

"Oh dear, I'm sorry, Dad, I thought I'd finished crying. I can't

3

believe Mum's gone, and we'll never see her again."

"Now, now, then. Chin up, love. Mum wouldn't want you to be sad, would she? I'll be fine, dearie. You have both been wonderful, but I fancy a little fresh air to stretch these old legs. Come over in the morning. I would be grateful for your company then."

Grace looks sadly at her dear dad's sweet, old face and relents, respectful of his wishes. "Well, you know where I am if you need anything tonight, and I'll pop over tomorrow then." Kissing the side of his cheek.

"I'd better be making tracks too, if that's all right with everyone?" Sam moved closer to his dad, shaking his hand firmly. The bond between father and son was unmistakable; no further words or gestures were necessary.

"Of course, son, and I hope Sal feels better soon. Give her my love, won't you?"

"I will, thanks. What a time to catch bronchitis. Sal was devastated that she couldn't be here today. I left Trish with her, who was happy to have a day off school to look after her mum! Why don't you come and stay for a bit? Sal and Trish would love that." Sam paused, realising it was probably the last thing his dad wanted to think about right now, and quickly added, "When you're ready, of course, just think about it and let me know."

Joseph reached out, taking a firm hold of each of his children's hands. "You are and always will be our greatest joy. We were very blessed, and that's no mistake. You get home safe now; Mum would have been so happy to see us all together." The emotion in Joseph's voice was evident, and he turned quickly, walking away to hide the desperate sadness which threatened to overwhelm him.

They watch him for a while, his limp more pronounced, relying heavily on his cane for support. Grace turned to her brother, as the sight of her father walking away alone was more than she could bear. "Keep in touch, won't you? We'll be up to see you all soon. Eleanor loves playing with her older cousin, and as for William, if there's a garden for him to run around in, he's happy."

"That sounds great, sis. I'll ask Sal to give you a call once she's feeling better. It's been wonderful seeing you. It's going to be hard to imagine life without our lovely mum, isn't it?"

"It doesn't feel real." Grace's voice broke, tears brimming. "Safe travels, Sam. See you soon."

Sam pulled Grace into a hug, holding on just a moment longer than usual. Then, with a final wave, he turned and walked toward his car.

Daniel had remained quiet, giving his wife time to say her goodbyes, but now he stepped beside her, wrapping a steady arm around her shoulders. "Come on, love," he murmured. "Let's get you home."

Alone with his thoughts, Joseph allows himself, just for a little while longer, to imagine that today was like any other day. A day when he had returned from his usual morning walk with the paper tucked under his arm, and Kitty was in the kitchen, humming softly as she prepared their breakfast. He pictured the large pot of tea, kept warm beneath a cheerful, multi-coloured knitted cosy, waiting for them to share. He could almost see her now, pouring the tea with care as he recited snippets from the news; some met with a nod, others sparked one of the lively debates he cherished.

Breathing in the crisp spring air, he stopped momentarily to admire the tree-lined avenue where they had lived for over fifty years. The cherry blossoms were in full bloom, and in his humble opinion, that was when Victoria Avenue looked its best. The front gardens were small, but each garden would always have a bright display of spring flowers, presenting a cheerful canvas for anyone to admire as they passed by.

His thoughts drifted to Kitty's funeral. It had been a beautiful service. Her final resting place was a peaceful spot overlooking the River Mersey, which brought him some comfort. It was the right place. Special, even. After all, it was the Mersey that had brought him to her all those years ago, and he had never once regretted the path he chose, no matter the cost. From the moment he met Kitty, he knew, without doubt or hesitation, that his future would begin and end with her.

Reaching into his trouser pocket for his key, he paused momentarily to stare at the front door. It had been painted blue many years ago, Pacific Blue, to be precise. Kitty had set her heart on the colour when he had just wanted to paint it black to match the other front doors in the avenue. Eventually, he relented, as he always did, and was pleased, for it was a beautiful colour and certainly a talking point for every visitor who had ever crossed their threshold. Then, placing his keys in the chipped Worcester pottery dish on the hall table, as he had always done since they had first moved into the house as newlyweds, a wave of tiredness overwhelmed him. His damaged leg was 'shouting' as he used to say to Kitty when it gave him grief.

Sitting heavily in his armchair, he scanned their cosy sitting room, except there was no 'their' anymore. He looked at the empty armchair opposite, choking back the tears. He remembered when he had first bought them. Kitty had set her heart on the matching pair of Queen Anne armchairs decorated in a floral pattern. He couldn't afford them then, and Kitty had told him that it didn't matter, and second-hand would do the job just as well. On his next shore leave, Joseph returned to the furniture shop and could not believe his luck as the chairs were still for sale. He bought them there and then, and Kitty's joy when they were delivered that afternoon meant everything to him. Well-worn and faded over the years, what stories these chairs could share! He noticed Kitty's knitting bag was still on her seat, and her shawl hung over one of the arms. Had it only been two weeks ago when he had thought she was sleeping, her knitting lying on her lap? He had brought her a cup of tea and tried to wake her, but she had gone. Just like that, no warning. Her heart, the doctor said, was a blessing, some might say, but not for Joseph. Kitty was only seventy-two, and they still had a lot of living to do. Trying to shut out the memory of that last day, he closed his eyes and returned to the day they had first met. *Who would have thought that a snap decision to call in at a café one afternoon for a cup of tea and a piece of cake would change the course of his life forever?*

Chapter 2

Liverpool, England - November 1907

Captain Clayton-Barr stood on the deck of the RMS *Carmania*, his hands clasped behind his back as he inspected the four young officers standing to attention before him.

Safely docked in Liverpool, the passengers had disembarked earlier that day, and the crew were already preparing for the next voyage to New York. But for now, the Captain was honouring the four engineers for their bravery in discovering and containing a serious fire in the engine room.

Joseph tried to concentrate as the Captain spoke, but excitement buzzed through him as he was about to transfer to Cunard's brand-new flagship, the RMS *Mauretania*.

"Because of your brave actions, you helped your fellow crewmen escape without injury. Realising the fire was spreading, your quick thinking prevented severe damage to the engine room. The Cunard directors have asked me to award each of you the company's Commendation for Bravery, along with a formal note in your service record."

Joseph stepped forward and saluted as he received his medal. The captain paused, then looked directly at him.

"I believe you're leaving us today, Ellwood?"

"Yes, sir. I'm transferring to the *Mauretania*."

"Well, they're lucky to have you. May you find fair winds and following seas."

The Captain's words touched Joseph, and he stammered out his thanks as the ceremony continued. Once the medals had been awarded, Joseph sought out his shipmate and closest friend, Spider Mason. Of all the crew, he would miss Spider most. They'd been assigned the same cabin when they first joined the

Carmania, and despite being complete opposites, they'd become inseparable.

"Like chalk and cheese, we are!" Spider would often laugh. Joseph had often wondered how Spider had managed to make it through officer training. But beneath the jokes and mischief was a sharp mind and a generous heart. About a week into their first voyage, Joseph finally plucked up the courage to ask, "Spider, was that the name you were christened with?"

Spider had laughed so hard that Joseph had to beg him to stop. "I'm sorry, mate, it's just I thought everyone knew why I'm called Spider!"

"Well, obviously not everyone," Joseph muttered, cheeks flushed.

"It was during my first days at sea. I was about sixteen, and they gave me the job of cleaning out one of the galley stores. I opened the door and there it was—the biggest spider I'd ever seen, just sitting there bold as brass. I went after it with a mop, and I swear on me dear old Nan's grave, the bloody thing turned and chased me!"

"You're winding me up," Joseph said, shaking his head.

"I swear it's true! The crew dined out on that story for weeks. Been Spider ever since."

"What's your proper name—the one your parents gave you?"

"Jack Mason," he said proudly, standing to attention. "Born and raised in Liverpool. Mason men have worked the docks for generations. I'm the only one to go to sea. My pa was that proud—God rest his soul."

Joseph smiled. "I wish you were transferring to the *Mauretania* with me. We make a good team, and I shall miss that ugly mug of yours."

"You cheeky sod! Nowt wrong with this handsome face!" Spider said, gently slapping each side of his face with his hands.

"Anyway, you'll make new mates soon enough," Spider

replied, a mischievous glint in his eye.

Joseph narrowed his gaze. "What are you grinning about now? It was a good idea, and it wouldn't hurt your career, especially as you're about to become a father."

Spider leaned back, looking smug. "Well, it's lucky then that I sent in my papers and got accepted, isn't it?"

"You bugger!" Joseph burst out laughing. "Why didn't you tell me?"

"Thought I'd surprise you. And we couldn't be happier. It means more money, which'll be a real help. Mary's due any day now, and we're praying the little one arrives before we set sail again."

Joseph reached for his cap. "It's going to be a busy stretch, getting her shipshape. I can't wait to get on board and see what she's made of."

"Right. That's enough talk of ships and babies. Let's celebrate. It's high time I showed you the sights of Liverpool. Just go easy on the rum, though—or the missus'll have my hide."

At The Harbour Spoon, Kitty Brown stared wearily at the clock, which ticked on without the slightest regard for her aching back and feet. Across the kitchen, her friend Maude stood at the sink, up to her elbows in soapy water, methodically washing and rinsing delicate cups and saucers. She dreaded a breakage that would surely be docked from her wages by their kind but rather strict employer, Mrs Whitlow.

The café could be found just a short walk from the bustling Albert Dock, tucked between a tobacconist and a newsagent. Clara Whitlow's late husband, Thomas, had been a foreman at the Cammell Laird shipyard across the Mersey. After his death from pneumonia seven years earlier, Clara was left with a modest pension and a small inheritance.

With four children to feed and a reputation for brewing tea strong enough to *'wake the dead and soothe the living,'* Clara had been encouraged to open a small café. Over the years, it had become a popular spot for sailors, dock workers, and local residents, all eager for a hearty cup of tea and a slice of the delicious cakes Clara baked fresh each morning.

Clara had been a close friend of Kitty's mother, and when Kitty was left bereft and alone after her mother's death, Clara took her under her wing. She found Kitty respectable lodgings and offered her work. Kitty enjoyed her job, but on days like today, she longed for work that would be kinder to her aching feet. With only fifteen minutes of her shift left, she thought hungrily of the lamb stew Mrs Croft would undoubtedly be serving that evening, as she always did on Wednesdays.

She sighed as the doorbell rang, announcing the arrival of more customers. Kitty glanced at Maude, hoping she had heard it, but Maude seemed oblivious, quietly humming a tune. Fixing her brightest smile, Kitty grabbed her pad and pencil and stepped into the café.

Her customers were two Merchant Navy officers, dressed in the dark blue uniform of the Cunard Line, complete with brass buttons and peaked caps. That in itself was nothing unusual, but Kitty found herself struck by how handsome the younger of the two was. He stood tall and broad-shouldered, with a strong, athletic build. When he removed his cap, his neatly cropped light-brown hair framed a face that was both confident and inviting. His companion, by contrast, was shorter, stockier, and slightly older, with a shock of curly black hair.

Kitty observed them from a distance as they chose a table by the large bay window, which perfectly framed the docks and the wide expanse of the River Mersey beyond. When they had settled into their seats, she walked over to take their order.

"What can I get you, gentlemen?" she asked.

Joseph was deep in conversation with Spider and hadn't noticed the waitress. When he finally looked up, a pair of cornflower-blue eyes met his with an intensity that stole his words. He simply stared.

Spider chuckled. "I'll order, shall I? What do you recommend for two hungry sailors?"

"We're closing soon, but we still have some Victoria sponge freshly made by Mrs Whitlow this morning." As Kitty jotted down the order, she stole a glance at the younger officer. He was watching her with a warm, lingering smile. The kind that made it impossible not to smile back.

"You're not from around here, are you?" she asked, intrigued.

Spider replied quickly, "It's my accent. Always confuses people." He grinned, making Kitty laugh—it was obvious he was a Liverpudlian.

"I'm Jack, by the way, and this here is Joseph."

"I'm from New Zealand," Joseph said.

"I thought you were, or possibly Australia. It's always hard to tell, isn't it?"

Joseph looked mildly annoyed. "Well, no, not really. Our accents are quite different from the Australians."

"Oh, I'm sorry. I didn't mean to offend," Kitty said, blushing slightly. "I'll go and fetch your tea. It won't take long."

Joseph immediately felt embarrassed. He hadn't meant to sound defensive, wishing, not for the first time, that he could be more relaxed and easy-going like his friend.

Kitty entered the kitchen, calling out for Maude, hoping she'd take over and serve the two men instead. Maude pulled her soapy arms out of the sink and shouted, "What on earth, Kitty! I nearly dropped the cup."

"Sorry, Maude, but we've got customers who want two servings of Victoria sponge and a pot of tea."

Noticing how flustered Kitty seemed, Maude asked, "What's up with you? Have you forgotten how to serve tea and cake?"

"You idiot," Spider chuckled at his friend. "I told you to go easy on the rum! Let's hope the cake and tea sober us up before I get home to the missus."

Kitty watched the two men, puzzled by their amusement. She hoped their laughter wasn't at her expense, as she already felt foolish enough. Over the years, The Harbour Spoon had become a popular stop-off for seafarers from around the world. *You'd think I'd be able to tell the accents apart by now,* she thought, shaking her head. Steadying her breath, she lifted the tray, balancing two generous slices of cake alongside a pot of tea. With careful precision, she carried it to the men, set it down smoothly, poured their tea, and placed the cake before them.

"This looks delicious," Joseph remarked with a warm smile, clearly hoping to smooth over the earlier awkwardness.

"Which ship are you off?" Kitty asked.

Spider spoke before Joseph could answer, knowing it would annoy his friend. "The *Carmania*. Well, we were, but soon we'll join the crew aboard the *Mauretania*."

"Oh yes, the new ship! It's been in all the newspapers. Maude and I went to see it yesterday. It's ever so grand."

This time, Joseph replied quickly. "Yes, we're preparing for her maiden voyage, sailing to New York. We're engineers, and it'll be up to us to get the ship's huge engines running. She's fitted with Parsons turbines, you know. We're aiming for the fastest-ever crossing. Can't let that German ship keep winning the Blue Riband!" Joseph paused, feeling a bit foolish about his sudden burst of enthusiasm. But he was so excited about his new posting and the chance to prove how fast the new engines could move the great ship that he couldn't help himself.

"Well, I hope you win, then. Enjoy your tea, and Maude will see to your bill when you've finished," she said, nodding toward her friend, who had come into the café area to find out who had made Kitty so flustered. Joseph looked crestfallen.

"Are you leaving?"

"My shift's just ended, and I'm off home." She smiled at him and added, "I'll be back tomorrow, though. My name's Kitty, by the way." And with that, she walked back to the kitchen and left them to it.

Joseph watched her go, then turned to his friend, who was happily savouring his cake. "Spider, you've just met the woman I'm going to marry."

Spider snorted, then laughed with a mouthful of cake. "You're barmy, you are!"

Chapter 3

Liverpool, England - Spring 1960

Joseph woke with a start at the sound of knocking. Disoriented, he realised it was morning, and he had fallen asleep in his chair. His leg ached, and a deep shiver ran through him as he realised the fire had gone out. "It's only me!" Grace called through the letterbox. With some effort, he hauled himself from the chair and hobbled to the door, opening it to find his daughter's bright, smiling face.

"Sorry, dearie, my bones are slow this morning," he said with a tired chuckle.

Grace embraced him warmly, noting his rumpled clothes from the previous day and the chill that lingered in the dimly lit house.

"Shall I get the kettle on?" She asked, already making her way to the kitchen without waiting for an answer. "I didn't sleep well and decided to stop trying, so I did some baking instead. Look, I've made some of your favourite biscuits," she said as she pulled a small tin out of her bag.

Although worn in a fashionable bob, Grace's hair was the same golden-brown colour, and her blue eyes and the freckles on her cheeks were almost identical to the precious image he held in his mind's eyes. *So, like her,* he thinks to himself. He sighs, wanting to say something, but stops himself quickly. Instead, he smiles at her and says, "Thank you, love. I'll look forward to eating those later."

Moving towards the empty hearth, Grace says, "Why don't you freshen up a bit, and I'll get the fire lit and a pot of tea brewing."

"Yes, I'll do that, dearie, and change my clothes. I won't be too long." Gripping the handrails on each side of the narrow staircase, he pulls himself up slowly. It was fitted only a month ago by Daniel after Grace had unsuccessfully tried to persuade her parents to move to a bungalow or a flat, as she hated seeing how her father struggled to climb the stairs. Both of them flatly refused to move. The only thing they agreed on was the addition of the extra rail. As the staircase was so narrow, Joseph could reach both rails and haul himself up more easily.

After lighting the fire, Grace put the kettle on and tidied the dishes left on the draining board. There were reminders of her mum wherever she looked, and it took all her strength to hold back the tears that were threatening to fall again. Grace carefully removed the knitting bag and shawl from the armchair, placing them in a cupboard. They will do a proper clear-out when Dad is ready. She could hear him moving about upstairs, and her heart broke again. *What will he do without her? What will I do without her?*

Grace looked fondly around the cosy room and then over at the two armchairs on opposite sides of the fireplace. She had lit the fire as her dad had taught her, and it glowed red and orange, making crackling noises as the fire devoured the kindling sticks and bits of paper to get to the coal. The gleaming fire irons stood smartly on the left. Kitty insisted they should be polished once a week in the winter, relenting to just once a month in the summer. Grace often helped her dad with this job when she was a little girl, spreading the newspapers out on the table for him and handing him the different rags he needed—a comforting routine that brought her joy. *It's funny the things you remember.*

Grace remembered her mum telling her that they had only planned to rent the house, hurriedly searching for somewhere to live before Dad had to return to sea. Just as they were about to sign the lease, the landlord remarked how relieved he was to have found tenants, since the house had been on the market for several years with no buyers showing the slightest interest. Without hesitation, Joseph used the inheritance from his grandfather, received on his twenty-first birthday, and purchased the house then and there. With a twinkle in her eye, Kitty would always laugh at that moment in the story and say, "So you see, this house was waiting for us all along. We were blessed indeed that it became ours."

It had three bedrooms, two of which were a good size, and a small box room. When Sam turned fourteen, he announced that his sister should have his larger bedroom, as he only needed a place to sleep and study. Grace remembered how excited she had been, only to have to wait patiently, as, according to her mum, it needed to be painted in a more feminine colour. Grace only ever remembered laughter and happiness growing up. Not that she wouldn't get a good telling-off when needed, but growing up, she always felt her home was full of love and laughter and a place where she could be herself.

Downstairs, most of their days had unfolded in their cosy sitting room. In addition to the two armchairs, a small settee had been squeezed in along the interior wall as the children grew. Its faded cushions still held the imprint of their childhood: of elbows jostling for space, tangled limbs, and laughter. Despite their pleas, neither of her parents felt that a television was necessary, so the evenings were spent quietly doing homework, reading, and recounting the day's adventures to one another. Grace could almost hear the echo of their voices, causing her to sigh as she smiled, as the memories came flooding back.

At the front of the house was the 'best room,' which Kitty kept spotless for special occasions, where the family gathered for birthdays, Christmases, and to welcome visitors. It featured a bottle-green settee and armchair, and a glass cabinet where her mum's 'special ornaments' were kept safely out of harm's way. The walls held an array of photographs: Sam and Grace at various ages, Mum and Dad's wedding portrait, both sets of grandparents, and the one that always caught Grace's eye—her mysterious Aunt Adelaide, poised at a grand piano, elegant and distant.

Whenever Grace asked about her, Joseph would smile and say, "Your aunt is a famous musician and far too busy performing all over the world to visit us lot!"

Sam and Grace, knowing the tale by heart, would exchange amused glances before chiming in, "We know, Dad. You've told us at least a hundred times!"

Feeling the tears threatening again, she busied herself in the kitchen, making breakfast. A few minutes later, Joseph came down the stairs looking more refreshed. He had changed his shirt and trousers and added a forest green woollen waistcoat. He wore the tartan slippers that Grace had given him last Christmas. Grace had made him toast and had set the table. "Eat some toast first, then later, we can have another brew and try the biscuits!" As they sipped their tea and ate the hot, buttered toast, they discussed the funeral and expressed their gratitude for the many people who had attended the service.

"Mum was well-loved, wasn't she, and not just by us."

Joseph nodded in agreement, "She was, and no mistake. There wasn't an unkind bone in her body, and she was a saint putting up with me for all those years." He chuckled, trying to disguise the grief that wanted to consume him. When they had finished eating, Grace wondered if there was anything he wanted her to do.

"Perhaps you could tidy a few of her things away upstairs? I can't face it right now, seeing her things breaks my heart. Maybe just a few of her bits and pieces, though, not everything. I'm not ready for that yet."

Grace begins to tidy away the breakfast things when Joseph stops her. "I'll do this, dearie, need to keep busy. You go upstairs and see to your mum's things." Grace smiles and goes upstairs to her parents' bedroom.

Kitty's nightdress still lay on the bed, neatly folded and resting on her pillow, just as it had ever since Grace could remember. Tears welled in her eyes as she realised her dad hadn't been able to bring himself to sleep in their bedroom. Grace couldn't even begin to imagine how her dad was feeling. Apart from when he was at sea during the early days, Grace didn't think they had been apart for more than a day at most. She lifted her mother's lavender-scented nightdress and pressed it to her cheek. With a sigh, she opened the cupboard in the bedside table, deciding it was the best place to tuck her mum's belongings away—for now. Out of sight, out of mind, until the time felt right. As she placed the nightdress inside, her hand brushed against a muslin-wrapped parcel tied with a blue ribbon. Curious, she pulled it out and peeled back the cloth, revealing an ornate silver box. Tracing the decorative filigree birds on the lid before opening it, she was torn between guilt and fascination. It was a music box. Feeling for the key beneath, she wound it gently until it stopped. The melody, though crackling with age, was unmistakable: Beethoven's *Für Elise*.

Rushing down the stairs, she called out, "Look what I've found inside Mum's nightstand! I promise I wasn't snooping; I just noticed it when I was tidying things away."

"Well, that's a surprise," Joseph remarked. "I'd completely forgotten about it." Taking it from her, he moved towards the window, turning the box over in his hands and examining it more closely in the light. Then, with deliberate care, he lifted the lid, as though afraid to disturb the memories carefully tucked within. Inside was an old sepia photograph, a delicate floral brooch, and a gold locket.

Curiosity sparked in Grace's eyes as Joseph handed her the faded photograph, showing a young couple laughing as they looked towards the camera.

"Is this an old picture of you and Mum?" she asked, studying the two youthful faces.

Joseph's smile was gentle, touched with nostalgia. "No, it's your Aunt Adelaide. She must have been about eighteen or nineteen there."

Grace looked again, more closely this time. "And who's the young man with her? They look so happy together."

Joseph frowned; his memory was not as sharp as it once was. "I think this was taken at a family picnic. I remember Adelaide writing to me about it. I was already at sea by then and married to your mum. The young man beside her, if I recall correctly, was Valentine Spielmann. He was Adelaide's piano tutor before she went to study at the Royal Academy of Music in London. It was all quite tragic in the end, but that's a story for another day."

"How romantic yet sad at the same time," Grace replied as she kept staring at the photograph.

"You said Aunt Adelaide studied music? I knew she was a renowned pianist, but I didn't realise she actually studied at such a prestigious place as the Royal Academy of Music?"

"Yes—the pianoforte, if you want the formal term, and she earned a degree," Joseph said with pride.

"That's incredible. I didn't realise women could study for degrees back then!"

Joseph smiled. "Not many did, and it certainly wasn't easy for her. She was a determined and gifted woman. I was so proud of her." His voice wavered slightly as a memory he preferred to keep buried surfaced, momentarily interrupting his thoughts.

It's time, Joseph thought. Then, turning to Grace, he said, "We'd better put the kettle on as I think it's about time I told you all about my sister Adelaide and the significance of this music box, and its contents."

Chapter 4

It was the perfect summer's evening. After a day of sweltering heat, a salt-tinged breeze drifted in from the harbour, carrying with it a welcome coolness that settled over the elegant garden belonging to Robert and Marie Ellwood. As the light waned, candles were lit in readiness for their daughter Adelaide's twelfth birthday.

Marie Ellwood felt her usual flicker of disappointment with her daughter's choice of celebration. Adelaide had dismissed her suggestion of a picnic in the Botanic Gardens with her friends, opting instead for a quiet gathering at home. To Marie, such reluctance to engage with her peers seemed unbefitting of a young girl from a good family. Yet Adelaide remained resolute, preferring to be in the company of grown-ups rather than the chatter of her peers. Marie constantly fretted over her daughter's solitary nature, while Robert quietly indulged his precious daughter's need for solitary pursuits.

The only exception was Adelaide's closest friend, Charlotte. Born only months apart, the girls had shared their earliest steps and secrets, forming a bond that far surpassed the fleeting alliances of the classroom. Charlotte's parents, Susannah and John Montgomery, had been longstanding friends. John, a senior official at Government House, worked with Robert, handling matters both colonial and domestic. Meanwhile, Susannah and Marie enjoyed Wellington's growing social scene. At afternoon teas and charity galas, they were fixtures of a refined society, their names frequently appearing in the civic columns of the Dominion and the Evening Post.

Marie shifted her attention to the guests gathered around the dining table, which had been beautifully arranged by their capable housekeeper, Peggy Doyle. At the head of the table, Robert was expertly carving an impressive leg of lamb, the silver carving knife catching the glow of the candlelight. Marie presided at the opposite end, ensuring that glasses were filled and that everyone helped themselves to the generous bowls of buttered potatoes, glazed carrots, and freshly shelled peas. Laughter rippled across the table, sparked by a joke from Charlotte's brother, Miles, which had particularly amused the younger guests. Eighteen-year-old Joseph was seated beside Miles, and he found himself at odds with where he fitted in. Expected to adopt the air of a young gentleman, he struggled to feign interest in his parents' genteel conversation about politics and diplomatic receptions. In truth, he found it all dreadfully dull. Miles reminded him of his own fourteen-year-old self, curious and occasionally prone to chaos. Joseph chuckled at the memory of a misadventure involving a science kit and a disregard for the instruction booklet that had resulted in a chemical mishap so noxious that Peggy had refused to clean his room for weeks.

He glanced toward his sister, now deep in animated conversation with Charlotte. Whatever they were discussing had sent both girls into an irrepressible fit of giggles, making Joseph laugh along with them.

When the main course was finished, Peggy swiftly cleared the table and returned a little while later, carefully carrying Adelaide's birthday cake. She placed it at the head of the table where everyone could admire it. Peggy had enlisted her sister's help in baking it, knowing there was no way to keep a secret from Adelaide for long. But the look of complete joy on Adelaide's face made all the secrecy worthwhile. It was a beautiful cake, covered in white icing and decorated with pink rosebuds, with twelve small candles arranged on top. As she made to return to the kitchen, Peggy quickly glanced back at Adelaide, who looked lovely in her plain cream dress and long, golden-brown hair tied with a blue ribbon. Peggy made a hasty exit before they could see her eyes fill with tears. *Everything will change now with Adelaide starting at that fancy school in January,* she thought to herself.

Peggy had been with the Ellwood family since Mr and Mrs Ellwood were newlyweds and had offered her a place to live and work when Marie found her one day sitting on the only thing she was allowed to fill, a carpet bag, crying as the bailiffs took away all her precious belongings and turned her out of the home she had shared with her husband before he ran off and left her all alone. She acted as a lady's maid, cook, housekeeper, and nursemaid when the babies arrived. Mrs Ellwood was a kind and generous lady, and Peggy was content with her life. She had given up any ideas of remarrying and having children of her own, as, technically, she was still married to her husband, Patrick, who had run away because he couldn't keep a job or stop spending the little money they had on beer and card games. As she began to wash the dishes, Peggy secretly hoped that Adelaide would not consider herself too old to sneak into the kitchen after school for milk and biscuits and sit in her favourite chair with Mrs Whiskers, the kitchen cat, purring on her lap, chattering like a ha'penny book and unable to stop the words tumbling from her mouth as she told Peggy all about her day.

In the dining room, Robert lit the candles and said, "Come on, Adelaide, blow your candles out and make a wish!"

Adelaide took a deep breath as she prepared to blow out the flickering candles. With a determined exhale, the flames danced for a moment before surrendering to the darkness. A wave of applause erupted around her, filling the room with warmth and celebration. Her eyes sparkled, reflecting the glow of love and joy that surrounded her.

"Well, my dear, would you like to know what else we've got for you for your birthday?" Marie looked over at her daughter, smiling affectionately.

Adelaide nodded enthusiastically. "Yes, please, I wasn't expecting another present!"

"There's just one more surprise for you. I hope you know how proud your father and I are of how accomplished you are becoming at playing the piano, and it is obvious how much you enjoy your piano lessons."

"That's a matter of opinion." Joseph piped up, which caused a ripple of laughter and a frown from his father.

"Now, where was I?" Marie pretended to be confused.

"You were about to tell me about my birthday present!" Adelaide shouted, glaring at her brother, who was grinning broadly next to Miles, who was trying not to laugh.

"Yes, indeed. So, we felt it was time for you to learn from someone perhaps more qualified than Miss Merton, who, of course, has done a wonderful job so far," Marie added swiftly.

Marie smiled warmly at her daughter and continued, "So, I've arranged for the music teacher at your new school to tutor you. She comes highly recommended by the headmistress, Mrs Easterwood.

"Really? I don't know what to say except thank you so much!" Adelaide exclaimed, throwing her arms around her mother in an enthusiastic hug. Marie chuckled, but as Adelaide's excitement nearly sent them tumbling, she gently grasped her daughter's shoulders and pushed her back. "I think you've thanked me enough now. You'll have us both over!"

Later that evening, as the house settled and their guests had departed, Robert poured himself a nightcap and sank into his chair.

"Well, I think that went well," he remarked, swirling the amber liquid in his glass.

Marie sighed, a wistful smile playing on her lips. "It was a wonderful evening, dear, yet I fear our children are growing faster than I care to keep up with."

Robert nodded, sipping his whiskey in quiet agreement.

The following Saturday, after a restless night, Adelaide felt a wave of relief as the early morning light filtered through her bedroom window. Sitting up and stretching her arms, she murmured happily, "At last, today's the day for my piano lesson!" She dressed in a flurry of excitement and was already pestering Peggy for breakfast by seven o'clock.

"You're far too early!" Peggy chided. "If you eat now, you'll be hungry again by nine. Why don't you go back to your room and find something to do until it's time for breakfast?"

Adelaide clasped her hands together, her excitement spilling over. "But Peggy, I'm far too excited. Please let me stay in the kitchen with you."

Peggy sighed, shaking her head. "Oh, all right then. But don't get under my feet. I must make sure your father and brother have a good breakfast this morning, as they are off to watch a cricket match today."

"Cricket is boring. It goes on and on and on forever." Adelaide said, pulling a sulky face.

"And how would you know? You've never even watched a cricket match!" Joseph retorted as he appeared in the kitchen.

"Joseph, you are up! I couldn't sleep. I am so excited, and Peggy says I can't have breakfast yet."

"Well, she's quite right, but as Father and I are having an early breakfast, I'm sure it will be all right for you to join us."

Adelaide jumped up and followed her brother to the dining room. Mr Ellwood was already there, drinking from a teacup and reading his paper. Peggy followed them in and began to set another place for Adelaide.

"Good morning, Father. Can I join you for breakfast? I am far too excited to wait any longer."

"Adelaide, sit quietly. You know better than to interrupt your father," Peggy admonished.

Adelaide, looking a little sheepish, turned to her brother, hoping he would share her excitement. Instead, Joseph was struggling to stifle a laugh—a reaction Adelaide did not appreciate. She shot him a sharp look before sticking out her tongue in defiance.

"You're certainly up with the larks this morning." Robert's voice emerged from behind his newspaper, which formed part of his cherished morning ritual. His children had learned from an early age that interrupting him was simply not done. Yet today, he found himself unable to suppress a quiet smile, moved by his daughter's boundless enthusiasm.

Hidden behind the folds of his newspaper, he remained acutely attuned to his children's activities. With a soft sigh, he reflected on how much was changing. He still wrestled with the reality of Joseph embarking on an apprenticeship in Engineering, clinging to the hope that his only son might reconsider and pursue a career in law. And as for his daughter. How swiftly those twelve years had flown by. Her extraordinary talent for the piano filled him with pride, yet he couldn't help but wonder where it would all lead.

He realised Joseph had said something to him. "What was that, Joseph? I didn't hear you?"

"I was just saying I hope Wellington wins today after losing to Auckland the other week."

Folding his newspaper meticulously, Robert had concluded his normal, peaceful morning routine was at an end.

"I hope so, too. It was such a close-run thing. Let's hope Wellington is better prepared today."

Adelaide interrupted their talk of cricket, too excited to be quiet any longer. "Father, did you know I have my first piano lesson today?"

Robert turned his attention to his daughter, "Well, no, I wasn't aware of any such thing. Are you sure? I don't remember your mother mentioning it to me."

Adelaide's face showed her disappointment just as Marie entered the room and put Robert straight. "Don't be a tease. You know full well Adelaide has a piano lesson this morning. But it is not until nine o'clock, young lady. Why are you up so early?"

After breakfast, Adelaide sat at her piano, her eyes fixed on the clock. Its hands seemed to slow deliberately, teasing her impatience as she eagerly awaited the arrival of her music teacher, Miss Ivery. Suddenly, a wave of nerves swept over her. In all her excitement, she hadn't stopped to consider what Miss Ivery might be like. What if she were terribly old, like Miss Merton, or strict enough to rap her knuckles with a ruler when she made a mistake, just as Edith's teacher did? Worse still, what if she lacked the skill to teach Adelaide the music she so desperately longed to master? With butterflies flapping around her stomach, Adelaide toyed with the idea of fleeing to her bedroom. But her thoughts were interrupted by the sound of the doorbell. Moments later, her mother and Miss Ivery appeared. Summoning her courage, she stood up and approached them, managing a shy "Hello" as she met Miss Ivery for the first time.

"Hello, Adelaide. It's a pleasure to meet you, and I'm very much looking forward to teaching you. What a beautiful piano you have."

Adelaide barely heard Miss Ivery's words. Relief flooded through her as she took in the young woman's warm smile and the blonde curls that peeked rebelliously from beneath her hat.

"It belonged to my grandfather," Adelaide explained, her voice barely a whisper. "He gave it to me because he said I showed real promise and encouraged me to practise regularly."

A brief silence passed before Miss Ivery spoke again, gently steering the moment forward. "Why don't you play something for me? I'd love to get a sense of where you are in your musical journey."

Uncertain, Adelaide turned to her mother for guidance. "What do you think I should play, Mother?"

Marie smiled reassuringly. "Why don't you choose one of the pieces you enjoy most? Miss Ivery only wishes to gauge your level. Now, I must take my leave. Enjoy your lesson, Adelaide."

Adelaide hesitated for only a moment before sitting at the piano, carefully lifting the fallboard to reveal the ivory keys. She considered her options, then chose a simple arrangement of *Ode to Joy* from Beethoven's Ninth Symphony, the last piece she had worked on with Miss Merton.

Positioning her hands carefully, she concentrated as she tried to recall the opening. She played steadily for a few minutes before pausing, uncertain how long Miss Ivery expected her to continue. Miss Ivery rose from her seat and approached with a thoughtful look. "Are you sure that's your favourite piece of music?"

Adelaide hesitated. "I'm not sure. It's what my previous teacher had me working on, but I don't think it's my favourite."

Miss Ivery gave a kind nod. "Then let's try something different. Can you read music at sight?"

Adelaide's stomach fluttered. "Yes," she said at last, though her voice betrayed a trace of nervousness.

From her elegant leather case, Miss Ivery drew out a sheet of music and laid it on the stand. "Here is a little German folk tune, arranged by Beethoven. It's quite simple. Don't worry about being perfect; enjoy the music."

Adelaide bent over the page and began to play. The melody was light and cheerful, and before long, she found herself smiling. When she finished, she let out a sudden laugh—half relief, half delight and Miss Ivery's eyes softened in approval.

As the lively music drifted through the house, Marie prepared to depart for her meeting with the Wellington Ladies' Society, where she holds the position of President. Peggy helped her into her coat, a small smile dancing on her lips as she listened to the melodies from the library.

"I think it's going well, Mrs Ellwood," Peggy remarked as she passed Marie her gloves.

Marie nodded, though her agreement was hesitant. "It does seem that way." Yet, as laughter floated through the doorway, she found herself pausing. Piano lessons, in her experience, had never involved laughter. She couldn't help but wonder what had amused them.

The hour slipped away too quickly, and Adelaide felt a pang of sadness as the lesson drew to a close.

"Remember, Adelaide," Miss Ivery said gently, "music is more than just playing an instrument well. As you grow and learn, it will become a part of you — almost sacred. Before you share it with others, you must first learn to treasure it yourself."

Adelaide stared at her teacher in quiet wonder. A lightness replaced the usual tension she felt when she longed to express what the music meant to her. Here, at last, was a kindred spirit to guide her.

Later that day, a jubilant Joseph returned from an exhilarating cricket match in which Wellington had finally claimed victory. At the same moment, Marie arrived home from her meeting, and the two entered the house together. Joseph helped his mother off with her coat and asked how the piano lesson had gone.

"I'm not sure yet, as I had to leave just as the lesson began. It all sounded rather frivolous for a piano lesson in my mind, but Miss Ivery seems very capable. I'm sure Adelaide will want to tell us all about it!"

"Well, hopefully it wasn't a total disaster then," Joseph said with a mischievous twinkle in his eyes.

"Joseph! What are you talking about? I'm sure it wasn't. Miss Ivery believes there is considerable potential in Adelaide after speaking with Miss Merton. Go and freshen up, then come to the kitchen, and you can ask Adelaide all about it yourself."

"Miss Ivery? Her name is Miss Ivery?" Joseph burst into laughter, clutching his sides in exaggerated amusement.

"What's the matter with you? What's so funny?" came the sharp response. "Miss Ivery is a highly respectable young lady, personally recommended by Mrs Easterwood. And I'll have you know, her father was a vicar with his own parish!" Exasperated and utterly baffled by her son's uncontrollable laughter, Marie shook her head and made her way to the kitchen, certain that was where she would find her daughter. As Marie entered, a smile tugged at her lips. The cosy kitchen exuded warmth, filled with the comforting aroma of baking. Peggy was carefully lifting a tray of golden fruit scones and a perfectly baked apple pie from the oven, all the while listening attentively to Adelaide, who sat curled up on a chair with Mrs Whiskers purring contentedly on her lap.

"Oh, hello, Mother. I've been waiting ages for you to return! I had the most wonderful piano lesson with Miss Ivery. Am I to have another one next week? Is Joseph home? Did Wellington win?" Adelaide's chatter was like the sound of a fast train, her words tumbling from her mouth. Marie held her hands up in mock surrender. "Slow down, young lady, and give me a chance to answer! Yes, you have another lesson next week, and your brother is home. I'm surprised you didn't hear him. For some reason, your piano teacher's name has sent him into fits of laughter."

Peggy and Adelaide exchanged a glance, their eyes sparkling with mischief, before dissolving into giggles.

"It's her surname, Mrs Ellwood," Peggy said, stifling a laugh. "Miss Ivery teaches piano."

Mrs Ellwood blinked, unamused. "I fail to see the joke. I think you're all being rather—oh! Ivery. Ivory! Well, I never. What an exquisitely apt name for a piano teacher."

Joseph wandered into the kitchen just as Marie let out a delighted laugh, the realisation dawning. He took one look at her and burst into laughter himself.

"That's enough, all of you," Marie said, pulling herself together. "It's not right to laugh at someone's name. She must be tired of hearing the same jokes. I want you all to promise not to make fun of her surname again."

"We promise," they chorused, and Joseph wasted no time in swiping several scones from the cooling rack. Peggy playfully swatted at his hands in protest.

"Now, where has your father got to? We're invited to dine with the Lawsons, and I don't want to be late."

Chapter 5

Dunedin, New Zealand – January 1905

Hands gripping the handlebars, Joseph skidded to a halt at the entrance to the Foundry, where he would spend the next two years learning his trade. He dismounted, feeling a mix of awe and anticipation tighten in his chest. With a deep breath, he pushed his bicycle through the towering iron gates and stepped into the noisy, energetic world of a working foundry.

Today marked Joseph's first official day as an apprentice at Joseph Sparrow and Sons, and he was eager to begin. Convincing his parents to support his chosen path hadn't been easy, but he had held firm. Even now, he shuddered at the memory of the day he told his father…"

After a full day at Government House and on evenings when he wasn't at his Club, Robert liked to retreat to the sanctuary of his study. His large oak desk was cluttered with books, and he was halfway through one, reading glasses perched precariously on the bridge of his nose. He traced each line with the tip of his right index finger. A glass of whisky stood within easy reach while a well-used pipe rested in an ashtray nearby. The room was heavy with the scent of old books and tobacco. *If there were ever a scent called 'My father,'* Joseph thought, *this would be it.*

Robert was so absorbed in his reading that he was unaware of Joseph standing in the doorway. Joseph gave a gentle cough to announce his presence.

"Joseph, what are you doing hovering by the door? Come in, boy. How was school today?" Robert relished hearing about Joseph's academic progress. He had grand aspirations for his son to follow in his footsteps to study law at Oxford, as he had and as his own father had before him.

"School was fine, thank you. We had Science this morning—my favourite subject." Joseph's voice faltered as unease flickered across his face. He shifted his weight, fingers twitching at his side, the words he'd rehearsed suddenly tangled in hesitation. After a shallow breath, he stepped forward and stammered, "Could I talk to you about my plans… after I leave school?"

"Of course, sit down," Robert said, gesturing to the leather armchair opposite him. "Have you been reading the material I gave you about Oxford? I can't tell you how proud it would make me to see you go there."

"Yes, I'm sure it would," Joseph replied, his voice quieter now. "But there's something I need to tell you."

Robert set his book down, narrowing his eyes slightly. "Well? Spit it out."

Joseph swallowed hard. In the space of a few heartbeats, he knew without any doubt that he was about to disappoint his father.

"It's like this, Father," Joseph began carefully. "You know how I've always loved taking things apart and putting them back together again? Even when it got me into trouble?"

Robert raised an eyebrow. "Don't I just. Especially with my clocks—always fiddling with them. But I'll give you credit, you usually managed to get them ticking again."

Suddenly, Robert snapped his book shut with a loud thud. "Good grief, Joseph, you haven't broken one of my antique clocks, have you?"

Joseph raised his hands in surrender as if his father had drawn a weapon. "No, no, nothing like that. I'm trying to explain. What I mean is... my passion lies with machines like automobiles and trains... but especially ships."

Robert's expression darkened. "Where is this going, Joseph? Are you trying to tell me you don't want to become a lawyer?"

"Yes, I am," Joseph said, steadying his voice. "And I don't

want to disappoint you, truly I don't. But what I want, what I've always wanted, is to be an engineer. Especially if I could work aboard one of the great ships, like the ones that sail to and from New Zealand or even to New York."

As Joseph spoke, the colour in Robert's face deepened steadily. He gripped the arms of his chair, clearly struggling to contain his temper. But restraint gave way to fury, and he finally erupted in a torrent of words.

"Ungrateful! All that money, wasted! You'd throw your life away to tinker with engines? It's shameful, Joseph! Deeply disappointing! And what on earth am I supposed to tell your mother?"

Each word struck like a slap, and Joseph flinched under the force of them. But he held his ground.

"I'm sorry you feel that way," he said quietly, "but this is what I want. Engineering is my path, whether you understand it or not."

Robert's eyes narrowed. His voice was cold now, clipped and final.

"Go to your room. I'll speak to you in the morning. You can forget about joining us for dinner; Peggy can bring you a tray. I don't want to see you again tonight."

"But Father …"

Enough! I don't want to talk to you right now. Go to your room!"

Joseph bolted from the study, brushing past Marie so fast he nearly knocked her over, then thundered up the stairs and slammed his bedroom door shut behind him.

"Robert, what on earth just happened?" Marie called from the hallway. "I could hear you shouting all the way from the garden."

Robert stood rigid, fists clenched. "Do you know what your son just told me?"

Marie raised an eyebrow. "*My* son? I was under the impression he belonged to both of us."

"Yes, yes, of course he does," Robert snapped, waving a hand impatiently. "Don't interrupt me. I'm too angry right now. Maybe I should calm down and speak to you later."

"You'll do no such thing," Marie said firmly, stepping into the study and closing the door behind her. "You will sit down, take a deep breath, and tell me what's going on—now."

Marie was a strong-willed woman, her voice calm but commanding, the kind of woman Robert usually admired. Today, however, his temper was still smouldering, and all he wanted was to shout in frustration over what he saw as Joseph's foolish ambition. But he knew from experience that arguing with Marie in this state would get him nowhere.

With a heavy sigh and a muttered curse, he dropped into his chair, right onto the edge of his whisky glass, which tipped and shattered on the floor.

"Damn and blast it, Marie. Now look what's happened."

"Damn and blast all you like. Peggy will clean it up later. Now, talk to me. What did Joseph say?"

Robert exhaled sharply, dragging a hand through his hair, and calmly tried to explain what had just transpired between them.

"I just can't believe he'd throw his life away like this," Robert muttered. "Why would he want to work on a ship when he could study law and build a successful career in government, like I have? It offers so much more than a grubby engine room. I don't understand what's gotten into him."

Marie's tone was calm but pointed. "Did Joseph say he wanted to work in a grubby engine room, or did he say he wanted to become an engineer?"

Robert frowned, rubbing his forehead. "What are you getting at?"

"I'm saying there's a difference," she replied. "Have you not been aware of where his interests lie as he has grown up?

35

Remember that year he won first prize at the science fair and the cart he built for himself and Adelaide, complete with working brakes and a steering wheel? Need I go on?"

Robert sighed. "Yes, yes... and my poor clocks—always disappearing, only to be found in pieces on his bedroom floor."

"Exactly. So, what does that tell you?"

"I know, I know," he admitted, running a hand through his hair again. "He enjoys building, creating, and fixing things. And he's never shown the slightest interest in law books or sitting behind a desk for hours like I do. But that's not the point. Tinkering won't earn him status. It won't lead to a respectable income, at least not the kind we've worked hard for."

Marie moved closer, gently wrapping her arms around his shoulders. With a sigh, she leaned her head against his.

"We always knew this day would come," she said softly. "When our children would begin carving their own paths, just like we did. We were fortunate to have found each other, and we have built a wonderful life together. Is it really for us to say what our son should do? We could certainly persuade him to attend Oxford. And being the good son he is, he would go on to become a successful lawyer. But he wouldn't be happy, Robert. You must see that."

Robert tilted his head slightly, looking up at her. Then, slowly, he reached for her hand. "I suppose I've known for a while that Joseph might choose a different path. I just always hoped, when the time came, he'd change his mind."

"I know," Marie said softly. "It reminds me of your brother Edward. He defied your father's wishes, didn't he? You've never really talked much about him. Even Henry rarely mentions his older brother."

"Poor Edward," Robert murmured. "He died so young, living in poverty."

"But you once told me that Edward was happy and content to

be living his life on his own terms."

Robert shook his head slowly, and Marie moved to the armchair across from him. She folded her hands in her lap and tilted her head slightly, inviting him to speak.

He nodded, gathering old memories from the corners of his mind. "I remember the arguments as if they were yesterday. When they started, Henry and I would slip out into the garden, taking little Alice with us. Father was beside himself, furious that his eldest son preferred painting to studying. He couldn't understand it."

He paused, his voice softer now. "Eventually, Edward ran away. He ended up in Barcelona, poor but happy. We never saw him again. He died far too young, and his friends paid for his funeral, but Father refused to attend, and it broke Mother's heart. It's something he regretted for the rest of his life."

Marie listened in silence, her expression softening.

"I was in my first year at Oxford when we heard the news of his passing, and Henry was working in London. We used all our spare money to travel to Barcelona to meet some of his friends. They were very Bohemian," he added with a faint, rueful smile. Marie returned it knowingly.

"They'd kept all of Edward's paintings. You know the rest. We shipped them all back to New Zealand, and our parents found some peace in displaying them throughout Woodlands."

Robert pointed across the study to a large oil painting. An elegant rendering of Oxford's spires bathed in evening light. "This one's my favourite," he said quietly.

Marie was silent for a moment, then turned to her husband and said, "If that's not an example of the importance of following your dreams rather than living to please others, I don't know what is. Not everyone's path is the same. Why don't you go and talk to him? Suggest we help him find an apprenticeship with a reputable company so he can learn the trade properly."

Robert looked at his wife, shaking his head in frustration. "If only Edward had focused on his studies and chosen a 'proper' career, he might still be here. I won't let our son waste his life. He needs to go to Oxford, and if he still wants to become an engineer after that, we can talk again."

Marie inhaled sharply, frustrated by her husband's stubbornness. Weeks of cajoling and discussions followed. With the help of her brother-in-law, Henry, they eventually secured Joseph a place at a successful engineering company in Dunedin, which was willing to offer him an apprenticeship. Robert, though reluctant, finally relented but gave his son a stern warning, "Don't come crawling back when you realise you've made a mistake. You've burned your bridges now."

So, that was how Joseph came to be standing outside Joseph Sparrow and Sons on a sweltering hot day in January, gripping the handlebars of his bicycle, rooted to the spot.

Ted Griffiths, the foreman responsible for overseeing the two new apprentices, spotted the boy standing like a statue, sweat glistening on his forehead. "Good God," he muttered to himself. "He's going to get himself flattened the minute the shift bell goes." Cupping his hands to his mouth, he bellowed, "Hey, you! What do you think you're doing, standing in the middle of the road like that? You'll get yourself crushed. The shift bell's about to go, and in a few seconds three hundred men are going to come pouring through those gates—move your skinny arse!"

Joseph was so shocked by the roar of the foreman's voice that it shook him out of his stupor. He leapt to the side just as the siren screamed. The great iron doors swung open, and a swarm of tired, grimy men poured through the gates.

"You daft bugger," Ted said, pretending to cuff him but

deliberately missing. "Are you trying to get yourself killed on your first day? Which one are you, anyway?"

"Joseph Ellwood, sir. Sorry about that, first-day nerves, I suppose. It won't happen again."

"Hmm. Well, make sure it don't. Welcome to Sparrows, Joseph. You've got the right name for the job, that's for sure." Ted chuckled at his own joke. Joseph wasn't sure whether to laugh, but did so anyway, immediately warming to the man.

A flat cap shaded Ted's eyes from the morning sun, and his face bore the rugged texture of tanned leather, weathered by time and work. He wore blue overalls, and on his feet a pair of well-polished hobnail boots coated in a layer of foundry dust. "Come on, lad," said Ted. "I'll show you where the locker room is. You can stash your things and change into your work gear there. You'll be issued two pairs of overalls each year you're with us. If you lose or damage them, it will be deducted from your pay. If your parents can afford it, they can buy you a spare set. The same goes for the boots; keep them clean. I like to see a bit of polish, so you'd best learn."

"Yes, sir," Joseph replied, pushing his bicycle and hurrying to keep pace with the foreman's brisk stride.

Inside the locker room, the other new apprentice had already changed into his overalls and was busy tying his bootlaces.

"Ah, you must be the other one," Ted said. "Joseph Ellwood, meet Jethro Gilbert. My advice? Help each other. This ain't a competition. Work together, and you'll learn faster. Got it?"

"Yes, sir," the boys chorused.

Ted gave a wry smile. "And just so you know, this isn't the bloody Army. My name's Mr Griffiths. If, after a year, I think you've earned it, then and only then, you can call me Ted."

There was a lot to take in that first day, but Joseph was in his element. The vast workshops buzzed with noise and energy, and he found the machinery and the organised chaos utterly fascinating.

At lunchtime, he sat with a few of the older men and soaked up all he could. That's when he learned that Joseph Sparrow, the company's founder, was a mechanical engineer who, along with his brother Robert Spiers Sparrow, had established the Victoria Ironworks back in 1879. They had built everything from bridges and gold dredges to steam engines and brass castings. It was a lot to absorb all at once, but what stood out most to Joseph was the talk of steam engines. His eyes lit up at the very mention. Steam engines were exactly what Joseph dreamed of working on. But when he said so, Ted chuckled, lifted his flat cap, and scratched his head. "Slow down there, lad. You've got to walk before you can run. There's a lot to learn before I'll let you anywhere near one of those big beasts." Still, Ted was quietly pleased by the boy's enthusiasm.

For now, Joseph's duties included sweeping the work areas, fetching tools, running errands, and observing without getting in the way. But that didn't bother him in the slightest. He was finally learning the trade he had dreamed of, and his future as a ship's engineer was no longer a fantasy. It was just over the horizon, and he could hardly wait. Joseph cycled back to Woodlands at the end of his shift, elated. He skidded into the driveway just as his uncle Henry was returning from a day at the office.

"How was your first day?" Henry called out.

Very interesting, Uncle Henry. There's so much to learn, and I'm eager to get started properly. The foreman, Mr Griffiths, seems like a decent sort. I'm working alongside another apprentice—he's called Jethro Gilbert.

"Excellent, excellent," Henry said with a nod, following Joseph into the house, where a servant stepped forward to take his hat and cane.

Joseph glanced at his uncle, immaculate as always, and then down at his own dusty clothes, suddenly aware of how different his own future would be from that of his father and uncle.

Henry Ellwood was a man of quiet influence. As a member of a British bank's board, he oversaw the Dunedin branch and its smaller outposts across the South Island. Following his father's death, Henry inherited Woodlands, a grand colonial-style house perched above the ocean, surrounded by gardens that grew more refined and graceful each year. Having only inherited the house because of Edward's passing, Henry made it clear that Woodlands would always welcome his siblings. Alice had left home many years earlier after marrying Hugh Brokenshire, a close friend and colleague of Henry's who had swiftly whisked her off to London. Robert and Marie, however, continued to bring their children to stay during the summer months so they could play with their cousins and enjoy the beautiful home created by their parents, Thomas and Grace Ellwood, all those years ago when New Zealand was still in its infancy.

The household was lively, thanks to their three children: seventeen-year-old Helena and seven-year-old twins, George and Douglas, whose constant noise and antics often prompted their father to threaten them with boarding school if they didn't learn to behave. Joseph loved staying with his aunt and uncle. As a child, he had treasured his summer holidays at Woodlands. Swimming in the sea, hiking the hills, playing tennis, and exploring the sprawling gardens with a freedom he had never experienced at home.

Back in his room, he washed away the day's dirt and made a mental note to polish his boots later, then slipped out into the garden, eager to enjoy the last of the evening sun. He spotted Aunt Victoria among the flower beds, snipping blooms for the many vases scattered throughout the house. When he waved, she looked up and smiled.

"How was your first day?" she called.

"Excellent, thank you. There was a lot to take in, but the foreman was friendly, and I'm working with another apprentice as well."

"Sounds like a productive start," Aunt Victoria said warmly.

"You should write to your parents. I'm sure they'll want to hear how it went."

"I doubt it," Joseph replied with a faint smile.

"Nonsense. Your father will be secretly curious about what you're learning, even if he doesn't admit it. In the end, Joseph, all you can do is work hard, do well, and prove him wrong. That's my advice, for what it's worth."

"Thank you," Joseph said quietly but steadily. "I'll write at the end of the week when I have something worth telling him. I do still want to make him proud."

By the end of his first week, Joseph had become familiar with the approved areas of the workshop. He quickly discovered that the foundry could be a dangerous place if you didn't follow the rules. Every corner seemed to hold hazards for the careless or inattentive. He was also getting to know Jethro better. Jethro, a Dunedin boy, was set on a career at Sparrows. Sometimes Joseph envied that kind of clarity. Jethro's plan was straightforward and grounded, while Joseph's ambitions soared further. He dreamed of earning a place with one of the great shipping lines, such as Cunard or the White Star Line. He knew he had to put in the hard work, but he was determined to succeed.

On Friday afternoon, Ted called them into his office just before the end of their shift. "Well, lads," he said, settling back in his chair, "you've just about survived your first week. What do you think of us so far?"

Joseph and Jethro both began speaking at once, their voices overlapping with enthusiasm. They agreed it had been a great start and were eager to learn more about the production of the enormous steam engines. Ted raised his hands as if to calm a runaway horse. "Whoa there, lads—one at a time!"

Joseph smiled and nodded to Jethro, letting him go first.

"I've enjoyed it, Mr Griffiths," Jethro said. "Can't wait to get into the more technical parts of the job."

Joseph added, "Same here. I was wondering if there are any books I could read over the weekend. I'd really like to get ahead on the theory side."

Ted was quietly pleased. It had been a while since he'd had apprentices this eager. The last pair had been a disappointment, and he'd caught flak from the higher-ups because of it. But these two showed promise. No one had ever asked for books before. They usually waited until they began part-time studies at the Technical School, only to turn to him in panic when they were unprepared for the academic side of becoming an engineer.

"Right then, before you go, tidy up all the metal strips scattered around the workshop floor. They need to be put away. And don't forget, be back here Monday morning, eight o'clock sharp, or you'll know about it."

Chapter 6

Wellington, New Zealand – June 1907

On the eve of Joseph's farewell party, the late autumn sun dipped low on the horizon, casting long golden rays that filtered through the trees and streamed into the dining room. A gentle, pine-scented breeze drifted through the open windows, stirring the lace curtains. The waning light reflected on the polished surfaces of the furniture that Peggy had worked on so diligently that morning. She was already hot and flustered as she showed her niece, Lucy, how the table should be laid and what would be expected of her that evening as the Ellwood family sat down to dine with their guests. Peggy thought her niece a capable child, efficient and willing to learn, which was a mighty relief.

"This room is so pretty, Aunt Peg," Lucy sighed, taking in her surroundings.

"It is the best room in the house, in my humble opinion. But come along now; we've no time to admire the scenery!"

"Sorry, Aunt Peg. I've never seen such a pretty room, that's all."

"Fetch me the lace tablecloth on the dresser, will you? Let's get started. I've got lamb roasting in the oven and a dessert to make."

Marie was in the garden, selecting flowers for the centrepiece. She overheard Lucy's admiration of the dining room and had to agree with the girl. She loved nothing more than to entertain there, whether for the Women's Political League or the charities she organised. Decorating the room with an abundance of seasonal flowers while Peggy baked to impress the ladies was one of her greatest pleasures.

"Shall I pick some of the flowers at the back of the garden?"

Adelaide asked, bringing Marie back to the task at hand.

"Yes, that will be lovely. I was thinking perhaps some of the chrysanthemums. The white, yellow and orange ones would look quite pretty in the entrance hall."

Adelaide made her way toward the little orchard, where two cherry trees grew, forming a sheltered nook perfect for retreating with a blanket, a favourite book, or the music sheets she often studied before lessons with Miss Ivery. She welcomed the distraction as she placed the chrysanthemums in her basket. But a heaviness stirred in her chest, an aching knot she had not been able to shake all morning.

Tomorrow, Joseph would be leaving home, and the reality of not knowing when she would see him again weighed heavily on her. Mother had already scolded her for being selfish, insisting she ought to be proud of Joseph and everything he had achieved. But no matter how hard she tried, the thought of celebrating his departure felt unbearable.

That evening, Marie surveyed the dining room with quiet approval. The table was set for twelve. Henry and Victoria had arrived earlier with Helena and her fiancé, Gabriel, though Victoria had drawn the line at including the boys. "Who knows what mischief they'd get up to? I swear they're becoming utterly uncontrollable!" She had exclaimed upon receiving the invitation from her sister-in-law.

The Montgomery family completed the guest list. Marie preferred an even number at her table, and twelve felt just right. Before dressing for dinner, she paused to adjust the arrangement of gerberas and alstroemeria on the sideboard. The vivid orange blooms lifted her spirits—if only briefly. The thought of Joseph leaving home weighed on her too, but unlike Adelaide, Marie felt a quiet pride in all her son had accomplished, despite Robert's persistent efforts to sway him.

In the kitchen, Peggy had everything under control. There

was French onion soup, freshly baked bread, and a splendid leg of lamb with all the trimmings. Marie also requested Robert's favourite dessert, a sherry trifle, in an effort to lift his spirits, as he still struggled with their son's career choice. Lucy was absorbed in carefully chopping mint for the lamb when the doorbell rang.

"That will be the Montgomery family, no doubt," Peg muttered, flushed with the heat of the range. "Lucy! Quick now, answer the door, take their coats and hats, and escort them to the drawing room. Then come straight back and help me with the soup."

"Yes, Aunt Peg," Lucy answered nervously as she hurried to greet the guests.

Robert was pouring drinks in the drawing room, ensuring the adults were comfortable and enjoying their chosen beverages. Joseph, Adelaide, Helena, and Gabriel stepped forward to welcome Charlotte and Miles, glad to see younger company after an hour of Robert and Henry debating politics, while Marie and Victoria discussed their eagerly awaited visit to the Prime Minister's residence to take tea with Lady Ward. A tap at the door brought Lucy back to announce dinner. Once everyone was seated, Peggy and Lucy began to serve the soup. Robert said a simple prayer of thanks, and the hum of conversation resumed. The talk soon turned to Joseph's new adventure.

"When do you join your ship, Joseph?" asked John Montgomery.

"Not until January. I must get to England first, then I'll enlist with the Cunard Line and join the *Carmania* in Liverpool."

"So, how will you get there? Do you plan to swim?" Miles asked cheekily.

"Well, that was an option," Joseph replied with a grin. "But instead, I'm joining the steamship *Surrey* and will work my passage to England. I've already spent some time on board to gain experience in an actual working engine room, and Ted

Griffiths, who trained me, put in a good word for me with the captain. We should reach England in late August, and after I've completed my training with Cunard, I am looking forward to spending Christmas in London with Uncle Hugh and Aunt Alice. I can't wait to see the sights and enjoy a proper cold Christmas. Then, if all goes well, I'll join the *Carmania* in the New Year."

"It all sounds very exciting," Miles declared. "I think I might go to sea when I'm older!"

"We'll see about that, young man," John Montgomery said sharply. "First, you must pass your school examinations." Miles took the hint and lowered his head as a slight flush appeared on his cheeks.

Adelaide whispered to Charlotte, "It's like I'm losing Joseph forever. Who knows when or if I'll ever see him again."

Charlotte frowned. "Oh, Addie, don't think like that! You should be happy for him. He's worked hard to earn his place. I read an article recently in *The Lady* about the rich and famous who travel on the *Carmania*. The interior looked so elegant, it was like a floating hotel. Imagine travelling on her—it would be wonderful." Adelaide couldn't find the right words to make Charlotte understand how she felt, so she just stared into her soup. She knew Charlotte was right, but the sadness pressing on her chest would not lift.

As the evening progressed, Helena talked animatedly about her engagement, while Charlotte and Joseph teased Miles, and Adelaide sat quietly, feeling invisible. She noticed Lucy clearing dessert dishes and whispering encouragement to her. "Tell your aunt everything was perfect and well done, you've been brilliant." Lucy beamed, unused to such kindness from those she served, and hurried back to Peggy with the praise. When the door closed behind her, Robert rose, tapping his glass.

"Dear friends and family, thank you for coming to wish Joseph a bon voyage. Marie and I are proud of all he has achieved. As they say on the high seas, we wish him good health, calm seas, and a happy life. To Joseph!"

"To Joseph!" came the chorus.

Joseph grinned, nodding his thanks, his gaze lingering on his father. He hoped the unspoken tension between them was easing. But when he glanced at Adelaide, her downcast face dimmed his joy. He made one of his silly faces to cheer her, but it only deepened her frown.

"Come, let's take our coffee by the piano," Marie announced. "Adelaide has prepared something for us."

Adelaide froze. She had not. But her mother's calm, expectant look said otherwise—a subtle rebuke for her melancholy.

Heart pounding, she moved to the piano, stalling as she shuffled her music. At last, her fingers found the keys, and as she began Debussy's *Arabesque*, her sadness softened, swept away by the delicate rhythm. When the final notes faded, applause filled the room. Joseph's proud gaze found hers, and for the first time that night, she smiled a genuine smile, meant only for him.

The next morning, Adelaide woke early, acutely aware that Joseph would be leaving soon after breakfast. She drifted toward the library, longing for the piano. But when she sat before it, frustration overcame her, slamming the fallboard down, she ran out of the room and straight into Joseph.

"Steady on, Addie! Where's the fire?" His teasing voice stopped her in her tracks, and her frown melted at his grin. "Don't be sad," he urged gently. "Be happy for me. I've worked hard for this. I can't stay home forever."

She looked up at him, struggling to find the right words. Despite their seven-year age gap, they had always enjoyed each other's company. Joseph would craft fantastical adventures. Sometimes, they were pirates searching for buried treasure; other times, they were brave explorers risking their lives in the jungles of Borneo. As they grew older, they studied together, and

Joseph would read her stories, such as Treasure Island and The Jungle Book. His voice, mimicking pirates, apes, and various other creatures, reduced Adelaide to tears of laughter. He was her greatest supporter whenever she was asked to play the piano in front of their parents' many guests, and she couldn't bear the thought of not knowing when she would see him again.

At breakfast, Adelaide could barely eat. Afterwards, she sat in the library, pretending to read, while Joseph prepared to leave. "It's time to go, Joseph," Robert called. Joseph hugged his sister tightly—and then he was gone.

The following morning, as Marie sat at her writing desk, her thoughts were interrupted by Adelaide entering the room, looking as though she carried all the world's worries on her small shoulders; her expression was solemn and distant. Choosing not to indulge her daughter's melancholy, Marie adopted a cheerful tone.

"Are you ready for school? Charlotte will arrive any moment, and you mustn't be late!"

"Yes, I'm ready," Adelaide murmured, avoiding her mother's gaze as she walked towards the piano. "I just need my sheet music for school, as I'm playing a piece during the morning assembly." Placing the sheet music into her school bag, Adelaide hurriedly kissed her mother's cheek and rushed towards the door just as the doorbell rang, signalling Charlotte's arrival.

Shaking her head and shrugging off the cloud of sadness that followed Adelaide out of the room, Marie continued writing a letter to her sister-in-law, Alice, informing her that Joseph had set sail and was expected in London for Christmas. Putting her pen down, she straightened her aching shoulders and looked around to admire her favourite room. When Robert was promoted to

Senior Legal Advisor to the Government, his new role brought a changed lifestyle. As part of Wellington's social elite, they were expected to host parties. Their two existing rooms were transformed into a cosy study for Robert and an elegant drawing room for receiving guests. Meanwhile, an extension was added at the back of the house. The new dining area featured a large oval mahogany table, a matching sideboard, and two elegant doors opening onto the garden. In the centre, a rich blue Turkish rug divided the room visually into two halves. A large wooden bookcase formed an L-shape across two walls. Marie's small walnut writing desk was positioned at one end facing the window, so she could gaze into the garden while organising her thoughts before replying to correspondence and committee work. In the corner created by the bookcase, a comfortable seating area had been arranged for guests to relax after dinner, often entertained by Adelaide at the piano. The elegant Bechstein piano stood near the back wall. Marie was glad her father had lived long enough to hear Adelaide play properly. He had always believed in encouraging his granddaughter's talent, convinced she had a natural gift. Marie was beginning to see how right he had been.

Although shy by nature, Adelaide seemed transformed when she played. Her posture relaxed, her features softened, and her delicate fingers danced across the keys. Marie had grown to admire Miss Ivery's teaching methods and was grateful she had set aside her initial misgivings. She would often see them sitting in the garden after a lesson, drinking lemonade and discussing books or Adelaide's latest writing project. It pleased Marie to see her daughter happy, though she could not help but feel a little envious. If only she had more time with Adelaide. Yet her social responsibilities kept her away from home during the week. She often felt conflicted, torn between the need to be socially active and the desire to spend more time with her daughter. Still, she reminded herself, *these duties were expected of the wife of a senior Government official.*

Adelaide's progress at school flickered into her thoughts. Easterwood Academy for Young Ladies had been the perfect choice for her quiet young daughter. Adelaide thrived there and took great pleasure in her studies. *With Mrs Easterwood's influence, we shall shape you into a confident young lady yet, dearest daughter,* Marie thought to herself.

Chapter 7

Easterwood Academy for Young Ladies, Wellington – September 1907

Every morning at exactly nine o'clock, Kathryn Easterwood stood outside the school's elegant oak-panelled doors to greet her girls. Punctuality and discipline were strict requirements. Mrs Easterwood would not accept tardiness or disobedience. To her, education was a vital part of a girl's growth, and if a girl showed no interest in learning, she had no place at her school. In exchange, the girls were cared for and prepared for the roles expected of them: adulthood, marriage, and managing a proper home. That was the message Mrs Easterwood shared with prospective parents seeking a refined, private education for their daughters. Yet behind the formalities, she harboured a deeper belief. If any of her students showed academic promise, she made it her mission to ensure they had every chance to pursue a scholarly path if that was their calling.

Kathryn moved to New Zealand with her husband, Frederick Easterwood. They married a week before setting sail, eager to begin a new life in the colonies. Frederick was an accountant and had already secured a position at a firm in Wellington. They planned to stay in a guesthouse temporarily until they could buy their own home. Kathryn was excited about the prospect of a new life with her husband. She had been a teacher at the school in the village where she grew up, and she had known Frederick for most of her life. It had always been expected that they would marry, but not that they would then leave for the other side of the world. Kathryn had no qualms and embraced the idea of such an adventure. Having to give up teaching simply because she was a married woman did not sit well with her, and she hoped

New Zealand would give her more freedom than living in a small village in the English countryside ever would.

Unfortunately for Frederick, he fell seriously ill during the long sea voyage and died, never setting foot on New Zealand soil. Kathryn was distraught and terrified of what would become of her once they docked in Wellington, praying that her husband's employers would somehow assist her. Fortunately, Kathryn was spared that indignity. Having spent eight weeks at sea, Kathryn had made friends with some kind and decent people. There was Mr and Mrs Grimshaw, a couple from Yorkshire who were starting a new life in Wellington, and with whom Kathryn enjoyed the occasional game of whist after dinner or a stroll around the deck, where Connie Grimshaw would regale her with tales of life in the grand home of the Wetherby family, where she was the housekeeper, and Albert was the Head Gardener. She would encourage a shy Albert to talk about the gardens and woodland he created for the old Mr Wetherby. Kathryn was horrified to learn that the reason they were leaving their old life behind was that, after old Mr Wetherby's death, his son and heir decided to dismiss all the staff who had loyally served his late father over the years and replace them with younger people, who wouldn't tell him how it was done. "Silly young fool" was all Albert would say about his feelings on the matter, and he was excited to start a new adventure.

Kathryn also enjoyed the company of Andrew and Julia Lawson, who were returning home to Wellington with their young daughter, Emily, and their baby son. They found the long journey home challenging. The children's nanny had fallen ill with severe seasickness and could not leave her cabin, so Kathryn offered to help with Emily. She had won the child over with stories, walks around the deck, and playing games with her. The Lawsons were so grateful that when they heard of Kathryn's husband's death, a week before the ship's expected arrival in Wellington, it was now their turn to support the woman who had cared so well for their daughter. Julia and Andrew had discovered that Kathryn was a schoolteacher, so without hesitation, they told her they planned to find a governess to teach Emily at home and would like to offer her the position. It was a live-in role, as they often travelled with Andrew's job. Kathryn gratefully accepted, and Emily flourished under her excellent care.

Due to the distance and the length of time it took to settle her husband's estate, a whole year had passed since his untimely death when Kathryn received a letter summoning her to the offices of Messrs Weir, Abercrombie and Jacobs. As Mrs Easterwood sat nervously, flicking at her black leather gloves, she wondered what on earth her late husband could have left her. Mr Weir peered over his round spectacles at the rather stern-looking young widow and swallowed. Delivering such news was never easy, and people's reactions were seldom what he expected.

"Mrs Easterwood, thank you for attending today. I now have your husband's will, and it gives me great pleasure to inform you that Mr Easterwood has bequeathed his entire estate to you."

Kathryn's eyes widened in shock. "I wasn't aware my husband had anything to bequeath! We brought everything we owned with us when we came to Wellington."

"On the contrary, Mrs Easterwood," Mr Weir replied with measured gravity. "His parents left him well provided for. The money was placed in trust to be released upon his marriage. Over the years, it has grown into a considerable sum—making you, madam, a lady of comfortable means."

All Kathryn could do was stare at Mr Weir, causing him to turn bright red. "Mr Weir, are you telling me that my husband became wealthy after we married? I can't believe he didn't tell me! Nevertheless, this changes everything, and I know exactly what I plan to do with the money."

Shortly afterwards, Kathryn bought a house on the outskirts

of Thorndon and turned it into a school. Easterwood Academy for Young Ladies opened its doors on 23rd January 1899. Her first student to enrol was Emily Lawson, who had begged her parents to let her attend Mrs Easterwood's school to continue her education.

Kathryn also discovered that Albert and Connie Grimshaw were finding life in the 'new country' quite challenging. After much persuasion and reassurance that it was not charity, they agreed to join her household and quickly settled into her beautiful new home, helping her turn it into a school.

The house came with three acres of previously neglected land, which spread into the hilly wooded area that bordered the property. Albert eagerly set to work creating something special for his kind employer. Much to his joy, the garden's most redeeming feature was a large greenhouse, which he planned to restore and use. Kathryn gave him free rein to design a peaceful and beautiful space for the young ladies to enjoy, with one stipulation: the garden must include an area where the girls could tend plants, grow seeds, and maintain a kitchen garden to contribute to the pantry.

Alongside her housekeeping duties, Connie prepared the girls' lunches and a simple evening supper for Mrs Easterwood, as well as providing the girls with basic cookery lessons. Sometimes, she found this task quite the challenge, as it was clearly evident that some of the girls had never set foot in a kitchen before.

Adelaide always looked forward to going to school and loved learning. Music and English being her favourite subjects. Mrs Easterwood had a magical way of discussing books, and Adelaide became an avid reader thanks to Mrs Easterwood's encouragement—and the beautiful library she had curated over the years. Of course, having extra music lessons with Miss Ivery was the best part of her day. Adelaide was often found helping Miss Ivery tidy up after class, or simply escaping to play the piano in her free time.

When Mrs Easterwood announced that there was to be a concert, an excited buzz of chatter filled the room, causing her to clap her hands to quieten the eager girls.

"I will expect everyone to be involved, whether it is performing, guiding people to their seats, making the programme, or decorating the room. It takes a lot of people working together to create a concert worthy of Wellington society." Charlotte was practically bouncing with excitement. "Oh, Addie, I hope I get to sing, and you can accompany me on the piano."

On the day of the auditions, the girls' excitement was calmed by Mrs Easterwood and her teaching staff: Miss Davenport, Miss Ivery and Miss Phelps. Mrs Easterwood had everyone say their morning prayers and sing a hymn, accompanied by Miss Ivery on the piano.

As Mrs Easterwood surveyed the eager faces of her girls, a quiet happiness filled her. But, as always, her expression remained composed, revealing nothing. She straightened and, in her usual firm tone, announced, "We will now begin the auditions. I will call each of your names, and you will share how you wish to contribute to the concert. Before we start, however, I have one more announcement. Hush now, everyone will have their turn."

She paused, making sure she had everyone's full attention before proceeding. "We have a new student joining us today." Looking directly at the newcomer, Mrs Easterwood raised her hand to make the young girl stand, "Please introduce yourself to everyone."

The girls had already noticed the sullen newcomer. As the girl stood, fifteen pairs of eyes fixed upon her. Clearing her throat, she stood stiffly, her posture precise and controlled. She spoke sharply, her voice carrying just enough for everyone to hear, "Guten Morgen. Mein Name ist Eva Müller, und ich bin gezwungen, hier zu sein." Her eyes swept over the assembled faces, meeting their polite smiles with none of her own. She knew she was expected to speak English, yet she deliberately chose German, carefully measuring each word to make her unwillingness obvious. There was no warmth in her tone, only the quiet assertion that her presence was an obligation, not a pleasure.

"What did she say?" Cordelia Fairchild whispered rather too loudly. "I don't understand what she's saying." There was an eerie silence, and everyone looked towards Mrs Easterwood for guidance.

Mrs Easterwood looked sternly at the defiant Eva and said, "Thank you for eloquently welcoming everyone in your mother tongue. However, you are now in New Zealand, where English is the primary language spoken. Shall we start again?"

Eva's face flushed a deep red, her expression tight with frustration. But after a brief hesitation, she seemed to reconsider, forcing a stiff smile. In a thick German accent, she muttered, "Good morning. My name is Eva Miller," and then quickly dropped into her seat.

Adelaide studied her and attempted to offer a small gesture of welcome, but before she could speak, Eva suddenly stuck out her tongue and turned away, deliberately avoiding her gaze. Adelaide frowned. *Why would someone come to school if they disliked every part of it?* Eva seemed miserable, disconnected, and completely out of place. It didn't make any sense. Adelaide knew Eva's parents well, as they owned her favourite bookshop. She smiled, recalling the warm, inviting store where books and kindness filled every corner. Theodore and Elisabeth Miller were always so welcoming. It was hard to believe this sullen girl was their daughter and sister to Hugo and Louis, cheerful, polite boys full of easy laughter.

Recovering from Eva's outburst, Mrs Easterwood continued with the auditions, making a mental note to speak to Eva's parents as soon as possible. "Right, let's finally begin these long-awaited auditions. Alice, please come forward and tell us what you wish to do for the concert." And with that, it was as if the whole incident had never happened.

Eva was not easy to befriend, and the girls tried to include her in their small groups at lunchtime and in lessons. The rehearsals for the concert were in full swing, and with only a day to go, Adelaide and Charlotte were in the school hall helping Albert with the decorating and setting out the chairs. He had brought in a basketful of flowers to decorate the hall. As it was a spring concert, there were plenty of daffodils, hyacinths, and tulips. Connie was arranging a beautiful glass vase of peonies, which would be placed on the piano. Adelaide sighed with pleasure, "Doesn't it look perfect, Mrs Grimshaw!"

"Bless you, child, it certainly does. Mr Grimshaw has worked wonders in the garden, and everywhere looks grand."

Charlotte was busy sweeping up a few leaves and stalks left over from the arrangements when Eva walked in. She had heard Adelaide utter her words of appreciation and, in her usual sarcastic tone, said, "All this fuss over the Mayor visiting. I am so glad I do not have to perform like a monkey before him!"

Charlotte was quick to send back a spikey retort. "You keep your opinions to yourself! We've all worked hard to make this concert special for our parents, and there's nothing wrong with that!"

Eva shrugged her shoulders, poking a finger into one of the flower arrangements before wandering off.

"She's an odd one, that girl. Can't put my finger on it, but there's a darkness about her." Mrs Grimshaw said, shaking her head, as she continued arranging the flowers while Mr Grimshaw put out chairs, his face neutral, unwilling to speak out of turn.

On the afternoon of the concert, the late spring sun shone brightly. Mrs Grimshaw laid out refreshments on a large trestle table beneath an open-sided canvas tent. The parents began to gather on the lawn and were greeted warmly by Mrs Easterwood. The students, smartly dressed in grey skirts, white blouses, and straw boaters, wandered around offering refreshments to their parents and guests. Adelaide had taken a moment to read through her music. She was to play Beethoven's *Sonata No. 14 – "Moonlight"* and had been practising with Miss Ivery. It was a beautiful piece of music, and she could hardly wait to perform it. Afterwards, she would accompany Charlotte, who was to sing *Home! Sweet Home!* Finally, the school choir would take the stage, accompanied by Miss Ivery.

As everyone filed indoors and took their seats, Adelaide felt a mixture of excitement and nervousness. She spied her parents seated just behind the Mayor and his wife, and felt sorry for her poor father, whose view was impeded by her rather large, but undeniably elegant, hat.

The concert was a resounding success, and the girls gave their best performances, receiving rapturous applause from the audience. Afterwards, the Mayor rose, thanked all the girls for what he declared to be the most enjoyable few hours, and congratulated them on their delightful performances.

The following Monday, Mrs Easterwood reiterated the Mayor's praise and, as a special treat to thank everyone for their hard work and commitment, she announced that jelly and cream would be served after lunch. The girls erupted in cheers and clapping, forcing Mrs Easterwood to calm the girls before their morning prayers.

Chapter 8

Wellington, New Zealand - December 1908

It was summer, and the early December sun blazed in a cloudless sky. Marie was already regretting her decision to walk home after the Wellington Ladies' meeting. She was grateful for her parasol and the foresight to wear her linen coat. As her home came into view, a wave of relief washed over her. Approaching the front door, she caught the melodic strains of a Beethoven sonata drifting through the open window. *Adelaide is so talented—but where will it lead?* Marie wondered. Adelaide had turned sixteen in November and had pleaded to remain at school, but Marie had hoped she might leave and join her in some of her charitable work, and more importantly, begin to socialise a little more. The Victoria League was excellent for young ladies. *Surely Adelaide could be persuaded to join that, at least.*

Peggy heard the door and went to greet Mrs Ellwood. Knowing she would be hot and tired after her meeting, she prepared some lemonade, which had been kept cool in the kitchen. "How was your meeting, Mrs Ellwood?"

"Very good, Peggy. After the meeting, the guest speaker provided me with some excellent tips on caring for my roses, so I am eager to put them into practise. But not now, I'm far too hot and bothered!"

"I've made some lemonade. Would you like to freshen up? Then I'll serve it in the drawing room. I've closed the shutters, and it's nice and cool in there."

"Oh, Peggy, you're a wonder. Thank you. I take it Adelaide is having a piano lesson with Miss Ivery?"

"Now, what made you think that?" Peggy laughed as the

solemn chords of Beethoven's *Sonata Pathétique* echoed through the house.

Adelaide was concentrating on a new piece Miss Ivery had asked her to try. The opening octaves, struck with her left hand, were proving painful.

"Don't you think the beginning sounds rather gloomy?"

Miss Ivery approached the piano with measured steps. *"Grave*, Adelaide. Not gloomy. The first movement is marked *Grave – Allegro di molto e con brio*, the second *Adagio cantabile,* and the third *Rondo: Allegro.* It is important to refer to the music by its proper names. As I've said before, playing notes is only part of the task. You must grasp the character and intention behind them."

Adelaide pulled a face as she stumbled through the unfamiliar chords, prompting Miss Ivery to shake her head in gentle reproach.

"It brightens soon enough," she said with a smile. "Played in its entirety, it is a marvellous piece of music. But let us take it in stages, for now."

Adelaide tried again, her fingers thundering out the introduction. By the end of the lesson, her hands ached, but she felt she had given it her best effort.

"That was not a bad first attempt. But you must play the chords in exact time if they are to sound dignified and courageous, as I believe Beethoven intended. I don't want you to touch the introduction again until you can manage the *Allegro.*"

"Yes, Miss Ivery," Adelaide replied, though reluctantly. She had recently discovered a book in Theodore Miller's bookshop about Beethoven, which explained that he had begun to lose his hearing around the time he composed this very piece. *How dreadful that must have felt,* Adelaide thought, her heart heavy with sympathy.

"I think we'll leave it there for today. I'll see you at school on Monday."

"Thank you, Miss Ivery. I enjoyed the lesson. Learning a new piece is hard work, especially this one, but I do enjoy the challenge."

"That's good to know. That reminds me, have you spoken to your parents yet about staying on at school next year?"

"I've mentioned it to Mother in passing, but we haven't talked about it properly yet. I couldn't bear it if they made me leave."

"Well, if you don't talk to them, matters will be taken out of your hands, so I suggest you speak to them soon. You never know; you might be pleasantly surprised."

Adelaide had a lot to consider after her lesson, so she chose to seize the opportunity and talk to her mother.

"Adelaide dear, have you been learning a new piece? Was it Beethoven? It was rather wonderful once you had got the hang of it." Marie said graciously.

"Thank you, but I have much to learn to get it right, and I will persevere. Can I talk to you? It is important, and if I don't talk to you now, I never will." Adelaide hurried her last sentence, feeling tears form, and one dropped onto her cheek.

"Adelaide, what is wrong? Come sit down next to me and let me pour you some of Peggy's delicious lemonade. It's so refreshing." Marie fussed around her daughter, giving her time to recover.

"Nothing is wrong as such, but Miss Ivery reminded me today that I should think about what I want to do next year. Charlotte will be leaving school at the end of this term. What do you think I should do?"

"Do you know what you want to do, Adelaide? I should think that would be a more important question, don't you? Within reason, of course."

"What I'd really like to do, if I am allowed, would be to stay on at school until I am at least 18 and also continue with my piano studies, and if I am good enough, I would like to apply to the Royal Academy of Music to study and gain my teaching certificate. I have read an old prospectus Miss Ivery lent me, and I know if I work hard, I can do it."

"It means I would have to go to London." Adelaide quickly added.

"Yes, I know where the Royal Academy of Music is, my dear." Marie paused and watched her daughter's anxious face as she waited for her to reply.

"Well, I wasn't expecting you to say that. You are such a homebird, and London is so far away. How long would you have to study?"

"For me to earn my teaching certificate, the course takes only one academic year. Mrs Easterwood is eager to guide me through the academic side of things, and of course, Miss Ivery will help me with my piano studies. I've come as far as I can here, but to truly advance, I need to take further examinations in England. If I pass, I'll earn my qualification and be able to use the initials L.A.R.M. after my name, which would allow me to teach."

"Well, you certainly have it all planned out." Marie paused briefly, her expression thoughtful. "I can't deny that I'm a little concerned. It's a big decision, and I had hoped you might join me in the Women's Social and Political League or some of the charities I work with. It's extremely rewarding, you know. And then, of course, there's marriage. I realise it's not something you want to think about now, but eventually, you'll meet someone and want to settle down. I met your father when I was eighteen. You must be sure you're not closing off all your options." Then her expression softened, and reaching for her daughter's hand, she said, "That said, I am so proud of you. I hope you know that. I never studied to the extent that you have."

Adelaide smiled, her voice gentle. "Thank you. That's all I want to do is to make you both proud."

"Well, you definitely do," her mother said warmly. "I suppose what I'm trying to say is that I can only imagine the level of dedication and practise this will require. The competition to gain acceptance at these institutions is surely fierce."

"Yes," Adelaide admitted. "But I'd like to try, at least."

"I will need to speak to your father about this, and I am uncertain about his response. It was difficult for him to accept that Joseph didn't want to follow in his footsteps as a lawyer, but perhaps he might allow you to pursue further studies. At least your Aunt Alice and Uncle Hugh live in London, and I'm sure they wouldn't mind you staying with them."

"Thank you. As it happens, Mrs Easterwood would like to speak to you both next Saturday if you are free. She would like to reassure you and answer any questions you may have."

"I see. Well, I will need to rearrange a few things in my diary, but we must get this sorted before the end of term and before we go to Woodlands for Christmas, and, of course, we have your cousin Helena's wedding to look forward to."

The following Saturday, Robert and Marie stood in the hallway, preparing to leave to meet Mrs Easterwood at the school. Marie was putting on her outdoor clothes and adjusting her hat, trying to ignore Robert's mood, which had surfaced during breakfast. He made it quite clear to anyone who would listen that he did not appreciate having to give up his precious Saturday afternoon.

"Marie, I am having difficulty understanding the point of all this extra education. It's ironic, isn't it, that it is our daughter, not our son, who is the academic one. If it had been the other way around, Joseph would be graduating from Oxford and beginning a promising career in law instead of ferrying the rich and famous on a floating hotel across the Atlantic Ocean."

"Robert! You do exaggerate. Joseph is an Engineering Officer onboard the *Mauretania*, a prestigious ship, as you well know." She picked up her gloves and stood by the door, waiting patiently for her husband to open it. Taking the hint, Robert opened the door, allowing his wife to pass. "Anyway, this is not about Joseph." Marie continued, "This is about Adelaide and her future. I have tried to include her in all my committees and charitable endeavours, but it has been hopeless. Yet the transformation is incredible when I watch her at school, performing at concerts, or teaching piano to her cousins. So, we must find out what Mrs Easterwood has to say. At this point in our daughter's life, I will listen to anyone who can help!"

Robert shrugged and allowed Marie to take his arm, and they strolled along the road towards the Academy. As if it were a normal school day, Mrs Easterwood stood in her usual spot at the top of the steps, waiting to greet them. "Mr and Mrs Ellwood, welcome! Come in, and I'll get Mrs Grimshaw to make us some tea." Marie and Robert were ushered into Mrs Easterwood's cosy little sitting room, which doubled as her office, and she gestured towards some chairs placed around a circular coffee table.

"Thank you so much for coming to see me on a Saturday. I'm sure your time is precious, but I felt it was important to get these things sorted out before the end of term, so we know where we are."

Robert felt even more confused. Settling himself, he looked around the room. Memories flooded back of the many times he had been sent to the Headmaster's Study for misbehaving, and he felt as if he'd entered a trap. Had he not supported his daughter's ideas of academia enough? Marie had been very vague about the purpose of the meeting. At that moment, Connie Grimshaw entered with a large tea tray, which she expertly placed on the table in front of Mrs Easterwood.

"Ah, Mrs Grimshaw, perfect timing, as always. Thank you, and I see you have been baking."

"Yes, Ma'am, I thought you might like some shortbread. I've been showing the girls how to make it."

"Perfect, and what a treat. Leave the tea, and I'll pour it in a moment." Connie Grimshaw smiled at Mrs Easterwood's guests and left them to it, closing the door softly behind her.

"I haven't had shortbread since I went to Scotland as a young man!"

That has finally put a smile on Robert's face, Marie thought to herself. "We must get the recipe from Mrs Grimshaw and ask Peggy to make some for you, dear." She smiled at her husband, who was in the process of picking up one from the plate.

Mrs Easterwood focused on pouring the tea. Passing the dainty cups and saucers to her guests, she continued her thoughts about Adelaide. "I'm sure I don't need to tell you what an exceptional student your daughter is."

Marie and Robert both nodded in agreement. *They look so uncomfortable. This isn't going to be as straightforward as I thought. At least the shortbread had softened Mr Ellwood up a little—it never failed with the fathers.* Mrs Easterwood smiled inwardly at her successful ploy.

"Adelaide excels in all her subjects, particularly Music and English. Miss Ivery tells me she is a natural and exceptionally gifted. Did you know that Adelaide has also done exceedingly well in several writing competitions, and her poetry is quite beautiful. Has she ever shown you any of her work?"

"No, she hasn't." Came Robert's quick response. "What sort of competitions?"

"Just a few we run with other schools around Wellington, and the Wellington Gazette runs one every three months, with a generous prize and the winner's work is published in the newspaper. Adelaide hasn't achieved first place yet, but she came in an impressive third the last time she entered. However, I believe music is where her heart lies. For such a shy and reserved young lady, watching her transform as she plays so confidently is a joy. I am also impressed with her ability to tutor the other students when they need extra support, which is commendable. I have spoken to Adelaide about her plans, and I'm not sure whether she has shared her thoughts with you, but if you agree, I will wholeheartedly offer my support to help her reach a standard of education that allows her to be accepted."

"Accepted?" Robert looked confused and carefully placed his cup and saucer on the table, realising his hands were shaking.

Mrs Easterwood smiled, "I didn't think she had mentioned it to you. She worries you won't approve and is torn between her desire to play music and her loyalty to you both."

Robert raised his hand as if to stop Mrs Easterwood from speaking further. "Please explain yourself. I have no idea what you are trying to tell us, and I would prefer plain speaking."

Marie looked on sheepishly. *I should have told him, oh dear, I should have just told him.*

Mrs Easterwood was accustomed to dealing with difficult parents and graciously replied, "Of course, Mr Ellwood. Adelaide has shared with me that she would greatly appreciate the opportunity to study at the Royal Academy of Music in London. The entry requirements are strict, but I would be willing to help Adelaide, and of course, Miss Ivery would too." Pausing to allow Mr and Mrs Ellwood time to process this information, Mrs Easterwood continued. "I understand it is a lot to take in, but I am completely confident of Adelaide's capabilities."

Robert's face began to redden, his confusion hardening into frustration. "For what purpose would Adelaide need to study? Eventually, she'll marry, and she won't need to work."

Mrs Easterwood's words had taken him by surprise. As a lawyer, he disliked being caught unawares, especially on matters as important as his daughter's future. He turned to his wife, his tone sharp.

"Are you aware of this?"

Marie met his gaze with calm composure. "Yes, Adelaide has shared her wishes with me, but Mrs Easterwood is simply discussing possibilities. Let's hear her out."

As Marie spoke, Mrs Easterwood poured more tea and placed another piece of shortbread carefully on Robert's plate. Then, in a measured and thoughtful tone, she replied.

"I fully understand your concerns, Mr Ellwood. However, we have entered a new century—one in which women have the vote and are beginning to forge their own paths. While Adelaide may choose to marry someday, why shouldn't she also have the opportunity to discover where her talents may take her?"

Robert listened attentively and, true to his diplomatic nature, conceded, if only slightly. "I'm not opposed to Adelaide continuing her studies if that's truly what she wants," he said. "She's only sixteen, and I know how much she enjoys school."

He paused as though a memory had suddenly surfaced.

"When Adelaide was born, it felt as though we'd been given a gift after so many years of loss. I've always known she was different. I believe that perhaps God has had a special plan for her from the beginning. She's a sensitive soul, and Joseph's departure hit her hard. Maybe we have indulged her more than we should have... but there it is."

He looked between the two women, his wife and Mrs Easterwood, their faces quietly expectant. With a heavy sigh, he pressed on. "So, this is what I propose, and I hope you'll agree. Adelaide may stay in school, but on a part-time basis. I'd like her to get involved in some of her mother's charitable work and, at the very least, start socialising more. It would do her good."

Marie nodded in agreement, feeling relief that her husband had taken charge. She felt quite emotional as she listened to Robert speak about Adelaide and how precious she was after losing so many babies beforehand, desperate for a sibling for young Joseph, and despite the warnings from the doctors, they kept trying. After seven years of heartbreak, Adelaide had finally completed their family.

Robert's speech also moved Mrs Easterwood. "I can see you want the best for your daughter. We need to guide her along the right path, not just what we think is right. I am more than happy to allow Adelaide to continue her studies part-time. However, I have another proposal to make. If she continues her studies here part-time, would you permit her to work here for the remainder of the time? I am always short of good, educated ladies to support our students. The school is expanding, and I would like to take on more pupils. Adelaide could assist Miss Ivery and help the younger students with their reading and writing. Would that be acceptable?"

Marie and Robert looked at each other and found no logical reason to disagree. Both nodded approvingly. Then

Robert said, "I think that would be a perfect solution. But I would like to add one caveat. Could you please try to build her confidence around people? We try our best, but it is hopeless. My work at Government House involves many social events, and Adelaide is old enough to attend with us. I would like her to come willingly and try to make new friends."

"Yes, of course, that is something we can work on. I will leave you to share the good news with Adelaide. I can picture her pacing in your hallway right now, waiting to find out if she can stay at school!" Smiling, Mrs Easterwood stands, and the meeting is over.

"Mr and Mrs Ellwood, it has been a pleasure to see you, and I appreciate you taking the time to talk to me. I look forward to welcoming Adelaide back in January."

Marie and Robert walked home in silence, content to bask in the summer sunshine. Robert was secretly pleased, thinking he had dealt with the situation well. He would allow his daughter to enjoy her education for the time being and was confident that before the time came for her to go to England, she would have met a decent young man and would be happily married with a home of her own. His niece, Helena, was to be married in Dunedin soon, and he was sure that when Adelaide saw how happy her cousin was, she would want that for herself, and any ideas of further education would soon be forgotten.

As Adelaide walked to school on the last day of term, the thought of the summer holidays brought a lightness to her step. She felt a sudden urge to skip, but thought better of it as someone would likely see her and tell her mother. She had eyes and ears everywhere with her loyal band of committee ladies.

It was also extremely hot, making her cheeks glow. Adelaide tugged at her blouse in an effort to cool down. Seeking the shade of a tree, she stood beneath it for a minute. There was a lot on her mind. Charlotte would soon be leaving for England, and after a short holiday, she would travel with her parents to Switzerland, where she would spend the next year in Geneva at a finishing school. She would miss her friend, but she was also happy for her. Anyway, she had her future to consider, and now that she knew her parents supported her plan to attend the Royal Academy of Music, she felt as if all her dreams were coming true. Her head spun with so much to think about, and then, realising she would be late for registration, she said aloud, "Come on, Adelaide Ellwood, get this day done and dusted!"

"Talking to yourself again, Adelaide?"

"Oh, hello, Eva. I suppose I was! I'm just so happy it's the last day of term. Aren't you? I can't wait to play my piano more. My cousin is getting married just before Christmas, too, and we'll be spending the holiday with my aunt and uncle in Dunedin. What about you?"

Eva scoffed, folding her arms. "It's all right for you, with your rich parents who let you do whatever you want. I have to start work in my father's shop. There are no choices for me. No fancy friends to drink tea with and giggle together."

Adelaide frowned. "Why are you being so mean, Eva? Everyone deserves a holiday, and working in your father's shop will be wonderful. I'll be working too. I'm only returning to school part-time and will be teaching the rest of the time."

Eva's expression hardened. "No need to be so defensive. You have no idea what it's like to be me. One day, I plan to return to Germany, but my father forbids it. I have to wait until I'm twenty-one or marry someone willing to go with me."

"Eva, I didn't mean to upset you! Come on, or we'll be late."

"Who cares!" Eva shouted, roughly brushing past Adelaide. The sudden shove caused her to stumble, nearly crashing face-first into the sturdy trunk of the tree she had been sheltering under.

By the time Adelaide had moved away from the tree, Eva had already gone down the road. Adelaide let out a sigh. She would never understand why Eva always seemed so angry. Adelaide and her friends had tried to include Eva in their games and activities, but she always managed to spoil the fun. Adelaide even invited her to her birthday picnic last year, which turned out to be quite a disaster. Eva sat in the garden, glaring at everyone and refusing to join any of her carefully planned activities. When Adelaide was asked to play the piano and her friends gathered around to sing, Eva suddenly said she had to go home and left without so much as a thank you. They all grew tired of Eva's endless complaints about her father's decision to move to New Zealand. Despite Miss Davenport's persistent efforts during elocution lessons, Eva's German accent remained, almost as a symbol of her defiance.

When Adelaide shared her concerns with her father one evening after a particularly tough day with Eva, he told her not to worry and said that, in his view, the German settlers were all very hardworking and decent people who usually achieved great success, just as Theodore had.

"It was a tough time for ordinary German citizens, which is why many decided to settle here. New Zealand truly is a land of opportunity for everyone, Adelaide. I'm confident Eva will come to realise this as she grows older."

At the time, Adelaide wasn't quite sure what a 'land of opportunity' was, but she liked the sound of it. Miller's Bookshop was one of Adelaide's favourite haunts. Every Saturday afternoon, she would slip away to its quiet charm, wandering through rows of overflowing shelves, each one brimming with books on every subject she could dream of. Over time, she grew close to Theodore and Elisabeth Miller, who delighted in selecting curious and captivating titles for her to explore.

Quite often, Elisabeth would bring over a pot of tea and mind the shop while Theodore shared his extensive knowledge of literature, and Adelaide would sit contentedly, soaking up every word. She frequently imagined herself working there, surrounded by stories and kindred spirits. Why Eva resented the place and her parents, she couldn't understand.

Chapter 9

Woodlands, Dunedin, New Zealand – December 1908

Helena's wedding and the Christmas festivities were almost upon them. The journey to Dunedin would take two days, as Marie did not want to arrive at Woodlands travel-weary and unable to enjoy the wedding. They would catch the ferry to Picton and stay overnight at their favourite guesthouse overlooking the stunning lake. It was somewhere they had often stayed, and Mrs Pengelley, the owner, had become a good friend. Picton was a vibrant town, with tall ships anchored at the wharf. Adelaide enjoyed wandering down there to watch the exotic cargoes of bananas and pineapples being lowered onto the pier.

Marie fussed and asked Peggy many questions: "Have all the plants been watered? Are the windows all locked up? What about Mrs Whiskers? Who will feed her? Has the food store been emptied of perishables?"

"Everything has been taken care of, Mrs Ellwood. I'll only be at my sister's house down by the harbour. I will check the house every day and feed Mrs Whiskers." Peggy reassured her, adding, "Just have a wonderful Christmas! I'll look after the house. Don't you be bothered about anything!"

Marie gave her housekeeper a weak smile. She was exhausted already, and she hadn't left the house yet. "Adelaide! Are you ready?" She called her daughter.

"Yes, all packed and ready!" Came Adelaide's reply further down the hallway.

"Excellent. All we need now is for your father to return home on time, and we can finally be on our way."

Adelaide was eager for them to be on their way. The lingering unease from yesterday's fright with the automobile still clung to her, and she longed for the calm of the coast, where she could unwind by the ocean and lose herself in her cousins' company. The incident had occurred just after her visit to Miller's Bookshop. She had gone to collect a book she'd ordered as a gift for her mother after Theodore had sent word that it had just arrived. As she stepped into the shop, the familiar scent of vanilla, old paper, and beeswax polish enveloped her like a comforting shawl. She breathed it in with quiet delight and waved cheerily to Theodore and Elisabeth. The shop was bustling with customers hunting for last-minute Christmas gifts, and Elisabeth's gift-wrapping station was drawing quite a crowd. Theodore returned her wave and briefly disappeared into the back room to fetch her order. Adelaide had chosen a book titled *Native Flowers of New Zealand*, knowing her mother would adore it. When he returned, he handed her the book with a warm smile, and then, unexpectedly, pressed another into her hands.

"This one's for you, Adelaide," he said. "A gift from Elisabeth and me, to thank you for helping Hugo with his piano studies, and for being so patient with little Louis. He absolutely loves it when you read to him."

Adelaide turned the book over in her hands, her heart lifting as she read the title: *A Christmas Carol* by Charles Dickens. The cloth binding was faded, and the pages had softened from use. It was a well-thumbed treasure. "Thank you so much," she said warmly. "The perfect seasonal read. I shall look forward to enjoying it nearer to Christmas."

"I thought you might," Theodore replied. "I found it at a house sale last week. The seller told me the original owner was an avid reader, and I came away with a fine collection I expect will sell well in the lead-up to Christmas."

Suddenly, she became aware of movement behind her, and then she saw Eva standing behind one of the bookcases, listening to their conversation. Adelaide was puzzled as Eva looked furious and muttered something in German that made Elisabeth gasp. "Eva, that is enough!" Theodore responded sharply, but Eva merely shrugged and walked out of the shop.

Theodore recovered quickly. "I apologise for my daughter's rudeness. She has no appreciation for books. It's such a shame. At least the boys enjoy reading, and that's thanks to you. Now go, enjoy your Christmas holidays!"

"You too, Theodore, and I look forward to seeing you in January! Thank you again for the book." Adelaide left the bookshop feeling very happy. Christmas was her favourite time of year, and with her cousin's wedding as well, this Christmas would be very festive. On her way home, however, a strange sensation that someone was following her began to creep in. Turning suddenly, she startled a passing couple. The man tipped his hat and apologised while the woman gave her a look of pure indignation. Feeling foolish but still uneasy, Adelaide continued walking, clutching her books tightly. *I'll be home soon. Everything will be fine.*

Reaching the final road before reaching her house, she waited to cross as an automobile approached. Without warning, she felt a hand on the small of her back, which, with one quick shove, sent her stumbling into the road. A man yelled, and strong arms caught her just as the car sped past, the driver shaking his fist angrily. "Watch where you're going, why don't you!" the driver shouted.

Dizzy and trembling, Adelaide could barely process what had happened. The man who had saved her looked deeply concerned.

"Are you all right, Miss? You were nearly a goner."

"Thank you," she stammered, still shaken. "I... I don't know what happened. I felt as if someone had pushed me, but I can't be sure."

The gentleman retrieved her books from the ground, carefully dusting them off with his jacket sleeve before handing them back to her. "Where do you live, Miss? Would you like me to escort you home?" He offered kindly.

Before she could reply, Eva's voice cut through the air, making Adelaide's confusion deepen.

"That won't be necessary. Adelaide and I are friends. I saw what happened and wasn't able to help in time, but I'll make sure she gets home safely."

The man hesitated but ultimately stepped aside, letting Eva take Adelaide's arm. Adelaide struggled to compose herself as she thanked him.

"Eva, what are you doing here?" she asked, bewildered, as Eva led her across the street toward her house.

"I saw you about to step in front of the car. Why would you do that? You could have been killed."

"I didn't! I felt someone push me, and I couldn't stop myself. If that man hadn't been there, I don't know what would've happened."

"Well," Eva replied coldly, "I guess we'll never know now, will we?"

"Here we are, what do you English say, 'home sweet home.' Will you be all right to get safely through your door without any more mishaps?"

"Yes, thank you, Eva. Oh, and Merry Christmas."

But Eva had gone, leaving Adelaide with a terrible feeling in the pit of her stomach. Terror seemed too dramatic, but the feeling unnerved her, making sleep that night impossible.

Trying to shake off the memory, she continued packing her bag for the journey, focusing on more exciting things.

"Goodness, Adelaide, you are as white as a sheet!" Marie exclaimed.

Adelaide told her mother what had happened to her the previous day and about Eva's peculiar behaviour. Completely ignoring the part about Eva, Marie gave her a lecture about road safety. "With so many of those awful automobiles on the road now, you must be more careful when crossing the road."

Peggy stood at the door to wave them off. She had overheard Adelaide's conversation with her mother earlier and thought she was right to worry. *There was something about that girl Eva that gave her the shivers*. While Robert and Marie busied themselves with the luggage, Peggy quickly hugged Adelaide and tucked a Christmas present in her bag.

"Just a little something for you to open on Christmas Day, and don't worry yourself about Eva. She is a troubled one, that's for sure, but if she sees you are worried, she will only give you more attention with whatever silly game she is playing."

"Thank you, Peggy. I will try. I wish you were coming with us. It won't be the same without you."

"Nonsense! With Helena's wedding to enjoy and all the fun and games with your cousins, you won't even notice. My sister has invited me to stay, and I intend to put my feet up and enjoy a quiet Christmas. Now, off you go and have a wonderful time!"

Adelaide enveloped Peggy in an affectionate hug before dashing out the door and down the steps. She turned and waved as she shouted, "Thank you for my present and Happy Christmas! Look on the kitchen dresser; you might find a little surprise waiting for you! Bye, Peggy."

They arrived at Woodlands late the following afternoon, greeted by a scene of carefully coordinated chaos. A large white marquee dominated the garden, where workmen were busy with final adjustments. Gardeners and various other workers moved through the grounds in a flurry of last-minute preparations. Then, cutting through the chaos, came Helena's familiar voice, warmly welcoming the tired travellers.

"Hurray, you're all here at last. Welcome to all the wedding chaos! I wonder if it will all come together in time. Mother has retired to her room, and Father is supervising a delivery of champagne for the reception. Let me get you settled in, and then I'll tell them you are here."

After freshening up, Adelaide wandered downstairs to find her cousins. George and Douglas greeted her with their usual exuberance, both talking to her at the same time. "One at a time, please. I can't hear what you are both saying." Adelaide said, laughing at them.

George, the eldest by twenty minutes, jumped in first and explained that their father had organised a tennis tournament on New Year's Eve to celebrate their thirteenth birthday and that she must join in.

"Of course I will, sounds fun. Is there a prize if I win?"

Douglas scoffed dramatically, "You won't win, but if you did, Father has bought a special trophy to give to the winner and will even get it engraved, and for the runner-up, a bucket of tennis balls!"

"Goodness, it's going to be quite the competition then. I'm glad I bought my tennis racket. I will have to get in some practise."

After the boys dashed across the lawn to explore the marquee further, Adelaide thought Uncle Henry was quite mad to organise a tennis tournament so soon after Helena's wedding. However, as he later explained to her himself, he was determined to celebrate the twins' thirteenth birthday properly. What better way, in his view, than with a lively game of tennis for everyone? Aunt Victoria then chimed in, announcing that once the tournament finished and everyone had rested for a few hours, they would ring in the New Year with a dinner party for their remaining guests and a handful of neighbours. She had even agreed, somewhat reluctantly, to let the boys stay up until midnight on the strict understanding that they keep out of the way and behave themselves.

Adelaide had no desire to socialise and dreaded the inevitable moment her mother would insist she join in. She preferred the company of the younger children much more. Slipping away with a polite excuse, she wandered outside to take a closer look at the marquee. The vast, white structure stood at the far end of the main garden, providing an elegant backdrop to the artfully arranged rose bushes, which bloomed in shades of pink, red, and peach. It was a breathtaking sight. Nearby, a gardener was diligently watering the flowers, clearly anxious about their well-being in the sweltering heat. Just beyond him, Adelaide noticed Helena seated on an upturned crate, a notebook balanced on her knee as she scribbled intently.

"Hello, Helena, you look busy. Is there anything you would like me to do?"

Staring up at her cousin whilst shielding her eyes from the sun, Helena smiled and said, "Believe it or not, everything is under control. Mind you, there are a great many decisions to make; it's quite exhausting! I want to ask you something important, though, and it would make me so happy if you said yes."

"What is it you'd like to ask me?" Adelaide asked, curious and hoping she'd be able to agree to whatever Helena had in mind.

"Would you play the piano at the reception?" Helena asked. "You'll be busy with your bridesmaid duties during the ceremony, but afterwards, while the guests are settling in the marquee. What do you think? Please say yes. I'd be so proud to have my cousin play at my wedding."

"Would you really?" Adelaide was astonished and genuinely taken aback by Helena's praise. "Well, I'd love to! Do you have anything particular in mind?"

I will leave all that up to you—just gentle, relaxing music, nothing too loud or plonky.

"Plonky! What on earth does that mean?" Adelaide laughed.

"Oh, you know what I mean, perhaps something by one of the romantics like Debussy or Beethoven. Think about it, and we'll talk later. Now, I must speak to the caterers and double-check they know what they are doing."

"Where's Gabriel? Is he doing anything to help, or does the groom just turn up dressed in a smart suit?"

Helena laughed, "My brothers seem to have kidnapped poor Gabriel, which is fine if it keeps those two monkeys away from the marquee. I'm terrified it will collapse, as they can't resist messing with the ropes and wooden beams holding it all up!"

"They're not so little now." Adelaide laughed as she thought of the two exuberant boys who were now at least a foot taller than she was.

"Gosh, I know, and look at me, soon to be married and have my own home to run. Anyway, I must dash. See you later at dinner."

Helena began to leave but hesitated and ran back to give Adelaide a big hug. "You are wonderful, and I love you dearly. I hope you know that."

Adelaide didn't get a chance to reply as Helena had already dashed off, calling out instructions to the staff who were busy decorating the marquee. Left alone, Adelaide suddenly felt a surge of emotion, overwhelmed by the noise and excitement swirling around her. She took a deep breath to steady her nerves. A walk, she decided, was just what she needed. Apart from playing the piano, walking in nature was the one thing that almost always brought her calm. Returning to the house, she collected her book and a blanket, then made her way through the garden to the path that led down to the beach.

Her grandfather, who had built Woodlands a few years after settling in New Zealand, had also commissioned a private path that led directly from the garden to the beach. It began at the edge of the lower lawn and wound its way down into a wooded area, where tall trees had been purposefully planted to shield the property from the harsh winds that often blew in from the ocean. As Adelaide stepped into the shade, the stifling heat of the day gave way to a cool, refreshing stillness, and her spirits lifted. The sound of waves crashing against the shore and the distant cry of gulls grew louder as she followed the path to its end, where the ground turned sandy and sloped gently down to the sea. Adelaide never tired of the view that greeted her. The cove's clear waters blended in a dazzling palette of blue, turquoise, and aquamarine against the soft golden sand. It was a small, secluded bay protected by rocky outcrops that formed a natural horseshoe shape. Finding a cool, shady spot, Adelaide laid her blanket carefully on the sand and settled down. The salty breeze filled her lungs and soothed her nerves like nothing else. She was just about to open her book when she noticed the corner of an envelope sticking out from between the pages.

"Joseph's letter!" she exclaimed aloud.

She had completely forgotten that she'd tucked it there on the morning they left Wellington, intending to read it later when she had time to savour her brother's news. That moment had come, and with a smile, she eagerly opened the envelope and began to read.

Mauretania, somewhere in the Atlantic Ocean
November 1st, 1908

Dear Addie,

By the time you receive this, your sixteenth birthday will have passed, and I wish you the happiest of birthdays! Please write to me soon and share your plans. I hope Father allows you to stay at school a little longer. I imagine he sometimes wishes I had your intelligence.

It'll be Helena's wedding soon, too. I hope her fiancé, Gabriel, is a decent sort. When the engagement was announced, Helena sent me a newspaper clipping with their photograph, so at least I know what he looks like. I wish I could be there.

Life aboard the Mauretania is more rewarding than I had hoped, and I have already been promoted. The steam turbines are incredible, and the ship can really move. We get all sorts of passengers on board, from Royalty to famous Actors and everything in between. One day, Spider and I were asked to take a group of ladies from First Class to the Engine Room, as they wanted to see the engines; goodness knows why! One of the ladies asked about the large pipes that ran from the turbines.

I couldn't resist it, but I told them that was where the soup for steerage was made. The funniest bit was that they all believed me! I was worried for a good week or so afterwards, hoping the ladies wouldn't mention their newfound knowledge to the Captain. I think I got away with it!

Adelaide rested the letter on her knee for a moment, laughing at the thought of her brother daring to spin such a ridiculous yarn, and it didn't surprise her in the least. Looking at the letter again, she continued to read.

I had better finish this letter now, as duty calls, but before I sign off, I must tell you about Kitty. I met her last year, just before I joined the Mauretania. Spider and I had a few hours of shore leave, and after exploring the city of Liverpool, we decided to visit a café. It was Kitty who served us. Several weeks passed before I could see her again, but when I did, I bravely asked her if she would like to walk with me to the local park. From the moment we started talking, it felt like I had known her forever. I know you'll love her just as much as I do, and perhaps one day, I can bring her to Wellington to meet you all. If she accepts my hand in marriage, that is.

Adelaide stopped reading and gazed at the letter. Joseph's familiar handwriting blurred as tears welled in her eyes. She tried to understand what her brother had written, but couldn't or wouldn't. She wasn't sure. Who was this waitress he had met in Liverpool? Adelaide threw the letter onto the sand and stared out towards the horizon.

On the morning of her wedding, Helena woke to a breathtaking sunrise. Wispy clouds, tinged with a soft pink glow, drifted across a canvas of blue sky. Sunlight streamed through her window, bathing the room in warm, golden light. She sank back into her pillows with a contented sigh. From somewhere below, a gentle melody drifted in, graceful and familiar. She smiled, instantly recognising her cousin Adelaide's distinctive playing. Helena was grateful Adelaide had agreed to perform at the reception, though she wished her mother would share her pleasure.

"I'd like Adelaide to play the piano as guests walk from the church to the marquee," Helena proposed eagerly to her mother a few days before the wedding.

Victoria, who was occupied arranging a large display of garden flowers, did not share her daughter's enthusiasm. "Being a bridesmaid is more than enough," she said curtly, not looking up.

Helena frowned. "Why are you always so dismissive of Adelaide? She's such a sweet girl. Why wouldn't you want her to play for us?"

Victoria stopped what she was doing and turned to face her daughter, her expression softening slightly. "You are so kind-hearted, always thinking of others. But it's your day, and I don't want Adelaide to overshadow you."

"Overshadow me!" Helena replied, horrified.

"Mother, how could you say such a thing? Firstly, it is not just my day but Gabriel's, too. Secondly, I am proud of Adelaide's talent, and so should you be. She's such a quiet, shy little thing, and I wanted her to feel included. I know she only agreed to be my bridesmaid to please Aunt Marie, and knowing Adelaide as well as I do, the last thing she wants is to follow me down the aisle with over a hundred pairs of eyes watching her!"

"That may well be, but we really should hire a professional pianist. Say she gets nervous and makes a mistake. I couldn't bear it!"

"I can assure you with absolute certainty that Adelaide won't make a mistake," Helena said, firmly defending her cousin. Her mother merely shrugged, continuing to jab the flowers into the large vase.

Helena had at least won the argument. Choosing not to let her mother's attitude toward Adelaide upset her, Helena let the soothing strains of *Clair de Lune* wash over her and calm her mind. Too excited to stay in bed a moment longer, Helena climbed out and immediately caught sight of her wedding dress hanging on the wardrobe door. Bathed in the soft morning light, it looked stunning, and the sight brought a smile of delight to her face. Her maternal grandmother had brought the dress all the way from Scotland, carefully wrapped in muslin and paper, in the hope that if she ever had a daughter, she might one day see her wear it on her wedding day.

Victoria had refused even to consider it. But Helena had seen the dress once, when she was about ten, and had fallen in love. She'd thought it the most beautiful dress in the world and declared that she would wear it on her wedding day. Her grandmother, Cordelia Belvoir, had laughed and said, "We'll see. You might hate it when you're all grown up."

But when Helena became engaged, she hadn't hesitated. She went straight to her grandmother and asked if she could wear the dress. Now, as Helena gazed at the dress, it felt almost unreal that she would soon be wearing it. She hoped Gabriel would love it as much as she did. She smiled, remembering the moment she'd nervously confessed her worry that he might not like the dress. He had taken her hand, smiled, and said, "I'd love you in an old seed sack, my darling. It's you I'm marrying, not the dress."

The full-length gown was crafted from delicate chine silk taffeta, trimmed with lace, and subtly altered to accommodate Helena's taller frame. New silk was seamlessly blended with the original fabric, and the neckline was edged with lace, into which tiny pearls had been meticulously sewn. Helena couldn't help but admire the skill of the seamstress her mother had hired. Not only had she tailored the vintage gown beautifully, but she had also created the two bridesmaids' dresses with equal care. *I'm the luckiest person alive today,* Helena thought, spinning in a joyful pirouette across her bedroom.

Adelaide had woken early, feeling a mixture of anxiety and excitement. She was eager to rehearse her music properly, just as Miss Ivery had taught her. "It's no good just memorising the music, Adelaide. You must read it and understand it." So, Adelaide always sat and carefully read her music before a concert or when asked to perform for her parents' many guests. She would memorise each note and play it mentally. Today was no different, and more than anything, Adelaide wanted to play well enough to please Helena and Gabriel. Thinking of Helena's happiness, Adelaide didn't understand the ways of love and wondered if she ever would. Most of her friends had started attending tea parties and balls around the city, and Adelaide had been invited a few times but refused, not letting her mother persuade her otherwise. She didn't feel ready. When Helena began courting Gabriel, she gradually lost interest in playing the piano. She only played on rare occasions, usually when the whole family was gathered. Once the wedding was announced, it became Helena's main focus and something she discussed constantly. Adelaide, meanwhile, found the whole affair rather dull and couldn't quite understand all the fuss. *No, marriage is not for me...*

Still, when Helena asked her to perform at the wedding reception, Adelaide was overjoyed. She wanted to play something truly special for her cousin. After much thought, she decided on Debussy's *Clair de Lune*, a dreamy and romantic piece she felt would be ideal for the newlyweds. Though she had played the piece many times before, Adelaide felt nervous that morning. While the others were at breakfast, she slipped into the marquee, where the piano had been moved the night before, for a quiet moment to practise. Sitting at the piano in the marquee felt quite different from playing inside a solid structure, and she wondered what the sound would be like. As she struck the first chord, she was relieved to find that the piano was well-tuned and the acoustics more than acceptable. As the final chord faded into silence, gentle clapping broke the stillness behind her.

"Bravo, my dear, bravo. That was beautiful."

"Good morning, Uncle Henry. I hope I haven't disturbed you. I just wanted to try the piano in the marquee to hear how it sounds."

"It sounds perfect to me, just perfect."

"What a relief. Thank you. I have been worrying about the acoustics all night." Adelaide said, smiling at her uncle.

"Are you looking forward to being a bridesmaid today?"

I am indeed, and my dress is quite pretty. Although it's not as stunning as Helena's, I still feel incredibly special wearing it.

Henry chuckled at his young niece. "It'll be your turn before you know it. Any young suitors on the horizon?"

Adelaide blushed bright red and shook her head. "Absolutely not. My focus will be on playing the piano for the next five years. All I care about is becoming good enough to study at the Royal Academy of Music in London."

Henry shook his head but didn't contradict her, tell her she was being silly, or suggest that she should abandon her ambitions. It was one of the many reasons Adelaide adored her uncle. He never fussed over things like that, preferring to leave 'the difficult questions' to his wife or his sister-in-law.

"Right, my dear, I must be off. There are 101 things to do before the wedding, and if I don't start ticking these things off my list, your Aunt Victoria will have my guts for garters."

Laughing at her uncle's peculiar remark about guts and garters, she closed the fallboard and gathered her music books. She hesitated, unsure whether to leave them ready on the piano. Then, she began to worry that the breeze might send her books fluttering across the marquee. *Perhaps Jenks could help?* As she scanned the marquee for him, she spotted him meticulously checking off items and instructing a few young servants to remove glasses from a crate and wash them with care. Her aunt and uncle had hired Jenks to oversee the wedding celebrations and supervise the additional staff they had to hire for the occasion. Not knowing him very well, Adelaide approached him nervously.

"Good morning, Jenks. Would you mind keeping these safe for me and placing them on the piano when the guests return from church? I'm worried the breeze might carry them away if I leave them here now."

Jenks was tall and notably angular. His prominent nose reminded Adelaide of an eagle's beak. He looked down at her, and with a sniff, he nodded and said, "Of course, Miss, I will make sure your music is left on the piano in time for your performance."

"Thank you. I imagine you are terribly busy, so I do appreciate it."

"Well, thank you, Miss, and it is no problem at all."

Jenks watched Adelaide walk away, and although her kindness touched him, he was far too busy to worry about some music books. Once Adelaide was out of sight, he set them down on a nearby table, not giving them another thought.

Adelaide returned to her room, knowing it would soon be time to get ready. An hour later, Marie stepped back, admiring Adelaide as she fastened the final button. Though the dress was simple, it draped gracefully over Adelaide's petite frame, lending her an effortless elegance. Helena had chosen a soft lavender hue for her bridesmaids, the empire waistline allowing the fabric to flow with gentle movement. Adelaide's hair was gathered into a delicate chignon at the nape of her neck, accented with tiny cream rosebuds. Around her throat, she wore a single strand of pearls — a gift from Helena, as a thank-you for being her bridesmaid.

"You look beautiful, darling."

Adelaide did a little twirl and gave her mother a huge smile. "Thank you, isn't the dress lovely? Mind you, I can't wait to see Helena in her dress. I'm sure she'll look like a beautiful princess." Smiling at her daughter's imaginings, Marie said, "Every bride feels like a princess on their wedding day, Adelaide. Now remember, chin up, back straight and glide like I taught you, no skipping or stomping."

"I promise." Adelaide nodded at her mother. "Anyway, I could only ever glide in such an elegant dress." Laughing and twirling around her exasperated mother.

Adelaide stood at the foot of the staircase, anticipation thrumming in her chest as she awaited Uncle Henry and Helena's arrival. Beside her, Helena's best friend, Daisy, stood poised in a matching dress. Helena had insisted on having just two bridesmaids, and she had refused to include her mischievous brothers as page boys. George and Douglas had offered no protest, feeling relieved to be spared the ordeal.

Adelaide and Daisy gasped in unison as Helena finally descended, her father walking proudly at her side. Draped in the elegance of her wedding gown, Helena was a breathtaking vision of grace and serenity. "Oh, Helena, you look beautiful," Daisy murmured, her voice full of awe. Adelaide, utterly spellbound, could only nod, incapable of finding words to match the moment.

Their journey to the church was in a horse-drawn carriage hired specially for the occasion. Ribbons in soft pink and white decorated its polished frame, winding around the delicate floral arrangements that echoed Helena's bouquet. Even the horse had been part of the celebration, its mane plaited and threaded with white ribbons that fluttered gently in the breeze. When they arrived, Henry descended first, offering his daughter a steady hand as she carefully stepped down from the carriage, and then he returned to assist Daisy and Adelaide.

As the first notes of the wedding march echoed through the church, Adelaide took a steadying breath and followed Uncle Henry and Helena, keeping in perfect stride with Daisy beside her. The hushed reverence of the congregation settled around them, a quiet anticipation threading through the air. Ahead, Gabriel stood at the altar, his best man, Tommy, at his side. The Vicar presided just above them on the raised platform, but Gabriel noticed nothing else; his gaze was locked onto Helena, unwavering, as if nothing else in the world existed. Adelaide glanced at her cousin, radiant in her gown, and felt something shift inside her. Watching Gabriel's expression, tender, unguarded, utterly lost in Helena, she thought, *This must be what love looks like.*

After what Adelaide thought was one of the loveliest wedding services she had ever attended, everyone made their way back to Woodlands. Outside the marquee, guests began to gather while servants circulated, offering drinks. The bridal party stood in a neat line to greet them.

Adelaide took her place dutifully, as was expected, but the rigid formality soon began to wear on her. The endless stream of unfamiliar relatives, the constant smiling, and the small talk were overwhelming. If she had to endure one more conversation with a distant cousin she didn't know, she feared she might go mad. Escaping to the sanctuary of her bedroom, she was grateful for the brief moment of solitude. Her thoughts drifted to Joseph's letter, still tucked inside her book. She was tempted to read it again, but his last words about Kitty intruded on her thoughts. No, she would save it for later, as now she had more pressing matters to attend to. It was nearly time to return to the marquee and prepare to play the piano.

Downstairs, the celebration was well underway. Guests milled about, sipping champagne and nibbling on canapés served by waitresses in black dresses and crisp white aprons. As Adelaide approached the piano, she felt a ripple of unease. The music she had carefully selected and asked Jenks to place on the stand was nowhere to be seen. Her chest tightened, and panic began to set in. *Oh no, what am I going to do?* She stood frozen, her mind scrambling.

"Everything all right?" came a familiar voice from behind. It was Tommy.

"My music book is missing, and I'm supposed to be playing the piano now while the guests mingle."

"Never fear, Tommy Broadstairs is at your service. Where do I need to go to get it?"

"Oh, thank you. Jenks, the butler, was supposed to put it here for me. Better start with him and see where it has gone."

Tommy gave a mock salute, turned around and went purposefully on his mission.

"Adelaide, why aren't you playing the piano?" Aunt Victoria's sharp voice penetrated Adelaide's thoughts.

"I'm sorry, Aunt Victoria, the music is missing. Tommy has just gone to find it for me. He won't be long, I'm sure. Mr Jenks had it and was supposed to put it out ready for me."

"Well, this is not good enough, young lady. Why did you expect Jenks to put the music out for you? He has other, far more important duties to attend to today."

"I'm so sorry."

"Well, so you should be. I knew this would happen! Can't you play anything by memory?"

Adelaide gave her aunt a small, embarrassed nod before settling onto the piano seat, her hands trembling. She hated the thought of disappointing anyone, especially her family, on this day of all days. Adelaide took a deep breath. *Come on, Adelaide, you can do this*.

She focused on what Miss Ivery had taught her before any performance. She had no music to guide her, but she envisioned the notes clearly in her mind. "Stretch your fingers and get comfortable. Then play …" And play she did. That day, she played with her heart rather than her head. Because there was no music to remind her what to do, she simply played from memory and quickly became lost in the music. When she finished, she paused with her fingers gently resting on the keys and took a deep breath, feeling relieved. She had done it. Spontaneous applause echoed around the large marquee, causing Adelaide to look around in surprise. She was so absorbed in the music that she hadn't noticed the gathered guests had stopped talking to listen to her. Standing, she offered a small curtsey. Scanning the room for her parents, she moved toward them—her steps quick, drawn by the safety of their presence.

"Adelaide, my dear, that was beautiful." Robert had been genuinely surprised as he listened to his daughter perform. He hadn't heard her play for some time as he had been so busy at work, but as he listened to the beautiful melody his daughter was creating, he felt immensely proud. A letter he had just received from Joseph had left a sour taste in his mouth. One moment, he felt anger, and the next, he felt as if he were grieving the loss of his son, or perhaps the son he had hoped for. Desperately trying not to allow it to spoil the enjoyment of his niece's wedding, he found listening to his daughter play so beautifully had soothed him.

That night, when all the guests had gone home and the bride and groom had been waved off ceremoniously to begin a two-week honeymoon on the North Island and in the privacy of their bedroom, Robert could no longer contain his feelings. He was angry, hurt, betrayed and everything in between. "A waitress from Liverpool!" Robert yelled at his wife. "What is he thinking? Stupid, stupid boy. I will write to Alice and Henry in London, and maybe they can intervene."

"Robert, please don't shout so loudly! We don't want the whole house to hear our business. He hasn't married her yet, and we know nothing about her. We must not judge until we know the facts."

"The facts are that our irresponsible son has allowed his heart to rule his head. He could be a ship's captain one day, but not with an uneducated waitress by his side!" Robert's face had turned a vivid red with rage, and his eyes were almost bulging out of his head. Marie had never seen him so angry.

"Robert, please try to calm yourself. Before we pass judgment, let's find out more about this woman he wishes to marry; perhaps she is a woman of good breeding but has fallen on hard times. We must ascertain the facts first, or we will lose our son forever."

"Marie, we have lost our son forever. That much is clear."

All Marie could do was hold together the pieces of her own broken heart and comfort her husband until he finally fell asleep, exhausted.

Marie lay awake, staring at the ceiling, her mind filled with thoughts of Joseph. Sleep remained elusive, and after what seemed like hours of restless turning, she finally surrendered to wakefulness. Carefully avoiding waking her husband, she eased herself out of bed, slipped into her dressing gown and slippers, and silently padded across the room. Despite the warm night,

Marie thought a cup of hot milk might comfort her. As she entered the dimly lit kitchen, a familiar figure stood by the range; the flickering candlelight cast long shadows on the walls.

"Adelaide? Is that you?" Marie murmured, her voice low in the quiet hush of the night. "Can't you sleep either?"

"Oh, hello, Mother. No, I can't. A letter I received from Joseph is playing on my mind."

"I know, my dear. We have had one, too. Your father is in a rage, but thankfully, he has worn himself out and fallen asleep. Add another cupful in there for me, will you?"

"I'm worried, are you? Do you think he intends to marry this woman? She must be very special for Joseph to fall in love without considering his career or our feelings."

"It does sound like it, but he has not married her yet. I will write to him in the morning and ask him to tell me more about this woman he is so smitten with. In the meantime, take your milk to bed with you and try to get some sleep. It's Christmas in a few days, and then the twins' birthday celebrations, so we must make the most of our holiday, and I shall tell your father to do the same!"

Chapter 10

Wellington – January 1909

Adelaide found it hard to settle back into her normal routine after all the excitement of Helena's wedding, Christmas, and the twins' birthday celebrations on New Year's Eve. Her brother's news also weighed heavily on her mind. Her parents refused to talk about it, leaving her feeling very alone. She knew she must write to Joseph soon, but wondered if there was anything she could say that he would want to read. She was grateful that Miss Ivery was coming that morning to give her a piano lesson and to discuss lesson plans for the new term. The thought of the new school year made her stomach flutter, but in a good way. She couldn't wait to go back to school and enjoy the routine and structure that came with it. This time, however, she would enjoy the best of both worlds: studying and helping students with their learning. She felt very lucky and thankful that her father had given his blessing. The mere thought of joining her mother's many committees made her feel quite nauseous.

The trill ringing of the doorbell announced Miss Ivery's arrival, and Adelaide went to greet her, but Peggy had beaten her to it, catching them as they wished each other "A Happy New Year."

"Miss Ivery, it's so good to see you. Did you have an enjoyable Christmas?"

"I did. Thank you, Adelaide. Aunt Susan and I were invited to spend it with Mrs Easterwood, and Mrs Grimshaw spoilt us with a traditional Christmas dinner with all the trimmings!"

"What about you, Adelaide? Did you enjoy Helena's wedding and Christmas at Woodlands?"

Adelaide told Miss Ivery all about the wedding, including

how she had to play from memory and how many of the guests complimented her on her performance. Miss Ivery was impressed and pleased for her. She made Miss Ivery laugh when she regaled her with the goings-on surrounding the twins' birthday tennis tournament and how competitive the boys had been.

"They didn't win, though, the final was between Tommy, the best man, and Stephen, one of the twins' friends. Tommy won the trophy, and Stephen won a bucket of tennis balls!"

"What a lovely family you have, Adelaide. You are lucky," Miss Ivery said.

"Do you have family near?" Adelaide asked shyly, not wanting to pry. She had often wondered who, if anyone, was waiting for Miss Ivery when she left the school at the end of the day.

"It's just Aunt Susan and me now. My mother died when I was twelve years old, and my father a few years ago. He was much older than my mother, and he never really recovered after losing her, so Aunt Susan stepped in to take care of me."

"I'm sorry, and I hope I haven't upset you. Mother is always scolding me for my inquisitiveness." Adelaide blushed slightly, hoping Miss Ivery didn't think her insensitive.

"Heavens, there's no need to apologise. I am very content, and Aunt Susan and I are like two peas in a pod, according to Mrs Easterwood." Miss Ivery laughed. "Right, we'd better begin your lesson. We have much to do to get you up to the standard required for entry to the Royal Academy of Music! Oh, and Adelaide, as you will be a part-time member of the staff when we return to school, please call me Violet. We have known each other for a while now, and I hope you know I consider you more than just a pupil. You are a dear friend, too."

"Yes, Miss Iv … I mean, Violet. I would like that very much."

"Mind you, when we are at school and especially in front of the girls, you must call me Miss Ivery. Right, let's get on, shall we? I have a piece of new music for you to try."

The following day, Adelaide decided to take a walk to visit Theodore and Elisabeth and find out if their Christmas had been enjoyable. As she arrived at the Miller's bookshop, she opened the door, setting off the bell, and searched for Theodore's familiar face. He hadn't looked up as she walked in because he was deep in conversation with a man she didn't recognise and who had his back to her. Not wanting to interrupt Theodore when he had a customer, she busied herself, gazing at a variety of enticing books on the shelf nearest her. Eventually, she heard Theodore's familiar voice. "Welcome, Miss Ellwood. Did you enjoy your Christmas break?"

Feeling rather shy and tongue-tied as she was so near the stranger, she swallowed and remembered her manners. "Happy New Year, Mr Miller. I had a wonderful Christmas, thank you."

The stranger turned, his curiosity piqued by whoever had captured Theodore Miller's attention. As his gaze settled on Adelaide, discomfort stirred within her. His light grey suit, impeccably tailored, spoke of quality, and the deep red, almost burgundy, necktie provided a striking contrast against his crisp, round-collared shirt. Yet, despite his formal attire, his long blond hair rested just past his collar. At the tips of his elaborate moustache, delicate curls added to his eccentric air. Adelaide had never encountered anyone quite like him. Theodore Miller's voice broke the moment, "Forgive me, Adelaide, this is Mr Valentine Spielmann. His father is an old friend who owns the Gentlemen's Tailors, just across the street." Theodore said, pointing his finger towards the shop door.

Adelaide made herself speak, but inwardly, she desperately wanted the stranger to disappear so she could resume her normal routine of book-browsing and talking to her friend. "Good morning, Mr Spielmann."

Valentine turned his full attention to Adelaide, offering a small bow, his heels clicking together with effortless grace. As he straightened, Adelaide's gaze was drawn to his eyes, which were pale blue and utterly mesmerising. Combined with his long hair and imposing stature, he was undeniably striking. There was something undeniably handsome about him, though not in the conventional sense. He had the effortless allure of a bohemian artist, reminiscent of the photographs she had pored over in her many art history books. He didn't look like a tailor, she mused. When she had visited on occasion to collect several orders for her father, she had only seen an elderly, impeccably dressed gentleman and a young girl about her own age.

"Good morning, Miss Ellwood. I'm pleased to make your acquaintance." His speech was formal, with a strong German accent. He bowed slightly towards her again as he spoke.

"Valentine plays the piano like you, Miss Ellwood."

"Do you?"

"Yes, Miss Ellwood, I do. I studied at the Royal Conservatory of Music in Leipzig until we moved here, and now I am a tutor and occasionally give recitals if invited."

Like a proud father, Theodore told Valentine of Adelaide's plans to study at the Royal Academy of Music in England.

"How interesting, Miss Ellwood. I wish you well in your endeavours" Bowing again, he said, "Apologies, but I must take my leave now as I have a student waiting."

Adelaide could only nod and stare at Valentine as he paid for the book, said farewell to Theodore, and left.

Once he had departed, Theodore eased back into their familiar, more relaxed manner. "Now, to what do we owe the pleasure of your company today? Have you set your sights on another book?" His broad smile, partially concealed by his large, bushy grey beard, was difficult to discern, but the unmistakable twinkle in his eyes gave it away.

"I wanted to thank you for the book you gave me for Christmas. I have already read it! It was a wonderful story."

Theodore laughed, "Well, that won't do, will it? We need to find you another one to read."

Adelaide grinned and said, "Please don't tempt me to buy another book. Mother wouldn't be pleased. My books already take up a large section on the family bookcase!"

Laughing, Theodore shouted for his wife to come through, but all of a sudden, Eva swooped in ahead of her mother. "Adelaide, how good it is to see you. I suppose you had a wonderful holiday?"

"I did, thank you, and my cousin's wedding was wonderful. Now I am looking forward to returning to school next week. What are your plans?" Adelaide tried to sound confident and kind, but as always, when she spoke to Eva, her voice wavered slightly, and Eva would smile one of her satisfied smiles as if she had won a prize.

"Oh, this and that. I can't think why you would want to stay at school. I am so lucky not to be going back. I will, of course, be helping my mother and father in the bookshop, and I have a few other plans as well. But I'm keeping them to myself for now."

Theodore shook his head, words failing him in the face of his daughter's rudeness. All he could do was watch as Eva swept from the room, the swish of her skirt punctuated by the smug smirk she left in her wake. He turned to his wife and then to Adelaide, searching for some explanation, some understanding of his daughter that he had never quite grasped. "Eva has always been secretive," he murmured, more to himself than anyone else. "Even as a child, she never spoke to us, never let us in. She was only ever happy with her beloved Oma. The stories she could tell, I'm sure."

After meeting Valentine and enduring Eva's rudeness, Adelaide decided to go home. She felt an odd sense of foreboding and made an excuse to leave. After saying her goodbyes, she opened the shop door and stepped into the busy street and the warm sunlight.

Adelaide enjoyed her walk to school, admiring the bronzed hue that had appeared on the trees and feeling grateful for the cooler breeze after a hot summer. Autumn had finally arrived in Wellington—her favourite time of year. Her book bag was full to the brim with the lesson plans she had worked on over the weekend, and Monday morning brought many pleasant possibilities for the week ahead: a week of music, learning, and the challenge of engaging her students and watching them improve.

Her first few months as a student and teaching assistant had been perfect. For the first time since her brother left home, she started to feel happy again and realised she had a purpose. Joseph's surprise announcement still unsettled her, but not as much as she expected. He had a right to be happy, even if their parents disagreed. The other day, she was horrified to overhear her father telling her mother that he would disinherit Joseph if he went through with it. But none of that mattered today, as she looked forward to tutoring her new students, Harriet and Mary, enjoying Schubert, and getting them to work on their scales again. Violet had asked Adelaide to take these students under her wing and prepare them for their piano grades in July, and that's what she meant to do!

As always, Mrs Easterwood was at the top of the steps, welcoming both teaching staff and pupils with a bright "good morning" to everyone who walked past her. "Good morning, Hazel. How was your visit to your Grandmother yesterday?" A small girl with glasses smiled at Mrs Easterwood. "It was very enjoyable, thank you. We had ice cream."

"What a treat." Mrs Easterwood smiled down at the child

as she entered the main door. Adelaide and Violet passed her next, smiling at the little girl's comment. After greeting Mrs Easterwood, they went through the door together.

"Are you prepared for your lessons with Harriet and Mary this morning?" Violet enquired. Laughing, she added, "You don't need to answer that. I can see by the expression on your face how much you are looking forward to it!"

"Oh yes, I have been preparing all weekend." She tapped her book bag as they walked to the music room. The music room was situated on the ground floor, featuring two large windows that overlooked the garden. Mrs Easterwood had decided this was the ideal location for a music room so as not to cause too much noise for her neighbours. An elegant grand piano, a gift from a grateful parent, recently replaced the original upright. A well-polished wooden floor had been laid to improve the acoustics, and Violet was allowed to arrange the room to her liking. Opposite the windows, Violet had requested a bookcase to display a selection of music books and scores for students to borrow for home practise. Some of these books were her own, as she believed it was important for students to learn about the composers, not just the music they played. Six desks and chairs were arranged neatly in a row in front of the bookcase. The rest of the area was kept clear, with chairs set out for students to sit and play various instruments. This year, students were learning to play the violin, clarinet, and flute. It was not quite an orchestra, as most of Wellington society preferred their daughters to be able to play the piano, at least acceptably, before leaving school. Other instruments were usually only encouraged if the parents themselves played. It was not Violet's place to change her pupils' parents' minds, but if a girl showed interest in another instrument, she always allowed them to try. Fortunately, she had several instruments at her disposal, funded over the years by Mrs Easterwood.

Harriet and Mary were waiting in the music room as Adelaide entered, both sitting at the piano and giggling together about something Adelaide had no idea of.

"Good morning, girls. You both appear to be in good spirits. Are you ready for your lesson?"

"Yes, Miss Ellwood." They both said in unison. It still felt strange for Adelaide to be called Miss Ellwood, but she liked it. Adelaide spent an enjoyable hour tutoring the girls. Even though they could be giddy at times and inclined to practise sparingly, they were easy to teach, and Adelaide was sure they had enjoyed their lesson.

After the girls had departed, Violet had just finished her lesson with four twelve-year-olds, teaching them about the history of the Tudors, focusing on King Henry VIII for the next two weeks. The girls loved the mnemonic she taught them to remember all his wives: 'Divorced, beheaded, died. Divorced, beheaded, survived.' It never failed to amuse them, and they always remembered it! Miss Phelps, who usually taught the girls history and geography, had fallen ill, and Violet was more than happy to take over since she enjoyed history and was confident teaching it.

"How was the lesson?" Violet enquired as she entered the Music Room, where Adelaide sat at one of the desks, writing down her notes in a book.

"It went very well, thank you. I think the girls are almost ready to take their next Grade. I've given them some music to practise at home and emphasised the importance of keeping their hands strong by doing their scales. It makes playing so much easier. I'm so glad you insisted I practise hard with my small hands." Adelaide held her hands aloft, wiggling her fingers with a proud little flourish. "Now I feel I could play almost anything and not worry about my hands getting too tired."

"I'm sure you could, but you must not become complacent.

I'll give you some homework to study the Hungarian composer Franz Liszt, followed by writing an essay on his life and works. After that, I will teach you *Liebestraum No. 3*. It's very dreamlike, and I believe it will suit you perfectly. We can start practising it next Saturday."

"I look forward to it. Oh yes, I almost forgot. Mother asked if you and Susan would like to join us for afternoon tea. She has invited a few friends from the Women's Political League to plan additional fundraising events for their charitable causes. Please say you will come. I hate these things, and having some familiar faces to sit with will be such a relief!"

Shaking her head in mock frustration, Violet replied, "You are hopeless! But thank you, I'd be delighted to join you, and I'll also check if Aunt Susan is available. I do hope Peggy's making her famous lemon syrup cake!"

Chapter 11

Eva
Wellington, New Zealand - February 1910

Eva sat at her desk, idly thumbing through the pages of her precious red leather notebook, a slow smile curling at the corners of her lips. Here was where she studied her next "victim" with the meticulous precision of a hunter. Each detail noted, each weakness catalogued. She tapped the edge of the page thoughtfully, as if weighing the moment of pursuit. The desk, once intended as a dressing table, had been a gift from her parents on her sixteenth birthday, crafted by a local carpenter and adorned with delicate floral carvings along its edges. It was elegant, meant for refinement, but Eva had never cared for such things. She had accepted the gift with grace but had inwardly scoffed when her foolish mother had gushed, *"For you, mein Liebling, to sit and prepare yourself for the day ahead."* As if "preparing herself" could change anything. She had long since learned that beauty was something she did not possess. The girls at school had made that clear, taunting her with cruel suggestions—smile more, be softer, be prettier. But what was there to smile about? The only thing that would bring her happiness was returning home to Germany.

So, the dressing table had become something far more useful: a desk where she crafted her plans and recorded her observations. Over time, she built a business out of people's indiscretions, astonished at their stupidity. Her talent for lurking in the shadows, listening to whispered secrets, had followed her from the ship all those years ago. Now, at eighteen, she understood far more than she once had, often revisiting her earliest notebooks and laughing at the humiliations she might have inflicted. Her trunk, which had once carried her belongings to New Zealand, now contained something far more valuable: a stash of money acquired from those who had underestimated her. She kept it locked away, hidden deep within her wardrobe, ensuring that no one entered her room. Catching her reflection in the mirror, her steel-grey eyes were sharp and calculating. They could pierce through the bravest of liars and unravel the confidence of the guilty with effortless precision. As the thrill of power surged through her, electric and intoxicating, she smiled.

Today, Eva's chosen victim was Emilia, a woman she had first encountered years ago on the ship that carried her family to New Zealand. The voyage had been long, monotonous, and wearisome, leaving Eva little amusement except for observing others. Heavily pregnant, Emilia had caught her attention early on, and for a time, Eva had followed her, studying her movements and filing away details with ease. One evening, she had caught sight of Emilia kneeling at a makeshift altar, whispering a desperate prayer. The woman begged God to delay her child's arrival and vowed, in return, to devote herself to being a good Christian, a dutiful wife, and a loving mother. Eva had kept her distance, watching and listening. When the journey ended, Emilia was still pregnant, and they parted ways, leading Eva to conclude that God had indeed answered her plea.

Now, years later, fate had delivered Emilia into the bookshop one afternoon, accompanied by a boy of seven or eight. As Eva observed them, the pieces clicked neatly into place. And when she later recognised Emilia's husband as the very same man from the voyage, excitement flared in her chest. *This is going to be fun,* she thought, clapping her hands together in delight. Without hesitation, she had raced upstairs to retrieve her old notebook from the depths of her trunk. She began to carefully read the notes she had scrawled all those years ago. Pursing her lips and furrowing her brow, a habit whenever she devised something particularly ingenious, she decided that a letter would be far more effective than mere words. Taking plain notepaper, she set to work, copying Emilia's whispered prayer exactly as she had heard it, every word preserved. At the end of the note, she added her demand: three shillings to be left inside the old oak tree that had been struck by lightning the previous summer. Then, tucking the letter into her skirt pocket, she returned downstairs. When her father asked her to mind the shop while he made deliveries, Eva seized the opportunity. She quickly scanned his client register, her fingers trailing over the names until she found the confirmation she sought. She suppressed a grin as her eyes fell on the entry she needed: *Tobias and Emilia Trafford, 10 Carter Street, Wellington*.

"I'm so clever," she murmured to herself, barely containing her satisfaction.

As Emilia Trafford dressed and made her way to the kitchen early the next day, before the rest of her family woke up, she noticed the handwritten note on the doormat. Puzzled, she opened it and gasped, dropping the letter as if it were red hot. Picking it up quickly, she shoved it in her pocket and went to the kitchen to start breakfast for her family. She had regained her composure by the time her sleepy family entered the kitchen. No one would have ever guessed the turmoil she was feeling inside.

Satisfied with her plan, Eva sat at the breakfast table, absent-mindedly picking at her food while wondering what was unfolding at the Trafford household. The anticipation sent a small thrill through her, a secret delight she carefully concealed. Her father's voice suddenly interrupted her thoughts.

"What's put a smile on your face today, Eva?" Theodore's gaze was gentle, his big, kind face filled with quiet curiosity.

"Nothing," Eva snapped, cutting off any further questions. Then, relenting just enough, she added, "It's a lovely day, so I was thinking of taking a walk later." Before any response could be given, the trill sound of the doorbell alerted them to a caller. Hugo shot up from his chair.

"I'll see who's at the door," he said, already slipping down the corridor before anyone could object. Minutes later, he returned, his usual lively energy noticeably dampened. Without a word, he handed a telegram to his father. Theodore read it, his expression changing as something heavy settled behind his eyes. When he finally looked up, his voice was quiet and measured.

"It's your Oma. I'm afraid she has passed away." He exhaled as though absorbing the weight of his own words. "I think we should not open the shop today. It's only right." Rising from his chair, and without another word, he left the room.

A strangled cry escaped Eva as she bolted upright, fleeing to her bedroom. The door slammed shut behind her.

Hugo and Louis sat frozen, uncertain. Hugo barely remembered his grandmother, and Louis had no idea who she was. Both turned instinctively to their mother, seeking reassurance. Elisabeth composed herself, her voice quiet yet steady. "It is all right. Oma was very old, and it was her time. She's in heaven now, with Opa. I imagine they have much to talk about." The boys, content with their mother's explanation, went off to get ready for school.

Left alone in the kitchen, Elisabeth carefully cleared the breakfast dishes, giving herself time to absorb the news. Once everything was tidied away, she placed a note on the shop door explaining that there had been a family bereavement and pinned a length of black cloth across the entrance.

When she returned, she found her husband sitting in his favourite armchair by the counter of his beloved bookshop.

"Are you all right, my dear?" she asked gently.

Yes, I am fine. Honestly, I'm not sure how I feel. We were never close, and as you know, she was a difficult woman, which only worsened over the years. It's Eva I'm worried about. She was so close to her Oma, and I fear she will take this very hard.

"I will go and see if I can comfort her." She kissed the top of her husband's head and left him to his thoughts. Knocking on her daughter's bedroom door, she called out her name. "Eva, can I come in?"

"Go away. I don't want to speak to you. Leave me alone."

Eva was curled up on her bed, crying. She never cried, but today, it felt like all her hopes and dreams had been destroyed. Her dear Oma had gone, even though she had promised to be there for her when she returned to Germany. *Everyone lets me down in the end.*

Over the next few days, Elisabeth tried everything she could to comfort Eva. Then Theodore tried. Then Hugo. Yet nothing could coax her out of her bedroom. Elisabeth was at her wit's end. Eva would only speak German, shutting herself off from the family completely. The boys were upset and confused by Eva's behaviour. Hoping to lift their spirits, Elisabeth suggested they go to the promenade, instructing Hugo to buy them both an ice cream and, if there was any money left, to enjoy themselves at the penny arcade. Eva was another matter, and she needed to do something to pull her daughter out of the terrible melancholy she had sunk into—and then Elisabeth had an idea. Crossing the road to Spielmann & Son Gentlemen's Tailors, Elisabeth's stride was purposeful. If anyone could draw Eva out of her grief, it was Giselle.

The contrast between the two siblings was striking. Where Valentine was blond, reserved, and effortlessly formal, Giselle was warm with a gentle expression. She dressed in understated elegance, often designing her clothes from photographs she had cut out of fashion magazines. She wore her dark brown hair in an attractive chignon and looked older than her eighteen years. As Elisabeth entered the shop, Giselle greeted her with her usual warmth. "Hello, Mrs Miller. What can I do for you today?"

"Hello, Giselle. I've come to ask for your help," Elisabeth answered, her voice tinged with worry as she stepped inside the shop. "We received a telegram from Germany to tell us Theodore's mother has passed away."

Giselle's expression softened with sympathy. "Oh, I'm so sorry to hear that," she said, her tone warm. "Please, sit down. Would you like some tea?"

"That's very kind of you, but no, thank you," Elisabeth managed a weary smile before sighing. "It's Eva. I'm afraid she's taken her Oma's passing terribly and won't eat or leave her room. I was hoping you might invite her to do something with you. Anything really to help take her mind off the sadness?"

Giselle hesitated. She had never particularly liked Eva, who often targeted her with her moodiness. Still, her affection for Elisabeth and Theodore outweighed any reservations. After a brief moment, she nodded. "I'll do what I can. Valentine is performing in a small fundraising concert with a few other musicians; perhaps I could invite her to come with me?"

Relief flickered in Elisabeth's eyes. "Thank you, that sounds perfect. I'm afraid I've run out of ideas." She exhaled, her voice quiet. "I can't tell you how worried I am."

"Are you, Mother?" Elisabeth and Giselle spun around, their breath catching as Eva materialised in the doorway. She stood with her hands resting on her hips, her gaze sharp and commanding, surveying them with an air of imperious disdain.

"Oh, Eva! How are you feeling? I came to see Giselle to discuss making you a new dress. How would you like that?" Elisabeth knew she was babbling, and it was obvious that they'd been talking about Eva, but what else could she say? Elisabeth looked beseechingly at Giselle, who took her cue and walked over to where Eva was standing.

"Eva, I'm so glad you're here. I was just about to ask your mother if you'd like to join me for a concert this Friday evening. Valentine is performing, and it's for a good cause as we're raising funds to contribute to the major fundraising that has begun for a Children's Hospital to be built here in Wellington."

Silence. Elisabeth gave a nervous cough and looked at her daughter.

"That sounds lovely, Giselle. How thoughtful of you to ask me," Eva replied, betraying no trace of the week spent railing against life and mourning her cherished Oma. Giselle shivered and felt a sudden chill. *No, I do not like you, Eva Miller. You have a cold heart*. Then, fixing one of her best smiles, usually reserved for difficult customers, Giselle turned to Eva and said, "Wonderful. Should we call for you at about six o'clock on Friday? I promised to go a little earlier to help Valentine set up and see if any of the committee ladies needed help."

Eva smiled in agreement and excused herself, saying that she had an urgent errand and that was that. Elisabeth sighed and looked sadly at Giselle. "You have a kind heart, thank you."

The grief of losing her beloved Oma had momentarily driven Emilia Trafford from Eva's mind, but urgency seized her as she recalled her plan. She had to reach the oak tree at once. She hurried to the spot where the gnarled roots sprawled like the legs of a monstrous spider. Digging into the hidden hollow beneath, her fingers closed around an envelope. Tearing it open, she let out a gasp as money spilt into her hands. A jubilant laugh escaped her, and in an instant, the sorrow for her Oma vanished, replaced by cold determination. Her focus sharpened as she vowed to channel every ounce of energy into her next target. Germany beckoned like an unyielding dream, and nothing, neither loss nor obstacles, would deter her. All she needed was a new plan.

Chapter 12

Marie's heart swelled with pride as she surveyed the music salon at Josiah Westfield & Son Music Emporium, which was packed to capacity for the Children's Hospital fundraiser. As a member of the Mayoress's Committee, she had been entrusted with organising the concert, and she had done so with meticulous care, determined that every detail be perfect. She moved swiftly, adjusting the towering vases of poppies and the delicate sprays of pink and blue lupins, ensuring they formed a vibrant summer backdrop for the small, raised stage where the grand piano awaited.

Adelaide had spent the previous hour placing a programme on each seat. Excitement thrummed through her as she set down the neatly printed yellow leaflets, her gaze lingering on her own name. A quiet thrill ran through her. Seeing it in print felt momentous, as if she, too, belonged to the magic of the night. The programme opened with Gwendoline Pelham singing *She Walks in Beauty,* with Adelaide at the piano. Next, Violet would perform Debussy's *Arabesque*, followed by Valentine, who had chosen Beethoven's *Piano Sonata No. 1 in F Minor*. After a short interval, during which refreshments would be served, Josiah Westfield himself would begin the second half with a recital of Rudyard Kipling's poem *If*, a choice he claimed would inspire the audience. And, since he had so generously donated the music salon for the concert, no one dared to disagree. The programme would then continue with Mrs Easterwood's school choir, accompanied by Violet Ivery, and conclude with Delia Howard performing Beethoven's much-loved *Für Elise* on the piano. Adelaide had secretly hoped for a solo herself, but when she had voiced her desire, her mother had gently reminded her that the evening was already crowded with performers. She should be content with accompanying Gwendoline, and Adelaide tried her best to swallow her disappointment.

Meanwhile, Peggy was arranging an enticing selection of cakes and buns, generously donated by households across Thorndon eager to support the fundraiser. With quiet pride, she placed her prized lemon syrup cake and a plate of freshly baked strawberry scones at the centre of the display. Adelaide, determined to steady her nerves, resolved to read through her music one last time. Across the room, Gwendoline was already seated, softly humming the melody to herself. Just as Adelaide was about to take her place, Marie appeared, her face etched with worry.

"Adelaide, you'll need to step in for Delia Howard. She's just sent word that she's unwell. She's included her music with her letter of apology, so you must do your best," Marie said, her tone brisk but pleading.

Adelaide's eyes widened. "But I haven't practised properly, I don't—"

Raising her hand to silence any further protest, Marie stopped her. "Adelaide, you're perfectly capable of playing *Für Elise*. I've heard you play it many times. Please, no arguments. You've half an hour to familiarise yourself with the music. I must make sure everything else runs smoothly and try to prevent any further disasters!"

Violet, seated nearby, had been silently watching the mother and daughter exchange. She leaned forward and said softly to Adelaide, "May I say something?"

"Yes, Miss Ivery," Adelaide replied, reverting nervously to their tutor–pupil formality.

"Your mother is right. You can do this. She is only upset because her plan has gone awry. Try not to overthink it. Sit quietly, focus on your music, and play the notes in your mind, just as I've taught you. I believe in you, Adelaide. I promise it will be fine." Adelaide tried not to cry. Her sensitive nature had never coped well with her mother's sharp temper, and now, to be suddenly asked to do something for which she was unprepared, felt overwhelming. Yet Violet's calm, soothing voice worked its usual magic. Adelaide took a deep breath and began to read through the score. It wasn't that she doubted her ability; she could play the piece well enough, but her mother and the committee had chosen Delia to perform it, and in Adelaide's mind, that meant they considered her not good enough. She was the second choice. And echoing in her thoughts was her mother's earlier word: *Disaster.*

As if reading her mind, Violet whispered, "Adelaide, you are not second-best. It was only decided that you were the better choice to accompany Gwendoline."

Adelaide smiled. "I'm sorry. You know how I hate surprises. I am all right now. All will be well."

"That's the ticket," Violet said with a grin.

Josiah Westfield's wealth was entirely self-made. He arrived in Wellington as a penniless sixteen-year-old, working his passage aboard a ship with nothing but the clothes on his back, a few coins, and a burning ambition. For several years, he took on any work he could find, and then, during the Otago gold rush of the early 1860s, luck favoured him. With his earnings, he returned to Wellington, where he opened his emporium while the city was still in its infancy. Over the years, his business flourished, and he became one of its leading citizens.

Now a portly middle-aged man with a quick smile and a friendly glint in his brown eyes, he took his place at the front of the stage. Pulling a gold watch from his waistcoat pocket, the chain barely stretching across his ample belly, he checked the time and prepared to welcome the gathered audience. His loud, genial voice resonated through the hall, and the audience hushed as he welcomed them to his store, and especially to his music salon, where he hoped many more concerts would follow. He announced that all proceeds would go towards the construction of Wellington's new Children's Hospital, and he thanked everyone warmly for their generosity. Then he handed over to Marie to introduce the performers.

Adelaide observed her mother, poised and confident as she addressed the gathering. How wonderful it would be, she thought, to possess such assurance. Her own certainty extended only as far as the piano; beyond that, the world felt confusing and difficult. Her mother's voice cut into her thoughts. "To begin our programme, Miss Gwendoline Pelham will perform *She Walks in Beauty,* accompanied on the piano by Miss Adelaide Ellwood."

Adelaide and Gwendoline rose to polite applause and took their seats. The familiar sensation of the keys beneath Adelaide's fingers grounded her, easing the tension in her shoulders as the music began. Gwendoline's voice soared, pure and elegant, filling the salon with beauty. When they finished, the applause was warm and enthusiastic. Adelaide and Gwendoline bowed slightly before returning to their seats, where Violet met Adelaide's gaze with an encouraging smile.

Violet then performed her own piece with elegance, her fingers gliding effortlessly over the keys. As she finished, the audience responded with eager applause, and Adelaide could not help but feel proud to be studying under, in her opinion, Wellington's finest teacher.

Next came Valentine. As he rose to the piano, an unexpected nervousness swept over Adelaide. Why should she feel this way about a relative stranger when he had trained at the prestigious Leipzig Conservatoire? She could not look away as he began. The music poured from him, reaching deep into her. His performance was extraordinary, drawing rapturous applause and several spirited cries of "Bravo!" Valentine bowed, then turned and caught Adelaide's gaze. Her cheeks flushed. Was he flaunting his talent, reminding her how it should be done? The thought unsettled her. She dreaded following such brilliance, yet knew she had no choice.

After a brief pause, Adelaide found solace in Mr Westfield's recitation of Kipling's *If*, delivered with remarkable eloquence. Mrs Easterwood's young pupils then followed, their light-hearted giggles illuminating the room. Violet gently silenced them before striking the opening chords, and their cheerful singing soon had much of the audience smiling and even joining in. Adelaide's spirits finally lifted. When the choir had finished and the children returned to their seats, Violet sat beside Adelaide, squeezed her hand, and whispered, "You can do this."

Confidence restored, Adelaide moved to the piano. She carefully placed the music on the stand and took a steadying breath. As her fingers made contact with the keys, the music took control. The audience's presence faded away. When the last notes died away, applause erupted once again. Glancing across the salon, Adelaide saw Valentine smiling at her, clapping eagerly. His sister Giselle joined in warmly, but beside them sat Eva, her arm linked possessively through Valentine's, staring at Adelaide with a look that made her shiver.

"Well done, Adelaide!" Violet, Marie, and Mrs Easterwood's voices carried above the applause.

Mr Westfield returned to the stage for the closing remarks and invited the Mayoress, Mrs Wilford, to join him.

"Mrs Wilford," he began, "thank you for entrusting me with the honour of hosting this concert in support of your fundraising campaign. I am pleased to announce that the princely sum of five pounds has been raised from ticket sales. And it is with my greatest pleasure that I would like to double that amount and present you with a cheque for ten pounds." The room erupted in cheers and applause as a visibly moved Mrs Wilford accepted the cheque with heartfelt appreciation.

"This is indeed a most generous contribution toward the establishment of a much-needed hospital dedicated to the care of Wellington's children," she said. "I must extend my sincere thanks to Mrs Ellwood for her splendid organisation of this evening's concert, and congratulations to all who took part—it has been thoroughly delightful."

As the audience dispersed, Adelaide bade farewell to Gwendoline, who left with her mother. Violet was helping Mrs Easterwood guide the last of the pupils to their parents. Then Valentine, Giselle, and Eva approached. "Well done, Adelaide," Valentine said. "That was an impressive attempt at Beethoven's masterpiece. I would gladly offer you some lessons if you wished to improve your skills." Before Adelaide could reply, Eva spoke. "Isn't that kind of Valentine, Adelaide? But you already have a tutor, don't you? A Miss Violet Ivery. We heard her play earlier, didn't we?" Adelaide was struggling to find a suitable reply when Valentine answered on her behalf. "Indeed, and I enjoyed her interpretation of Debussy's *Arabesque*."

Giselle shot Eva an annoyed look but quickly turned her frown into a cheerful smile. "Adelaide, you are a gifted pianist, too. You accompanied your friend beautifully, and *Für Elise* was wonderful!"

"Thank you, Giselle. That is kind of you," Adelaide replied, doing her best not to blush or stutter.

Eva seized her chance. "Oh, Adelaide, you still blush, just like when we were at school. Isn't that so endearing, don't you think, Valentine?" Valentine only nodded, showing no emotion in response to Eva's unkind remark.

A strange feeling welled up inside Adelaide. She was used to Eva's constant criticism, but Valentine? Was he being critical of Violet's playing and of herself? How rude of him. Eva stood at his side, wearing that half-smile, half-smirk, and Adelaide was suddenly overcome by the urge to say something sharp in return. It took every ounce of self-control to remain silent. Anger—that was what it was. She was angry.

Looking up at Valentine, cursing inwardly at her small stature, she forced herself to respond with composure. "Well, anyway, it was generous of you to play to help raise funds for such a worthwhile cause. I'm sure they appreciate you giving up your precious time."

Valentine nodded and looked at her with a puzzled expression. Eva remained silent, simply watching as Adelaide turned and hurried away as fast as she could.

"Adelaide, dear!" Her mother's voice broke into her thoughts. "Are you ready to go now? I am exhausted."

They walked home together in comfortable silence. The evening air was pleasantly cool after the heat of Mr Westfield's salon. Finally, Marie spoke. "I thought Valentine Spielmann's performance was particularly good. I do think, however, that he should cut his hair. It's a little too long for my liking!" Adelaide smiled, slipped her arm through her mother's, and at that moment, all was forgiven.

Chapter 13

Wellington – November 1910

Early mornings were Adelaide's favourite time of day. An early riser, she would open the shutters in her bedroom, listen to the dawn chorus, and enjoy the sight of the trees and plants filling their back garden. It wasn't as grand as Woodlands, but Angus the gardener had made it look lovely all the same. Adelaide was especially excited because that evening she was to attend her very first opera with Violet at the Wanganui Opera House, a thoughtful eighteenth-birthday gift from Violet and her Aunt Susan. Afterwards, Susan planned to treat them to a late supper at Dustin's Tea Rooms on Victoria Avenue. Susan smiled as she announced her plans: "You are only eighteen once!"

Violet had gone to see Marie to ask for her permission first, and since Marie was not particularly fond of opera, she was more than happy for Violet and her aunt to take Adelaide with them. Marie, instead, busied herself with planning a birthday party for her daughter, inviting a few friends and family to celebrate, and she insisted that Violet and Susan be included as well. Despite Violet's polite protests, Marie would not take no for an answer.

"Adelaide thinks the world of you, so you must come and celebrate with us!" she said warmly.

Violet was secretly delighted and was eager to tell Aunt Susan, for neither of them had many opportunities to be welcomed into the elevated circles of Wellington society.

That evening, the Opera House glowed with light as the audience settled into their seats. The performance was Puccini's relatively new opera, *Madama Butterfly,* and Adelaide sat entranced. From her seat, she could see the orchestra as well as the stage, and she hardly knew where to look—at the singers in their colourful costumes or at the musicians below. The music was beautiful and deeply moving. At one point, Violet leaned in close and whispered, "One day, that will be you," her eyes fixed on the pianist in the orchestra pit, who played with exquisite precision. "Not here in Whanganui perhaps, but on a far greater stage. You have the gift, Adelaide. Never forget it." Adelaide's answering smile said everything, her eyes shining with the secret hope that Violet's words might one day prove true. Violet felt a quiet pride in her young student, convinced she was witnessing the first spark of a remarkable career.

Later, the three ladies made their way along Victoria Avenue to Dustin's Tea Rooms, a fashionable establishment that had recently added an upstairs supper room. The supper room was softly lit, its tables set with crisp linen and shining silver, the air fragrant with coffee and warm pastries. Gentle conversation mingled with the clink of china as other operagoers arrived, prolonging the evening's pleasure with light suppers of oysters, sandwiches, and delicate cakes. As Adelaide sat with Violet and Aunt Susan, she barely touched her food at first, still adrift in the spell of Puccini's music. The soaring melodies echoed in her mind, each note mingling with the glow of lamplight and the low murmur of voices around her. It seemed to her that the night had woven together music, friendship, and promise, and she longed to hold onto it for as long as she could. For Adelaide, it was the perfect end to a night she knew she would never forget.

When Adelaide returned home, she noticed the light was on in her father's study. Too excited to sleep, she tapped lightly on the door. "Come in," came his familiar voice. She pushed it open and almost flew inside. "Oh, Father, I have just been to see *Madama Butterfly!* It was the most wonderful thing—the costumes, the music, everything! Tomorrow I must go to Mr Miller's bookshop and find out more about Puccini and his life. I must know how he writes such music!" Her words tumbled out in a rush, her eyes sparkling as though the performance still lingered before her. Robert, seated in his worn leather chair, cradling a glass of whiskey, had been unwinding from a particularly demanding case. He looked up at the whirlwind that was his daughter and couldn't help but laugh out loud. She was a joy, brimming with life and promise, but she was no longer his little girl. Soon she would be eighteen, and it was time to put all childish things away. Yet, watching her so alight with wonder, he worried if she was ready for such changes. He made a mental note to speak to Marie about it.

"Good heavens, young lady, slow down! You are making me quite dizzy," he chuckled, setting aside his glass. Pointing to the leather armchair by the bookcase, he rose and moved to the one opposite. "Come, sit here, and start again, properly this time. Tell me everything from the beginning. You entered the Opera House and…"

Adelaide obeyed at once, smoothing her skirt as she perched on the chair, her whole face alight. For the next hour, she recounted every detail. The swell of the overture, the brilliance of the soprano, the moment Violet whispered her dream for her future. Robert listened, amused and touched in equal measure, as his daughter relived her evening with breathless enthusiasm, eager for him to share in her joy.

On the morning of her eighteenth birthday, Adelaide had been awake since dawn. She stood at her window, watching the sunrise, inhaled the cool morning air, and gazed at the garden as she always did. Later, she would help her mother pick flowers to place around the house. Angus had been teaching her how to care for the plants and the proper way to deadhead the roses, and he had promised to dig over a small area for her to create a miniature garden. She had been so thrilled that she hugged him, making the poor man blush.

"Now, now, Miss, there's no need for that. Everyone should learn how to tend a garden." But the small grin on his weathered, nut-brown face as he continued his weeding made Adelaide smile.

A sharp, insistent knocking at her door jolted her from her thoughts. "Adelaide, dear, are you awake? Your father is leaving for work soon and wants to see you before he goes."

"Coming, Mother."

Having already dressed, Adelaide opened the door and nearly collided with her mother.

"Adelaide, slow down! I sometimes despair. You are now eighteen, a young woman. Please try to behave like one!"

"Sorry. I'm just excited about my birthday. Is there anything in the post? I was hoping Joseph would have written to me by now."

"Well, let's go and see, shall we?"

Robert was finishing his breakfast, and Peggy was clearing away some of the dishes.

"Ah, here's the birthday girl!" Robert rose to greet his beaming daughter.

Peggy smiled at her discreetly before leaving the room.

Several envelopes lay on the table. Adelaide tried to see if one had a British postmark, but she could not find any. She tried not to look too disappointed, but she could not help feeling sad that her brother had not remembered.

"Are you looking forward to your party this evening?" Robert asked.

"I am! It's a beautiful day, too, and I can't wait to see everyone. When are Helena and Gabriel arriving?"

"I'm not sure, Adelaide. We couldn't decide whether to come or not!"

"Helena!" Adelaide almost screamed as her cousin entered, and everyone laughed.

"But how — when?"

"I'm afraid we arrived quite late, so we decided to surprise you this morning instead. I can happily say our mission was accomplished."

"It certainly was! I had no idea."

Everyone sat down, and Peggy brought in a trolley laden with fruit, bread, hams, cheeses, and a jug of orange juice. Marie had asked Peggy to forgo their usual cooked breakfast for Adelaide and their guests, knowing it would only go cold with all the birthday distractions.

"This is the best birthday ever!" exclaimed Adelaide.

Robert handed her a small box decorated with a pink bow.

"This is for you. Happy birthday."

Adelaide carefully undid the bow and lifted the lid, revealing the most exquisite gold locket nestled on blue silken fabric.

"Oh, Father, it is beautiful."

"I'm glad you like it. Your mother and I deliberated long and hard over what piece of jewellery to buy you, and when we saw this, we thought it would suit you perfectly."

Adelaide held the locket up to the light, admiring the intricate flowers engraved on the front. Turning it over, she read the inscription:

For our precious daughter, with love. 4th November 1910.

"Let me help you put it on," Helena offered, taking the locket from Adelaide. She lifted her cousin's hair from her neck and fixed the clasp.

"There, it looks lovely on you."

Marie and Robert looked on fondly.

Turning to her father, Adelaide smiled. "Thank you, and I will treasure it always. I wish you didn't have to go to work today."

"Do you? Well, in that case, I won't!"

"Really?" Adelaide's shocked expression made everyone erupt into laughter again.

Robert smiled warmly at his daughter. "Turning eighteen deserves to be celebrated! After breakfast, I suggest we take a walk along the esplanade. It's a beautiful day, and we could even treat ourselves to some ice cream, then return home to prepare for this evening's party. How does that sound?"

Adelaide sat, watching her dear family. Helena and Gabriel appeared blissfully happy, and Marie was eager to hear how they were settling into their new home and how Gabriel's job at the bank was progressing. Adelaide wished she could bottle this moment to keep forever—her family was all she needed to be happy.

She then spied a box at her father's feet.

"What's in the box?"

"What box?"

"The box right by your feet!"

"Oh, this box. Let me see who it is for." Robert made a show of picking up the parcel to read the address label.

"Is it from Joseph?" exclaimed Adelaide.

"Oh yes, I think you are right. And it's addressed to you, too. Here you are." He handed it over to his daughter.

Adelaide was overjoyed. "May I be excused? I'd like to open it alone. I'll be right back to show you my present once I've opened it!"

She raced out of the room, followed by her mother's exasperated voice: "Adelaide, walk, for heaven's sake!"

Once in her bedroom, she ripped open the top of the box. Inside were parcels of varying sizes, neatly wrapped in brown paper and tied with string. Sitting on top was a blue envelope, her name written neatly in the centre in her brother's familiar hand. She eagerly pulled out the letter and began to read.

Dearest Addie,

Happy Birthday! I hope this arrives well in time and that you like the enclosed gifts. I must confess that it was Kitty who helped me. She decided I was rather hopeless at knowing what a young lady might appreciate for her eighteenth birthday!

Kitty and I have settled into our new home, and Victoria Avenue is a welcoming neighbourhood. Everyone has neat little gardens, which have inspired me to learn about bulbs and to plant seasonal flowers. Our little front garden is now up to standard!

I am enjoying married life, but it's challenging when I have to go away to sea so often. Kitty is wonderfully patient and accepting of my work. She enjoys caring for our home, and when I'm on shore leave, I have to go around the house guessing what little changes or additions Kitty has made.

I have been promoted to 3rd Engineer, which I am told is quite an achievement for someone of my age. I am embracing the challenges and extra responsibilities that come with it. As much as I would like to, I won't bore you with all the details of the ship's engines, which never cease to fascinate me!

I've enclosed a photograph of our special day, which I hope you like. Our only witnesses were my shipmate, Jack Mason, and his wife, Mary. Kitty and Mary have become great friends, which is a relief when I am away at sea, knowing she has someone to call on if she needs anything.

Write soon. I want to hear all your news.
With fondest wishes,
Joseph

Adelaide could almost hear her brother's voice speaking to her. With all her heart, she wished she could see him and meet Kitty. It made her even more determined to be accepted at the Royal Academy of Music when the time came, and then, hopefully, she would finally get to visit her brother and get to know Kitty, the source of all his newfound happiness. Putting the letter aside, she turned to the selection of presents in the box. The first gift was a set of hand-stitched mats for her dressing table. They were exquisite, and Adelaide loved them. She then unwrapped a book about the history of Liverpool, with a little note from Joseph: "I thought you would like to read all about our hometown, and when you visit one day, you will know its history!" Adelaide wasn't sure how to feel about the book, despite its interesting appearance. Joseph's words had upset her a little, as he now considered Liverpool home. Placing the book back in the box, she opened a smaller package containing special soaps and a pretty hair clip. Finally, there was an envelope holding a photograph. It showed Joseph and Kitty looking blissfully happy on their wedding day. Staring at the photograph, Adelaide could tell from Joseph's smiling face how happy he was—he looked grown-up, handsome, and smartly dressed in his uniform. She then turned her attention to Kitty and begrudgingly admitted that she looked happy, too. Kitty was attractive in a simple, unassuming way, wearing a modest but pretty gown with a satin sash around her small waist. Her shoulder-length hair was adorned with a circlet of flowers. "I am happy for you, dear Joseph," Adelaide murmured to the photograph, hugging it tightly to her chest.

Placing all the presents back in the box, Adelaide returned to the dining room. As she was about to enter, her mother's voice stopped her in her tracks. She was speaking about Adelaide's presents.

"I wonder what Joseph has bought Adelaide. At least he hasn't forgotten her birthday. It's all so disappointing; he could have done so much better for himself."

"He's happy, Aunt Marie. Isn't that important too?" Helena replied.

"Happiness doesn't pay the bills, does it?" Marie shot back.

"I understand, Aunt Marie, but I believe Joseph has been promoted. He writes sometimes and sounds so content with his life."

Adelaide took advantage of the brief pause in conversation to enter the room, fixing a broad smile to conceal her sadness at hearing her mother speak of her brother in that way.

"Adelaide, dear," Helena said quickly, patting the empty chair next to her. "Come and show us what Joseph has given you!"

Adelaide gratefully sat beside her cousin, displaying all the beautiful gifts she had received. The photograph was passed around, accompanied by exclamations about how happy the couple looked and how pretty Kitty's dress was. Marie had to admit the stitching on the table mats was quite fine, but she only gave the photograph a cursory glance, unwilling to acknowledge her son's happiness. Robert had remained notably silent throughout. Adelaide took a deep breath, letting the moment sink in. Surrounded by the warmth and laughter of her family, she felt a quiet satisfaction she had never known before. Joseph's gifts, Helena's cheerful encouragement, Gabriel's easy smile, and even Marie's sharp remarks all reminded her of the varied ways love and care could be expressed. She realised that happiness did not always look the way one expected it to. It could be found in small acts, thoughtful words, and the shared joy of those who genuinely cared for her. Holding the photograph of Joseph and Kitty again, she smiled softly, feeling proud of her brother and grateful for the life she had at home. In that moment, Adelaide understood that family, in all its imperfections and tenderness, was all she truly needed to feel complete and content.

After an enjoyable stroll along the promenade and the

promised ice creams, the party returned home to prepare for the evening's entertainment. Adelaide had been told that, as the 'birthday girl,' there was no need for her to do anything to help, so she took the opportunity to find Peggy. Hoping she wouldn't be too busy to share a cup of tea, Adelaide discovered Peggy kneading some dough at the kitchen table.

"Hello, Peggy. Hello, Lucy." Lucy was also there to help her aunt prepare for Adelaide's party and would later serve drinks and canapés.

"Ah, there's the birthday girl! Perfect timing, too. I don't know about you, but I am ready for a cup of tea. Put the kettle on again, Lucy, would you, please?"

"Yes, Aunt Peg." Lucy was smiling because the minute Adelaide had walked into the kitchen, she had placed the big kettle on the range, knowing the next request would be for a cup of tea. "Happy Birthday, Miss Adelaide," Lucy said, then discreetly left them alone, not wishing to intrude on their conversation. Smiling, Adelaide walked up to Peg and hugged her.

"Goodness! What was that for? Be careful, or you'll get your lovely dress covered in flour!"

"I am missing Joseph, and being here with you reminds me of our childhood and how close we were."

"Well, we still are, and nothing will change that. You must try to be happy for your brother. Everyone has to make their own choices in life. If you had been the eldest, you would have gone to London, wouldn't you? And you wouldn't have thought twice about leaving your brother to follow your dreams. That's what Joseph is doing. It's all part of growing up."

"Oh, Peggy, I hadn't thought of it like that."

Peggy wiped her flushed face with the back of her hand. "If I have learned anything about life, it is this: no matter how well you try to map it out, there'll always be the odd, unexpected bend in the road you must take. Sometimes it's a painful choice, but other times it can be an unexpected gift. I think Kitty is Joseph's unexpected gift."

"What a lovely way to think of life," Adelaide said.

"My pleasure, dearie. Right, let's have that tea before it gets too busy, and you can show me that photograph you're holding!"

Adelaide's recollections of her eighteenth birthday party were mostly joyful until her father spoiled it all. Marie had ordered a bolt of sky-blue satin from England and had asked Giselle to make a dress for her daughter. Giselle was delighted, as it was a refreshing change from the men's suits she worked on so diligently every day. Marie and Giselle agreed on a simple yet elegant design—a tubular column dress with an empire line that suited Adelaide's petite frame perfectly. Giselle added a cream lace collar and lace trimmings around the three-quarter-length sleeves. Adelaide attended the fittings but was more than happy to leave the decision-making to her mother, confident that Giselle would create a beautiful dress for her.

That evening, Helena styled her cousin's hair into a loose plait, threading in some pretty ribbon made from some of the leftover material of her dress. Adelaide had to admit she was enjoying the attention that becoming eighteen brought with it. She didn't often like such attention, but today, it felt good, and she felt loved. All the guests were arriving, and the doors were wide open to let in the cool evening air. Angus had hung about half a dozen lanterns from the trees, creating a fairyland-like scene. In Adelaide's mind, anyway. A few guests made their way outside to enjoy their drinks in the cool evening air. Henry and Victoria had just arrived with the twins. Henry had some business to attend to in the city over the next few days, so they had decided to turn their visit into a mini-holiday and booked into a hotel. As Henry worked, Victoria would show the twins around Wellington. Adelaide had offered to join them on a few excursions, and her Aunt was delighted and relieved to have another pair of hands to supervise their youthful exuberance. Now fifteen years old, they had suddenly shot up in height and seemed to fill the room. After a loud and cheerful welcome, they wished their cousin a "Very happy birthday." After which, they were persuaded by their mother to go into the garden and play cards, anything to keep them out of mischief.

John and Susannah Montgomery were the next to arrive, and they greeted Adelaide with a beautiful bouquet of delphiniums and a pretty set of lace handkerchiefs that Charlotte had embroidered for her friend. "Thank you. I love delphiniums, and look, they go with my dress! The handkerchiefs are beautiful. Has she mentioned when she is coming home yet?"

Susannah sighed before explaining, "She hasn't shown any interest in coming home yet, I'm afraid. She has fallen in love with London, and a gentleman called Matthew Hibbert, as he is all she writes about."

Adelaide laughed, saying, "I must write to her. I haven't heard from her for some time, and now I know why. Is university life suiting Miles? Joseph was asking if I knew how he was faring."

"He has embraced university life, and so far, it's going well. Although I must say his letter-writing is appalling, we rarely hear from him. I am relieved he chose to study in Christchurch and not abroad; otherwise, we might never see him again!" Susannah shook her head in mock despair.

"Happy Birthday, Adelaide!" The cheerful voice of her friend Gwendoline Pelham could be heard, making Adelaide turn to greet her. Gwendoline was the first of Adelaide's school friends to get engaged, and she proudly showed off her engagement ring and her new fiancé in that order. Adelaide had made the mistake of telling her mother at the time of Gwendoline's engagement that eighteen was far too young to get engaged, causing a lecture to ensue about how love doesn't always come first. "Meeting the right person is what is important." Her mother explained. Adelaide decided not to argue. It wasn't worth it, and she nodded sagely at her mother. Cecil Gilmore seemed to make Gwendoline happy, and they both appeared excited about their wedding next summer. After making sure Gwendoline and Cecil were supplied with drinks, Adelaide excused herself to find Violet and Susan. She discovered them sitting at a table on the terrace, hiding their nervousness by admiring the roses.

"There you are!" Adelaide said, sitting in one of the empty chairs. "I've been looking everywhere for you."

"Happy Birthday, Adelaide!" Violet and Susan spoke simultaneously. Violet tapped a beautifully wrapped box. "This is for you, from both of us."

"For me?" Adelaide gasped.

Laughing, Violet said, "Well, yes, unless another young lady here is celebrating her eighteenth birthday!"

"But you have already treated me to the opera, which, I might add, I cannot stop thinking about!" Grinning, Adelaide carefully opened the box. As she lifted the lid, she gasped in surprise. Nestled in a bed of black velvet lay the most beautiful brooch she had ever seen. Adelaide stared at it, unable to speak.

"Do you like it? It was my mother's," Violet explained. "The brooch is one of three I have, and I would like you to have this one. Wear it when you are performing; hopefully, it will bring you luck, as it has for me."

Adelaide held the dainty brooch in her hand. Its design was a floral spray set with rose-cut diamonds, sparkling in the candlelight.

"Oh, Violet, thank you. It's beautiful, and I will wear it always."

"Adelaide, dear, you have two unexpected guests. They are

here now, so please, can you go and welcome them?" Marie sat down next to her daughter, looking rather put out. Ignoring her mother's agitation, Adelaide showed her the brooch. "Look what Violet has given me. Isn't it beautiful?"

"How lovely. Yes, it's very pretty indeed. Now, please go and greet your unexpected guests."

Adelaide knew by the sound of her mother's voice that she must obey, so she reluctantly excused herself from her friends and hurried toward the hallway. Her heart sank at the sight of Valentine and Eva standing there. Valentine looked distinguished in a dark suit, and Eva wore a green dress that, for a change, suited her remarkably well. Eva smiled as she spoke. "Adelaide, I am so sorry we are late. Unforgivable, really, but we are here now, so no harm done."

"Happy Birthday, Adelaide," Valentine said kindly. "It was very thoughtful of you to invite us."

Adelaide hesitated. She had not invited either of them and was puzzled as to why they believed they were included. Yet, not wishing to seem rude, she greeted them warmly. As Valentine and Eva started mingling with the other guests, Eva pressed a book into Adelaide's hands. "This is from my father, by the way." Threading her arm through Valentine's, they moved towards Lucy, who was carefully weaving among the guests with a tray of drinks.

Adelaide opened the book, "The History of the Pianoforte." Inside, she read the inscription:

"To Adelaide, may this book inspire you to follow your dreams, always."
Theodore and Elisabeth Miller, November 1910.

Her anxiety about the unexpected arrival of Valentine and Eva began to ease. Instead of dwelling on Eva's peculiar behaviour,

Adelaide chose to focus on happiness, smiling at the familiar, dear faces of her family and friends.

The delicate tapping of a spoon against a champagne glass rang out, growing steadily louder until Adelaide could make out her father's voice.

"Ladies and gentlemen," he began warmly, "it's a pleasure to welcome you to our home. Thank you for joining us in celebrating Adelaide's eighteenth birthday. I promise to keep this brief." As he paused, a ripple of laughter stirred through the crowd, and then Robert pressed on.

"It's hard to believe our youngest is now eighteen. The years have flown. I still remember Adelaide's seventh birthday, when all she wanted were piano lessons, books, and more books."

Another wave of laughter rolled through the guests. Adelaide felt the heat rising in her cheeks, bracing herself for what might come next.

"But in all seriousness," her father continued, "Adelaide has made us incredibly proud. She's excelled at school, and I see no sign of her slowing down—whether in her own studies or in tutoring younger children. Yet what stands out most is her music. From the endless scales we endured in those early years to the graceful performances she now gives, including Beethoven, Strauss, and beyond. Her playing fills our home with beauty. Marie and I couldn't be prouder."

He turned towards Adelaide, his eyes softening. "I am not certain where all this study will lead, Adelaide, but your determination and persistence are remarkable." Looking around the room, he continued, "Adelaide has often told me how much she would like to study at the Royal Academy of Music, but not for a few more years yet. So, I have reflected long and hard about what she could do in the meantime, as there is only so much piano study a person can do, and my dear, your mother and I wish to see you 'finished' as a young lady should." Robert looked straight at Adelaide, and she gave him a weak smile. *What was her father about to say?*

"And so, Adelaide," Robert declared with theatrical cheer, we have secured you a place at a distinguished Ladies' College in Christchurch, which will give you every advantage: music, languages, etiquette, all the things that will help you shine when the time comes for you to take your place in society. It is a fine opportunity, and though it may seem daunting now, I truly believe it will be the makings of you."

Robert looked proudly at Adelaide, clearly pleased with his announcement. The guests erupted into applause, clinking glasses and offering congratulations. Adelaide tried to smile, but the shock hit her like a wave, swift and suffocating. Her cheeks burned with humiliation. She glanced toward Helena, whose furrowed brow betrayed concern. Eva, by contrast, was laughing, raising her glass with gleeful approval. Valentine's face remained unreadable, carved in quiet restraint. Around the room, a hum of excited chatter swelled.

"Adelaide? Adelaide, are you all right?" Marie's voice broke through the haze, gently tinged with worry.

Adelaide managed a faint, "Thank you. What a surprise."

Robert, oblivious to the storm behind her eyes, beamed at her. "I thought you'd be delighted! You'll still have time for your books and studies, of course, but more importantly, you'll learn all the useful things a young woman needs to make her way in society."

He raised his glass high. "Now, after all that excitement, let us toast to Adelaide. Happy birthday, my dear. May the year ahead bring joy, growth, and new adventures."

Adelaide felt numb and wished the ground would swallow her whole. She tried to focus on what was happening around her as the guests congratulated her and raised their glasses, while Peggy brought in the cake. From that moment, the rest of the party became a blur, the laughter of her parents echoing as if they had given her the whole world. Someone gently took her arm and guided her towards the garden. It was Violet. Adelaide breathed in the heady scents of jasmine and roses and felt tears prick her eyes. "Why has Father done this to me? What am I going to do? I don't want to go."

Violet's concerned expression said it all, though she chose not to voice her thoughts on Adelaide's father's startling announcement. Instead, she said softly, "Perhaps it's best to sleep on it for now. You've had quite a shock. Don't forget to thank them for this lovely party. I'm sure they believe they're doing what's best for you. Maybe tomorrow would be a better time to share how you really feel."

Adelaide's voice trembled as tears streamed down her cheeks. "I'm so confused. It's as if they don't know me at all. Do they expect me to go to London like Charlotte and find a husband? If I did, there'd be no question about the Royal Academy, would there? I can't bear it."

"Come, let's take a walk in the garden." Violet's soothing tone calmed Adelaide slightly, and together they wandered to the farthest corner, where her favourite tree stood, offering a quiet refuge. After a while, Adelaide thought, reluctantly, they had better return to the party, not wishing to appear ungrateful. As they neared the terrace, Eva suddenly emerged from the shadows, making both of them step back in shock.

"Well, aren't you the lucky one? I couldn't imagine my father paying for me to attend a fancy private school. Just think—a year of learning to walk and drink tea properly, so you can find yourself a man and give up having to play the piano all the time. Won't that be wonderful? Mind you, I think they'll have their work cut out with you." Eva's cruel laughter pierced Adelaide's already fragile mood.

"Eva! That is quite unnecessary. How unkind of you." Violet

sounded genuinely angry. "Adelaide will always play the piano. She's far too talented ever to stop."

"Heaven's, Miss Ivery, how shocking that you presume to understand the ways of the upper classes. I think it would be up to Adelaide's parents to decide what she can and cannot do, and then it will be up to her husband." Eva laughed, thoroughly enjoying Adelaide's misery.

"Eva, why are you so mean to me all the time? I have no intention of getting married, even if I have to endure a year at this school to be 'finished.' After that, I will return to Wellington. Nothing is going to stop me from going to the Royal Academy!"

Just then, Lucy appeared, trying to catch Adelaide's attention. "Sorry to interrupt, Miss, but a few of the guests are starting to leave, and Mrs Ellwood wants you to come and say goodbye."

"Thank you, Lucy." Adelaide turned to speak to Eva, but she had already vanished into the night. Shivering, Adelaide followed Lucy into the dining room to find her mother.

When all the guests had departed, Adelaide feigned tiredness. "Would you excuse me? All this excitement has rather caught up with me." Helena hugged her extra tightly as she said goodnight, and Adelaide felt comforted that her cousin understood without needing words.

The grandfather clock in the hall chimed midnight as Adelaide sat at her writing desk, composing a letter to her brother. She always found it easier to put her feelings on paper than to verbalise them. Her pen scratched furiously, her hands smeared with ink. She shared her true feelings with her brother, who was on the other side of the world, living the life he wanted. After three pages, she crumpled them and threw them in the wastepaper basket. She knew she couldn't even tell her brother how she felt — it somehow felt disloyal.

Exhausted, Adelaide eventually drifted into sleep. As dawn broke and sunlight seeped into her bedroom, the memory of her father, his bright smile and proud announcement that she was to go to Christchurch, overwhelmed her again, and she buried her face in her pillow, sobbing. When the tears finally slowed, she lay still, whispering to herself that it wasn't the worst thing in the world, but at that moment, it felt like it was. She did not feel ready to leave home. Not yet.

Then she remembered Violet's advice. Straightening slightly, she took a deep breath and said aloud, firm despite the tremor in her voice, *"Adelaide Grace Ellwood, get out of bed, pull yourself together, and go and tell them how you feel!"*

Eva sat at her desk the morning after Adelaide's party, feeling pleased with herself. She thought back to when Valentine had walked her home and how pathetic he sounded when he expressed his concern for Adelaide, believing the school in Christchurch was not right for her. She had to contain her fury when he dared to question whether, in fact, they had been invited to the party, considering how surprised Mr and Mrs Ellwood were to see them there. She brushed off his concerns. "What if it's true? We should have been invited. I went to school with her like Gwendoline, and anyway, they didn't seem to mind."

The satisfaction of seeing the startled expressions on everyone's faces when the maid announced their arrival made the deception well worth it. Who did they think they were, treating her with such disregard? Mr Ellwood's little speech had been particularly amusing, and the look of utter shock on Adelaide's face felt like a reward in itself. Let her taste some of the anguish she'd endured when her parents had ripped her away from her home and forced her to live here. Even if it were only for a year, at least Adelaide would experience some of the hardship she had faced. Her thoughts then shifted to Miss Ivery. That woman wielded far too much influence over Adelaide, and her meddling could easily derail everything. The piano teacher was a threat. She needed to be dealt with. *Fix it—do something about it!* Staring into the mirror, her narrowed eyes and a twisted grin formed a grotesque mask of resolve. She nodded at her reflection, sealing the decision.

In Robert's opinion, life in the Ellwood household had become unappealing and fraught with tension. He was growing exasperated, unable to understand why his daughter was so upset, as he felt she was being ridiculous and ungrateful. He had not spoken to her for days and spent most evenings at his club rather than returning home to confront his family. Marie wasn't making his life any easier, either. After the party, he had planned to share a glass of whiskey with his wife, as they would normally do after such an occasion, but instead, she had turned on him.

"We should never have made such an impetuous decision like that. I knew Adelaide would hate the idea, and now we have embarrassed ourselves in front of our friends."

"Might I remind you, dear, that when I suggested the Ladies' College in Christchurch to you, you thought it to be the perfect solution for our shy, young daughter? She must grow up eventually and take her place in society, and hopefully, in time, marry."

Marie could not deny that, at the time, she thought it was a good idea, but she also knew her daughter, and as much as she wanted Adelaide to be as fortunate as she had been in finding a suitable husband, she knew deep down that Adelaide would choose a different path than the one she desired for her.

"Oh, why do my children choose to make my life so difficult?" Marie shouted at Peggy as she brought in a tray of tea one afternoon. Peggy carefully placed the tray down and gave Marie a sympathetic nod, understanding that Mrs Ellwood did not require an answer.

"I can feel one of my headaches coming on, Peggy. Could you please ensure I am not disturbed for at least an hour? If Adelaide is going to continue her education in Christchurch, there is so much to be done, but I need time to think and make some lists."

"Of course, Mrs Ellwood. I'll make sure you are not disturbed." Peggy then decided to return to the safety of her kitchen, her own troubled thoughts swirling around her head. It wasn't her place to offer an opinion, but having cared for Joseph and Adelaide since they were born, she sometimes felt she knew them far better than their parents. Shaking her head, she busied herself with preparing the evening meal in the hope that Mr Ellwood might decide to return tonight and life would return to some semblance of normality.

Before Adelaide spoke to her mother, she decided to talk to Peggy. She was such a good listener, and even if she didn't always have the answers she needed, simply voicing her worries to someone she could trust seemed to help. Entering the kitchen, the familiar smells of a ham roasting and an apple pie cooling on the table transported her to a time when life felt easier. She settled herself into her favourite chair, and although Mrs Whiskers had long gone, their new cat, Toby, was now in charge of the kitchen, doing a sterling job of ridding the place of any wayward mice. He jumped onto Adelaide's lap and curled up, sighing as he did so. Peggy looked over at Adelaide, and her heart broke for her.

"I think it's time for a cup of tea. Things always look better after a cup of nice, strong tea, don't they? And I have baked a batch of oatmeal biscuits this morning, too." They sipped their tea in companionable silence.

"I feel awful, Peg. I have upset my parents, but I can't go. I know I will be hopeless, and all those silly girls worrying about their hair and clothes and learning about deportment and manners!"

"Hush now, love. Stop fretting. That's not going to help anyone." Peggy patted Adelaide's hand gently.

"What should I do? I'm really worried they will make me go, and I don't think I can bear it."

However, Adelaide's worries would soon pale into insignificance as she was about to receive some devastating news that would change her forever …

Chapter 14

A few days after Adelaide's party, Violet and Susan sat in Violet's cosy sitting room, enjoying their weekly catch-up with a cup of tea and some leftover birthday cake Marie Ellwood had insisted they take home. The events that had unfolded at the party were very much on their minds. Violet was a little more annoyed than her Aunt. "It's as if her parents have never really understood their daughter. Either that or they have let their disappointment with Joseph cloud their judgment."

Susan sat back, calmly sipping her tea as her niece vented her feelings. Putting her teacup down, Susan offered her opinion. "I think you are right, my dear. Joseph's decision to marry 'below his station,' as Mrs Ellwood keeps telling us, has left them determined to ensure Adelaide doesn't do the same."

"But why would wanting to train at the Royal Academy of Music be so terrible? If I'd had that opportunity and the money to study there, I wouldn't have hesitated to go."

"Unfortunately, even though we have now been given the vote, women are expected to give up work after they are married, and if they aren't at least engaged by the age of twenty-one, they are still considered to be an old maid. It is quite ridiculous in this day and age, but it is what it is, and Mr and Mrs Ellwood are traditionalists and want to see their daughter settled with a respectable and wealthy husband."

Violet sighed and shook her head, taking a sip of her tea. "The notion that a woman must belong to her husband, bound to serve and bear children, is outdated. Perhaps that is why I have never married, as the idea of yielding such authority to a man is quite intolerable to me. From the very first lesson I gave Adelaide, I recognised in her a rare gift, a sensitivity to the piano that goes far beyond mere technical skill. She has always sought to understand the music, not simply to play it. We share a quiet understanding, she and I. At times, I feel she is the daughter I shall never have, and the prospect of her spending a year at a Ladies' College fills me with dread. We had planned hours of practise and careful preparation for her to meet the standards required by the Royal Academy. It is all rather disheartening."

Susan regarded Violet with quiet sympathy. Although she agreed with every word, she felt compelled to speak with candour. "Violet, as unjust as it may seem, I do not believe it is our place to pass judgement. Adelaide's parents have made their decision, convinced it is what she requires at this juncture in her life. If, after the year, she remains certain of her desire to study in London, then at the very least, they will have equipped her with the accomplishments expected of a young lady of her station."

"Aunt Susan, do you truly believe that? Would you send your own daughter away, knowing how wretched she felt?"

"No, darling, I wouldn't. But I am not Adelaide's mother, am I? All we can do is help her come to terms with what's been decided. Sharing in her distress may feel kind, but it will only deepen her sorrow."

Violet was about to reply when Susan's husband arrived to take her home. "It's only me. I let myself in. I hope that was all right."

Harry Robinson had the look of a man who had spent countless hours tucked away in the dim corners of libraries. His face, framed by spectacles and weathered by time, was partly hidden beneath a thick, unruly beard. Strands of silver hair stood untamed, and his waistcoat was almost always buttoned incorrectly. Susan would often sigh, adjust it for him with a smile, and press a gentle kiss to his cheek. Violet had been overjoyed when her aunt and Harry married four years ago. Until then, Susan had never imagined she would marry and had been content to care for her young niece, especially after her brother's passing. Yet she and Harry were perfectly suited. Susan delighted in looking after him, frequently reminding him of the time and urging him to put his books down and eat. Violet always enjoyed her Sunday visits to their cosy cottage on the grounds of the private boarding school where Harry taught history. They enjoyed lively discussions, a walk before lunch, and the promise of a traditional British Sunday roast, even in the warmer months.

"Hello, Harry, dear. Would you like a cup of tea and some delicious birthday cake from Miss Ellwood's birthday party?"

"That does sound tempting, but we really should be going. I have a History Department meeting at four, so I mustn't be late." Harry said, casting a longing glance at the cake.

"Well, in that case, I will wrap a slice for you to enjoy later." Violet busied herself in her little kitchen as Harry helped Susan with her coat. Violet lingered on the doorstep, waving farewell to her aunt and Harry, watching until they turned the corner and vanished from view. Returning indoors, she cleared away the cups and saucers, wrapped the remaining cake and set it aside. Then, with a glance at the mantel clock, she gathered her music folios as she was expected at Adelaide's for a lesson shortly. But first, she intended to stop at Miller's bookshop to collect her order for a few new scores for school.

The bell above the door chimed softly as she entered. Theodore looked up from behind the counter and greeted her with familiar warmth.

"Ah, Miss Ivery," he said, "I was wondering when you might appear. Tell me, how did Adelaide's gathering go? Eva mentioned she seemed rather out of sorts. A pity, is it not?"

"She enjoyed most of the party, Mr Miller. Only at the end, when they were about to cut the cake, her father told her something she wasn't expecting. But I'm sure all will be well soon. I'm heading there now to give Adelaide a music lesson. Playing the piano always cheers her up!"

Eva walked slowly down the steps that led from their flat

above the shop. She had heard Violet's voice and, feeling a little bored, decided to cause some trouble. "That's not what Adelaide told me, Miss Ivery." Eva's voice caused Theodore and Violet to look towards the staircase, where Eva was standing. She pretended to be busy with a few books on a nearby shelf but was smirking, thinking about how much fun the next few months would be watching Adelaide Ellwood's misery. "I heard Adelaide had a terrible tantrum, and Mrs Ellwood is making her stay in her room until she calms down."

Violet found it difficult to control her anger. Instead, she swallowed hard and responded as calmly as she could. "I don't think that's quite right, Eva. Adelaide wouldn't behave like that. I was one of the last to leave, and she bravely said goodbye to her guests, even though I knew how shocked she was at her father's news. I'm on my way there now. I have some new music for Adelaide to play, which will cheer her up, I'm sure."

"You would say that. Adelaide has always been your favourite; she could never do anything wrong in your eyes. I remember at school, she always received the best grades and awards."

"That's enough, Eva," Theodore said firmly, his voice low but commanding. "There's no need to speak to Miss Ivery like that. I'm sure Adelaide got the best grades because she worked hard. I always remember her coming into the shop after school to find a book about the latest topic you were all working on. She was like a little sponge, eager to soak up knowledge." Theodore turned to Violet with an apologetic expression, then turned to his daughter and shot her a warning look. He had already heard from Valentine that they had not been invited to Adelaide's birthday party. Valentine was very embarrassed and appreciated how welcoming Mr and Mrs Ellwood were, even pretending nothing was wrong.

Eva, on the other hand, felt heartily sick of how 'perfect' Adelaide always seemed. She often wished just once her parents would praise her like Adelaide's did. Even her father was defending her. She muttered something in German towards Theodore, too quietly for Violet to make anything of it. Whatever it was had made Theodore grow red with anger, and before he could answer, Eva slammed the book she was holding onto the desk and left the room.

"I must apologise for my daughter's behaviour. She harbours a very unhealthy jealousy towards Adelaide, and Adelaide has never done anything to warrant it."

"I think you are right, Mr Miller. Adelaide has always tried to be friendly towards Eva, yet it has never been reciprocated. Eva harbours a lot of resentment towards Adelaide. I wonder why that is?"

Eva could hardly believe what she was hearing from the other side of the door. Eavesdropping had always been her way of staying in control before life controlled her. But as she struggled to hold in her temper, that familiar voice inside her, growing louder with each passing month, whispered its relentless demand: That woman can't treat you like that… *Violet Ivery needs to be put in her place and soon!*

Violet paid for the music scores and placed them in her smart leather case, which held all the music she needed for the day. It had been a gift from Aunt Susan when she began her teaching career, and it was something she treasured. Saying goodbye to Theodore, Violet made her way to Adelaide's house, contemplating what she would say and how she could make Adelaide feel better. As she walked towards Thorndon, Violet passed several shops before the local park came into view. It was a beautiful summer's day. Couples strolled arm in arm, children enjoyed ice treats, and babies were pushed in perambulators. Suddenly, she stopped as a strange feeling enveloped her, causing her to shiver. Turning to look behind, she was certain that someone was following her, yet no one was there. She told herself she was being silly, yet the sensation lingered like a shadow at her heels. Holding her case tightly, she quickened her pace along the pavement. At the crossing, she paused, watching the horse and carriage approach. A few others gathered beside her, waiting patiently. Then, without warning, she felt a firm pressure at the small of her back... A voice cried out sharply, and a stranger's hand reached out in vain as Violet lost her balance and fell in front of the horse, which reared up in fear, its heavy hooves coming down hard on Violet's body. It unfolded in an instant. The man who had tried to help her cried out for a doctor. A woman knelt beside Violet's motionless form, her sobs punctuating the chaos, while someone else draped their jacket over her lifeless body. The music case had landed across the road, spilling its contents, the loose and twirling pages playing out a symphony of death at the loss of their guardian. Amid the commotion, no one noticed the young woman hastily retreating from the scene, heading toward the park. She sank onto the nearest bench, trembling. The sight of a lifeless body was something she'd never experienced before. She hadn't intended to push so hard, but these things happen for a reason, and no one lives forever. Relief flooded through her as the angry, insistent voice finally quietened. If anyone had observed the woman, they wouldn't have guessed they were now looking at a cold-blooded murderer.

In time, there had been an inquest, witnesses had been questioned, and, in the end, it was declared an accidental death. No one had been at fault, and the coroner was satisfied that it was a tragic accident.

Without Harry's unwavering care and love, Susan would never have managed to cope with the grief that overwhelmed her on that tragic day when a young policeman came to her door, tears in his eyes as he delivered the dreadful news. Harry had also been informed by the headmaster, who received a message from another police officer and immediately told the professor to hurry to his wife. Harry hurried home as fast as his old legs would carry him. All he could do was hold his beloved wife and let her cry, murmuring comforting words. Not once did he say, "It was God's will," for which Susan would always be grateful. Later, she endured visits from people offering condolences, saying unhelpful phrases like, "Life is so fleeting. It shows how you must make the most out of every day." Susan wanted to scream at them. Instead, she tried to stay composed and silent, but inwardly, she wept for what could now never be.

Violet's funeral was one of the hardest things Susan had ever had to face. How she wished it had been her lying in the cold earth instead of her dear niece. St. Paul's Church was overflowing with mourners, a testament to how many lives Violet had touched. Susan was deeply moved by the sheer number of people who had come to pay their respects to a much-loved teacher. Mrs Easterwood and the entire school community were present, including Albert and Connie Grimshaw, along with everyone who had been part of Violet's life, both past and present. Determined to honour Violet's memory, Mrs Easterwood insisted on offering the school hall for the wake. Her students arrived in the early morning, adorning the space with seasonal flowers and arranging tables and chairs for the mourners. Meanwhile, Mrs Grimshaw spent the morning baking, joined by Peggy and Mrs Easterwood's two remaining teachers, Louise Davenport and Georgiana Phelps, who were eager to channel their grief into something meaningful. Amid such heartfelt generosity, Susan and Harry couldn't help but be deeply moved. As tea was being served, Susan was anxious to find Adelaide. Since Violet's death, Adelaide had not called on Susan, and although it had upset her, it also worried her, given Violet and Adelaide's close friendship. Marie Ellwood had written a note, sent flowers, and explained that Adelaide was too upset to visit, sending her apologies. She spotted her sitting in a corner with her mother. Adelaide's white face stared into space. She looked thinner and had a haunted look. The poor child, she thought. Violet and Adelaide were so close, and Susan guessed Adelaide had probably been blaming herself, as it was Adelaide she was going to see when the tragic accident happened. Susan stood and made her way to where Adelaide was seated. "Adelaide, I wonder if you wouldn't mind staying behind when everyone has left. I have something for you." Adelaide's tear-stained face managed to stutter, "For, for me?"

"Yes. Please, Adelaide. It would mean a lot to me if you could wait until everyone has left. If that is all right with you, Mrs Ellwood."

"Of course we will, and if there's anything you need or anything we can do, you only have to ask."

The wake had lasted several hours, longer than Susan and Harry had expected, and it had been exhausting. Eventually, as the final guests departed, Mrs Easterwood approached Adelaide, her hand settling gently on her arm. "Promise me, Adelaide, don't let this sorrow steal your future."

Adelaide lowered her gaze, a faint shake of her head the only reply—silent, but unwavering. Mrs Easterwood let her hand fall away and turned to Marie. Their exchanged glance held all the concern words could not express. Susan looked on, her heart aching at the sight of Adelaide's devastation. Seizing a quiet moment, she stepped forward and addressed her gently.

"May I have a private word with you, if your mother does not object?"

Marie offered a soft smile and nodded, encouraging Adelaide with a touch to her arm. Obediently, Adelaide followed Susan towards a door that led to a small classroom. Susan paused, steadying herself, and blinked back tears. "Today has been a most difficult day," she said, her voice low, "but the presence of so many has brought a measure of comfort." Adelaide's eyes brimmed with tears. She could only nod. Susan reached for

Violet's leather music case, which had been placed on one of the desks earlier, and held it close. "I know Violet would have wished you to have this. It was among her most cherished possessions. Keep it, not only as a token of your friendship, but as a reminder of how deeply she believed in your gift. She was certain you would become an exceptional pianist. From what Mrs Easterwood just said, I gather you told her you would never play again. Was she correct?"

Adelaide knew she had to answer, and with great effort, she finally found her voice. "Oh, Susan, I couldn't. Not without Violet. She taught me so much and gave me courage when I thought I had none." Susan passed her a handkerchief and guided her to a chair. Sitting beside her, she said gently, "Adelaide, the fact that Violet is no longer here does not mean she cannot still guide you. You must remember what she taught you. I promise she will be with you in spirit. When doubt comes, think of Violet, and she will give you strength."

"I... I will try. My heart hurts, Susan. Does yours?"

"Yes, it does. It hurts very much. But Violet would want us to be brave and carry on. You must utilise the skills she has given you to inspire others. That is what you were meant to do. She often spoke of how excited she was for you to study in London. She wished she'd had the chance herself."

"I still wish to go, one day, but it seems Mother and Father have other plans for me. And now that Violet is gone, I have no one to confide in."

"You still have me. I would find comfort if you came to visit, so that we could remember Violet together and you could share your progress with me. But do speak honestly with your parents. It is clear to me that attending this ladies' college in Christchurch is not the right path. You must show them your determination to complete your studies and pursue the Royal Academy. That is what Violet longed to see for you."

Adelaide's face brightened slightly for the first time since Violet's death, and a glimmer of hope shone in her eyes. "You are right, and I know Violet would have said the same thing to me."

"She would indeed, I'm sure of it. So, please take this case and look after it, and I'm sure it will bring you luck and memories of Violet."

"Thank you so much, and I will take great care of it. I will visit as soon as I've sorted out my little predicament with my parents. You are so kind and thoughtful. I can only imagine how you must feel, yet you still have time to care for me."

"You are a dear friend, Adelaide, and I want only the best for you. Now go and talk to your parents!"

Adelaide stood and hugged Susan hard and ran out of the room before Susan could see the tears escaping from her eyes. Susan watched Adelaide go and felt a kind of peace flow over her. Today had been incredibly hard, but the outpouring of love and respect for her niece was quite humbling, and she would carry that with her through the difficult days ahead.

Chapter 15

Wellington - December 1910

Summer arrived with bright blue, cloudless skies, and the coastal breezes softened the heat as Peggy laboured in the sweltering kitchen, baking mince pies for Mrs Ellwood's Christmas fundraiser, which would be the final social event before the family departed for their holiday at Woodlands. The house was hushed as Marie was taking her customary post-lunch nap, and Adelaide had gone to Easterwood Academy.

Peggy felt a quiet relief that Adelaide had returned to her studies, though it saddened her that the piano remained untouched. She missed the music that used to drift through the rooms, whether Adelaide was practising or simply playing for joy. Adelaide had declined all invitations to perform at the Christmas concerts, a decision no one questioned after Mr Ellwood's shocking announcement at her party and, soon after, Miss Ivery's tragic death. For weeks, Adelaide had barely left her room. But now, she seemed more improved and had started taking her meals in the dining room, a small but hopeful sign.

There had been heated discussions, however, about her refusal to attend the Ladies' College in Christchurch, where her parents were convinced would serve as a suitable finishing school. Mr Ellwood's booming voice carried from his study. "What is it with our children, Marie? What did we do to deserve not just one ungrateful child, but two? It's hard to fathom, it really is!" He shouted, slammed doors, and then declared he would spend the next few days at his club, citing important business before Government House closed for Christmas. Everyone breathed a sigh of relief once the house returned to its normal, peaceful routine.

A few days later, Adelaide was delighted to receive a note from Charlotte, announcing that she had returned home to visit her parents and had brought along her fiancé, Matthew Hibbert. She had been eager for Adelaide to meet him, but having learned about Violet, Charlotte reconsidered and decided to visit Adelaide on her own. The very next day, she breezed in, sweeping Adelaide into a hug and spinning her around the hallway.

"Oh, Addie, how wonderful it is to see you! It feels like ages since we last met." When Charlotte finally released her, both girls were laughing so much that it seemed no time had passed at all. Charlotte, smartly dressed and radiating confidence, carried herself with grace. As they sat together in the drawing room, Adelaide was happy to let her friend do most of the talking; her cheerful chatter was strangely comforting. When it was Adelaide's turn to speak, she couldn't bring herself to mention Violet, so instead she explained how her parents had wanted her to go to Christchurch. "I have told them I do not wish to go, and in doing so, I have caused a great deal of upset. Life feels rather strained at present."

"Well, I think you are quite right," Charlotte replied. "What were they thinking? You would loathe it. You are not like me. You have a gift, and you ought to pursue it, not waste time preparing for marriage."

"Oh, Lottie, do you truly think so? I only hope you haven't rushed into your engagement. You deserve to fall in love and enjoy married life, and if Matthew is the one, then he's a very fortunate man indeed."

Charlotte's smile widened, her voice bubbling with joy. "Matthew and I are deliriously happy, I promise. I'm not like you, Addie. At school, I was always just middling, and that was mostly thanks to your help. But my year in Geneva was the happiest time of my life, and my London season felt like a dream. Then I met Matthew, and suddenly everything seemed exactly as it ought to be. I adore him." She leaned forward, eyes alight. "He's a little older than I am, but that doesn't matter in the least. His parents, Lord and Lady Hibbert, are kindness itself. Can you imagine it?" Charlotte laughed, her excitement spilling over. "In time, Matthew will inherit their estate, but for now he's establishing himself in politics, so we'll be living in London."

"Where is the family home?" Adelaide asked, caught up in her friend's joy, feeling lighter than she had since Violet's passing.

"In Devon, near a place called Ottery St Mary. It is idyllic, but for now, we plan to live in London and spend some weekends and holidays at Ottery Manor. Then, when the time comes, we shall raise our children there."

"Oh, Lottie, it all sounds absolutely delightful. I am so happy for you."

All too soon, Charlotte had to leave. Adelaide hugged her tightly. "It has been such a joy to see you, and just think, by the time I reach London, you will be a married lady!"

Charlotte departed in a flurry of laughter and perfume, and Adelaide sank back into her chair, the old sadness creeping over her once more. *Everything was changing, and she felt she could scarcely endure it.* Rising suddenly, she sought the comfort of Peggy's kitchen, where Toby, the cat, promptly curled into her lap the moment she sat down.

"Those mince pies smell delicious. Is there a spare one?"

"You remind me of your brother, always coming into the kitchen to see if there was anything to eat. Always hungry, he was."

"Those were the days, weren't they, Peggy? Why do we have to grow up? I feel so unsettled. I'm only eighteen, and already I've lost my brother, Violet, and now Charlotte is getting married! It feels quite unbearable at times."

"Now then, that's foolish talk, that is. You haven't lost your brother. He's happy and living his life. When did you last write to him?"

"Not since before my birthday, I haven't even thanked him for my presents. Everything just felt too difficult after Violet's death."

"Well, I hope you don't mind, but I wrote to him to tell him about what had happened, and I received a letter from him the other day. Do you want to read it?"

"Yes, please, I would like that."

"Now, where did I put it?" Peggy went to the large pine dresser that held all the crockery and kitchen paraphernalia and opened one of the drawers. Rummaging around, she suddenly picked up the letter, still in its envelope. "I have it!" she cried.

Peggy handed it to Adelaide, who read it eagerly, desperate for news from her brother.

Dear Peg,

Thank you for writing to me. What a tragic thing to happen to one so young. My heart goes out to her family, and to poor Addie. She is too sensitive for this world, and I can only imagine how she feels. I hope she is well.

I will write to her soon, but in the meantime, please let her know that she is in my thoughts. I am not proving to be a particularly good older brother, am I? I ought to be looking out for her. It is hard indeed, at times, being on the other side of the world.

I do not know whether my next bit of news will please or distress her, but I am to become a father! The baby is due in the spring; I have already begun work on the nursery, and I am eager for the day when I can meet our little one.

You are all in my thoughts, and Addie most especially.

Yours fondly,

Joseph

Adelaide sat staring at the letter. "He is to be a father. That is such important news, Peggy. It is hard to be cross with someone when they are so happy, isn't it?"

Peggy nodded in agreement as she poured boiling water from the large kettle into a teapot.

Adelaide gently tickled Toby's head as he purred contentedly. "I remember what Violet once told me when I was upset about Joseph meeting Kitty. She said that everyone has a right to be happy, and even if you don't always agree with their choices, the important thing is to accept their decisions in life and be happy for them."

Peggy gave her an affectionate smile. "Well, I think that's absolutely right, Adelaide. Don't you?"

"Yes, I do. I think I will go to my room and write to Joseph instead of waiting for him to write to me." Adelaide unceremoniously evicted Toby from her lap, leaving him feeling very put out. "Don't you want tea and a mince pie?" Peggy shouted after her, but Adelaide had already gone. Peggy shook her head at Toby in a fellowship of sympathy.

Adelaide finally finished her letter to Joseph at around five in the evening. She had told him everything, and setting her thoughts down on paper had been a deeply cathartic experience. Rubbing her arm and flexing her fingers, which ached after filling three pages with her sadness, grief, joy, and reflections on life, she felt lighter than she had in days. She pushed open her window and drew in the cooling evening air. Below, her mother's prized roses were in full bloom, their fragrance intoxicating at that hour. As the grandfather clock in the hall began to chime, she heard her father enter the house at last, returning from his self-imposed exile.

Adelaide had missed him desperately and reproached herself for having upset him. Buoyed by her improved spirits, she went to seek him out. She found him in the library, holding tightly to a medium-sized box, while Peggy deftly relieved him of his hat and coat.

"Ah, Adelaide, there you are." Robert's unexpectedly cheery voice startled her. "Come and see what's in the box. It's for you." He placed it gently on the floor.

Intrigued, Adelaide knelt and lifted the lid. Two large brown eyes peered up at her.

"Oh, my goodness!" she exclaimed, carefully lifting the tiny puppy from the box.

It wriggled joyfully, licking her face and scrambling up to her shoulders, its tail wagging madly. Adelaide laughed, holding it close.

Robert watched fondly. "You've had a sad time, and I know how much Violet meant to you, and I've not helped matters, have I? So, shall I take it you'd like to keep her?"

"Oh yes, please. She's adorable."

"Well then, she'll need a name. What shall you call her?"

After several more enthusiastic licks, the puppy curled contentedly in Adelaide's lap.

"I shall call her Elise after Beethoven's *Für Elise*. It's one of my favourite pieces to play, and one of Violet's too." Her voice caught, and she quickly swallowed her sadness, unwilling to spoil the moment.

"It suits her," Robert said warmly. "Elise, it is. She sleeps in the kitchen at night, mind—I won't have her in the bedrooms."

Gathering her courage, Adelaide ventured, "Does this mean I don't have to go to Christchurch to be 'finished,' and all that nonsense?"

Her father regarded her with quiet sympathy. "It does, my dear. I still believe it would have been a fine opportunity for you, but I accept that now is not the right time. I'm sorry it caused you such distress, especially after all that has happened."

Peggy appeared at the door. "Mrs Ellwood has asked for

dinner at seven o'clock, Mr Ellwood. Can I bring you anything in the meantime?"

"No, thank you, Peggy. I need to do a little work before dinner. I'll help myself to a whisky." He gave the puppy a pat on the head before disappearing into his study.

Adelaide turned to Peggy, still in disbelief. "Oh, Peggy, I can't believe Father has just given me this gorgeous puppy."

"How wonderful. If I'm not mistaken, she's a King Charles Spaniel. Those big floppy ears are a dead giveaway. Bring her into the kitchen, and we'll get her settled. She'll need to be fed, and you must teach her to do her business outside. I hope Toby won't be too put out."

Chapter 16

Wellington - January 1912

They say time heals, and Adelaide clung to that hope, doing her best to recall the joyful moments with Violet rather than the sorrow that still caught her off guard. Mrs Easterwood had gently urged her to continue teaching, and her parents, quietly watchful, understood how much the comfort of routine steadied her. Even Susan, with her usual tact, had persuaded Adelaide to take on a few of Violet's private students. It was a small step, but one that marked a quiet return to purpose.

Adelaide also announced her wish to offer music lessons to children less fortunate than herself. With her mother's help, she secured the use of St James' Church hall in Newtown for a few hours every Saturday morning, from nine until noon. The hall, with its polished timber floor and tall windows, was ideal for teaching, and the large upright piano provided by the parish ensured that every child could participate.

Her mother, however, had reservations about Adelaide travelling alone to a less affluent part of Wellington. It was therefore agreed that Peggy would accompany her, supervise the children, and serve refreshments after each lesson. Adelaide, too delighted to argue, accepted her mother's conditions and looked forward to Peggy's company beyond the kitchen.

The children, aged between six and twelve, were eager and attentive. Adelaide structured the sessions with care: the first hour focused on scales, finger exercises, and the fundamentals of reading music, followed by short pieces to practise technique and expression. She encouraged ensemble playing whenever possible, pairing children so they could learn to listen to one another, and often included simple folk tunes or hymns to keep the lessons joyful.

Each child was praised for their progress, and Adelaide made sure that even those who struggled with rhythm or finger placement left with a sense of quiet triumph. The sessions soon became the highlight of her week. She relished watching the children grow in confidence and skill, and the genuine gratitude of their parents made every effort worthwhile.

It was a modest endeavour, but one that brought music into the lives of those who might otherwise have none, and allowed Adelaide to honour Violet's teaching legacy while quietly nurturing the next generation of young pianists.

There was a period after Violet's death when all kinds of rumours and opinions circulated in Wellington's parlours and tea rooms, and Adelaide started to worry that something did not add up. According to a witness, Violet seemed to have been startled by something; another witness mentioned seeing a woman walk hurriedly away from the scene, though they were too far away to describe her. However, the coroner would not change his mind. He was convinced it had been a tragic accident, and that was the end of it. Adelaide wasn't convinced, but she had no choice but to accept the verdict and carry on with her life.

One Sunday, after church, Adelaide decided to make the most of the summer sunshine and settled beneath her favourite cherry tree with a book. Elise was chasing a butterfly that had briefly landed on her nose, spinning in delighted circles as she tried to catch it.

"Oh, Elise, it's not even there now—you've frightened it away. Come here," Adelaide called, laughing softly.

Elise trotted back and collapsed on the blanket beside her, panting from the chase. Adelaide leaned against the tree's sturdy trunk, grateful for its quiet companionship and the refuge it offered her restless thoughts. The garden was peaceful, dappled with light, until Elise suddenly sprang up and began to bark, shattering the calm. Adelaide could hear someone attempting to enter the garden, but Elise's excitement made it impossible. Rising to her feet, she called out, "Elise, stop that and let our visitor in." To her surprise, it was Valentine Spielmann. He stooped to greet Elise, who instantly ceased barking, tail wagging at the discovery of a new friend.

"Good afternoon, Miss Ellwood," Valentine said with a warm smile, offering his customary bow.

His formal German manners always made her feel somewhat awkward, but she soon found her composure and greeted him politely. "Good afternoon, Mr Spielmann, this is an unexpected pleasure."

"I hope you don't mind me calling unannounced. Your housekeeper, Peggy, said it was all right for me to come through and that I'd find you in the garden, and here you are."

"Yes, here I am."

"Your mother suggested I call." He persevered. "She mentioned you hadn't played the piano for yourself for quite a while and that you might be interested in having lessons again. If you still wish to study in London?"

"I haven't given it much thought lately. I have been teaching but rarely feel like playing for pleasure."

"That is a shame."

"Miss Ivery was a good teacher and a dear friend. I really don't see how I could carry on with someone else. It would be like a betrayal of her memory."

"Miss Ellwood, I don't think Miss Ivery would agree with you. She wanted you to be the absolute best you could be, and she told me that."

"I wasn't aware you both knew each other that well?"

"We occasionally spoke at music functions, and if we happened to be in Miller's bookshop at the same time. She was very fond of you and would often mention your potential if only you believed in yourself more."

"I don't know what to say." Adelaide felt a lump in her throat, and as tears threatened, she managed to say, "I was very fond of her, too. She always encouraged me in a way that didn't make me feel self-conscious, and I always felt confident in her presence. Now, I don't know how I feel."

I'm very sorry. However, if you permit me, I would be honoured to assist you in continuing your studies. Please don't give up on your dreams. The Royal Academy's academic year begins in September, not January, as it does here. If we start now, I can help you with your application by January, allowing you to take your final examinations and begin your training at the Royal Academy the following September.

There was an uncomfortably long pause until Adelaide realised he was waiting for her to reply, but she wasn't sure what to say. As if Valentine knew what she was thinking, he said, "Just say yes and continue your studies; otherwise, all Miss Ivery's efforts will have been for nothing."

Adelaide could feel her cheeks flushing under his intense stare as he spoke; feeling a little uncomfortable, she managed to speak, "You have taken me by surprise, but you are quite right. Miss Ivery always encouraged me, believing I could do anything if I put my mind to it. So, thank you, and yes, I would be delighted to accept your offer to tutor me."

"Excellent!" Valentine's smile was warm. "And as I am now to be your music tutor, and we have known each other for some time now. Please call me Valentine."

"Valentine." She repeated his name softly. It was unusual, yet it seemed to suit him perfectly.

"If I am to call you Valentine, then you must call me Adelaide!"

She laughed, and a wave of relief and excitement bubbled inside her.

They started slowly, but Adelaide soon found herself enjoying the familiar rhythm once more. Every Sunday after church, Valentine would call on Adelaide. His teaching style was more formal than Violet's, yet he shared the same deep love for music and learning. Before long, Adelaide began to regain her confidence and started to look forward to their Sunday afternoons. If she were honest, it wasn't just the music. She also enjoyed Valentine's company. Without Eva around, he was easier to talk to. He had a genuine passion for music, not just for playing but for understanding and discussing it. One afternoon, after a particularly enjoyable lesson on harmony, Marie walked in and was quietly pleased to see her daughter looking happy again.

"Mr Spielmann, you must stay for some tea."

"Thank you, Mrs Ellwood, that is most kind."

As if on cue, a few moments later, Peggy came in carrying a tea tray. She set the tray down carefully, and Adelaide noticed the absence of the lemon syrup cake she had always made for Violet. However, an equally enticing fruit loaf had replaced it.

"So, how is my daughter doing under your excellent tutelage?"

"Very well, Mrs Ellwood. I believe your daughter has found her joy in playing again, and her ability is exceptional."

Marie practically beamed with pleasure at Valentine's enthusiasm about her daughter. Adelaide was secretly amused, as it was rare for her mother to show her feelings in such a way, especially to someone she hardly knew. They sat and talked amicably for about an hour, and then Valentine had to take his leave as he was expected at the home of Mr and Mrs Dunstable, who had decided their young son should have piano lessons.

"I shouldn't say this, but he is proving quite the challenge!"

After Valentine had left, Marie and Adelaide decided to stay in the sitting room to finish their tea, and they happily polished off two more slices of the delicious cake.

"You are doing well, my dear. I know it has been hard, but how wonderful that Mr Spielmann already thinks highly of you."

"He is very formal, isn't he?" Adelaide replied. "Mr Miller at the bookshop told me it has to do with his Germanic heritage, but he asked me to use his first name, Valentine. Perhaps you should, too, now that he has been teaching me for a few months."

"Indeed, but I think not, my dear. As much as I admire Valentine's teaching abilities, I find his name to be quite bohemian, and as for his long hair!"

Laughing, Adelaide admitted, "He certainly has a different way about him, but I think it suits him, and even though I find he has a more formal method of teaching than I am used to, his love of music is undeniable. He mentioned the Royal Academy of Music and how their term dates differ from ours. He believes that if I work hard, I will be ready to apply next year. Adelaide hadn't planned on blurting out her wish to go, as she hadn't spoken of going in such a long time."

Surprised at Adelaide's sudden announcement, Marie continued to sip her tea before saying anything. Smiling at her daughter, she said, "I think having something to work towards is just what you need, and there will be much to organise before you go."

"What about Father? Do you think he will still let me go, especially after everything that has happened?"

"You leave your father to me." Marie nodded at her daughter. "He only wants what's best for you, as I do. I will talk to him soon."

Chapter 17

Wellington – April 1912

Rising before the rest of the household, Adelaide would often settle at her small writing desk by the bedroom window, capturing her thoughts in the hush of early morning. After months shadowed by sadness and worry, she had made a quiet vow: her journal would hold only cheerful news and gentle reflections. Music that moved her, thoughts about books she had read, and glimpses of nature she'd savoured on walks with Elise. An hour passed in peaceful solitude before the house began to stir. From the kitchen came the familiar clatter of pots and pans as Peggy prepared breakfast, followed by the muffled tones of her father's voice, likely retrieving his newspaper before settling at the dining room table, as he always did. Setting down her pen, Adelaide realised she was hungry and ready to start the day. But, as she neared the dining room, a sharp exclamation stopped her in her tracks.

"Good grief, this can't be true."

Marie, just behind her, quickened her pace, concern etched across her face.

"My dear, whatever has alarmed you? You've given us all quite a fright."

Robert, pale and visibly shaken, held up the newspaper. Without a word, he turned it to reveal the front page. The headline blazed in bold type: *Titanic Disaster: Great Loss of Life*.

Marie gasped and sank into a chair. Peggy, mid-motion as she served Robert his breakfast, crossed herself. Adelaide stood frozen, staring at the paper, unable to understand why everyone appeared so shaken.

"What does this mean?" she asked softly.

Robert didn't answer her directly. Instead, he began to read aloud, his voice heavy with disbelief.

"The *Titanic* sank in the early morning hours of 15th April 1912 in the North Atlantic Ocean, four days into her maiden voyage from Southampton to New York City."

Marie's voice trembled. "Robert, isn't that the route Joseph takes on board the *Mauretania?*"

"Yes, my dear, but it says no other ships are involved. It's quite hard to fathom, but they are saying the *Titanic* struck an iceberg, causing the ship to sink, with 1,500 lives lost. Apparently, there weren't enough lifeboats. It's deplorable."

"Perhaps the newspaper is mistaken?" Adelaide asked, clinging to the hope.

"I don't believe it is," Robert replied gently. "But I'll go to the office and see what more I can learn. I can't believe such a thing could happen. They said the *Titanic* was unsinkable."

Breakfast was a subdued, routine affair. After such grim news, no one had much of an appetite. Robert left at his usual time for Government House, and Marie soon followed, heading to tea with her friend Dorothy Palmer, ostensibly to discuss the upcoming fundraiser, though Adelaide suspected it would be filled with the usual Wellington gossip.

She had a piano lesson scheduled that morning and briefly considered cancelling, but she couldn't bring herself to disappoint her student. Instead, she left the house earlier than usual and walked to Miller's Bookshop. The familiar hush and rows of carefully stacked volumes provided a quiet solace. Adelaide had always found comfort in the gentle companionship of books.

As she entered the bookshop, she was relieved to find the shop empty of customers. Theodore was standing behind the gleaming mahogany counter and raised a hand in greeting as she entered.

"I take it you've heard the news," he said, noting her pale face and sorrowful expression.

"Yes," Adelaide replied softly. "It's so shocking. All those poor people, and how could an iceberg bring down such a colossal ship? It doesn't seem possible."

Just then, Valentine and Giselle entered the shop. They, too, wanted some company and decided to check on their neighbours.

"Isn't the news just horrifying?" Giselle spoke first.

"Sit, sit, all of you, and I will fetch some tea. The shop can remain closed for a little longer."

Valentine looked at Adelaide. "Are you all right?"

"Yes, just a bit shocked. All I could think of was my brother Joseph and whether his ship was somehow involved."

"What ship is he on?" Valentine asked.

"The *Mauretania*. It also sails the North Atlantic to New York, but from Liverpool, not Southampton, like the *Titanic*. I know it's a big ocean, but you never know, do you?" Her voice trembled slightly; the loss of Violet was starting to creep back into her thoughts.

"Think how many journeys have been made along that same route over the years. It must surely be a freak accident. But to lose so many people is unforgivable. I think the owners of the ship will have many questions to answer," Valentine said, trying to reassure her.

Theodore gestured for them all to sit, and they drank their tea in silence. Despite the devastating news, Adelaide felt a quiet sense of peace—her friends were near, and she felt reassured Joseph was safe. Later, she would go to church and light a candle for the poor souls lost at sea.

Soon, Adelaide rose reluctantly, explaining that a student was waiting for a lesson.

"I hope you are practising. You have your Advanced Grade Practical in two weeks!" Valentine reminded her.

Before she could respond, Giselle scolded her brother. "Oh, Valentine, of course she is." Adelaide smiled, but at the same time, she felt a small pang of jealousy, wishing Joseph were there with her.

An eerie silence greeted her as she walked to her student's home. Apart from traffic noise, she felt a sense of shared shock as people tried to go about their business. The news placards and signs outside various shops all had the same headline: *"Titanic Disaster. Great loss of life."*

Arriving at her student's house on the outskirts of Thorndon, Adelaide took a deep breath and fixed her cheeriest smile as a little girl opened the door. "Hello Alice, are you ready for your lesson?"

"I'm not sure. Mama keeps crying."

"Where is she?"

"In the sitting room."

"Alice, why don't you make a start by practising your scales? I'll be in once I've seen your Mama."

Following the sound of crying, Adelaide made her way to the drawing room. Mrs Watkins sat on a luxurious, deep green velvet settee, dabbing at her face with a small white handkerchief. It was clear she had been crying profusely and could not even attempt to hide her distress when Adelaide entered the room.

"Mrs Watkins? I'm so sorry to disturb you, but Alice is worried."

"Oh, Miss Ellwood, I am in such a state of worry."

Without waiting to be invited, Adelaide sat next to Mrs Watkins. "Is it related to the terrible news about the *Titanic?*"

"My sister and her husband were travelling on it with their children. She wrote to me a month ago to tell me how excited they were about being the first passengers on such a luxurious ship. But I can't find out if they are alive or dead. We are so far away, and the time difference makes it difficult to communicate. We sent word to my sister in England, hoping that by some small miracle, they had decided not to travel. Mr Watkins has gone to

Government House to see if anyone could help. I'm not sure how they can, but you never know."

"It's certainly worth a try. My father works at Government House. If your husband is unsuccessful, I could ask him to see if he can help if you want. In the meantime, should I continue with Alice's piano lesson, or would you prefer to postpone it until you have news?"

"No, please continue. Poor Alice doesn't understand, and it will keep her occupied whilst I endeavour to compose myself."

Adelaide could hear Alice practising her scales diligently. Returning to the music room, she observed the young girl concentrating intensely on her scales, her small tongue sticking out with effort. It reminded Adelaide of herself at Alice's age. Music meant so much to her, and after reading in the paper how the *Titanic's* orchestra played until the very end, the thought of those brave men playing as the ship sank deeply touched her.

A few days later, a telegram had arrived from Liverpool, which Robert read out loud as Marie and Adelaide looked on, anxiously.

Joseph safe. Cunard has reassured families that Mauretania was docked in Ireland at the time. Returning to Liverpool soon. Kitty.

"How thoughtful of her to let us know," Marie said, feeling relieved.

"Indeed," Robert replied, unsure of his feelings but grateful that Joseph's wife was thoughtful enough to let his worried family know.

Adelaide visibly relaxed. The tension in her body that she hadn't realised she was holding faded, and she felt a surge of gratitude for her sister-in-law's thoughtfulness, which only strengthened her belief that Kitty was a kind and decent person.

During supper that evening, Adelaide asked her father, "Did you find any news about Mrs Watkin's sister and family? I have another lesson with Alice in a few days, and I know Mrs Watkins will be desperate for news." Adelaide looked at her father's face, and a feeling of dread seeped through her veins. "It's bad news, isn't it?"

"The information coming through is still shaky, but the *Carpathia,* the ship that picked up survivors, has now docked in New York, and there is a clearer picture of who survived and who sadly didn't."

"Are they all dead?"

"From what I have been told, the women and children were allowed into the lifeboats first, and Josephine Mulberry, Mrs Watkin's sister, is alive with their youngest child, Ernest. The two other children were separated in the chaos and have not been found yet. But hopefully, they were put in another lifeboat. Eric Mulberry, unfortunately, perished. There just weren't enough lifeboats. I am afraid we will be hearing many stories like this in the coming weeks. Mr and Mrs Watkins have been notified, so I think it might not be appropriate to be calling to give a piano lesson just yet."

"I hope the other two children will be found. Do you think I should call to offer my condolences, at the very least, and perhaps take them some flowers? I want to make sure Alice is all right."

Marie listened to her daughter and was taken by Adelaide's newfound maturity. It had been such a difficult time for her, and now this tragedy. It was as if these tragedies had somehow made Adelaide stronger. She wished her daughter didn't feel so much. It would only lead to more heartache over the years. Instead of saying all this to her daughter, Marie told her that taking flowers would be a kind gesture.

The following Sunday, St Paul's Church was full, and not a spare pew could be seen. It was as if the people of Wellington wanted to gather as a community and seek comfort through prayer. Marie, Robert, and Adelaide sat in a corner of the large stone church. The Vicar spoke about loss, love, and God's will, and Adelaide found it difficult to accept this terrible event as part of God's plan. Nevertheless, the hymns and prayers brought her peace, and she looked forward to seeing Valentine that afternoon for her piano lesson. Her final practical examination was scheduled for next Thursday, and she was eager to practise. It would be the furthest she could go in New Zealand with regard to her piano qualifications, and she so desperately wanted not just to pass but to earn a distinction.

As they walked home, the autumn weather remained sunny and the temperature pleasantly mild, though a gentle breeze stirred the fallen leaves. Marie suddenly announced that they must do something nice the following weekend.

"All this sadness is too much," she said. "We should organise a picnic at the Botanic Gardens next Sunday to lift our spirits! We could invite John and Susannah Montgomery. It would be lovely to see them properly before they begin their journey back to England for Charlotte's wedding."

Adelaide agreed enthusiastically. She wasn't sure why, but she suddenly said, "Could I invite Valentine and Giselle too?"

"Of course, my dear, the more the merrier. What about Eva? She always seems to be stuck like glue to the Spielmann siblings!"

Adelaide did not want to include Eva, but corrected her mean thoughts as Eva seemed to be more friendly towards her these days.

"I'll ask Valentine this afternoon after my piano lesson."

That afternoon, Adelaide sat at her piano half an hour before Valentine was due to call. One of the pieces she had chosen to play for the examination was Debussy's *Rêverie*, and to loosen her hands, she began playing an arpeggio of her own invention.

Valentine arrived at precisely two o'clock. After showing him into the library, Peggy murmured to herself, "You could set your watch by him!" Chuckling, she returned to the kitchen.

Valentine stood at the door, listening to Adelaide play, until she paused, aware of his presence. He quickly stepped forward to greet her, "Good afternoon, Adelaide. Are you ready for your lesson?

"Hello, Valentine. I've been practising and I hope I can do this piece justice."

"Whatever you were playing, it wasn't Debussy." Valentine's smile curved with quiet amusement, his eyes crinkling with mischief as he looked down at her.

"Well, no," Adelaide replied, a touch flustered. "I meant I've been practising while waiting for you. Just loosening up my fingers before our lesson."

"I'm teasing you, Adelaide. That was a lovely arpeggio." His voice softened, warm with reassurance. "Now, let's begin. We've only a few hours to perfect this, and you're nearly there."

He set the metronome ticking, its steady pulse filling the room. With an encouraging smile, he nodded for her to begin.

Adelaide drew a deep breath. Valentine's cheerful mood unsettled her, as he was usually so formal. She wondered what had caused such happiness, never considering it might be her presence that brought him joy.

Valentine observed intently, his right index finger counting the beats as a conductor would with his baton. He thought her hands were getting stronger, and the exercises he had given her were making a difference. Valentine was mesmerised by her dainty hands and how fragile they looked, yet she could still pound out the chords when she had to. He suddenly became aware she had stopped playing.

"Was that any better?" He heard her say.

"Yes, much. I was thinking how stronger and more supple your hands are getting, and I am glad you are practising like I told you to."

"Every day!" Adelaide smiled. "I'm determined to make my family proud of me!"

"You must make yourself proud, too, Adelaide. Remember, you are doing this for yourself. If you work hard, everyone else will be proud of you."

"You sound like Violet."

"Do I? I'm sorry, I didn't mean to upset you."

"No, you haven't. I only meant that Violet always knew what to say whenever I needed encouragement, and you are the same." Smiling at him shyly, she said, "I am glad you persevered with me."

Valentine smiled at her and nodded. His eyes said it all, Adelaide thought to herself, and she felt content and relaxed in another person's company for the first time in a long while.

"Mother is planning a picnic next Sunday to cheer us all up, and she wondered whether you and Giselle would like to come. Oh, and Eva, too, if she is free." She added quickly, wishing again that she didn't have to include her.

Valentine seemed surprised at the sudden change of subject but happily accepted her invitation. He felt sure Giselle would like to come, too. "I can't answer for Eva, but if I see her, I will ask her."

"Thank you, and it is quite possible I will be able to invite her myself, as I would like to visit Miller's bookshop to see if any new books have arrived."

"You are such a 'bookworm.' Is that what you call it? I enjoy reading, but I prefer music scores. Anyway, I think we can finish here. You played well today, but keep practising. You know what the examiners want you to play, so keep playing the pieces repeatedly. Read the music, memorise the notes, then if something doesn't go quite right, your memory will take over, and you will come across as confident and assured. Sit up straight and keep still, too. I noticed a slight tilt when you reached across the keyboard."

Adelaide found the week unbearably slow, her nerves wearing thin with each day. The newspapers remained filled with reports of the *Titanic's* sinking and the growing debate over who was responsible. Blame, she thought, would not bring back the lost souls. Yet her thoughts turned to Alice Watkins' family, and she decided to visit them, hoping for news of the missing children.

She had not sent a formal calling card, as her mother would have done when visiting friends, but she had brought a small bouquet of flowers. If the family were indisposed, she could always inquire discreetly with Betsy, the Watkins' maid, about the children's fate.

As it happened, Mrs Watkins was at home and received her warmly. Alice, too, appeared bright and cheerful, expressing how much she missed her lessons. Adelaide offered the bouquet, an autumnal arrangement of orange dahlias, white hydrangeas, peach roses, and sprigs of orange celosia, a quiet gesture of comfort and care.

Mrs Watkins lifted the flowers to her nose, a smile softening her features as she turned toward Adelaide. "Miss Ellwood, these are quite beautiful, and most thoughtful of you. Alice, my dear, please give them to Betsy to arrange in a vase, and ask her to bring some tea."

"Yes, Mama," Alice replied, taking the bouquet from her mother and hurrying down the corridor.

Adelaide settled herself on Mrs Watkins' deep green velvet settee, the fabric cool and smooth beneath her fingers, certain she would remember its richness for the rest of her days. The settee, with its deep cushions and dignified air, seemed almost out of place in the modest parlour, yet its splendour lent the room an unexpected elegance.

"I hope you do not mind my calling," she began, settling back into the cushions. "I just wanted to find out how you all were, and whether there has been any news of your missing niece and nephew."

"That is very thoughtful of you," Mrs Watkins replied. "It has been a dreadful ordeal, and for days we heard nothing, only what was reported in the newspapers. We eventually received word that the children had been found. A lady waiting to board a lifeboat saw what had happened, quickly gathered the distraught children, and kept them with her until they were safely on board the *Carpathia*. Emily, their eldest daughter, was then able to provide the authorities with her parents' names, and the two children were soon reunited with Josephine and young Ernest. It is just so tragic that she is now a widow and must make the journey back to England without Eric. I have suggested that they all come to New Zealand and build a new life here, but they are terrified of such a long voyage. It is bad enough that they must return to England by sea."

"My brother, Joseph, is an engineer on board the *Mauretania*. He mentioned in one of his letters that many of the deaths when the Titanic sank could have been avoided had the ship been equipped with sufficient lifeboats, and that there were already discussions underway about improving safety on all passenger vessels in the future. So, I feel confident that they will be quite safe on their voyage home."

"Well, what a relief, Adelaide! I never knew you had a brother."

"He is much older than I am, and left home when I was only fourteen. I have not seen him for such a long time, but I hope to study in England next year."

"You are going away?" A small voice came from the doorway.

"Alice, what have I told you about listening to adult conversations? That is not polite. Either come inside and sit with us or go to your room."

Adelaide smiled at the little girl and patted the green cushion beside her. Alice hurried over, settled next to her, and looked up with a bright smile.

"It is not certain yet, but if I am offered a place at the Royal Academy of Music, I shall travel to England next July to study for a year. Afterwards, I mean to return home, and my dream is to open a music academy here in Wellington, where I am sure you shall be my star pupil—that is, if you wish it."

"That is all right then. So long as you do come back. And yes, of course I shall be your star pupil!"

"Excellent. Then it is settled."

"Would you like me to continue giving Alice lessons? She is such a joy to teach."

"That would be wonderful. You would like that, wouldn't you, Alice?"

"Oh yes, please, especially if I am to be Miss Ellwood's star pupil!" Alice shouted, jumping up and down happily.

Chapter 18

The butterflies in Adelaide's stomach felt more like angry bees. Wearing her favourite outfit, a royal blue skirt and matching jacket, she pinned on Violet's brooch, remembering her dear friend fondly. Today, if all went well and she passed her final examination, she could begin arranging her trip to England.

As she made her way to the church hall, she savoured the vibrant autumnal foliage that had begun to colour the trees. A few other candidates were walking in the same direction, and they shared sympathetic, silent nods. All were preoccupied with nerves, waiting to be called one by one by the examiners.

Inside, a polished Bechstein piano dominated the left side of the hall, its ebony case gleaming in the morning light. To the right was a table with three chairs for the examiners. A lady with a clipboard approached, asking her name. She checked it off with a precise tick and gestured toward a side door, instructing Adelaide to wait in there until her name was called.

Adelaide found an empty seat and placed her music case on her knee. Inside were the carefully prepared pieces she had spent months practising: Debussy's *Rêverie*, a Bach two-part invention in C minor, the first movement of Beethoven's Sonata No. 8 in C minor, *Pathétique,* and a virtuosic étude by Chopin. Each piece bore neatly handwritten annotations—fingerings, dynamics, and subtle reminders Valentine had suggested.

When her name was called, Adelaide rose and entered the examination room. Three serious-looking examiners observed her: a rotund man with a large moustache and whiskers introduced himself as Mr Wallingford, flanked by Mr Carnegie and Mr Edwards. They nodded politely and asked a few questions about the composers, the era of the pieces, and stylistic considerations, as was customary for advanced-grade examinations.

She started with Debussy. The gentle arpeggios required

delicate finger work, precise pedalling, and careful control of tone—a subtle use of the una corda and soft pedal to create a dreamlike atmosphere. Mr Wallingford's sharp eyes observed her even touch, while Mr Carnegie made a small notation on his score sheet. Adelaide sensed Violet's presence in every phrase, every lingering note.

Next came the Bach invention. Each hand's voice needed clarity and independence, and Adelaide made sure her fingers articulated each note sharply while keeping the melody expressive. Mr Edwards whispered to Mr Carnegie, who nodded, impressed by her control and interpretation.

The Beethoven sonata demanded expressive phrasing and attention to classical form. Adelaide's fingers danced across the keys, balancing the lyrical passages with the stormier chords, subtly shading dynamics as she had been taught.

Finally, the Chopin étude arrived. The rapid runs and leaps tested dexterity and accuracy. Adelaide's fingers flew, but she maintained poise and evenness of touch. The examiners' pencils scratched across score sheets, noting phrasing, tone, rhythm, and overall musicality.

After the last note, Adelaide lifted her hands, heart racing. The examiners conferred quietly, making careful notations on their sheets before Mr Wallingford spoke.

"Very well, Miss Ellwood. You may step back." Mr Wallingford nodded. Adelaide rose from the piano stool, her hands still lingering briefly on the keys. "Your playing was most commendable."

Relieved and exhilarated, Adelaide allowed herself a quiet smile. She had survived the ordeal. Her meticulously annotated sheet music, hours of disciplined practice, and guidance from dear Violet and then Valentine had carried her through. The dream of travelling to England and continuing her musical studies now felt closer than ever.

In the waiting room, a hush of expectancy hung in the air as the students waited for their results. Adelaide walked towards a cheerful-looking woman serving tea.

"There you are, me duck. Get that down you and help yourself to a biscuit. It'll settle your nerves."

"Thank you," Adelaide managed, surprised but not offended at being called a duck. The woman's curious accent was unfamiliar, but her warmth was reassuring. Choosing a biscuit, Adelaide decided to sit by the tea trolley and chat with the woman rather than attempt conversation with the other students, who sat stiffly, their eyes lowered to their teacups.

"These biscuits look delicious…" Adelaide said, leaving a pause.

"Elsie McDuff, dearie. I keep the hall clean and running smoothly, and see to the tea on exam days."

"Did you make the biscuits?"

"I did indeed. Go on, have another. They're good, though I do say so myself!"

The two exchanged a few more words, and Adelaide found herself strangely comforted by Elsie's kindness. When she rejoined the other candidates, her hands still trembled a little as she lifted her teacup, but the warmth of the tea and the buttery biscuits steadied her.

At last, after what seemed an eternity, her name was called. Adelaide rose and entered the examination room once more. The three examiners looked up as she took her seat.

Mr Edwards, the senior of the three, spoke first. "Well, Miss Ellwood, we have considered your performance carefully." His manner was formal but not unfriendly.

Mr Wallingford adjusted his spectacles. "Your playing demonstrated both command and musical expression. You managed your programme with confidence, and it was evident you had prepared thoroughly."

Mr Carnegie inclined his head, and Mr Edwards resumed. "It is our pleasure to inform you that you have obtained 145 marks out of a possible 150, which places you in the class of distinction."

Mr Wallingford added gravely, "This is a very commendable result, Miss Ellwood. On behalf of the Board, allow me to offer our congratulations. We trust you will continue your studies and not neglect such a fine gift."

Adelaide could hardly believe what she was hearing. "A distinction?" she whispered.

"Yes indeed," Mr Edwards said with a faint smile. "You have every reason to be proud."

Clutching her rolled-up certificate a moment later, Adelaide stepped out into the autumn sunshine, her heart lighter than it had been for months. Since her mother wouldn't be home until later and was eager to share her good news, she decided to visit Valentine. She hoped he would be in his father's shop, but if not, she planned to share her news with Theodore instead. Entering the tailor's shop, Adelaide saw Giselle working on a man's jacket. Her beautiful but serious face was focused on the task at hand. Mr Spielmann was moving some rolls of cloth that had just arrived.

"Ah, Miss Ellwood, to what do we owe this honour?"

"Hello, Mr Spielmann. Is Valentine here? I have news about my examination." Lifting her rolled-up certificate for them to see.

Giselle answered, "I'm sorry he has gone out. He is with Eva, I think, as she called for him earlier this morning."

"Oh, that's all right. I only called on the off chance." Hiding her disappointment with a bright smile.

"So, how did you do?" Giselle asked.

"I passed!" Adelaide announced happily.

"Congratulations, Adelaide!" Giselle and her father shouted in unison.

A customer had just entered the shop, prompting Mr Spielmann to take his leave, but Giselle was eager to speak to Adelaide.

"Thank you for inviting us to your picnic on Sunday. I love the Botanic Gardens."

Adelaide had almost forgotten the picnic as she had been so wrapped up in the examination. "I am so glad you can both come. We will be a merry bunch, especially as I have much to celebrate now."

"Does this mean you can now take up your place at the Royal Academy of Music in London? Giselle asked.

"Well, I still have to apply and be accepted, but if all goes well, I hope to sail to England next year."

Giselle gave a wistful smile. "I think Valentine will be so pleased for you. I sometimes wish he dared to travel and take a post at a music academy abroad. His talents are rather wasted on the children of Wellington."

Giselle, not wishing Adelaide to feel included in her generalisation, quickly added, "That does not include you, of course. Teaching you has brought Valentine more happiness and fulfilment than he has known in a long time."

"That is a kind thing to say, but it's I who should be grateful to Valentine. He helped me so much after Violet died and encouraged me to play the piano again."

Their conversation was abruptly ended when Mr Spielmann needed Giselle's help with a customer. "I'd better go, but I will look forward to seeing you on Sunday!"

"Goodbye, Giselle. I'll see you at the picnic."

Adelaide's next thought was to share the news with Theodore and Elisabeth when an unexpected voice stopped her in her tracks. "Adelaide! Adelaide! Wait for me!" She turned, taken aback, to see her mother striding toward her, waving her closed umbrella to catch her attention.

"Mother, what a surprise!" Adelaide exclaimed, meeting her halfway. "I thought you wouldn't be back until later, so I didn't hurry home."

"I thought to surprise you. I went to the church hall, but you had already left. I ventured a guess that you might wish to visit either Valentine or Theodore. Let us take some afternoon tea, and you can tell me how it went."

"That would be lovely. Thank you."

They chose a table for two in a quiet corner of their favourite tea shop, The Willow Tree. Marie signalled the waitress and placed their order. Turning her attention to Adelaide with eager anticipation, she asked, "So, you walked in and ..."

"I passed with a distinction!" Adelaide declared, her laughter catching the attention of several other guests seated nearby, who all smiled at her.

Adelaide was so happy that, for once, she did not care if other people heard her.

"Well, of course, you did, darling. I never doubted you for a second," Marie replied with a proud smile.

Buoyed by her mother's enthusiasm, Adelaide launched into a vivid recount of her experience, describing the examiners, how she played, the warmth of Elsie McDuff, and the peculiar charm of her accent.

"I am very proud of you. I hope you realise that," Marie said, reaching out to pat Adelaide's hand gently.

"Thank you. That means a great deal to me, especially as I sometimes worry that you'd prefer I were more sociable like Charlotte and, of course, eventually find a suitable husband," Adelaide admitted, rolling her eyes.

"Oh, my dear, is that what you think? That's not it at all," Marie replied, a little put out by Adelaide's comments.

"I'm sorry, Mother, I didn't mean to speak out of turn." Adelaide's look of embarrassment softened Marie's reaction a little, but before she could answer, the waitress brought over their order and served their tea.

"This all looks delicious," Adelaide said quickly, not wishing to dampen the warmth of the moment any further. But there was one more thing she had to say before her confidence slipped away again.

"It will soon be time to apply to the Royal Academy of Music. I have sent off for the 1913 prospectus, and Valentine has kindly offered to assist me with my application."

Marie stirred her tea with composed assurance, a gentle smile softening her features.

"Excellent. There is much to consider if you are accepted. Though truly, there is no 'if' about it. I have no doubt you will be accepted—none at all. I have been giving much thought to our journey to England."

"Our journey?" Adelaide's eyes widened. "Are you coming with me?"

"Well, of course I am! You absolutely cannot travel alone. I shall treat it as a holiday. I have long wished to visit the Mother Country, and this will be a wonderful adventure for us both."

"But what about Father? Will he allow it?"

Marie waved off her concern with calm assurance. "Leave your father to me. He will likely relish a peaceful household with us out of the way. And who knows? If work permits, he may even join us for your graduation, and perhaps take a short holiday thereafter, before we return home together. It will be most delightful."

Adelaide clapped her hands together, beaming. "Oh, Mother, I can hardly believe it! My dream of studying in England is almost a reality."

As they finished their tea and scones, their conversation bubbled with excitement over preparing for the long voyage and their anticipated time in England. Nearby occupants at other tables exchanged curious glances, wondering what had made the two women so delightfully merry.

Chapter 19

Adelaide sprang from her bed, eager for the day ahead. Throwing open the shutters, she felt a sense of relief to see only a few light clouds drifting across the clear blue sky. It was a perfect autumn morning, still mild for the time of year. She was certain the Botanic Gardens would be at their best, and the thought of their picnic filled her with happy anticipation.

Her thoughts turned to Valentine, and she felt a pang of disappointment that he had not called to congratulate her. Even a note would have meant something. Adelaide was surprised by how much it mattered to her. Her parents had been happy for her, and Peggy, of course. But it was Valentine she had wanted to impress.

Peggy's voice could be heard in the kitchen, scolding Elise for getting under her feet. Feeling guilty, Adelaide made her way to the kitchen to rescue either Peggy or Elise or perhaps both. Peggy had been busy since yesterday baking all sorts of delicious treats, carefully wrapping them and placing them into a wicker picnic basket, along with a bottle of her homemade elderflower cordial.

"Good morning, Peggy. Is there anything I can help you with?"

"Ah, Adelaide, there you are! Perhaps you could kindly remove Elise from my kitchen. She is quite giddy this morning. Why don't you put her in the garden while you go and have your breakfast, and I'll finish packing the food?"

Picking up her wriggling dog, she tried to tickle her behind the ears to try to calm her. "Elise, what's got into you this morning? Are you excited for the picnic today?"

After securing Elise in the garden and leaving her happily chasing leaves and other imaginary delights, Adelaide wandered off to join her parents for breakfast. She found them already seated, enjoying their breakfast of scrambled eggs and toast. She took a plate and helped herself to a generous portion, along with plenty of toast.

"Good morning. Isn't it the perfect day for a picnic?"

Robert looked up from his breakfast, "It is indeed. It will be a nice change. But unfortunately, I have to go into the office this morning, so I will have to meet you at the Botanic Gardens instead."

"On a Sunday! Do you have to?" Adelaide shouted, unable to hide her disappointment.

Robert's reply was firm. "I'm sorry, but I do. I wouldn't go in if I didn't have to. But I promise I'll be at the Botanic Gardens by one o'clock. Don't worry." He then gave his daughter a sympathetic smile before continuing to eat his breakfast.

"What are your plans this morning, Adelaide?" Marie quickly changed the subject before Adelaide could say anything else to stir further ripples of dissent before the day began. She had already told Robert how disappointed she was that he had agreed to go to work, insisting that surely, being so senior now, meant he didn't have to. Robert had argued his case: "On the contrary, it means I must ensure I'm available whenever I'm needed. It's important that I set a good example to the men under me."

"I think I'll begin my application to the Royal Academy. The 1913 Prospectus has finally arrived, so I must thoroughly review all the information. Then I can show the application to Valentine when we have our next lesson."

"Your dream is becoming a reality, isn't it, my dear?" Her mother smiled at her as she buttered another piece of toast for herself.

Adelaide nodded, trying to swallow her eggs quickly before speaking. "I'm excited to send in my application finally. It's such a big step, but one I'm ready for!"

Robert, engrossed in his newspaper, said nothing as Marie and Adelaide talked excitedly about their potential trip to England the following year, should everything go as planned. Adelaide was aware of her father's silence and felt a pang of sadness that he wasn't as happy for her as she had hoped. *Is he as disappointed in me as he is with Joseph?*

As they prepared to leave, Peggy handed Adelaide the carefully packed picnic basket and tucked a folded blanket beneath her free arm.

"Goodness, Peggy, you've packed a feast," Adelaide said with a laugh. "I only hope I can carry it all the way to the Botanic Gardens."

"It's a pity your father had to work; we could do with his help," Marie added, still irritated that Robert had chosen to work on a Sunday. Giving her daughter a sympathetic smile, she asked, "Will you be all right?"

"I'll be fine. I'm stronger than I look," Adelaide replied, though the basket's handle was already digging into her delicate hands.

"Here, let me take Elise," Marie offered, reaching for the dog's lead. "She'll have you and the picnic basket on the ground if you're not careful."

Elise tugged enthusiastically, her tail wagging in anticipation of the outing. With the dog now under Marie's control, they set off toward the Montgomery house. John and Susannah were already on their way to meet them, and the two parties exchanged cheerful greetings and remarks about the glorious weather. Marie and Susannah soon wandered on ahead, their conversation trailing back in snippets of laughter and shared gossip.

Adelaide sighed as she watched them disappear around the corner, oblivious to her own awkward juggling of the basket, the blanket, and now Elise, as her mother had absent-mindedly handed back the lead just as she paused to greet John and Susannah.

"Here, let me take that for you," John said, reaching for the basket with an easy smile.

"Thank you," Adelaide breathed, grateful as she relinquished the weight. "Peggy's packed enough delicious food to feed an army, and Elise wasn't exactly helping."

"In that case, it will be a pleasure to help carry such important cargo." John smiled at her warmly.

"Are you sure? I can see you're already in possession of important cargo," Adelaide laughed, pointing to his picnic basket.

He lifted both baskets, gently bouncing them in each hand like a set of scales. "I can confirm," he declared merrily, "that the Ellwood picnic basket is indeed heavier."

Adelaide laughed again. John was like an uncle to her, always great fun to be with. A memory flashed in her mind of when she and Charlotte were about five years old, clinging to his back as he pranced around pretending to be a pony. They had laughed uncontrollably until Susannah scolded them all for such silliness and sent them off to Charlotte's room to play. John, flushed and grinning, had winked at them as they were shooed from the drawing room.

As they neared the meeting spot, Adelaide scanned the manicured lawns for Valentine and Giselle, hoping they had already arrived. To her relief, she spotted them beneath the shade of a flowering pōhutukawa, its crimson blossoms vivid against the blue sky. Relieved that Eva had not joined them, she waved enthusiastically, and they responded with cheerful smiles. Adelaide introduced them to Susannah and John, and soon the quiet hum of conversation gave way to a flurry of movement as the blankets were spread across the grass. At the edge of the lawn, a weathered bench offered a quieter place for Susannah and Marie to settle, their voices low as they continued to catch up on the latest goings-on around Wellington. Not long after, and much to Adelaide's relief, her father arrived. She had half expected him not to come, imagining him buried in work, and then she felt guilty as she saw the weariness etched into his face. She fussed over him gently, offering him a cold drink and cleared a place on the blanket for him to sit.

Giselle produced a game of quoits and invited everyone to play. Bursts of laughter echoed across the lawn as a pleasant hour passed. Then, through the trees, a voice rang out, clear and unapologetic.

"Sorry, I'm late!" Eva called. "I had to help my father at the bookshop, but I'm here now. Hope I haven't missed anything."

Susannah Montgomery looked at Eva with disapproval, wondering who this rude young lady was. Marie quickly explained that Eva had gone to school with Adelaide and Charlotte. Recognition flickered across Susannah's face as she remembered Charlotte's stories of the tension and the trouble Eva had caused, especially toward Adelaide.

Giselle, sensing the shift in mood, intervened with practised grace. "Eva, come join us, we're just about to start another round."

Eva smiled as she stepped forward, her eyes scanning the group until they settled on Valentine. She placed herself deliberately at his side, her presence almost possessive. Valentine inclined his head in a polite nod, but for the briefest moment, his expression flickered. Adelaide caught the tightening around his eyes and the slight stiffness in his posture. Eva had always been unpredictable, and her sudden appearance, together with that subtle air of possession over Valentine, left Adelaide uncertain of what she was truly witnessing.

When it was time to eat, Marie and Susannah insisted that the picnics be combined to create one large feast for everyone to enjoy. Eva helped herself freely, while Valentine and Giselle felt a little shy, as their picnic was quite modest compared to the others. However, their protests were ignored, and they both enjoyed the splendid array of sandwiches, pies, and cakes on offer. After lunch, Robert and John decided to go for a walk and smoke their cigars. Susannah and Marie chose to stroll by the rose garden, leaving the younger people to their own devices, with instructions to watch over the picnic baskets. Valentine finally had the chance to congratulate Adelaide on passing her exam. "I want to hear all the details and what the examiners said." Valentine was genuinely pleased for her.

"Of course, now, I will be losing my best student." Valentine teased.

"Well, not just yet. There's always room for improvement, and I have my application to submit. I was hoping you would help me."

"It would be an honour," Valentine replied happily, and Adelaide felt relieved as Valentine started to relax and seemed happier than he had been earlier when Eva first appeared.

Eva had been watching and listening to the exchange. The way they spoke to each other made her feel sick to her stomach. To contain the rising tide of anger, she clenched her hand into a fist, her fingernails pressing so sharply into her palm they nearly broke the skin. The pain was necessary, a reminder to stay calm, to focus, to plan her next move.

As it turned out, life had taken a turn for the better since Eva met a gentleman named Hermann Wagner in the bookshop one afternoon, while her parents were away at an estate sale seeking a highly sought-after book collection. Eva's remarkable knowledge of her neighbours had greatly impressed Wagner, and her unwavering loyalty to Germany and the Kaiser sparked his interest.

Hermann Wagner was an influential businessman with a commanding presence that attracted attention even in the modest gatherings he attended. He moved within a discreet circle of fellow entrepreneurs, mostly German immigrants, who met to preserve their culture, foster trade with the homeland, and, as some whispered, maintain a quiet loyalty to the Kaiser. He had quickly recognised Eva's unusual gift for overhearing snippets of private conversation. In a neighbourhood largely populated by German immigrants, she often crossed paths with those who quietly mourned the country they had left behind. Some were disillusioned, others resentful, and all appeared ripe for persuasion.

Lately, the demanding voice in Eva's mind had become louder and more insistent. After spending time with Wagner, she finally understood. It was his voice she had been hearing all along, whispering from the shadowed corners of her thoughts. It had to be. And he must be obeyed.

A few days ago, she had gone to Wagner with a plan—one that would serve their cause and finally secure her passage to Germany. Her first step was to send a letter to the Conservatoire in Leipzig, forging Valentine's handwriting and signature. However, she understood that to win Wagner's complete confidence, she would need to go further. Valentine would have to marry her, and smiling to herself with quiet satisfaction, she felt confident that, given what she knew, it would pose no difficulty.

When Robert and John returned from their walk, John produced a box camera and announced he would like to take a few photographs to capture the special day. Valentine and Adelaide were standing in front of a beautiful rhododendron, displaying elegant white blossoms. "Stand still, both of you!" John instructed as he set up his camera. They laughed and smiled towards the camera as he captured the moment perfectly.

Next, he took one of Robert and Marie, who were sitting together on the bench, and then Robert offered to take one of John and Susannah in return.

"Just one more and I'll leave you all alone." John laughed. "Adelaide, Giselle, Valentine, Eva … where's Eva?"

No one had noticed that she had left. Adelaide's heart sank, and she felt a little embarrassed, but not surprised, as it was what Eva did.

"Never mind, come on, the three of you. Stand together, and let's not forget Elise!"

They did as they were told, and as Giselle scooped up the excited dog, Elise promptly licked the side of her face, making them all turn to laugh just as John took the photograph. Click. A memory to last forever.

Chapter 20

Woodlands – December 1912

"You've outdone yourself this year, Victoria; the house looks so festive." Marie congratulated her sister-in-law. The hall and main rooms of the house had been decorated with garlands of fir, eucalyptus and dried red berries threaded with silver twine. A large Christmas tree stood grandly in the main drawing room, where they were seated drinking tea when Helena and Gabriel arrived with their newborn daughter, Isabella. Adelaide gazed into the deep blue eyes of the tiny baby swaddled in a pretty linen wrap as she was proudly presented to the admiring audience.

"She was so nearly born on my birthday," Adelaide said wistfully.

"I'm glad she wasn't. I think everyone should have their own birthday!" Helena declared, smiling fondly at her cousin. The twins, who for once had been quietly playing cards in the background, shot back in unison, "We have to share ours!"

"Hello, dear brothers! Still as cheeky as ever." Helena replied, laughing with them.

The twins began talking about how excited they were to celebrate their birthday with the traditional tennis tournament and a New Year's Eve Party. Sensing their enthusiasm, Elise started jumping around, which upset the baby, causing her to cry. Adelaide caught Elise and said she would take her to the beach. She was thankful for the chance to escape, as she had a lot on her mind, and finding a moment's peace in such a noisy household was impossible. Not that she minded, but an hour or so on the beach with her little dog sounded perfect.

Elise ran ahead as she reached the little footpath at the bottom of the garden and disappeared through the trees. Adelaide breathed in deeply, the salty air assailing her senses. The ocean was calm, and the waves rippled on the shoreline, making Adelaide quicken her pace. She was eager to reach the beach and find a quiet spot to settle down and think. Settling herself against a rocky outcrop, she watched Elise rush to the shore and bark at the waves. There is so much to think of and plan. Next year, she might be spending her first Christmas in England. Nervous excitement raced through her veins.

"Adelaide!" Her cousin's voice shouting her name made her jump.

"Helena! You are on your own. What have you done with Isabella?"

"I've left her with her Grandma and Great Aunt for half an hour so I could come and see my favourite cousin." Sitting down next to Adelaide, she grabbed her hand and became serious. "How are you? I feel like I've not spent enough time with this past year."

Adelaide smiled at Helena, "Well, you have been rather busy becoming a mother, haven't you? Isabella is gorgeous."

"This is true, and I was so sick all the time. I must be the only pregnant woman in the whole world who lost weight instead of gaining it!"

"Was it that bad?"

"Worse." Helena laughed. "But when I cuddle little Isabella, I feel so much love. It was all worth it!"

"Isabella is such a beautiful name."

"We think so. One of Gabriel's distant Aunts was an Isabella, so we borrowed it for our daughter.

"Do you know what her middle name is?"

"No. I never thought to ask. I was simply relieved that you and the baby were safe."

Smiling, Helena said, "Her full name is Isabella Adelaide Thornhill. What do you think of that?"

Adelaide drew her hands up to her face in surprise. "Isabella

Adelaide! Oh, Helena, it is so beautiful!" Suddenly, overwhelmed by Helena's kindness and the serenity of the sea, Adelaide began to sob, and Helena wrapped her arms around her.

"Let it all out and have a good cry. No one is watching."

When the tears had subsided, Helena produced a large white handkerchief. "I think you might require this more substantial one."

Blowing her nose loudly, Adelaide felt a pang of remorse. "Oh, Helena, I am so sorry. I cannot imagine what made me cry so suddenly."

It seems to me you haven't given yourself a proper chance to grieve. Our British 'stiff upper lip' is quite absurd. We are New Zealanders; if we want to cry, I see no reason why we shouldn't be allowed to.

"I believe I am finally coming to terms with all that has happened and starting to dare to look forward to the future." Dabbing at her eyes, Adelaide smiled. "I think I needed that!"

"I am so proud of you, Adelaide. I have no doubt you will bring credit to the Academy. And if ever you require assistance or simply someone to listen, I am always here."

"Thank you, Helena. You are a wonderful cousin and friend. I believe I shall miss you more than anyone, if they accept me."

"Oh, Adelaide, of course they shall accept you. You possess extraordinary talent and are thoroughly deserving. We shall write, and I shall look forward to hearing all your news. When you return with your degree, performing recitals and lecturing across the country, I shall attend as many concerts as possible. I promise you that! And, of course, I hope you will teach little Isabella to play the piano—when she is old enough, of course."

"Of course I shall. Isabella shall have no choice in the matter," Adelaide replied, laughing with her cousin.

The Christmas and New Year festivities passed quickly, and before long, it was time to return to Wellington. Robert wanted to leave early, so they said their fond farewells to everyone the night before. As they boarded the train, Robert and Marie were in a quiet mood, preferring to gaze out of the window as the urban landscape gave way to fields of corn and wheat, along with a meandering stream that ran beside the train as it sped towards Picton. Elise was content to curl up on a blanket next to Marie, who absentmindedly stroked her from time to time. Adelaide took the opportunity to read. Retrieving a large book from her bag, she smiled at the beautiful illustrations on the front cover. It was a Christmas present from her aunt and uncle. Making herself comfortable, she opened the book and began reading all about 'The History of the Austrian Composers.'

The following day, Peggy opened the door to the weary travellers. She had returned earlier in the day to air out the house and had spent the morning baking. The delicious aroma greeted them as Peggy took their coats and hats. Wishes of 'Happy New Year' were shared, and Adelaide sighed happily. "Home," she said, smiling at Peggy.

Adelaide relished returning to her familiar routine of giving piano lessons, attending Easterwood Academy, and, of course, resuming her lessons with Valentine. She even dared to hope that, at last, her dreams might soon become reality.

One afternoon, Adelaide resolved to visit Theodore and Elisabeth to thank them for the beautiful book they had given her. It had become something of a Christmas tradition for Adelaide to present the Miller family with a large box of chocolates, a luxury they would not ordinarily purchase for themselves, while Theodore would select a book for her. Sometimes it was a novel by a popular author; at other times, a scholarly volume on music. This year, he had chosen Persuasion by Jane Austen, which she had read with immense enjoyment and left her eager to explore more of Austen's work.

As she stepped inside, the brass bell above the door chimed softly, and she was greeted by the familiar mingling of scents: beeswax polish on the wooden shelves, the faint tang of ink, and the dry, papery fragrance of well-thumbed volumes. Sunlight filtered through the front windows, casting golden bars across neatly stacked books, some imported from England, others from local publishers in Wellington and Dunedin. The polished counter, with its inkwell and ledger, stood ready for the day's business, and Adelaide felt a familiar warmth, as though she were entering not merely a shop but a sanctuary of words and ideas.

Looking around the shop for Theodore, Adelaide's heart sank as Eva stood at the counter, staring at her. Eva greeted her. "Frohes neues Jahr, Adelaide!" Choosing to ignore that Eva had welcomed her in German, Adelaide returned the welcome in English. "Happy New Year, Eva. Is your father or mother home? I want to thank them for the book they gave me for Christmas."

"You are such a bookworm," Eva said, but there didn't seem to be any malice in her words for a change; however, Eva's words unnerved her even more. *Why was that?*

Having heard voices, Theodore rushed into the shop, happy to see Adelaide. "Adelaide, Happy New Year! Did you have a wonderful Christmas? Thank you so much for the chocolates; as always, they were delicious and have been devoured with Hugo and Louis's help."

"My pleasure, Theodore. Thank you so much for my beautiful book. It was a wonderful and very romantic story.

"Excellent. I thought you would enjoy some Jane Austen."

"Is there anything I can tempt you with today?"

"I am sure you could easily tempt me, but I only really came to thank you." Theodore laughed and put his hands up in defeat, knowing it would be too easy to persuade his best customer to purchase more books from him.

After enjoying Theodore's company and listening to Hugo and Louis excitedly tell her about their Christmas presents, Adelaide had to say her goodbyes. As she walked home, lost in thought about the upcoming school year, she could hardly wait to show Mrs Easterwood her application to the Royal Academy of Music. So much seemed to depend on her answers and cover letter that she feared she was overthinking every word. More than anything, she longed for Mrs Easterwood's steady wisdom to help her finish the application and finally send it off.

As Adelaide left the shop, Eva felt immensely pleased with Adelaide's news. Persuading Valentine to teach Adelaide was a brilliant decision, even though she couldn't bear to see them together. That didn't matter for now, as her plan was progressing smoothly. The forged letter applying for a teaching position had been sent off to the Leipzig Conservatoire, and Eva felt confident they would reply soon with an offer for Valentine to work there. She was impressed with how well she had forged Valentine's handwriting, and aside from writing a glowing testimonial, she added that he was to be married this summer and would like to bring his new wife with him. Eva had done her research and knew that to become a Professor and gain tenure there, being married was encouraged. Now, all she needed to do was make it happen. Laughing, she narrowed her eyes and grinned. *With what she knew about Valentine and his true nature, he could not refuse her!*

Two days later, Robert finally spoke to his daughter about going to England. The grandfather clock in the hall was striking nine. Adelaide was about to retire to bed to read, and Robert was in his study. The door was ajar, which was unusual, so Adelaide popped her head around the door. "Goodnight, father. I'm off to bed now."

"Adelaide, my dear, come in. Can I talk to you for a minute?"

She entered his study and quickly sat down in a chair, fearing her legs would give way.

"Do not look so glum. I merely wish to speak with you about your journey to England." He was seated at his desk, cradling a glass of whisky. "There is much to be arranged: I must book your passage and make provision for you to stay with your Uncle Hugh and Aunt Alice. I daresay your mother is quite as excited as you are!"

"Do you mean you are happy for me to go and study, and you haven't changed your mind?" Adelaide's face broke into a radiant smile. She leapt up and wrapped her arms around her father. "Thank you, thank you."

Robert patted his daughter's hands, which were hugging his neck. It pleased him to see her smile again.

Adelaide eventually removed her arms from his neck and began to speak hurriedly, almost stumbling over her words. "I haven't been accepted yet and must get my application in. I keep dithering about it and worrying if I have done it right, but knowing I have your blessing means everything to me."

Laughing at his daughter's enthusiasm, he couldn't resist teasing her. "Can I not try to tempt you into changing your mind to go to Christchurch instead?"

Adelaide's face fell, but she saw the twinkle in her father's eye and realised he was only joking. After hearing about Charlotte's adventures in Geneva and London, Adelaide had been put off for life. All the dances she had to attend, the young men hoping to dance with Charlotte, the dances themselves, and all the socialising and dressing up for every occasion made Adelaide shudder with horror. No, she knew she was making the right decision and was looking forward to working hard and proving to everyone she was worthy of a place at the Royal Academy of Music.

Chapter 21

Wellington – April 1913

Summer had slipped quietly away, leaving behind a landscape ablaze with colour. The trees, now dressed in brilliant shades of amber, crimson, and gold, formed a breathtaking tapestry that never failed to captivate Adelaide. She had decided to take a walk with Elise to the park to admire the trees in their autumn glory and, more importantly, to read two letters that had arrived in the post that morning. It hadn't been easy to intercept them at breakfast without her parents noticing, but with Peggy's discreet assistance, she had succeeded. One envelope was from Joseph; the other bore the crest of the Royal Academy of Music. One letter she longed to tear open, desperate to know if her life was about to change forever. The other, she wanted to linger over, to soak in her brother's latest news.

Choosing an empty bench that overlooked a beautiful, ornate pond, she sat down and reached into her bag—deciding to let fate choose which letter to read first. Eyes closed, she drew one of the letters out. It was Joseph's.

> *Mauretania (somewhere in the Atlantic)*
> *25th March 1913*

Dearest Addie,

So, your dream of becoming a concert pianist is starting to come true! I told you, didn't I, that by the time I am a captain, you'd be travelling on my ship and performing in concerts all over the world! Well, I'm nowhere near becoming a captain, but 3rd Engineer isn't bad!

Adelaide placed the letter on her lap and paused for a moment. Even after all this time, *he still believes I can do this.* The other letter in her bag tugged at her thoughts, its presence growing louder. Shaking her head, she returned to her brother's words, which were tinged with sadness as Kitty had miscarried. Though the loss had shaken them both, the doctor had assured them there was no reason why they couldn't try again once she had recovered. But as Adelaide read the final paragraph, a faint frown crept onto her face.

Seeing you again after all these years would be wonderful, but I hope you won't be shocked by how different our way of life is from yours. Our home is small, but it's ours, and we're happy there. Anyway, duty calls. I look forward to receiving good news!

Your loving brother,
Joseph

Adelaide placed the letter on her lap again. Frowning, she wondered what he meant. Was he worried she would disapprove because their home was small? Adelaide was upset that her brother would think that of her, but then she realised it was probably their mother to whom he was directing his worries. *Well, there's no point in worrying about that right now.* The next task was to find out if she was, in fact, going to England.

When Valentine spotted Adelaide in the park, she was seated on a bench, staring out across the pond. She seemed a million miles away, her hands gripping tightly to a letter on her lap.

He approached quietly and sat down with care, so as not to alarm her. Leaning closer, he whispered her name.

"Adelaide." No response. He spoke louder.

"Adelaide!"

She started and realised Valentine was beside her.

"Valentine! I am so sorry. I did not see or hear you."

"Is everything all right? I hope the letter does not bring bad news."

"The letter? Oh yes, the letter…" She looked down at the vellum paper, the Royal Academy crest gleaming at the top.

"It is from the Royal Academy."

Valentine glanced at the letter, a moment of concern passing across his face. "I am sorry, Adelaide. Have they rejected your application?"

Adelaide looked at him, moved by the genuine concern in his expression.

"Adelaide, I cannot bear the suspense. Have you, or have you not, been accepted?"

"Forgive me—I am still in shock." Handing him the letter, she said, "Here, you read it."

Royal Academy of Music
York Gate, Marylebone Road., N.W.

28th February 1913

Dear Miss Ellwood,

It gives me great pleasure to offer you a place at the Royal Academy of Music.

Your course of instruction shall comprise two weekly lessons in your principal study and one weekly lesson in each of your second, third, and fourth studies. Annual examinations are held during the Midsummer Term and are conducted by the Principal. Should the examinations prove satisfactory, you will receive a certificate of your qualifications as a teacher and performer. Should you display special merit and ability, and on the recommendation of the Committee of Management, you will be granted the privilege of using the letters A.R.A.M. after your name.

Evidence of students' progress is presented at fortnightly concerts held during Term at the Academy, in addition to Public Chamber and Orchestral Concerts, which are presented twice each term in Metropolitan Concert Halls appointed by the Committee. Friends of the students and subscribers to the Institution are entitled to tickets for these concerts.

Upon passing your final examinations, those students who display special merit and ability, and who are recommended by the Committee of Management, may present themselves for the Metropolitan Examination. Successful candidates shall have the right to use the initials L.A.R.M. after their names. Further particulars respecting your chosen studies may be found in the Prospectus for 1913.

On a personal note, your letters of recommendation and record of qualifications made a most favourable impression upon the Committee of Management. In consideration of your residence overseas, it has been resolved that we shall offer you an unconditional place based solely on your qualifications. Nevertheless, we must request that you be present for an Entrance Interview on Thursday, 18th September 1913. You will be required to bring music exemplifying your attainments in the subjects proposed for your principal and secondary studies. Upon arrival, you are asked to enquire for Miss Lupen, who will accompany you to the music studio and assist you with enrolment.

Kindly confirm receipt of this letter and indicate whether you wish to accept our offer of a place at the Royal Academy of Music. Michaelmas Term commences on Monday, 28th September 1913, and all fees must be paid prior to that date.

Pray accept my warm congratulations and every good wish for success in your forthcoming studies.

Yours faithfully,

Tobias Matthay
Tobias Matthay, Esquire
Chairman

Valentine had read the letter aloud, and even as she heard the words repeated, it was still hard for Adelaide to absorb it all. When she reached to retrieve the letter from him, Valentine gently took her hand and kissed it. "Adelaide, I am so very happy for you. I truly am. You deserve this, and I wish you every success."

Blushing and drawing her hand gently away, Adelaide found her voice. "That is so kind of you, thank you. I can scarcely believe I have been accepted; it feels like such a dream. I can't wait to tell my parents, Mrs Easterwood, and, of course, Theodore and Elisabeth. Everyone who believed in me. If only Violet were here to share in my happiness."

"She would be immensely proud, I am sure. I believe she is looking down on you and smiling."

"I like to think she is, and I am grateful for all your help, too. You have been so patient and kind to me, and I wouldn't have had the courage to continue without you."

"It has been my pleasure, but we are not finished yet. Believe me when I say there is more work to be done before you are ready to start your studies. So, I will see you on Sunday afternoon, and we will start your lessons with renewed purpose!"

Valentine took his leave and carried on his walk. He was so delighted for his student, happier than he thought he should be or deserved.

Standing concealed behind a cluster of karaka trees, Eva watched intently as Valentine and Adelaide engaged in conversation. Earlier, she had seen Valentine leaving his father's shop and had carefully planned an 'accidental' encounter for an opportunity to spend a leisurely hour wandering the park. Everything was going to plan until she spotted Adelaide and Valentine together, laughing and looking so happy in each other's company. A surge of uncontrollable fury welled up within her, so strong she could barely keep herself from voicing the venomous thought that crossed her mind. *I wish it had been you who fell under the horse that day*. But no, Eva reminded herself. She had much more satisfying plans in store for Adelaide.

Slowly and deliberately, she positioned herself behind the trees, her ears straining to catch every word of their exchange. The conversation was everything she had hoped for, bringing her dream of returning to Germany tantalisingly close to reality. But when Valentine kissed Adelaide's hand, his face lit with unmistakable joy, Eva's control teetered on the edge. Rage burned in her chest, yet she managed to stifle the urge to betray her hiding place. "I swear," she hissed silently, her resolve hardening, "once I have what I need from you, I will make you suffer."

When Adelaide returned home, eager to share her wonderful news with her mother, her excitement dimmed upon finding the house unusually quiet. Peggy greeted her at the door, a warm smile on her face.

"Your mother's not back yet, I'm afraid," Peggy said. "She should be home in about an hour."

Peggy raised an eyebrow and gave her a knowing look. "Goodness, Adelaide, you look like the cat that got the cream! I take it the letters you were so careful to sneak past your parents this morning brought good news?"

"Oh, Peg, they did. One was from the Royal Academy of Music, and I've been accepted!" Adelaide cried, grabbing Peggy's hands as they spun around the hallway in a burst of laughter and joy, skirts swirling and feet barely keeping rhythm. When they finally stopped, breathless and beaming, Peggy patted her chest and grinned.

"Well then, this calls for a celebration! And as it happens, I made a lemon syrup cake this morning. Come sit with me in the kitchen while I get on with the evening meal."

"That sounds perfect. I'll freshen up and be there in a few minutes. Put the kettle on!" Peg, chuckling to herself, watched Adelaide almost skipping as she disappeared from view.

After removing her outdoor clothes and tidying her hair, she glanced at the letter again, making sure it was real and that the Royal Academy of Music had just accepted her. No matter what happens in the future, nothing could take away the glorious sense of achievement she was feeling right now.

Settled in her favourite chair with Toby the cat purring on her lap, Adelaide's words tumbled out of her. Peggy stood chopping carrots, smiling down at her. It had been an age since she'd seen Adelaide so buoyant and looking forward to the future.

"I wonder what the journey at sea will be like. Joseph has always made his time at sea sound exciting."

"Well, you'll soon find out," Peggy replied as she placed the carrots into a large pan. "Right, now that's done, let's have some tea."

"I hope there will be time to visit Joseph and Kitty."

"Of course, there will. Surely, you won't be studying all the time."

"I shouldn't think so. There's so much to think about, but I will enjoy this moment for now. I hope Mother returns home soon. I can't wait to tell her!"

During supper, Marie and Robert made a toast to their daughter and discussed plans for the journey, and Marie added that she must write to Alice and Hugh to prepare them for their visit. "I wish you could come too," Adelaide said, looking over at her father.

"I do, too, but I have no time to finish some of the cases I am working on. But I promise I will be there when you graduate, and we will take a short holiday. I want to take you to where your grandparents were born and where I studied."

"Will you be visiting Joseph?" Adelaide regretted the question the moment it left her lips.

Robert glanced at Marie, his expression momentarily uneasy. "I don't think so. He will, in all likelihood, be at sea." He took a sip of wine and, with studied ease, turned the conversation elsewhere.

Adelaide longed to say more, yet she checked herself, unwilling to distress her father and mar the evening. Still, she could not comprehend how readily her parents contrived to put Joseph from their thoughts, when he had done nothing worse than to fall in love.

The next day, after a lesson with an uncooperative nine-year-old named Oliver, she decided to visit Miller's bookshop to share her good news with Theodore and Elisabeth. As she entered the shop, she was disappointed to see Eva serving instead of Theodore. Although Eva had become much kinder to her, there was something about her that Adelaide couldn't quite identify. She tried to slip out of the door to avoid speaking to her, but Eva caught sight of her and called out, "You are not leaving without saying hello, are you?"

"Hello Eva, sorry, I didn't want to bother you as you looked busy," Adelaide said quickly.

"What brings you here today? The desire for another boring music book or to bother my father?"

And there it was. Eva's quiet, insidious cruelty, the kind Adelaide could never stomach. Then, just as swiftly, her demeanour shifted, all warmth and charm. "I believe congratulations are in order," she said lightly. "Valentine tells me you're going to London to study music."

"Yes, I am, and I still can't quite believe it!"

"How I wish I could escape this place."

"You still want to go back to Germany?"

"Yes, of course I do. I hate it here."

"I will be coming back as soon as I have finished my studies. Wellington is my home, and I couldn't imagine living anywhere else."

Eva was about to say something, but Theodore returned to

the shop and welcomed Adelaide far more warmly than Eva had done. He at once called Elisabeth down from their flat, and tea was brewed. They chatted excitedly about Adelaide's news. Theodore dusted off an old book about London and all the wonderful sites she should visit. "Thank you, that is so kind of you."

"Our pleasure. We are so happy for you."

"I'll miss this wonderful shop and our stimulating conversations. You've always been so kind and welcoming."

"We'll miss you too," Theodore replied, his voice thick with emotion he was trying to contain. But wait until you get to London. You'll be amazed by how many bookshops are packed into one city."

"I can't wait. Mother will be accompanying me, so I'm sure we'll do plenty of sightseeing."

"Your mother is going with you?" Eva cut in suddenly. Adelaide had almost forgotten she was still in the shop, true to her nature, quietly listening from the sidelines.

"Yes. Since we'll be at sea for nearly eight weeks, my parents thought it would be inappropriate for me to travel alone and honestly, I agree. Elise is coming too, but she can't exactly join me at the Captain's table for dinner, can she?"

Theodore and Elisabeth exchanged nervous glances, unsure of what their daughter might say next. However, they relaxed when Eva smiled and said, "That's an excellent idea, and it'll be lovely for you to have some company. Anyway, I must be off now as I have my English class soon and need to get ready."

Once Eva had gone, Adelaide remarked on how good it was to see her finally embracing life in New Zealand and making such an effort to improve her English.

"Yes, it is very pleasing," Theodore agreed. "Her longing for Germany is rooted in a nostalgic memory of life with her Oma, and nothing like the reality she'd face if she went back now. She does worry us at times, but seeing her try to fit in is encouraging.

She even seems to be enjoying working in the bookshop."

If Eva had overheard them, she would have laughed. Her family had no idea what she was involved in. The English classes were just a convenient excuse, an alibi that allowed her to attend secret meetings at Hermann Wagner's house.

Hermann Wagner had recently declared that the group would be known as *Die Stille Hand*—The Silent Hand—the unseen force shaping Kaiser Wilhelm II's ambition for global dominance through relentless industrialisation and militarisation. Under the Kaiser's name, he urged members to channel their investments into shipbuilding and armaments, ensuring Germany's war machine remained formidable. Eva was rarely welcomed at their gatherings. Few women were. Yet they tolerated her, knowing her uncanny knack for uncovering valuable fragments of information, and what she didn't know, she very quickly managed to find out.

That evening, she shared a crucial update, thanks to Adelaide's plans; her journey to England and then on to Germany was now possible—a ripple of murmurs spread through the room. Wagner raised a hand to silence them. "Excellent. We must act quickly. Sell some of our investments and buy the diamonds, as they'll be easier for you to smuggle aboard the ship."

"Has Valentine proposed yet?" he asked pointedly. "You can only travel under the pretence of being a married couple. If not, we'll need to find someone else willing to marry you."

That's all under control, Herr Wagner," Eva replied coolly. "I've written to the Conservatoire in Leipzig, pretending to be Valentine, inquiring about any available teaching positions. If they offer him a post, he won't hesitate to marry me and return to Germany.

"Well," Wagner said with a slight nod, "I admire your confidence. Everything must be ready by the beginning of July."

"It will be," Eva assured him.

She left the meeting with her head held high, a strange

sensation humming inside her, one she hadn't felt in ages. It took a moment to recognise it. Happiness. Yes, that's what it was. She was happy.

Chapter 22

The journey to England was rapidly approaching, and Adelaide could hardly wait to depart. She had packed and unpacked her trunk several times and finally felt confident that she had all she needed for the long voyage and her stay in London. All that was left was to say farewell to those who mattered most to her.

Her first call was to Mrs Easterwood, who had invited her to take tea and wander around the school one last time. As Adelaide approached, it seemed as if the years had fallen away. Mrs Easterwood stood at the top of the stairs, waiting patiently. *How does she always know the exact time someone will arrive?*

Kathryn Easterwood welcomed her warmly, and together they made their way to the sitting room. A fire burned cheerily in the hearth, casting a comforting glow over the room. Soon, Connie Grimshaw entered, carrying a large tray of steaming tea and an assortment of cakes. Placing it on the table, she smiled at Adelaide.

"Good luck, Miss Ellwood," Mrs Grimshaw said, her voice bright with genuine pleasure. "Mr Grimshaw and I are that excited for you. You must promise to write to us often so we may hear of your adventures."

"Thank you, Mrs Grimshaw," Adelaide replied, her heart warmed by the kindness. "I shall write as often as I can, and I will be sure to keep you all updated as to life in London and my music studies, of course."

Kathryn Easterwood was eager to learn all the details. They talked for several hours, and anticipating Mrs Easterwood's many questions, Adelaide had brought the Academy's prospectus with her. Mrs Easterwood thumbed through it with delight, recognising some names of prominent teachers, professors, and musicians. "Adelaide, you are a lucky young lady, but you rightly deserve it.

You've worked hard and dreamed of this moment since you were a young girl. Do you remember when I used to find you sitting at the piano when you should have been in class?" Giving Adelaide one of her stern 'Headmistress looks.'

Adelaide laughed at the memory. "I was very naughty, wasn't I? I remember sneaking out of Mr Chidwick's maths lessons, and you would find me playing the piano or hiding somewhere reading a book."

Mrs Easterwood smiled, "Yes, you often found it difficult to follow the rules, and I probably should have disciplined you more than I did. However, I didn't consider going off to practise the piano or to read a book worthy of punishment somehow."

As Adelaide took her leave, conscious she had stayed far longer than she had intended, she couldn't help but give Mrs Easterwood a spontaneous hug, taking the poor lady by surprise. "Thank you for everything, Mrs Easterwood. You have taught me so much, including how not to let being a woman stop me from doing what I want. I am truly grateful for everything."

Mrs Easterwood squeezed Adelaide's hand, saying, "It has always been a pleasure having you as a student in my little school. Please write to me when you can. I will enjoy hearing all about your studies and your life in London."

"I will, I promise. Goodbye, Mrs Easterwood."

Adelaide walked down the steps and away from the school, which held so many happy memories, turning one last time to wave. Mrs Easterwood stood in her usual spot, waving back to her.

Violet's Aunt Susan was the only person she couldn't visit to say goodbye. Harry had decided to retire and felt they needed a fresh start by moving nearer to Harry's sister in Auckland. Susan had been worried at first, but once they had settled in, she began to embrace life again. She wrote to Adelaide often, and when Adelaide wrote to say she was going to study in London, Susan was overjoyed for her. Adelaide had mentioned that she had worn the brooch to her final examination and that the music case went with her everywhere. Susan had responded at once, telling Adelaide how much her thoughtful words meant to her, and she believed that Violet would somehow always be part of Adelaide's life, guiding her along the right path and helping her chase her dreams.

The next day, after visiting Mrs Easterwood, Adelaide felt compelled to see Theodore and Elisabeth before her departure. Theodore had worked wonders, managing to gather all the books she would need to begin her studies during the long sea voyage. Marie had decided to accompany her, as she needed a few more books of her own. The two set off together, eager to indulge in one of their favourite pastimes.

As they stepped into the familiar shop, Theodore looked up and beamed. "Ah, my favourite customers. Good afternoon, Mrs Ellwood, Miss Ellwood," he said, nodding politely to each of them. Adelaide returned his cheerful smile, biting her lip to stop herself from laughing. When she visited alone, he always called her by her first name.

"I think I'll close the shop for a little while," Theodore said, glancing around at the quiet store. "It's a slow afternoon, and I'd like to give you both my full attention before you set off on your grand adventure."

He turned the sign to *Closed* and locked the door. "I find myself in need of a cup of tea. Would you do me the honour of joining me?"

"That sounds like an excellent idea," Marie said just as Elisabeth entered from the back, carrying a tray with a pot of tea and a type of cake Adelaide didn't recognise.

As Elisabeth poured the tea and offered Marie a slice, Adelaide leaned forward, intrigued.

"That smells wonderful. What kind of cake is it?"

"I made it this morning," Elisabeth replied with a modest smile. "It is a German recipe my mother taught me—*Blechkuchen*, which means 'sheet cake.' Once you know the basic recipe, you may add any fruit you wish. Today, I used apples." She handed Adelaide a plate, her cheeks tinged a faint shade of pink under the praise. "It is a favourite with the boys, so I must be sure to save them some when they return from school."

"Please, tell us more about London, Adelaide, and about the ship on which you are to sail. Do you have sufficient books to read?" Theodore chuckled, well aware of how easily Adelaide could be tempted into acquiring another volume.

"Is there such a thing as having enough books?" Adelaide laughed. "We are sailing on the *Ayrshire*. Father told me it's already docked, and the harbour is filled with activity as its cargo is unloaded and replaced with more cargo. I have to pinch myself now and then, as it's hard to imagine that we will be boarding the ship soon. I promise I will write to you in great detail about all my adventures at sea, should I have any! Once we get settled in London, I will send postcards too of all the beautiful sights of London, like Buckingham Palace, the Tower of London and The Houses of Parliament."

Adelaide's enthusiasm was catching, and Marie and Elisabeth were smiling at each other. Theodore wore an expression of happiness, even though he felt a little sad on the inside, knowing he would miss Adelaide and her regular visits. He was just about to say all this to Adelaide when he was interrupted by Eva, who suddenly made a rather grand entrance from their living quarters. She had been listening behind the door, waiting for the right moment to share her news. It had been an eventful couple of weeks, but all her plans had finally come together nicely. There was just one more obstacle to remove. *Adelaide, you make things so easy for me.*

"Good afternoon, everyone! Are you here to bid your farewells before embarking on your grand adventure overseas?"

Marie watched Eva descend the narrow staircase from their flat, regarding her with a curious expression. Adelaide felt a sudden unease, dreading what was to come.

"Have they told you my news yet?" Eva looked at Theodore with mischievous delight, clearly enjoying the embarrassment she was causing him. Theodore shook his head, and his cheerful smile quickly vanished. He replied, sternly, "No. I have not. We mustn't keep Mrs Ellwood and Miss Ellwood too long, as they are busy preparing for their trip."

Ignoring her father's attempt at distraction, Eva was insistent, "But it is such exciting news, I must tell them."

"What is it, Eva?" Adelaide asked, bracing herself.

Eva raised her left hand, and a gold ring set with a small solitaire diamond gleamed on her third finger, catching a sunbeam that streamed through the shop window. "I am engaged, and we are to be married in a few days."

"Engaged!" Adelaide and Marie exclaimed in unison.

Adelaide quickly added, forcing sincerity, "Congratulations, Eva. We are so happy for you." She hesitated, then asked, "Who is the fortunate gentleman?"

Eva's lips curved into a triumphant smile, her grey eyes bright with excitement. "Why, Valentine, of course."

Adelaide felt her blood rush to her head. Hearing his name nearly sent her spinning, as though the world itself had tilted beneath her feet.

"Valentine!" Marie exclaimed, taken aback. "Well, you certainly kept that quiet. No announcement, no celebration, such a shame not to mark such a happy occasion."

"That is not our way, Mrs Ellwood," Eva replied, calm and confident.

Adelaide was stunned. Yet, there was something more, an undeniable shift. Eva no longer seemed bitter or resentful; she appeared triumphant, untouchable. Sensing the awkwardness, Marie turned to congratulate Theodore and Elisabeth, who tried to conceal their surprise and discomfort at their daughter's sudden announcement.

"You are marrying very quickly. What is the hurry?" Adelaide asked, regaining her voice.

"Well," Eva began, "Valentine has been offered a teaching position at the Leipzig Conservatoire. He is to be Professor of Music, and the post comes with a comfortable apartment and an excellent income, allowing us to start our married life. This is why we must marry promptly, as they expect him to begin by the end of September. And the most exciting part, I have not yet told my own parents!" Eva turned to her bewildered parents, delighted to be the centre of attention.

Theodore interrupted quickly, "Eva, we really must let Mrs Ellwood and Miss Ellwood be on their way."

Oh, but I must tell them the best part. As luck would have it, we managed to secure two passages on the *Ayrshire*. Isn't that exciting, Adelaide? We will be your travel companions!

When Eva paused, waiting for a reaction, there was just silence. No one spoke. Adelaide didn't know what to say. She felt this was wrong, all terribly wrong. Valentine had never even hinted at his feelings towards Eva. She couldn't understand why he would suddenly marry her.

Aware of Adelaide's discomfort, Marie quickly took control of the situation. "Well, I must say, this is indeed a surprise, and I'm sure Adelaide and I will enjoy your company on the long voyage. Will you be catching the boat train to Calais and on to Germany?

"Yes, I believe so. Valentine is thrilled to be returning home, and I am too. I have never felt settled here, and it's just wonderful that we can make our home in Leipzig."

Marie rose to her feet, deciding it was time to leave. They said their goodbyes, and as Theodore shook Adelaide's hand, he held on just a moment too long, his eyes searching hers as if there was something left unsaid. Adelaide turned toward the door, her mother following, only to find it still locked.

Before anyone could reach it, Eva darted forward to unlock the door for them. In her haste, she collided with Marie, who fell hard to the floor with a sickening thud.

"Mother!" Adelaide cried, her voice sharp with panic.

Marie lay motionless, her leg twisted at a strange angle.

"Mrs Ellwood!" Eva gasped, her face pale with shock. "Are you hurt?"

"My leg…" was all Marie could manage before she lost consciousness on the cold shop floor.

"Don't move her," Elisabeth instructed calmly but firmly. "Eva, fetch a blanket—quickly."

"I'll fetch the doctor," Theodore said, already unlocking the door and rushing out into the street.

Adelaide dropped to her knees, gently cradling her mother's head in her lap. She pulled the blanket over her with trembling hands, trying not to jostle her injured leg. Moments later, Hugo and his brother arrived home from school, and Hugo was sent to Government House to alert Robert.

To Adelaide, everything felt surreal. She was aware of people speaking and moving, but their voices sounded muffled and distant. All she could do was sit on the floor, holding her mother, silently waiting for the doctor to arrive.

When Dr Albright finally arrived, Marie was starting to stir, groaning softly from the pain. After explaining what had happened, Elisabeth nodded at both Theodore and Eva to leave the shop to give them some privacy. Dr Albright examined Marie carefully and then offered everyone a faint, reassuring smile.

"Your leg isn't broken, Mrs Ellwood. Which is good news, but I'm afraid you have a serious sprain with what I think are torn ligaments, which will take time to heal. I'll give you something for the pain so we can help you up."

Just then, the door flew open, and Robert rushed in. Looking in horror as his wife lay on the floor, he dropped to his knees beside her.

"My dear, it's all right, I'm here now."

Once the pain relief took effect, Marie was slowly helped into a sturdy, cushioned chair and a stool to elevate her damaged leg, which Elisabeth had prepared for her. She sipped strong, sweet tea while Robert spoke quietly with the doctor.

Adelaide, still kneeling, suddenly realised she could no longer feel her legs. Theodore helped her to her feet, and as the blood returned, the sharp pins and needles nearly brought tears to her eyes. Yet she felt nothing but gratitude—gratitude that her mother would be all right. But then she heard her mother's voice, soft but insistent. "But I'm meant to be travelling overseas in just a few days..."

Adelaide froze. Her mother's words echoed in her ears— *travel, ship, sea*—until their meaning hit her like a wave. She sank heavily onto the nearest chair, the colour draining from her face.

In that instant, she knew. Everything she'd been dreaming of was slipping away.

"I'm sorry, Mrs Ellwood, but you must rest your leg, or it may affect your ability to walk properly in the future." The doctor was firm and held up his hand in a gesture to prevent any further argument.

"I cannot believe this is happening! We shall have to cancel the journey. Adelaide cannot possibly travel alone. This is dreadful—but what are we to do?" Marie spoke to the doctor, her lace handkerchief pressed lightly to her mouth as she tried to ignore the acute pain she endured.

Adelaide wished the ground would swallow her. What purpose would her life hold if she could not go to England to study? She was deeply concerned for her mother, but also devastated at the thought of missing her chance to study in England.

"There is not much to do on board the ship for eight weeks; could she not simply rest and take care?" Robert asked the doctor.

"Mr Ellwood, you must understand that your wife's leg is seriously injured. Fortunately, there are no broken bones, but the limb is damaged, and the only way it will heal properly is by keeping it elevated and at rest. Travelling upon a vessel that moves in such unpredictable ways will do nothing to aid recovery, will it?"

Adelaide tried to speak, but Robert interrupted. "We will discuss this at home, Adelaide. Right now, we must get your mother home safely and get her comfortable and settled."

"Yes, Father," Adelaide whispered sadly.

It took some time to figure out how to get Marie home, as she had refused outright to be carried or to sit in a wheelchair. Marie was firm, "I'm not having people see me in this state."

In the end, Robert organised for an official government car to take Marie home, whilst Adelaide decided to walk home, needing some fresh air and time to think. Robert looked at his daughter, and the only platitude he could come up with was, "Accidents happen, my dear. There's nothing we can do about it but to stay positive."

"A lot of accidents keep happening, Father. That's the problem. It is as if the fates are conspiring against me."

Robert looked sadly at his daughter as he climbed into the car. There was nothing helpful he could say, and he needed to get Marie home as quickly as possible.

As Adelaide said goodbye to a distraught Theodore and Elisabeth, promising to let them know how her mother was faring, she left the shop and began to walk down the street. Eva, of course, was nowhere to be found.

"Adelaide. Adelaide! Is everything all right? What has

happened?" A familiar voice was calling her name.

She turned to see Giselle hurrying toward her. Concern etched across her face. Adelaide tried to smile but faltered. "It's my poor mother. Eva knocked into her as we were leaving the bookshop, and she fell, injuring her leg. Father's taken her home. She has to rest now, so our trip to England is postponed."

Her voice cracked, and before she could stop herself, the tears came. "And why on earth is Valentine getting married?" she cried, her voice rising with the anguish she'd tried to suppress.
Giselle stepped forward and wrapped an arm around her, guiding her gently into her shop.

"I'm so sorry," Adelaide sniffled. "It must be the shock."

"Come into my workroom," Giselle said softly. "I'll make you some tea. That cures everything, doesn't it?"

A little while later, the warmth of the tea and Giselle's comforting presence had worked some small magic. Adelaide sat quietly, her breathing steady again, a handkerchief clutched in her fingers as Giselle busied herself, fussing in a way that reminded Adelaide of an affectionate older sister.

"Thank you, Giselle. You're so kind."

Giselle gave her a knowing look. "So, I take it Eva told you about the engagement? And the rushed wedding?" Adelaide nodded, her expression still dazed.

"Yes. It was a shock, to say the least. I didn't even know Valentine cared for her that way. They never seemed close. Or maybe I didn't notice. I've been so preoccupied with preparing for the Royal Academy."

As she spoke, tears welled up again, and she struggled to understand why this news hurt her so deeply. *Had she fallen in love with him?* She wasn't even sure what that felt like. All she knew was the pain, the confusion, and the loss. Giselle watched her closely, her brows drawn with concern.

"Believe me, Adelaide," she said gently, "my parents and I are deeply troubled by this as well. It is as though Eva has cast a spell over him. The offer from the Conservatoire in Leipzig seems to have closed his eyes to everything else. As only married couples are permitted to reside on-site, he appears to believe this is his sole means of returning. He is not thinking clearly. My father and I have both tried to reason with him, but he will not listen. He insists it is a dream come true and refuses to speak another word of it."

"And what part does Eva play in all this?" Adelaide asked slowly. "I remember, even at school, how she despised living here. Is this merely her way of returning home, with a husband, a house, and a comfortable life laid before her?"

"I fear that is precisely what she is doing; I'm sure of it." Giselle stood and paced up and down her tidy little workroom. Adelaide became aware of the neat rows of fabrics in all shades of green, blue, brown, and black. Two male dummies stood in the corner, faceless. One was wearing a part-sewn jacket with no sleeves yet, and the other was wearing a nearly finished jacket.

"Have you ever thought of trying your hand at ladies' fashion? The dress you made for my eighteenth birthday was exquisite, not to mention the clothes you make for yourself. You have such a talent."

"That is so kind of you to say that, and I must admit I have thought about it often. I would have loved to study with one of the famous couturiers in Paris, but it's not for the likes of me. With Valentine returning to Germany, it is now left to me to continue the family business."

"I'm sorry, Giselle. It seems we have both had our hopes and dreams destroyed. Anyway, I'd better go and see how Mother is. They will be wondering where I am."

"Of course, let me show you out, and Adelaide, if you ever need someone to talk to, you know where to find me."

"You are very kind, and thank you for helping me today."

"My pleasure. Let me know how your mother is, won't you? Give her my regards."

In the quiet sanctuary of her bedroom, hidden from prying eyes, Eva watched through her window as a tearful Adelaide was ushered inside by Giselle.

"Perfect," she murmured, barely audible. "You really are brilliant, Eva. Who would've guessed that just a well-timed push could be the answer to everything?" A low, throaty chuckle escaped her lips, then abruptly stopped. A ripple of unease crept over her skin. The shadows were always there, silent and patient, watching. Waiting.

She stepped back from the window and turned toward the mirror, her gaze locking with her own reflection. A smirk curled at the corner of her mouth.

"No need to worry," she said softly. "It's time for the next phase."

That night, sleep eluded Adelaide. Only yesterday, she'd been eagerly packing her trunk, and now it stood untouched in the corner, its lid slightly ajar. Her books were stacked neatly on the desk, waiting to be tucked into her bag. Violet's old music case rested on the chair, already filled with the sheet music she'd carefully chosen for her studies.

Taking advantage of a distracted household, Elise had crept into Adelaide's bedroom and jumped onto her bed, licking her face with enthusiastic affection and wagging her tail like a metronome.

"Elise!" Adelaide groaned, half-laughing. "As if I needed another reason not to sleep." Resigned, she decided to check on her mother. Shushing Elise, she tiptoed carefully towards her mother's bedroom. Easing the door open, she observed her mother lying peacefully in bed, her injured leg elevated on a nest of pillows, a lightweight blanket carefully draped over her. Beside her, Peggy sat slumped in the armchair, her head tilted to one side in sleep. Adelaide padded softly across the room, picked up the blanket that had slipped from Peggy's lap, and gently tucked it around her shoulders. Peggy stirred but did not wake. Adelaide moved quietly downstairs to the kitchen to warm some milk, pouring a little into Toby's bowl and some into Elise's. Then she settled into the old wooden chair, the one she had sat in for as long as she could remember, and let the weight of the day settle around her. Toby leapt into her lap, purring as she absent-mindedly stroked his fur. Elise, defeated by Toby's claim to her favourite spot, returned to her basket by the stove, curled into a ball, and began snoring softly. As she stared into the darkness of the quiet kitchen, the warmth of the milk and the rhythm of Toby's purring offered a fragile comfort. The day had been long, and tomorrow loomed uncertain.

That was where Peggy found them all early in the morning. She shook her gently and whispered, "Good morning, Adelaide." Adelaide stretched, knocking Toby off her lap, and he ran off outside to sniff the morning air.

"Good morning, Peggy. How's Mother? I couldn't sleep, so I warmed some milk and must have dozed off."

"Your mother seems fine, but is ready for some more pain medication. She still believes she could travel, so I am glad Dr Albright will check her leg later and hopefully persuade her to rest." Her face strained from an uncomfortable night's sleep, Peggy then busied herself, putting the kettle on the stove and preparing breakfast for Marie.

"It's true then. Mother really can't travel?"

"I'm afraid so. Your mother is being very brave, but it's the pain medication working. Her leg is badly bruised, and it is hard for her to walk unaided."

"Poor Mother, I can't quite believe what happened. One

minute, we were walking towards the door. Eva moved forward to let us out, and the next thing, Mother was on the floor." Peggy nodded her head in agreement. She had her own thoughts about what had happened, but decided to keep them to herself.

After dressing and attempting to eat some breakfast, Adelaide tried to persuade Peggy to rest, but she refused. Adelaide had missed her father leaving for work, and she suspected that he was avoiding everyone. She guessed he would try to cancel their passage to England at some point that day. Adelaide felt uncertain about what to do. One moment, she was going to England; the next, she wasn't. After taking Elise for a long walk to clear her head, she went upstairs to see her mother and learn what Dr Albright had said.

As she entered the bedroom, it was obvious that her mother had been crying, and Peggy was comforting her. "Oh, Adelaide, I am so sorry this has happened. I thought I would be well enough to travel, but I can hardly walk, and Dr Albright is adamant that I should rest. We'll never get you to London in time now." Dabbing her nose with her lace handkerchief, Adelaide couldn't bear to see her mother so upset.

"Please don't worry, it's not your fault. I will write to the Academy, and I'm sure they will allow me to defer for another year."

"You dear child, I can't imagine how upset you must be. Did you speak to your father this morning?"

"Unfortunately, I didn't get the chance as he had left for work quite early this morning. He didn't even have breakfast," Adelaide replied, her voice heavy with disappointment.

Marie went quiet. Peggy started straightening Marie's bedcovers and said to Adelaide, "I think we should let your mother rest now. The doctor's visit has taken a lot out of her."

Adelaide took herself off to the library with Elise close by her heels. She thought about playing the piano but didn't want to disturb her mother, so she chose a book and settled down to read. Until her father returned home and told her for sure, she didn't feel that what had happened was real.

Adelaide was far away with Mary Lennox in *The Secret Garden* when she was startled by the ringing of the doorbell. Elise started barking and ran down the hallway, ready to greet whoever was waiting on the other side. Adelaide rose and shouted at Elise to move away from the door. She opened it and was surprised to see a nervous-looking Valentine standing there.

"Please, Adelaide, may I speak with you. It is important."

Adelaide wanted desperately to tell him to go away. She felt betrayed and confused, but looking up at his handsome, forlorn face, she couldn't be angry with him. She allowed him in, still not saying anything, and he followed her towards the library. They sat in silence for a moment, and then Adelaide spoke. "Did Giselle tell you what happened yesterday?"

"No, not Giselle. Eva did. I'm so sorry about your poor mother. How is she today?"

"She seems a lot brighter, but I know it is probably the medicine the doctor gave her, and now we cannot go to England." Fighting back the tears, she thrust her chin out like she did as a child and couldn't get her way.

Memories of the beautiful day at the Botanic Gardens and the photograph of the two of them laughing together, as if they hadn't a care in the world, flashed through her mind. Yet, all this time, he had known he would be marrying Eva.

Valentine took a deep breath. "I am sorry about what has happened, but I hope I may have a solution that your parents would be happy with?"

Adelaide looked straight at him, wanting to be angry, but the look in his eyes stopped her. He was smiling at her. "Why are you smiling? My life has been turned upside down again, and you are smiling."

"Let me explain, please."

Adelaide nodded and allowed him to speak.

"As you know, Eva and I are to be married tomorrow," Valentine began gently. "And I *will* explain why—one day, I promise. But not now. The idea was actually Eva's. She suggested that, as a married couple, we could accompany you on the ship and ensure you arrive safely at your aunt and uncle's. We plan to stay in London for a few days before continuing to Leipzig."

Adelaide blinked, momentarily stunned.

"Oh, Valentine, that's a wonderful idea! I don't see how Father could object. I'd certainly feel safe travelling with you." She smiled warmly, and the two of them began discussing the journey ahead with excitement.

Moments later, Robert returned home from a particularly trying day at the office. As he closed the front door, he heard laughter coming from the library.

"Well, you two sound cheerful," he called out. "Do share. After the day I've had, I could use some good news."

That evening, after Valentine had gone, Robert and Adelaide went upstairs to see Marie. Robert kissed his wife gently and sat beside her on the bed, recounting Valentine's proposal.

"Well," Marie said slowly, "I can see that it makes perfect sense. Still, I confess I have grave misgivings about Eva. She has always struck me as flighty and self-absorbed, and I cannot imagine what Valentine sees in her. Yet he is a respectable man, well regarded in Wellington society, and with his new post as professor at the Leipzig Conservatoire, he carries a certain stature, one that could prove useful during the voyage, should any difficulties arise."

Nodding in agreement, Robert was relieved. His visit to the shipping office during his lunch break confirmed that a refund at this late stage was unlikely. Valentine's offer presented the best solution for Adelaide and perhaps for them all. More than anything, he couldn't bear to see his daughter so heartbroken.

And so, it was decided. The newly married Mr and Mrs Valentine Spielmann would be Adelaide's travelling companions.

Overcome with gratitude, Adelaide threw her arms around her father, holding him tightly.

From that moment on, everything passed in a blur. Packing began again, with Marie orchestrating the entire operation from her bed. Two days later, they sent a telegram congratulating the newlyweds, and Robert arranged for a case of wine to be delivered for their wedding breakfast.

The ceremony was a modest one. Only close family, a handful of neighbours, and a few local shopkeepers attended. Yet, despite the festive air, Adelaide couldn't shake the oddness of it all. But perhaps, she told herself, it wasn't her place to know. Ultimately, the most important thing was that her journey to England was back on track. And if this marriage meant she could pursue her dreams, then she wished them nothing but happiness.

A shadowy figure, draped in a long black hooded cloak, arrived silently at the residence of Hermann Wagner. The door was opened by a manservant, who, without a word, stepped aside to admit the expected guest. With a nod, he gestured down the corridor and led the visitor to Wagner's study. There, he paused to open the door.

"A visitor for you, sir," he announced with quiet formality.

"Thank you, Carter. That will be all," Wagner replied without rising from his desk. Carter gave a discreet nod and withdrew.

Hermann Wagner remained seated, his manner devoid of courtesy. "What news?" he demanded, his voice curt.

The figure drew back her hood, revealing a composed and determined face. Eva met his gaze with a steely calm.

"All is prepared. We board the *Ayrshire* tomorrow and set sail by evening. I have come for the package and instructions."

A flicker of satisfaction crossed Wagner's face. He gestured toward a chair but did not wait to see if she took it. Rising, he went to the oil painting that hung behind his desk and swung it aside, revealing a large green safe embedded in the wall. With practised ease, he turned the dial and opened it, retrieving a small, carefully wrapped parcel.

As Eva reached forward, Wagner hesitated a moment, his grip lingering on the package. "You understand the importance of this, I trust. It is to be guarded with the utmost care and delivered directly into the hands of our contact upon your arrival in London. Inside, you'll find the details you need: your contact information, the location, and the time. Do not imagine you can slip beyond my reach, Eva. I have eyes in every port, ears in every crowd. Should you falter, or worse, betray me, you will discover that the consequences are far more dreadful than you can conceive."

Eva accepted the package with steady hands. "You have my word, sir. I shall protect the package with my life. I will not fail you."

Chapter 23

S.S. Ayrshire, Wellington Harbour

The day of Adelaide's departure finally arrived, bringing a mix of emotions. She felt very excited, yet a faint sadness lingered since her mother would not be accompanying her. Having shared her feelings with her mother, Marie would not entertain any sentimentality or tears. Instead, she oversaw Adelaide's last-minute packing, insisting she check her travel papers and requiring her to account for every item she had packed. Adelaide was taking Elise with her for company, and Marie wanted her to consider what Elise might need and whether food would be provided for her on board the ship. Adelaide assured her she had checked, and since it was only a small ship, there would be plenty of scraps. The chef was happy to save them for any passengers with canine companions.

"It's a big responsibility, that's all." Marie said, using her 'committee voice' as Adelaide and Joseph always called it, when she was serious and wanted them to listen.

"I know, and I have thought about Elise's welfare, I promise. Having Elise with me will make me go out on the deck to walk her, and she's so sweet. It's much easier to start a conversation with her in my arms."

Marie shook her head and, peering over the rim of her spectacles, said with a sigh, "Adelaide, my dear, you are quite impossible at times. Do try to be sociable, particularly if you are honoured with an invitation to dine at the Captain's table. You must remember, you are representing the Ellwood family, and it is expected that you engage in polite conversation. One never knows; you may even find yourself making some new friends."

"I promise," Adelaide responded, nodding at her mother, while secretly keeping her fingers crossed behind her back.

When the time came for her to leave, Adelaide wrapped her arms around her mother in an extra-long hug and, trying not to cry, she made herself walk towards the door. Turning to look at her mother one more time, she waved a final goodbye.

As she stepped into the hallway, her father's voice drifted from the drawing room. "Adelaide, is that you? Have you finished packing yet?" A sigh followed, accompanied by the rustle of a newspaper. Adelaide entered to find her father seated in his favourite chair, seemingly absorbed in the morning paper. The chair had been angled differently from its usual position, she suspected, so he might keep watch over the hallway, where signs of the upcoming journey had begun to collect.

A travelling chest stood by the front door. Its leather straps were tightly fastened, and its side bore a patchwork of stickers, faded emblems of the many voyages. The chest belonged to her father, who had carried it to England more than forty years ago while studying at Oxford. Before him, it belonged to her grandfather, Thomas. "Oh, the stories it could tell!" her father had said fondly when he brought it to her room a week earlier.

She placed a large leather bag beside the trunk, filled with last-minute items, including a few extra books she couldn't bear to leave behind. Hearing another sigh from her father, she watched as he lowered his paper with theatrical flair and exclaimed, "Is all that luggage truly necessary?"

She smiled and ignored his grumbling, knowing it was just a performance masking the pain of parting. His only daughter was leaving, and he wouldn't see her for nearly a year. She would miss him dearly and was both touched and grateful that he had arranged to take a few hours off work and had hired a carriage to convey them to the port.

The sound of the horse and carriage arriving in front of the house meant it was finally time to leave. Valentine and Eva were already in the carriage, and Valentine climbed down to help Robert with Adelaide's trunk. Eva greeted Adelaide warmly. Surprised, Adelaide thought that marriage seemed to be agreeing with her, and she supposed that Eva must also be feeling happy and excited to be returning 'home' to Germany. Valentine greeted her, too, as he lifted her trunk into the carriage. "Are you ready to begin your life as a music student?" His generous smile never failed to lift her spirits.

"Very much, but I will miss everyone here; it all feels so very real now. I must go and say goodbye to Peggy. I won't be long, and then we can go."

"Don't take too long. We need to leave now as the docks will be busy." Robert said impatiently.

Adelaide quickly handed Elise to Eva, not caring whether she wanted to hold her or not, and ran towards the kitchen. Peggy was busying herself as usual, but there was a distant look in her eyes, and Adelaide realised how much she would miss her. "I'm leaving now, Peggy. Just wanted to say a final farewell." Peggy looked up and, wiping her hands quickly on her apron, moved around the table towards Adelaide and hugged her tightly. "Oh, Peggy, I'm going to miss you and our cosy chats." Stepping back, Peggy was unusually flustered and wiped tears from her eyes.

"Bless you, child. I can't deny I will miss you too, but what an experience you will have back in the old country. Now, go before I get all emotional. Stay safe, Adelaide. You are very trusting, but sometimes people aren't always what they seem, so be careful and don't forget to write!"

Adelaide was slightly confused at Peggy's warning but had no time to digest its meaning. Instead, she promised she'd write often. Intending to join the others outside, she suddenly changed her mind and quickly ran back to her mother's room again.

"I'm off now, Mother. Just one more hug!"

"Oh, bless you, please look after yourself and make the

most of your time in England. Before we know it, you will have completed your studies, and your father and I will be joining you on more adventures! Now, do you have all the letters I gave you to post when you get there?"

Laughing at her mother's exuberance, "Yes, they are safely stored in my trunk." Then, hugging her mother one final time, she ran out to join the others. Valentine was standing on the pavement waiting for her. Helping her up, he then jumped up and sat beside a frowning Eva, who handed Elise back to her rather abruptly.

"Your dog, I think, does not like me," she said.

Robert was right; the docks were busy, but the carriage driver knew where he was going and expertly manoeuvred the horse to the correct mooring with time to spare. The docks were filled with sound. Adelaide found it slightly alarming as so many people of all shapes and sizes were milling about. Sailors, dockers and passengers, all intent on their various missions. Trunks, boxes, and even cargo lined the mooring, and there was the S.S. *Ayrshire* — an enormous backdrop for all the comings and goings. Adelaide felt like a small child again, scared and uncertain, as she allowed her father to guide her towards the gangplank that would lead them onto the ship.

"Be careful as you walk up and hang on to Elise tightly. There is a long drop down into the sea." His warning was not helping her nerves.

"What about my trunk?" She felt she had abandoned all her belongings on the dockside.

"Don't worry. A crew member will take it up and put it in your cabin." Came Valentine's gentle and reassuring voice. She followed her father and Valentine as they walked confidently up the ramp. Eva was just behind her.

"Adelaide, I meant to ask before, could you quickly put this in your bag for safekeeping? I don't have a bag, just our trunk."

"Yes, if you want me to, but you'll have to do it, though, as I can't let go of Elise."

"Of course. Thank you, Adelaide." Eva quickly undid the clip on her bag, placed a package into it, and closed it again. She took Adelaide's arm and quickly moved her up the gangplank. Robert looked worried. "Are you all right, Adelaide?"

"All is well, Mr Ellwood," Eva spoke before Adelaide could say anything. As they finally entered the boat, a member of the crew efficiently checked their papers and signalled to an eager young steward to show them to their cabins.

They arrived at Adelaide's cabin first, and as she entered, she was amazed to find her trunk was already there. Valentine and Eva were taken further down the corridor and disappeared from view. Adelaide looked around the room, which would be her new home for the next eight weeks.

"I think I will be very comfortable here, and I am glad to see I have a window to look out of. I wonder if I can open it to get some fresh air?" Robert smiled, surprised at Adelaide's confidence and that she did not seem worried about the long journey ahead.

"The window is actually called a porthole, my dear." That was all he could find to say for fear of showing any emotion.

"Oh, right. I have much to learn on my journey across the ocean!"

"I must leave the ship now. Will you be all right? Look after yourself and always lock your cabin door, won't you? I know you have Valentine and Eva to look out for you, but always remember to be cautious and think first. Act later."

"I will be careful, I promise. Anyway, I plan to spend a lot of my time in my cabin, as I have my pre-course studies to finish before arriving in England." Nodding with excitement at the decent-sized desk under the porthole. Hugging her father, he kissed each side of her cheeks and gave Elise an extra tickle between her ears. "Look after Adelaide for me, won't you?" Elise barked, making them both laugh, and then he was gone.

A sudden wave of loneliness washed over Adelaide. "Well, Elise," she said softly, glancing down at her. "What should we do first, unpack or explore? Everything feels so strange." She paused, then gave a small sigh. "I think I'll unpack for now. Maybe once I've settled in, I'll feel brave enough to explore a little." Elise gave a woof of approval and began sniffing around the cabin, investigating their new surroundings.

Opening her bag, Adelaide noticed the package Eva had hastily shoved inside. She pulled it out, turned it over in her hands, and felt the crinkle of the wrapping beneath her fingers. What was it? But before she could investigate further, a knock at the door startled her, causing her to drop the package on the bed. Elise sprang at the door, barking at the mystery visitor. "It's all right, Elise," Adelaide said, soothing her with a gentle pat. "Let me see who it is." She opened the door to find Eva standing there, as composed as ever.

"May I come in for a moment?" Eva asked, her voice cool and unreadable.

Adelaide hesitated for the briefest moment. "Hello, Eva. Yes, of course, come in."

Eva stepped inside, her sharp grey eyes sweeping the cabin with quiet precision. There was something in her gaze that always unsettled Adelaide, though she could never quite say why. The silence lingered a moment too long, compelling Adelaide to speak. "I trust your cabin is comfortable. I'm rather pleased with mine, and once I've finished unpacking, I daresay it shall begin to feel like home."

Eva offered a crooked smile in return. Or was it a smirk? Adelaide couldn't tell. A chill crept down her spine. "Indeed. Your cabin is quite luxurious. Ours is quite small, unfortunately, but no matter, it is adequate." *Eva, be polite. You must not make her suspicious.* Shaking off the demanding voice, she fixed her best smile on Adelaide.

Adelaide tried to avoid eye contact; instead, she nodded towards the package on the bed. "Would you like to keep it here, safe in my room? It looks like the drawers in the desk can be locked."

"If you don't mind. It would stop me worrying." Eva picked up the mysterious package and pulled out its contents. It was a small muslin bag containing a rectangular silver box decorated with elegant filigree birds.

"Oh, it's beautiful!" Exclaimed Adelaide. "May I see it?"

Eva handed the box to Adelaide, who traced her fingers gently over the tiny birds etched into its surface. With great care, she lifted the lid and gasped as the delicate notes of Beethoven's *Für Elise* filled the cabin. "Oh, how wonderful! I promise I shall lock it in my desk drawer, and it will be quite safe there until we arrive in England."

Eva forced a smile and replied with quiet politeness, "Thank you. It is a precious family heirloom, very dear to me, and I should be most distressed if anything were to happen to it. And Adelaide, perhaps it would be best not to mention this to anyone. Not even Valentine. I should not like him to fret."

"Of course, if that's what you wish," Adelaide said, though a flicker of unease had already begun to stir within her.

"Good. Now, I must go and unpack. We shall see you at dinner this evening, no doubt."

And with that, she was gone—leaving Adelaide standing alone in her cabin, the music box cradled in her hands.

Chapter 24

Adelaide was sitting in a deckchair, wrapped in a thick blanket with a cushion at her back and her journal on her lap. Elise was curled up at her feet, having wriggled under the blanket to keep warm, too. It had been over two weeks since the *Ayrshire* had left Wellington, and the Chief Officer had told them they were nearing Cape Horn. The weather had been so cold that a steward had offered everyone hot bottles to take on deck with them. The Captain had announced during dinner that evening that they should be around Cape Horn that night, and in about a week, they should be experiencing warmer weather.

The first few days at sea had been overwhelming. Between the constant motion and unfamiliar routine, Adelaide found it all quite terrifying. Thankfully, she hadn't fallen victim to seasickness, which both surprised and relieved her. Valentine, on the other hand, hadn't been so fortunate and had spent the early part of the voyage recovering in his cabin. She had barely seen either him or Eva. "So much for being my guardians," she thought to herself, but at the same time, she was perfectly happy and preferred to be left alone.

That particular afternoon, Adelaide was determined to sit outside, no matter how cold it was, as she felt a little trapped in her cabin despite its cosiness. She read her book for a while and then tried to study one of her music theory books. In the end, she decided to write in her journal instead. Adelaide had decided to keep a travel journal to record all the interesting places she visited and the things she saw so she wouldn't forget even the smallest detail when writing to her friends and family. As she opened her journal on her lap, her pencil poised, she thought for a moment and decided to write her observations of her fellow travellers so far.

First, there were Gerald and Agnes Willoughby, an elderly

couple making what they called one final journey 'Home' before old age made travel too difficult. Gerald, a retired army officer, spoke often and loudly of his days in the British Army, particularly his time fighting in the Boer War. He loved to roll up his sleeve and show off the long, jagged scar on his right arm, the result of a near-amputation. "Saved by a brilliant surgeon," he would declare with dramatic flair. His stories captivated young Phillip Fairchild, who was travelling with his parents, Julian and Sarah, and his younger sister, Lydia. Recently accepted to study medicine at Edinburgh University, Phillip eagerly seized every opportunity to bombard the old Major with questions, much to his mother's gentle chagrin. "Darling, perhaps save some of your questions for after dinner," Sarah had said one evening, trying to steer her enthusiastic son away from a particularly grisly tale.

Then there were Mark and Jane Sampson, whom Adelaide had grown especially fond of. They were on their way to England to settle Mark's late father's estate after his sudden passing. Jane often joined Adelaide for walks along the deck with her cheerful Airedale Terrier, Bernard. Elise had taken an immediate liking to him, and the two dogs happily trotted side by side on their walks, tails wagging in perfect harmony.

"One thing's for sure," Jane said with a smile one afternoon as the four of them strolled together. "Once all the legal business is sorted, we're going to borrow a car and drive all over the British Isles. My parents left for New Zealand when I was a babe in arms, so I have no memory of the place of my birth." Adelaide smiled at the memory and wrote it down. These snippets, these moments with strangers who now felt like friends, made the long journey feel a little less daunting and a little more like an adventure.

Lastly, there was a single traveller named William Armstrong, who remained something of a mystery to Adelaide. Like her, he seemed more of a listener than a talker, and although she thought he had a more military appearance, he told everyone he was an investment banker travelling for business. He was tall, but then most people seemed tall to Adelaide. Tapping her pen on her lips, she tried to think of how to describe him. She believed his eyes were his most striking feature, and she began to write once more. He had very kind-looking eyes that could appear green or blue, depending on the light. Adelaide often found herself mesmerised by them when he spoke. There was a 'story' behind those eyes, she was sure, but she decided that was all she'd write about Mr Armstrong for now.

One of the nicest surprises for Adelaide was the discovery of a piano tucked into a corner of the saloon. Adelaide couldn't believe her luck, and when he had recovered from his seasickness, neither could Valentine. The Captain and the rest of the passengers were more than happy for Adelaide and Valentine to play, but Eva was not impressed. "We are just married, Liebling. Surely you would prefer to spend more time with your wife?"

"Of course, Eva. But perhaps you would permit me to play the piano with Adelaide after dinner to entertain our fellow guests?"

Eva just shrugged her shoulders. "If that is what you wish, it is of no matter. We have a long voyage ahead of us and the rest of our lives to be together." *What does it matter? I only have to bide my time, and everything will work out for the best.*

The following day, there was much excitement as, at last, land was sighted. Adelaide had grown accustomed to a world of grey, where the sea had taken its colour from a leaden sky. She had just finished a delicious afternoon tea with Jane and Mark when the Captain, who had been seen pacing on the upper deck, suddenly cried out, "Land ahoy!" Everyone crowded towards the rail, straining their eyes. For a while, no one could make out anything; then, gradually, a faint outline appeared, disappeared, and appeared again. Gerald, the only one with binoculars, cried, "I see it—land ahoy!" he shouted.

The sight of land seemed to lighten everyone's spirits, and the evening had a party feel about it. Valentine had been entertaining his fellow passengers on the piano and was beckoning Adelaide to join him to play a duet. One of the waiters placed another chair beside Valentine, and Adelaide sat beside him. "What should we play?" Adelaide asked.

"Play something lively!" Shouted a brandy-fuelled Gerald.

Adelaide suddenly felt a wave of nervousness come over her. Although she had always been prepared and had rehearsed beforehand, this was a new experience for her. Valentine whispered in her ear, sensing her unease, "Let's play some Brahms. How about the Hungarian dances, that should wake everyone up!"

As they began, their audience clapped and cheered. Taking turns to play the different elements of the tune, sometimes their hands touched, and Adelaide could feel the electricity between them. She wondered if Valentine felt it, too, but his expression never showed anything but his enthusiasm and concentration on the music he was playing. After they finished and took their bows to rousing applause, they returned to the dining table. Valentine settled himself next to Eva, who immediately took his arm, and her flint-like eyes reminded Adelaide of the days when Eva had no time for her. Adelaide was seated next to William Armstrong. He leaned toward her and told her how much he enjoyed their performance. He added, "Were you acquainted with Valentine and Eva before boarding the *Ayrshire?*"

"Yes, Valentine is my piano tutor. Sadly, my previous tutor died in tragic circumstances, and she was so young. I had known her since I was twelve and miss her terribly."

"I'm sorry to hear that," William replied. He was about to ask more questions when Jane interrupted, wanting to hear all about the Royal Academy of Music.

"You are so lucky, Adelaide, to have this opportunity to study."

Instead of waiting for Adelaide to answer, Jane continued by explaining that she had only been allowed to study until she was sixteen, and then she was expected to help her mother run the home and care for her younger siblings. "Luckily, I met Mark on my nineteenth birthday, and as they say, the rest is history." Laughing, she kissed her grinning husband on his cheek.

More coffee was served, and the men helped themselves to a variety of brandy and port, which had been left on the side table. Gerald Willoughby stood up and announced his wish to recite a rendition of Alfred, Lord Tennyson's poem, *'The Charge of the Light Brigade.'* Everyone clapped enthusiastically except Eva, claiming she was feeling a little queasy and left the room as Gerald began to recite, "Half a league, half a league, half a league onward, All in the valley of Death rode the 600."

Eva moved swiftly along the deck. She felt nothing but contempt for her fellow travellers, laughing and drinking, acting as if nothing was wrong with the world. Gerald Willoughby, in particular, irritated her with his constant boasting about his time in the British Army. Valentine, annoyingly, was always trying to persuade her to give the man a chance, and she began to think her husband did not care about her feelings at all and was only interested in his new career at the Conservatoire. He was also distracted by Adelaide. "Verdammt die Frau!" *Damn the woman*, Eva muttered under her breath. Eva loathed Adelaide for everything she was not. As she watched them play the piano together, she became convinced that Adelaide was infatuated with her husband. But that only made her laugh out loud, "Oh, Adelaide, there are so many things you do not understand." Adding under her breath, "You are both stupid, weak fools." Calming herself as she walked further into the restricted areas of the ship, she reminded herself to stay focused on the plan; once she was in Germany, she could live her life on her own terms. Valentine could wallow to his heart's content in his music; she didn't care. Germany was on the brink of becoming the most powerful country in Europe, and she would play a significant role in making that happen. Valentine knew nothing of the money, safely hidden in her trunk. Eva would have loved to earn more money on board the ship, but all the passengers were dreadfully dull. She hadn't heard a single bit of gossip or intrigue. William Armstrong intrigued her, but not in a good way. There was something in his manner she didn't trust, so she resolved to be cautious in his presence. But for now, she had a job to do, as she edged further into the shadows cast across the deck, intent on completing the next part of the plan.

Adelaide began to feel tired and realised it was past eleven o'clock. She had thoroughly enjoyed the evening, and her fellow passengers had been very pleasant company. However, she was grateful that the night was drawing to a close, and one by one, the merry group of travellers began to return to their cabins.

Mr and Mrs Willoughby were the first to leave, Agnes insisting she had to get her husband to bed before he dozed off in his chair. Gerald didn't protest, making his theatrical goodbyes and waving like an old stage actor taking his final bow. Sarah Fairchild stood next, calling for Phillip and Lydia to follow her. Valentine rose shortly after, offering a polite nod before disappearing down the corridor. Only William, Mark, and Julian remained by the fire, deep in conversation and quietly sipping brandy and smoking cigars. As Adelaide stood to leave, Jane slipped her arm through hers.

"Come on," she said warmly. "Let's leave the boys to their drinks. I'm exhausted."

They walked side by side toward the cabin quarters, their steps quiet in the dimly lit corridor. But as they turned the corner and reached Adelaide's cabin, they stopped short. The door was wide open.

Adelaide let out a cry. "I'm sure I locked it!" she exclaimed, rushing inside, and her breath caught in her throat.

"Adelaide, what on earth?" Jane's voice echoed behind her.

Books were strewn across the floor; her carefully organised

music papers were scattered like fallen leaves. Worst of all, the small drawer Adelaide had locked and where she had hidden Eva's music box had clearly been forced open. But none of that mattered as it suddenly dawned on Adelaide that she couldn't see or hear Elise.

"Elise," she whispered, spinning around. "She's not here."

Panic surged through her. "Oh Jane, please can you help me find her! She's so small, and if she's wandered outside, she could fall overboard." Everything else was forgotten. Only Elise mattered now. Jane made Adelaide put on her coat because it was so cold, and she ran to her cabin to get hers. She returned with Bernard.

"Don't worry, Bernard will find her. I'll go back to the saloon and get the men. You head toward the lifeboats," Jane instructed, trying to sound confident.

Adelaide didn't hesitate and began to run along the deck, calling out for Elise with growing desperation. Before long, she could hear others joining in, voices echoing across the ship in a chorus of concern. The sound filled her with hope. Someone had to find her. But as she moved further down the deck, the ship grew darker and quieter. She was likely in a restricted area now, but she didn't care. Nothing mattered except finding Elise. She couldn't lose someone else she loved. Tears streamed down her face, the terrifying thought of her little dog tumbling into the cold, inky black depths of the ocean, tightening her chest like a vice. Slowing her steps, she reached out with both arms to feel her way forward, trying not to trip as she moved deeper into the shadows. Fear began to creep in. *Maybe she should turn back and wait for the others*. Then she suddenly froze as the sound of hushed male voices drifted up from a nearby stairwell marked 'No Entry.' Cautiously, Adelaide crept toward the sign and leaned over just enough to glimpse a narrow flight of steps leading into a dimly lit space. The faint glow of a cigarette illuminated two men, perhaps members of the ship's crew, she thought. And then she saw her. It was Eva. Adelaide held her breath as she watched Eva hand one of the men an envelope. She strained to hear, but her German was limited, and the muffled conversation eluded her. Not wanting to be seen, she quickly backed away and turned down another corridor, her heart pounding. *What was Eva up to now?* She wondered, but the urgency to find Elise quickly overtook her thoughts, and when she was certain she was out of earshot, she began calling Elise's name again, her voice hoarse and cracking. Another thirty minutes passed, bringing her closer to her cabin, and closer to despair. She was nearly ready to give up, the horrible belief that Elise might be lost forever pressing in on her.

Then, out of the darkness, a figure appeared. As the figure stepped into the glow of the corridor lights, she saw him clearly. It was William, and in his arms, wrapped in a towel, was Elise.

"Elise!" she cried, rushing toward them. "Oh, I thought I'd never see you again!"

William handed her the trembling little dog, who responded with an excited flurry of tail wags and whimpers. Adelaide held her close, her tears returning, but this time with overwhelming relief.

"She's been on quite an adventure," William said with a warm smile. "I found her down on the lower deck near the crew's quarters. She's a bit oily and definitely needs a bath."

"I can't thank you enough," Adelaide breathed. "I was so sure she was gone." Then, glancing back toward her cabin and the splintered door hanging ajar, she added, "I don't understand what's happened. My cabin's been ransacked, and the package I was keeping safe for a friend is missing."

William looked concerned and asked if he could check her room for any clues that might indicate who had committed the crime. But first, he wanted to inform the Captain. As William turned to leave, Jane was being pulled along by Bernard toward them. Bernard spotted Elise and enthusiastically jumped up at

Adelaide, while Jane tried to calm him down.

"Oh, thank goodness you've found her—poor little mite. Let's take her into the cabin and warm ourselves up. It's freezing out here."

A few minutes later, William returned with the Captain.

"This is very bad. In all the years I've been Captain of this ship, this has never happened. Please accept my sincere apologies, Miss Ellwood. You can rest assured we'll do our best to find out who the culprit was. Has anything been stolen?"

Looking around her cabin, she explained that apart from all her beautiful books being thrown on the floor and her papers tossed carelessly around the room, the only thing missing was a package that had been locked in a drawer. "Oh, what am I going to tell Eva? She gave me the package for safekeeping!"

Jane managed to speak, "Adelaide, let me take you to the saloon, and we'll get some tea made. You've had a nasty shock, and I'm sure Elise would enjoy sitting by the fire after her little adventure."

As she sat in the warm saloon, her cold hands wrapped around a hot cup of tea, she watched Elise and Bernard curl up in front of the fire. She sipped her tea. "That's better." She said, looking towards Jane. "I find it very strange that Eva's music box was taken, don't you think?" She said, looking at Jane. But before Adelaide and Jane could discuss the puzzle further, Captain Carter, William and Mark walked in. Jane took her cue from Mark, making sure Adelaide was all right and persuading Bernard to follow her; they said goodnight and left the saloon.

The Captain kept apologising, but Adelaide insisted it wasn't his fault and no harm was done except for Eva's music box. Even in her shocked state, she noticed how Captain Carter would often defer to William Armstrong as they talked about the break-in. Mr Armstrong also seemed extremely interested in Eva and Valentine, wanting to know when they were married and how long she had known them. As a fellow passenger, she felt he was asking too many personal questions and that it was none of his business.

"I took the liberty of having all your belongings moved to another cabin," Captain Carter said, his face softening like that of a protective father. "We can't have you sleeping in an unsafe room, and the door will need repairing."

Stifling a yawn, Adelaide smiled at him. "Thank you. That's kind of you. I must admit, I have no desire to return to a room where someone rifled through my belongings with such complete disregard."

"Quite so. I'm at a loss as to why this has happened. We will interview the entire crew tomorrow and, hopefully, find both the culprit and the stolen package."

William turned to Adelaide. "Miss Ellwood, may I escort you to your new cabin?"

"That is very kind of you. Thank you." Adelaide offered him a shy smile before turning back to Captain Carter. "You have been so thoughtful. Good night, Captain."

"My pleasure. Good night, Miss Ellwood."

The cabin wasn't far, and Adelaide and William walked in silence, both deep in thought. When they reached the door, a steward stood waiting and handed her the key.

"Is there anything I can get you, Miss?" he asked.

"No, thank you. All I want now is to settle Elise and get some sleep."

The steward nodded and left Adelaide and William standing in front of the door.

"Will you be all right?" William asked.

"I will once I get some sleep." She met his gaze with gratitude. "Thank you for being so helpful, and for finding Elise, of course. It has been quite an evening."

"It certainly has, and now I must let you get some rest." William smiled down at her, whilst giving the sleepy dog a playful tickle, earning a few affectionate licks in return. "Good night, Miss Ellwood."

After shutting the door to her new cabin, Adelaide placed Elise on the floor, locked the door behind her, and leaned against it. She took a deep breath. Elise jumped onto the bed, her sad brown eyes watching Adelaide's every move, ensuring she wouldn't be left behind again. Gazing around her new cabin, she noticed it was slightly larger and had two portholes side by side. An oak desk, with all her papers carefully arranged on top, was positioned beneath the portholes, while her clothes were hung neatly in the wardrobe and her toiletries had been carefully placed in the bathroom. Adelaide was touched by how much care had been taken to organise her belongings, which had been carelessly strewn across the floor only a few hours earlier. Next to the wardrobe was a small bookcase with four shelves and bars across each one, presumably to hold the books during rough seas. Adelaide smiled at the sight of all her treasured books displayed on the shelves, none of which were too badly damaged. She made a mental note to ask the Captain in the morning who had been responsible for moving her belongings so she could thank them. After giving Elise a very unwelcome wash and drying her with a towel, she sat on the bed, suddenly overcome by the events of the evening. It took all her strength to get ready for bed and change into her nightgown. Shivering as she climbed into bed, she realised the shock of the evening's events had upset her more than she had realised. Sensing her distress, Elise jumped onto the bed and cuddled up to Adelaide as closely as possible. The pair fell asleep almost instantly and remained so until the early morning light filtered through the portholes.

Rising, Adelaide felt refreshed, and the air felt warmer. Elise, who seemed to have forgotten last night's adventure, gave a little bark, eager for her early morning walk. Adelaide dressed quickly and stepped onto the deck, heading towards the designated dog area, which had been fenced off and contained a wooden bench, along with some old barrels and jumps to keep both passengers and their dogs happy. Adelaide entered the enclosure and removed Elise's lead, leaving her free to run and sniff to her heart's content. Jane appeared shortly after and, letting Bernard off his lead, she joined Adelaide on the bench. Patting her friend's gloved hand with her own, Jane asked, "How are you this morning? What a dreadful thing to have happened on board such a small ship. It must have been one of the crew, don't you think?"

"I don't know what to think. All that was taken was an item Mrs Spielmann had asked me to look after, and she told me it had no value, only sentimental. None of it makes any sense. I am grateful to Captain Carter, though, who has been so thoughtful. He insisted that I should have a new cabin, which was such a relief, and a kind person unpacked for me, doing it so neatly. I must find out who they are and thank them."

"You're very welcome," Jane replied with a big smile.

"It was you! Oh Jane, I am so grateful. You put everything away so carefully, even my precious books. I don't know how I can ever thank you."

"No need; the fact that you are feeling better and no harm was done is all the thanks I need. Right, I must go and wake that lazy husband of mine. Will we see you at breakfast?"

"Definitely — I've quite an appetite this morning! Oh, and Jane, thank you again."

Jane smiled and attempted a wave as Bernard led her rather briskly along the deck.

Enjoying the sun on her face after weeks of greyness and cold, Adelaide didn't feel like moving just yet. Elise was still happily exploring, so she sat with her eyes closed, listening to the waves and the sounds of the ship, waking up to begin another day.

"Good morning, Adelaide." Opening her eyes, Adelaide was surprised to see Valentine standing by the gate to the enclosure.

"May I talk to you?"

Still always so formal, she thought. "Yes, of course, come and join me. I am enjoying the sunshine. Isn't it lovely, a rare treat!"

"Indeed, it is very pleasant to come out on deck without wearing layers of clothing to stay warm. How are you, Adelaide? We had an early-morning visit from Officer Hughes, who informed us that your cabin had been broken into, with the only item stolen being a package Eva had given you for safekeeping. Eva is distraught and refuses to leave her cabin. What was it that Eva gave you, and why would anyone want to steal it?"

"My cabin was quite a mess; it was all rather upsetting, and yes, the only item that was stolen was the package Eva left in my safekeeping. I am so sorry. It was a very ornate music box, and she said it belonged to her family and had great sentimental value. I feel awful about it, and I hope Eva understands it wasn't my fault."

"I beg your pardon?" Valentine asked, frowning.

"It was a music box which Eva told me belonged to her grandmother," Adelaide replied, looking puzzled.

Adelaide watched as his face shifted from confusion to anger to sadness. "Can you describe it?" he finally asked.

"Well, it was quite elegant and about the size of a cigar box. Made of silver, I think, with birds engraved across the lid. When you opened it, it played *Für Elise*."

Valentine rubbed his forehead with his hand, "I'm not sure what to think. Perhaps you misheard Eva. The music box you described belongs to my mother, and it has been in our family for many years. It was intended to be passed on to Giselle upon her marriage. Why has Eva got it?"

Adelaide was even more confused by Valentine's explanation. She was sure Eva had said it belonged to her grandmother, but perhaps she had been mistaken. Before Adelaide could ask Valentine any further questions, he rose quickly. Bowing slightly, he looked flustered. "I must go and talk to Eva."

Adelaide sat still for a while longer as she tried to understand Valentine's behaviour and why Eva had lied. However, her grumbling stomach soon reminded her it was time for breakfast. After taking Elise back to her cabin with the promise of some bacon later, Adelaide made her way towards the saloon.

As Adelaide entered, she was met with concern and kindness. Gerald was outraged that such a thing could happen, and he hoped the culprit would be suitably punished. Jane smiled at Adelaide— no words were needed. William rose to greet her and asked if she was all right.

Looking around at all the concerned faces, she said, "I'm fine—really, I am. No harm done. It's all very puzzling, but I'm sure the Captain will get to the bottom of it in due course."

As she spoke, she was conscious of Valentine and Eva's absence, and she felt another pang of guilt for failing to keep the music box safe.

"Where are Mr and Mrs Spielmann this morning? It's a bit strange that they haven't joined us for breakfast, don't you think?" Phillip said, hoping there was more intrigue to be had.

"I'm sure they'll be along presently," William answered. Adelaide was grateful that William prevented further talk about last night's events. She wondered whether she should tell William about Eva's secret meeting with the two crew members that same night, and when she saw Valentine earlier, why hadn't she pressed him for more information about Eva's strange behaviour? Adelaide's mind was whirling with so many questions as she tried to eat her toast while doing her best to maintain a calm exterior.

Later that morning, while Adelaide sat on the deck reading her book, Eva slumped heavily onto the chair beside her. "So, you managed to lose it," she snapped, her face thunderous.

"I didn't lose it on purpose, Eva. Someone broke into my cabin, made an awful mess and stole your music box."

"Well, I have complained to the Captain and told him I expect to be compensated for the distress and loss of a precious family heirloom!"

Adelaide sighed. Eva had reverted to her usual contempt for her and showed no concern that Elise had gone missing and her belongings had been carelessly tossed about. Before Adelaide could say anything else, Eva stood up and disappeared along the deck and towards the cabins.

As more days at sea passed, the warmer weather encouraged everyone out on deck. Quoits was a popular choice among the younger passengers, and there was a memorable chess competition, which Phillip won after a showdown against William, who took his loss to an eighteen-year-old in good humour. Lydia was sitting beside Adelaide when the final match was being played, and Adelaide sensed she was trying to ask her something, but was too shy. Understanding how she felt, Adelaide spoke first. "Are you enjoying life onboard the ship? I must admit, I will be glad to see land again. The sea seems to stretch on forever!"

"It does, doesn't it," Lydia replied, hesitating over her next words.

"Is there something you want to ask me? Feel free to ask me anything, and I'll do my best to answer!"

Encouraged by Adelaide's kindness, Lydia managed to speak. "It's just that I have enjoyed listening to you play the piano so much, and I would really like to learn. I tried, but my tutors soon gave up on me because I wasn't improving. I wondered if you wouldn't mind giving me a few lessons?"

Lydia reminded Adelaide of her younger self, awkward and shy, so she said, "I'm glad you have enjoyed listening to me playing, and yes, I'd be delighted to teach you!"

Later that afternoon, Adelaide waited in the saloon for Lydia to arrive for her first lesson. She had spent a good hour beforehand going through all the music she had with her, pondering the best way to begin the lesson. Not knowing how well she played, or not, as the case may be, Adelaide decided to choose an easy option and see how it went. Lydia arrived promptly and was eager to start. Adelaide encouraged her to take it slowly and asked her to begin with a few scales. Lydia dutifully complied, and she was indeed terrible. She couldn't remember the simplest scales, became frustrated, and blamed the piano for being out of tune.

"When was your last lesson?" Adelaide enquired.

"I'm afraid it was about a year ago when my tutor became so impatient with me that my parents said it was a waste of money and refused to let me continue. I know I'm terrible, and I shouldn't blame the piano. Is there any hope for me?"

Adelaide couldn't help but warm to the poor child. They had three weeks left at sea, so Adelaide promised to do what she could in the time they had. "Let's meet here every day, and we'll spend an hour on the basics, then we'll progress to some simple tunes and take it from there."

And so began Lydia's lessons. At first, the other passengers complained, and Adelaide pleaded with everyone to bear with them, which they did under sufferance. Eventually, Lydia started playing passably. Her parents were delighted and promised to find a tutor for her upon their return home.

For Adelaide, it was a welcome distraction from worrying about Eva and the mystery of the music box. Nothing more had been said. She had asked William and Captain Carter several times, but they both had nothing new to report.

Chapter 25

Puerto de Las Palmas, Gran Canaria

It wasn't long before they reached the Canary Islands. Everyone, except Valentine and Eva, stood on the deck gazing at the port of Las Palmas. Officer Hughes had joined them and announced, "We will be moored in Las Palmas until tomorrow morning, and if you would like to go ashore and explore, I will arrange transport to take you to the town, but please make sure you are back on board by eight o'clock at the latest. We will have taken on more cargo and supplies, and we would like to close up the ship and prepare for sailing tomorrow at dawn."

The idea of a few hours off the ship was met with much enthusiasm, apart from Valentine and Eva. Valentine apologised, explaining that Eva wasn't feeling very well, and he didn't want to leave her alone. Adelaide felt unsure about what to do as they were supposed to be her chaperones. Turning to Jane, she said, "Perhaps I shouldn't go ashore, either?" She was also worried about leaving Elise again after what had happened. "Nonsense!" Replied Jane. "You are with friends, and we will look after you. As for Elise, she can keep Bernard company in our cabin. I will pay the steward well to let them have some exercise, and anyway, we won't be out for long. So, no need to worry. Come on, let's go and enjoy the delights of Las Palmas!"

Adelaide couldn't help but be swept up in Jane's infectious enthusiasm. She changed into a blue cotton skirt, a cream-coloured blouse, and a pair of lightweight yet sturdy walking boots. Placing a straw hat on her head and collecting her bag, she looked forward to stepping off the ship for a while. She had written letters to everyone, describing her adventures so far, including vivid portraits of her fellow passengers, carefully omitting the break-in and Eva's strange behaviour.

The town was lively with a colourful array of market stalls. Unfamiliar smells and sounds overwhelmed Adelaide's senses as she entered. Traders dressed in bright clothing called out to attract attention, urging people to browse their goods, while fishermen busied themselves preparing their catch for sale. Lively music drifted in and out of cafés, and Adelaide didn't know where to look first.

Mark suggested they visit the monastery, which wasn't far but involved a walk uphill. Everyone agreed, except Gerald and Agnes, who preferred a gentle stroll around town and planned to meet them at the designated restaurant for lunch. The walk was quite a trek, but Adelaide enjoyed the exercise after so many days at sea. She felt the ground shift slightly beneath her and recalled her father's advice about 'sea legs' and 'land legs.'

William joined her, slowing his pace to match hers. "It's hot, isn't it?"

"It is. I hope I can make it to the top!" Adelaide exclaimed, already quite breathless.

William shaded his eyes with a hand. "I can see it coming into view now," he said. His cream linen suit was both smart and practical, and the Panama hat perched on his head gave him the air of an adventurer straight from one of Joseph's Boys' Own books. Adelaide couldn't help but notice how handsome he looked, though her breathlessness left little room for distraction.

The monks greeted them warmly, offering cups of cold water drawn from the well at the centre of the courtyard. As Adelaide sipped the cool water, it soothed her parched throat, and it was, she thought, the most refreshing drink she had ever tasted. Inside the monastery, a welcome coolness settled around them as they wandered its halls, exploring relics that whispered stories of times long past.

After an enjoyable hour exploring, they sat beneath a shady

canopy while the monks served wine made from grapes grown on the monastery's land, accompanied by cakes that, surprisingly, paired well with the wine. Adelaide let the conversation wash over her as she watched the monks go about their daily chores. Some were working in the kitchen garden, while others tended to vines in the distance. From the church came the sound of beautiful chanting. She had no idea what they were singing, but it was mesmerising.

"Isn't it wonderful?" William whispered.

"It is heaven," Adelaide replied.

Soon, it was time to head down the hill to the restaurant for lunch. Gerald and Agnes had secured a table and were waving eagerly at them. They enjoyed large, juicy red tomatoes, fresh fish caught that morning, and bread baked in the restaurant's own ovens. She asked William about the wine they were drinking, wondering if it was possible to buy some to take to London to give to her Uncle Hugh. William spoke to the restaurant's owner, and a case of wine was brought up from the cellar for her. William promptly offered to carry it back to the ship for her. Adelaide had begun to enjoy William's company and wanted to get to know him better. She was still sure he wasn't a banker and wanted to solve the puzzle before arriving in England.

Once back on board the ship and feeling refreshed after a few hours of rest, Adelaide looked forward to the evening with her fellow passengers. Her time on land had done her a world of good, and as they gathered for dinner, a festive atmosphere filled the room. The meal was a feast of fresh chicken, fish, vegetables, fruit, and warm bread. Each delicious mouthful demonstrated their newly replenished stores, ensuring they would be well-fed for the final leg of their journey.

The Captain joined them at the table, along with the ship's doctor, Michael Cranfield. Dr Cranfield had been especially kind to Philip Fairchild, granting him access to the medical room and the small space that served as the ship's infirmary. He had even allowed Philip to study his medical books and had promised to write a letter of recommendation for him to take to Edinburgh University as proof of how diligently he had used his spare time. A true Scotsman, Dr Cranfield spoke with a broad accent that made conversation somewhat difficult, but his good humour and easy-going nature made him a welcome presence.

After dinner, Gerald and Agnes asked Adelaide if she would play something for them. She had already selected a piece she felt suited the mood of the evening, Schumann's *Romance*. Valentine had only come to collect some food to take back to his cabin, meaning Adelaide would have to play on her own. Since the break-in, he had barely spoken to her, and Eva remained in her cabin, leaving Valentine to offer vague excuses on her behalf. The whole situation troubled Adelaide, and she resolved to speak to him the following day.

Pushing her worried thoughts aside, she sat at the piano, straightened her back, and gently rested her fingers on the keys before beginning to play. She had persuaded Lydia to sit beside her to turn the pages of the music book. "It'll be good for you to practise reading music," Adelaide encouraged a nervous Lydia.
As the soft, melodious strains of Schumann filled the room, the gathered group fell silent, captivated by the music's tenderness. When the final chord faded, enthusiastic applause erupted.

As she returned to the table, William rose and asked if she would like a glass of wine. She declined but was grateful to sit down and catch her breath.

"You played that beautifully," he said, his voice warm. "You're incredibly talented. Now I understand why you're so determined to pursue your studies, and I admire you for it."

"Thank you; that is very kind of you to say. I have been playing the piano for a long time now, and my dream is to one day teach and perform all over the world!"

William looked impressed. "That is an ambitious plan, and I hope your dreams come true. I really do."

Adelaide had begun to feel a subtle nervousness around William, although it was not unpleasant. In fact, she often found herself looking out for him, hoping to catch a glimpse of him in the saloon or on deck. That evening, buoyed by the relaxed and cheerful mood, she gathered the courage to ask him if there had been any progress in the investigation of the break-in and the missing music box.

William hesitated, clearly reluctant to dampen the atmosphere, but he saw the concern in her expression and answered gently, "I'm afraid not. From what I understand, the crew have all been questioned, and according to the Captain, everyone was accounted for at the time of the incident."

"But I saw two crew members behaving suspiciously …"

Adelaide wished she could have swallowed her words, but it was too late.

"You saw two crew members?" William replied with a look of surprise. "Why didn't you say anything before?"

"Because I wasn't sure what I saw. I had been hoping to speak to Valentine and Eva, but they are acting so strangely, I find it all very confusing."

"That begins to make sense," William replied, his forehead pulled into a frown.

"Mr Armstrong, do you know more than you are telling me?"

"Miss Ellwood, we've been at sea for more than six weeks. I think you can call me William now."

Adelaide blushed slightly, feeling very out of her depth and unsure how to proceed. Taking a deep breath, she decided to be honest. "I sense that you aren't what you seem, and I would very much like to know what is going on."

"I see. If you're so determined to ask questions, we'd better go somewhere we won't be overheard."

William stood politely as she rose and draped her shawl over her shoulders. He escorted her to the door leading to the outside deck. He held the heavy door open for her, letting a gust of fresh night air flow in, which felt invigorating on her skin. He guided her to a sheltered corner, pointed to a chair, and remained standing as she sat down. From the back of the chair, he took a blanket and gently placed it around her shoulders. Adelaide shuddered to think what her parents would say if they ever found out she was sitting alone with a man she hardly knew at ten o'clock at night!

"What is it you want to know, Miss Ellwood?" William asked, his voice low and steady.

Caught off guard, Adelaide hesitated. Her thoughts were swirling. "Well, to start with, if I am to call you William, I think it is acceptable for you to call me Adelaide.

"Adelaide is a lovely name," William replied, smiling at her, which made her even more nervous, so she decided to be brave and speak her mind.

"For a start, who are you really? You're not a banker, are you?"

He raised an eyebrow. "You're questioning who I am?"

She gave a small shrug, the blanket slipping slightly, and she pulled it tighter. "The Captain treats you like an equal. I've seen you speaking with him more than once, and not about the weather or the ship's route. Certainly not the kind of conversation I'd expect from a fellow passenger."

William smiled. "You're very observant, Miss Ellwood."

"And you've suddenly become very formal, Mr Armstrong," she replied, the corners of her mouth lifting. Despite the gravity of their conversation, she found herself enjoying the back-and-forth. Her nervousness had shifted into a strange sense of exhilaration.

William began to laugh, raising his hands in surrender. "All right, I'll explain everything, but not tonight. It's late and very dark out here; anyone could be lurking about and listening in. Let's meet after breakfast on deck if the weather is good. We will have set sail from Las Palmas by then and hopefully will be enjoying fair winds and some hot sunshine."

"As you wish," Adelaide said softly. She hesitated before asking, "Would you mind walking me to my cabin? I'd feel safer with someone beside me."

"It would be my pleasure."

He offered his arm, and she took it, the two of them walking together through the night.

Unseen in the shadows, a pair of cold, steel-grey eyes watched them silently. "Interesting," came a quiet voice from the darkness. The hidden figure remained motionless, quietly observing until the pair disappeared from view. Only then did the watcher step out of the gloom and begin to wander the deck.

Chapter 26

S.S. Ayrshire, Atlantic Ocean – August 1913

Adelaide woke early. Sitting up, she stretched and yawned loudly. Elise looked at her with disgust and burrowed into her blanket. Her conversation with William had played on her mind all night, and she was eager to see him again to get more answers. As soon as daylight began seeping through the portholes, she felt movement below as the ship's great engines powered up. The ship was packed to the gunwales with coal, provisions, and cargo and was ready to set sail as soon as the Harbour Master gave his permission. She felt the ship sway slightly, then finally the rhythmic movement of the ship heading back out to sea. Looking at Elise, she gently tickled her head and said, "Only a few more weeks, Elise, and we'll be in England!" Feeling excited about her new life in London as a music student, she leapt out of bed, disturbing Elise, who let out a little woof to show her annoyance at being disturbed again. Ignoring her, Adelaide pulled on her dressing gown and sat at her desk to write in her journal. She made some notes and compiled a list of books she still needed to read.

Later that morning, Adelaide saw William gazing out to sea. He rested both hands on the railings and was lost in thought as he looked towards the horizon. There was nothing out there, just the vast blue ocean. "Good morning, William." Adelaide stood beside him, savouring the salt in the breeze as it brushed her face. She clutched her hat tightly with her left hand, expecting the wind to snatch it away and throw it into the sea. Her right hand held a firm grip on Elise's lead, and her little ears flapped furiously as she poked her nose through the railings, sniffing the air.

"Good morning, Adelaide and a good morning to you, too,

Elise." Giving in to the little dog's insistent nudging for a head rub. Looking out to sea again, he said, "I've been standing here, deciding what colour the ocean is today. I am thinking perhaps azure or possibly turquoise?" Smiling down at Adelaide, he asked, "How would you describe it?"

"Well, that is a question." Trusting the wind would not steal her hat away, she let go and tapped her finger on her lips and smiled, "I think cerulean would be the perfect description for such a beautiful ocean."

"Cerulean? That is a word I have not heard of before." William looked at Adelaide in mock bemusement.

"Cerulean is one of my favourite words. I've read many poems where the poet uses the word to describe the deep blue depths of the ocean or the cloudless sky. The ocean really is beautiful today." Blushing slightly, suddenly aware of William's intense stare.

"I couldn't agree more, and I am going to remember the word 'cerulean' and use it whenever I can!" he laughed.

Then, his expression grew more serious, and he said, "I hope you haven't been worrying about what I said last night. You look quite pale this morning." His show of concern and intense gaze had a strange effect on Adelaide. *He makes me feel safe.*

Smiling up at him, she replied, "I am all right, even after a restless night! I have so many questions swirling around in my head."

"Well, I'd better try and answer some of them for you then. The Captain has invited us to his stateroom, and he would like to talk to you as well if that's all right."

"Does he?" Adelaide said, surprised.

After returning a very disgruntled Elise to the cabin, Adelaide walked with William to the Captain's Stateroom. Captain Carter greeted them warmly and invited them to sit as a steward set a tea tray on the Captain's desk. Adelaide felt grateful that the

Captain shared her eagerness to uncover what had transpired. The stateroom was small yet tidy and comfortable. The walls featured wooden panelling, which Adelaide presumed was walnut. A large porthole was positioned dead centre on the exterior wall, and the Captain's desk was in the room's centre. On the other available wall hung a large map of the world. His desk was strewn with charts and measuring instruments. Adelaide could only speculate. Behind the desk was a bookcase, and beside it stood a drinks cabinet.

Captain Carter spoke first. "I believe you have called Mr Armstrong here to account and have decided he is not who he says he is."

"I'm afraid I have Captain Carter. I've decided he's not a banker, and Mr Armstrong has promised to explain everything to me this morning. I am waiting eagerly to hear what he has to say."

"Well, Armstrong, best get on with it then, hadn't you?" The Captain chuckled, though there was a sharpness to his tone, aware that this was serious business.

William offered a faint smile and raised his hands in a gesture of surrender. "I suppose I must," he said. He hadn't intended for things to unravel quite like this. His orders were simple: blend in, observe, and report back to Headquarters on his return to London. But in this line of work, things were rarely straightforward.

"You're right, of course," he continued, the smile fading from his face. "I haven't been entirely truthful, and you are quite correct, Miss Ellwood. I'm not a banker. If you must know, my full title is Major William Armstrong, and I work for British Intelligence."

He hesitated, considering his words carefully before proceeding. "For the past year, I've been stationed in New Zealand, working closely with the government. My mission has been to monitor certain German immigrants, especially those with substantial investments in German industry and infrastructure. Some, we have found to be deeply involved in the Kaiser's expanding military ambitions, which, as you can imagine, have the British Government, its colonies, and the rest of Europe on tenterhooks."

He hesitated once more before adding, "And there's something else. I know your father, or rather, I've had the privilege of meeting him, and he asked if I would look out for you during the voyage, and make sure you were all right."

Adelaide's expression changed with each revelation: surprise, confusion, disbelief. Of all the explanations she had thought of, this one hadn't even crossed her mind.

"You know my father?" she asked finally, her voice barely above a whisper. The shock had settled in, clouding her thoughts and leaving her momentarily speechless.

"Only in a professional capacity. He's been advising us in his role as Senior Legal Adviser at Government House," William replied softly, trying to ease Adelaide's growing unease. "He's been incredibly helpful with the work we've been doing."

"Oh, right, I see," she replied a little hesitantly. She was grateful that William was speaking to her as an equal, direct and to the point. However, she didn't entirely agree with what he was saying. Adelaide shook her head and said, "But I know many decent, hardworking German immigrants, especially Valentine and Eva's parents. They came to New Zealand for a better life, and I don't believe they would be doing anything untoward to jeopardise that."

"That is true, and it would be wrong of me to assume all German immigrants were up to no good. However, there are factions scattered around the country, and it is my task to identify them. One man in particular has caught our interest. His name is Hermann Wagner. Do you know him, or have you ever heard his name mentioned?"

Adelaide shook her head. It wasn't a name she recognised.

"I only asked because Mrs Spielmann has been seen calling at his home on several occasions. I wondered whether either Mr or Mrs Spielmann might have mentioned him?"

Adelaide hesitated at the mention of Eva's name. She still wasn't used to hearing her referred to as Mrs Spielmann, and it unsettled her.

"No, they haven't mentioned his name to me," she said, pausing to consider how to reply. But in the end, she chose to be honest. "For as long as I've known Eva, I mean Mrs Spielmann, she's been fiercely proud of her German roots. At school, she was always causing trouble, refusing to speak English, sneaking around, hiding in dark corners, and listening. She had a way of appearing out of nowhere, like magic. My friend Charlotte and I used to find it quite unsettling."

"That's an interesting insight into Mrs Spielmann," William replied. "Good to know. Can you tell me more about her?"

"I've known her since we attended the same school. She immigrated to New Zealand around 1904 with her parents, Theodore and Elisabeth, and her brother Hugo. They had another son, Louis, who was born shortly after they arrived in Wellington. Theodore and Elisabeth are wonderful people. They own a bookshop, and sometimes it's hard to believe that Eva is their daughter. It's her mood, you see. You never quite knew how she would behave towards you from one day to the next. Eva resented coming to New Zealand and leaving her grandmother, her 'Oma,' as she called her. She was constantly telling anyone who would listen how she planned to return home one day, and then, unexpectedly, she announced her engagement to Valentine and that he had been offered a position at the Leipzig Conservatoire as a music professor. I don't think their families were best pleased with the marriage; they thought they weren't suited, and I have to agree."

The Captain looked thoughtful, tapping his hands together as if carefully considering his next sentence. "I have tried to engage in several conversations with Mrs Spielmann, but she is very clever at avoiding my questions and is very insistent on receiving monetary compensation!"

"There is something else," Adelaide said quietly, turning her head to look behind her as if she was expecting Eva to suddenly appear behind her like she used to in the bookshop.

Encouraged to continue, Adelaide described the night of the robbery when she was out looking for Elise. "It was very dark, and I couldn't say for certain, but I think I saw Eva talking to two of the ship's crew. I couldn't see their faces, but she spoke to them in German. I didn't wait to find out what else they were doing as I had no wish to be discovered."

"Quite right," William said. "If Eva has been tasked with passing secret information, I imagine she will need to contact someone either in England or Germany. I suggest we don't let on that we know what Eva is up to and try to act as normal as possible around her, if you can."

Adelaide nodded, too stunned by the talk of secrets and spies to speak any further.

William continued, turning to the Captain. "I will alert Headquarters and have someone follow them once they leave the ship. We have two of the ship's crew under surveillance already, as they have German heritage, but conveniently, they have alibis for the night of the break-in, both covering for each other."

Finding her voice, Adelaide said, "Isn't this all a bit cloak and dagger? I am sure Valentine and Eva aren't up to anything sinister, and it's probably all a big misunderstanding. Valentine wouldn't jeopardise his new position at the Conservatoire, I'm sure of it."

"I understand your concerns, Adelaide, and we won't do anything unless we have absolute proof. I promise you." William had risen and was standing in front of the large map of the world. Looking at William and then at the map, she realised how much of the world and life she still didn't understand, and she desperately wished her mother were with her right now; she was sure none of this would have happened if only she hadn't had that accident.

William was speaking, and Adelaide tried to focus. She suddenly felt afraid and wondered whether her mother's fall had truly been an accident.

"So, Miss Ellwood. Do you feel a little better now that you know my secret?" He was grinning down at her, trying to make light of the situation.

"I do, thank you. I knew you weren't a banker!" she said, giving William and the Captain her brightest smile to avoid further talk of what seemed to be becoming more disturbing by the minute.

Tonight was to be Adelaide's last night aboard the *Ayrshire*. By tomorrow morning, the ship would be guided into Avonmouth by the tugs, and by lunchtime, if all went well, they would disembark. Adelaide was excited for her English sojourn to begin, despite everything. The Captain had invited everyone to dine with him, so Adelaide decided to wear her best dress. It was made of silk, in a shade of blue that complemented her eyes, or so her mother had said when they chose the fabric. Giselle had sewn it for her, using a pattern she'd copied from a Paris fashion magazine. As Adelaide looked in the mirror, she suddenly felt nervous about wearing it. She'd never been concerned with such things at home, but her mother had insisted she bring a few outfits for special occasions.

As she made her way to the dining room, she could hear the lively chatter of her fellow passengers, and a sudden wave of nervousness washed over her. She paused by the door, her hand resting on the handle. Taking a deep breath, she debated whether or not to turn around and go back to the safety of her cabin, even though she very much wanted to enjoy the last night with her friends. "May I escort you in, Miss Ellwood?" Surprised, Adelaide turned to see William standing behind her. "And may I say, you look very elegant tonight."

"Thank you, that's very kind of you to say," Adelaide managed to stammer. Offering her his arm, they walked in together. The steward showed them to their seats, and Adelaide felt relieved as she had been placed between William and Jane. "What a beautiful dress, Adelaide. You look quite lovely tonight; I do believe eight weeks at sea have done you a world of good." Jane was smiling and gave her a furtive nudge as she looked towards William. Not accustomed to such compliments, and Jane's assumption that William had something to do with her happiness, she looked at her friend, blushing slightly. "I'm just excited that tomorrow we will finally be able to disembark, and I can begin my studies, that's all."

"If you say so, my dear." Jane smiled, raising a glass of champagne towards her. "You must have a glass of champagne tonight to celebrate the end of our voyage. I've hardly seen you drink any alcohol!"

"I promised Father I wouldn't, and I actually don't really like the taste. The odd glass of wine is fine, but I'm really not that keen."

Despite Adelaide's protests, Jane beckoned the Steward to pour her a glass, "Tonight is a celebration, and I don't think one glass will do you any harm!"

Adelaide laughed and began to think perhaps it was the friendships she had made during the long voyage that had made her so happy, and once in England, she would miss Jane most of all. Raising their glasses, they both shouted, "Cheers!"

The Captain was seated opposite her and was deeply engaged in conversation with Jane's husband, Mark. Captain Carter looked splendid in his dress uniform, and Mark appeared very smart in a black evening suit and bow tie. As she looked around the table, offering a smile as a welcoming gesture, she spotted Valentine further down, seated next to Gerald. Eva had been placed beside Agnes and was not even attempting to conceal her sullen expression as Agnes prattled on, oblivious to Eva's resentment. Upon learning they would be living in Germany, Agnes was eager to share stories of her trip to the Rhine from her early days as a newlywed. Adelaide fixed her eyes on Valentine, who appeared quite haunted, his pale face gazing across the table. She kept her gaze on him a little longer, hoping he would notice her, but to no avail. William had been watching her and cleared his throat slightly to attract her attention. "Are you all right, Adelaide?"

Startled, Adelaide turned to look at William. "I'm sorry, I was just wondering what Eva was thinking of right now as she endures what looks like a very in-depth story from Mrs Willoughby."

William laughed. "Indeed, Eva doesn't look very amused, does she?" He then grew more serious, "Adelaide, I know how very worrying this must be for you, but please trust me. I will ensure Eva is watched at a discreet distance until I understand exactly what her involvement in all this is. As for Valentine, I don't think he knows what his wife is up to. I've noticed his personality change over the past few weeks, and I believe he may have discovered something that has deeply upset him."

"I think you might be right." Adelaide agreed. "We were so close in Wellington, and I enjoyed our lessons together. He is a talented pianist, but all the joy seems to have left him."

William was about to reply when the food and wine began to appear, and the evening took on an air of joy and laughter with the Captain and his officers, ensuring everyone was included in the conversations by asking each person to share the best parts of their time at sea. Adelaide decided it was a delightful way to end her first sea voyage, and she felt as though she had found lifelong friends. Jane gave Adelaide the address of Mark's family estate in the Cotswolds, insisting she would be very welcome if she had the time to visit; if not, she should write and let her know how she was doing. Lydia asked if she could also write to her, so Adelaide provided Lydia with her aunt and uncle's address in London. Adelaide had enjoyed teaching her, which was not only good practise for her future studies, but she also enjoyed watching Lydia blossom as she improved and began to believe in herself.

At the end of the evening, everyone decided to say their farewells, knowing that tomorrow would likely be extremely busy as they prepared to disembark. As always, William walked Adelaide to her cabin. He had taken on the role of chaperone over the past few weeks as Valentine was nowhere to be seen. She had hoped to wish Valentine well and to thank him properly for all he had done for her, but he had avoided her all evening, and it was difficult to hide her disappointment. Something that was not lost on William. "Adelaide, I'm sorry, but sometimes people aren't who they seem to be."

Looking up at William, Adelaide thought she might cry, but recovered quickly. "How do you always seem to know what I am thinking?"

"A special gift, I suppose," William answered, smiling at her. "Maybe you'll get a chance to speak to Valentine at breakfast, but you know where he will be working. Why not give it a few days and write a letter to him instead? Perhaps it would be easier for him to write down his thoughts and feelings?"

"I think that is an excellent idea. Thank you for seeing me safely to my cabin. Will I see you again?"

"I will be based at Whitehall for the foreseeable future, as I have orders to spend at least a year working on all things hush-hush. Sorry, that's all I can say. I do get some time off, though, so perhaps we could meet and go for a walk once you are settled. You are not far from Regent's Park, and I'd love to hear you play at one of your concerts at the Royal Academy, so keep an eye on the audience. You never know, I might be there!"

265

Laughing, she said her goodbyes and entered her cabin. She closed the door and leaned against it. Her heart was racing faster than usual, and she felt an overwhelming sense of happiness. Shaking her head, she walked towards her bed, calling for Elise. "Where are you, Elise? Aren't you pleased I'm back?"

Glancing at her basket, she let out a startled gasp as above it, stuck into the wall, was a large knife with a note pinned to it. "Elise! Where are you?" A muffled whimper came from near the bed. Did she imagine it? There it was again. It was coming from beneath the bed. Adelaide knelt and peered into the darkness. Suddenly, a cold, wet nose pressed against her cheek. Reaching in, she pulled out Elise, who was trembling and whining. "Oh, Elise, whatever has happened now?"

William leaned over the handrail, savouring the sea air as he smoked a cigarette before calling it a night. His thoughts drifted to Adelaide, a habit that was becoming increasingly frequent. There was something undeniably special about her. He sighed, catching himself as a familiar ache stirred in his chest. Was he falling for her? Perhaps. But he shook the thought away. She was far too good for him, and besides, he had a job to do. The sound of her voice broke his reverie.

"William! Oh, good, you're still out here." She appeared breathless, a hint of urgency in her tone. "Something's been left in my cabin. Elise is in a dreadful state. Can you come?"

William threw his cigarette overboard and followed Adelaide to her cabin. Elise was curled up in her basket, hidden beneath a blanket that Adelaide had draped over her. She had not touched the knife or the note. William pulled the knife from the wall and examined the note. The handwriting was sharp and spiky, and the ink was a deep, dark black. It gave the impression of something dark and sinister. It simply said, "You have been warned!"

"What does this mean?" Adelaide's voice sounded shaky.

"I don't know. It's a warning of some kind, but very cryptic."

An invisible line of tension ran between them as they stared at the note.

William spoke first. "This is quite serious, but I think we should still stick to the plan and act as if we don't suspect Eva or Valentine of anything. Let them go about their business and see what happens. If Eva does have a German contact, that's the only way to flush them out! I will add the knife and note to all the other evidence I have collected and share it back at Headquarters. Rest assured, we will get to the bottom of this."

Adelaide couldn't hide how worried she was. "I feel like I am in one of Theodore's detective novels that he sells in his bookshop. I usually lead such a quiet, simple life. This all seems unreal, and I dread what my aunt and uncle will say when they come to collect me tomorrow."

"It's all in a day's work for me. But I am sorry that this has happened to you. Anyway, we'd better get some sleep. Will you be all right? I'll prop up this stool next to the hole in the wall, so it doesn't remind you of what you found, and I'll ask the Captain to station a trusted member of the crew outside for your peace of mind."

"That really isn't necessary. I will be fine and thank you once again for coming to my aid."

William gave her a mock salute as he left her cabin. Deciding he would keep an eye on the deck near Adelaide's cabin himself, just in case. *This is becoming more sinister than I first thought.*

Adelaide walked back into her cabin and locked her door, checking it several times before getting ready for bed. Lying in her bed, she called out Elise's name, and the little dog jumped up, snuggled under the bedclothes, and gave a happy sigh before both of them succumbed to a deep sleep born out of complete exhaustion.

Concealed behind a steel column, a pair of watchful eyes scanned the shadows, alert and uneasy. Their owner whispered anxiously under her breath. *"Shouldn't have done it - too risky. Why did you make me?"*

The lone figure lingered for a moment, then slipped quietly away, muttering to herself as she went. With one last cautious glance to make sure William Armstrong hadn't spotted her, she disappeared into the darkness, heading back toward her cabin.

As Adelaide awoke, her eyes heavy with sleep, she could hear the sound of seagulls. We must be near land. Getting up, she washed and changed into her travelling clothes. Her trunk was packed and ready to be taken off the ship by a porter. Giving Elise a gentle tickle behind her ears, Adelaide told her, "What an adventure we've had, and I can't deny I am glad it is almost over!"

Making her way to the dining room for breakfast, she carried Elise in her arms. Today, Adelaide did not care what people thought about Elise joining them for breakfast. No one did, of course, as the news of the menacing note had spread swiftly.

"Adelaide, my dear, how are you this morning?" Gerald was the first to greet her.

"Good morning, Gerald. I'm really quite well. No harm done." She smiled brightly.

Her cheerfulness didn't go unnoticed in the far corner of the room where Valentine and Eva sat. Eva eyed her with suspicion.

"What's she got to be so cheerful about?" She muttered.

"That's enough, Eva," Valentine said quietly. "Don't draw any attention. Let's finish our breakfast and get off this ship."

Eva shrugged. "Very well, if that's how you feel."

As the time came to disembark, Adelaide saved her biggest farewell for Jane. "You have been so kind, and thank you for taking care of me. I will keep in touch, and I hope you will write to me, too."

"Of course I will. Take care of yourself, and good luck with your music studies. I'm sure it won't be long before I will be reading about your celebrated performances around the world, and I shall boast that you are my good friend!" Jane laughed.

A porter wheeled Adelaide's trunk through customs, and she stood in the waiting area for any sign of her aunt and uncle to arrive. The air felt cold and damp, and the English accents sounded unfamiliar. She suddenly felt like little orphan Annie, waiting to be claimed by kind strangers who would take her home. Then she saw them. A middle-aged couple were walking purposefully toward her. She recognised them instantly, though she had only ever seen photographs of them. Aunt Alice bore a striking resemblance to her grandmother and had the same kind eyes as her father. Without hesitation, she ran into her aunt's outstretched arms. She was home.

Chapter 27

London – September 1913

London was a sensory delight of unfamiliar sights, sounds, and smells of an ancient, historic city. Although Adelaide had read several books about London and listened to her father's many stories about his time in England as a student, she was unprepared for the reality of it all. It was loud, dirty, busy, and steeped in history, and she loved it!

Her aunt and uncle's residence was a stylish three-storey townhouse in Marylebone. Number 15 Dorset Square was among several dignified houses surrounding the oblong lawn that had once been the site of Lord's Cricket Ground, as Uncle Hugh had proudly told her. The square itself was enclosed by black iron railings and planted with cedars and rhododendrons. The front of the house was painted white. There was no front garden, only an iron gate, with steps leading down to the kitchen and scullery, and another flight rising to an elegant front door, painted black. From what she had observed so far, Adelaide was struck by the antiquity of many of the buildings and the sense of history that seemed to cling to them.

The house, which was to be her home for the coming year, was pleasantly furnished and kept scrupulously clean. The drawing room was spacious, with two sofas and three chairs covered in flowered cretonne. A graceful fireplace held pride of place, its mantel decorated with photographs of her cousins at various stages of their lives. In the alcoves on either side were fitted bookcases which, to Adelaide's delight, contained a good selection of her favourite books, along with volumes on art, music, and many other subjects she had not yet had time to explore.

The drawing room was covered with a soft, pale green square

carpet, placed in the centre of the room, leaving a border of dark, stained wood. The walls were wallpapered with green satin stripes on a cream background. There was only one picture on the wall. Adelaide guessed it was an oil painting of the English countryside, judging by the trees, and she noticed in the bottom right corner the signature of her late uncle Edward. Best of all, much to Adelaide's delight, stood a piano, an Érard with a particularly lovely tone, she thought, when she furtively lifted its fallboard and briefly touched the keys. It was a comfortable room, Adelaide decided, and she was looking forward to sitting there to read or study at the writing desk placed in the centre of the three windows that overlooked the Square.

The dining room, situated beside the drawing room, was furnished with a large oak table and matching chairs, along with a substantial dresser displaying delicate cups and saucers decorated with a blue floral pattern. The room was decorated with the same wallpaper and pale green carpet as the drawing room. Finally, a set of double doors led to a narrow yet charming garden.

The next room, situated at the very back of the house, was the kitchen, which could be reached by descending a small flight of stairs. Their housekeeper, Mrs Coates, managed the kitchen very efficiently, but Adelaide soon realised that Mrs Coates did not like to be disturbed or interrupted, and the kitchen certainly lacked the warmth of Peggy's back home. Adelaide decided it was best to avoid the kitchen altogether.

Adelaide's bedroom was small but comfortable and felt almost luxurious after eight weeks at sea. Positioned at the front of the house, it overlooked the central garden shared by all the residents of the square. The wooden furniture, painted white, included a single bed, a wardrobe, a chest of drawers, a small dressing table, and an oak desk carefully provided for Adelaide's studies. The wallpaper featured a pattern of pink roses on a white background, while the curtains were of a deep, dusky rose colour. When

Adelaide first noticed them, she couldn't resist stroking the fabric and pressing her cheek against it to feel its softness. Curtains were somewhat new to her, as at home she had only ever known shutters to keep out the night air. On the wooden floor lay a pretty rug that echoed the colours of the wallpaper.

That evening, sitting up in bed after her first busy day, Adelaide looked around her new room with quiet satisfaction. Elise was already asleep in her own bed, tired from an exciting adventure in the park with Cousin Rose, who had taken an immediate liking to her. Yes, she thought, I believe I shall be very content here.

Aunt Alice and Rose were wonderful companions, and she felt at ease with them, even though she had only just met them properly a couple of days prior. Often, as she walked around the gardens or the park, she would sway a little, having to grab onto an available arm to steady herself. "I think I still need to find my land legs." Adelaide laughed. Eventually, Adelaide grew accustomed to the hustle and bustle of city life. She had already visited the Houses of Parliament, Buckingham Palace, and the Tower of London and had enjoyed a river cruise along the Thames.

Rose was thrilled to finally have a dog to enjoy after her pleas for one of her own had always been met with an emphatic "No!" Adelaide couldn't resist teasing her, saying, "I do believe you are happier to have Elise as a guest than your cousin!" But secretly, Adelaide was thankful, especially when she needed to focus on her studies as she prepared for her enrolment interview. Her other cousins were away at university but would be home for Christmas. Lawrence, the eldest, was studying Archaeology, and Michael, the younger of the two by just a year, had chosen to study History.

Time passed quickly, and the day of her interview had finally arrived. Although a few nerves had crept in, Adelaide could not help but feel excited to start her studies. At last, she would become a student of the pianoforte! Over breakfast, Adelaide forced some toast down, knowing she would need to keep her energy levels up to perform at her best. She had also been practising several pieces by Mozart and Brahms, hoping at least one would be an acceptable choice to perform in front of the interview panel.

"How are you feeling today, my dear?" Aunt Alice's gentle voice interrupted Adelaide's thoughts.

"I'm well, thank you. Although I must admit to feeling somewhat apprehensive, I am also excited. I have studied and practised for my interview and look forward to starting the Michaelmas Term. If they accept me," Adelaide added, suddenly feeling uncertain of herself.

"Of course they will, my dear. I've so enjoyed listening to you practise, and you play so beautifully. I'm not just saying that because you're my niece; you have a natural talent. Besides, you've travelled an exceedingly long way to do this, so believe in yourself!"

Hugh had been listening behind his newspaper, and putting it down for a moment, he said, "I quite agree with your aunt, so there's no need for any nerves. Now, did you manage to open an account at our bank without any problems?"

"I did, thank you. Father's money has been deposited, and I also have my savings from teaching the piano over the past few years."

"Excellent. You shan't be a starving student like your father and me. We had to rely on the kindness of our professors' wives, who often took pity on us and invited us to Sunday lunch to feed us up!" Uncle Hugh chuckled, lifting his newspaper to continue reading.

Adelaide couldn't help but laugh at the thought of her portly Uncle Hugh as a thin and starving student. Aunt Alice joined in with a chuckle. "I daresay you can scarcely imagine your uncle like that now. His middle-aged spread has quite got the better of him. I do try to encourage him to be mindful of his diet, but alas, it always falls on deaf ears," she said, shrugging her shoulders in a gesture of helplessness.

Hugh ignored his wife's last comment, but Adelaide caught him grinning as he returned to reading his newspaper. Her aunt and uncle enjoyed teasing each other, much like her parents did, and a small pang of homesickness crept into her thoughts.

"Would you like some company on your first trip to the Royal Academy?" her Aunt asked. "I have a few errands to run nearby, so I'd be happy to accompany you and meet up afterwards. We could go to a tearoom where you can tell me all about your interview."

"That would be lovely. I should like that, thank you."

"Could I come too?" Rose pleaded.

"I don't see why not," her mother replied, smiling at her daughter.

"And Adelaide, can I take Elise for a walk while you get ready?"

"Rose! Elise is Adelaide's dog. The poor thing will forget who she belongs to. You have already spent so much time with her!"

"I don't mind at all. Rose has been a great help, and Elise seems rather taken with her. I've already taken her outside for a short walk this morning, but I'm sure she will be happy to have the chance to run around the park again."

Chapter 28

The Royal Academy of Music, London

The Royal Academy of Music was a short walk from Dorset Square, part of which was through Regent's Park. Although there was a more direct route, Adelaide decided the park would be a lovely walk on her way to her lectures. She found the park delightful and was in awe of the large, majestic trees, which could have shared so much history with her if only they could speak.

"I think I will enjoy my walk to the Academy even in the winter," Adelaide said enthusiastically.

Rose smiled at her cousin, "I'm not sure you'll say that when it snows and the temperatures fall below zero. Even the River Thames can freeze!"

"Is that true?" Adelaide was surprised at the idea of the River Thames freezing. Her brother Joseph had spent many winters skiing in the mountains back home, but she rarely experienced very cold weather in Wellington. "I'd better buy some warmer clothes in that case."

"And boots!" Her Aunt joined in. "Mind you, I'm sure Rose could lend you a pair. She habitually collects far too much footwear than is necessary for one small person!"

"Oh, Mother, you do exaggerate. I don't think you could ever have too many shoes."

"Well, in that case, you'd better find a rich husband to accommodate your fascination with them."

"I will bear that in mind," Rose replied, trying to look serious but breaking into a fit of giggles, which caused Alice to shake her head with mock frustration.

It wasn't long before the Royal Academy of Music came into

view. Adelaide couldn't help but admire the majestic building. None of the photographs she had seen in her books did it justice.

"It's rather grand, isn't it?" Rose said.

"It's stunning," Adelaide replied.

"Well, off you go and begin your exciting journey as a student!" Encouraged her Aunt as she noticed her niece hesitating slightly.

"Thank you, Aunt Alice. I will see you both later. Wish me luck!" Adelaide shouted as she joined the other students, who were making their way through the open doors.

The small entrance hall was a hub of activity, with people coming and going, and Adelaide noticed signs indicating where students should go to register, depending on the courses they had applied for. She admired the marbled walls and pillars before enquiring at reception where she should go. A porter pointed at the sign that said 'pianoforte' on it. "Just follow the sign, down the corridor and to the left." Feeling a little foolish at not seeing the sign before asking, she made her way down the corridor and eventually arrived at the correct room. As she walked through the door, she was greeted by an efficient-looking woman in a grey dress and blue hat, holding a clipboard. "Name?" the woman shouted briskly.

"Adelaide Ellwood." She said timidly.

Peering through her thick glasses, the woman spied her name and placed a purposeful tick next to it. "I am Miss Lupen. If you need anything or have any questions, I will be available afterwards. Head through that door and take a seat."

Adelaide obeyed Miss Lupen's instructions and sat down next to a young woman of similar age to herself, who, Adelaide decided, appeared far less nervous than she was. After a few minutes, the young woman asked gently, "Are you quite well?"

It was then that Adelaide became aware that she had been tapping her foot, a habit that always betrayed her anxiety.

"Don't be nervous. I've been told the tutors will only ask a few questions about your experience and then ask you to play a piece of music. They want to ensure you are proficient enough to attend the course."

"Thank you, that's very helpful."

"My name is Sonia, by the way."

"Hello, Sonia. I'm Adelaide."

Just then, another door opened, and a man entered. "Good morning, ladies. I am Mr Whitemore. Would Miss Sonia Kirkland please follow me?"

Without the calming presence of Sonia, Adelaide's heart thudded in her chest. She tried to calm herself by imagining a piece of music in her head, picturing Violet standing by the piano, gently correcting her posture, encouraging her to breathe and relax. *I'm here because of you, Violet*, she thought. *Don't let me fail now*. After about fifteen minutes, Adelaide heard Sonia beginning to play. "Beethoven, if I'm not mistaken," she whispered to herself, a flicker of nerves prickling at her stomach. *I hope I can play as well as she does*. As the music faded, she caught the muffled hum of voices and the shuffle of movement beyond the door. Her palms felt slightly clammy, and she took a deep breath, steadying herself. Soon, it would be her turn. Suddenly, the door swung open, and Sonia emerged, cheeks flushed but smiling.

"How did it go? I enjoyed listening to you play."

"Thank you! I think it went very well." Sonia grinned and held up crossed fingers. "Mr Whitemore asked me to tell you to go in. So off you go, and good luck! See you at the start of term." With that, she was gone. Adelaide felt her stomach tighten as the butterflies took flight. She stepped forward, each footfall echoing softly in the quiet hallway. *This is it. Don't falter.*

The next room was larger than the waiting area, with a highly polished grand piano at its centre. A man stood, ready to greet her.

"Good morning, Miss Ellwood. My name is Tobias Matthay."

Adelaide's breath caught. She had read so much about him—his methods, his exacting standards, and his reputation as an innovative teacher and composer. She shook his hand, trying to appear calm.

"Please sit down and tell us about your achievements so far," Mr Matthay said, gesturing to a chair with a gentle smile. Adelaide lowered herself onto it, smoothing her skirt, her mind racing as she recalled every lesson, every practice session, every correction Violet had ever given her. She began to speak, her voice trembling slightly at first, but confidence grew with each word. Music, she realised, was the only language in which she truly felt at home. Mr Whitemore asked about her life in New Zealand and the long voyage to England. Adelaide found herself talking about the seas she had crossed, the excitement and the loneliness of the journey, and the anticipation that had carried her across the ocean. Then came the crucial question.

"Would you like to play for us now?" Mr Matthay asked.

"It would be a pleasure. What should I play?"

"Do you know Mozart's Piano Sonata in B-flat major?" Mr Whitemore inquired.

Nodding, she moved to the piano, her heart still hammering in her chest. Seating herself on the stool, she closed her eyes for a brief moment, picturing Violet's calm, patient guidance. Her fingers touched the keys, tentative at first, then confident as the music began. The room disappeared, and all that remained was the piano, the music, and the memory of Violet. When the final chord rang out, she felt the weight of two pairs of eyes upon her. The scrutiny was intense; unlike any examination she had faced back home. Adelaide stood, curtsied lightly, and returned to her chair, pulse still racing but heart swelling with pride.

"That was delightful, Miss Ellwood," Mr Whitemore said warmly. "We are very much looking forward to welcoming a student from the colonies, especially one who shows such promise."

Adelaide felt her cheeks warm. She barely managed to nod. "Thank you. I am very much looking forward to learning and improving my technique during my time here."

"Excellent, excellent. The term begins on 28th September. Miss Lupen will ensure you receive your timetable and any further instructions."

As she left the studio, Adelaide felt a heady mix of exhilaration and relief. Her dreams were no longer distant hopes; they were within reach, and she could hardly wait to begin.

"How did it go?" Rose asked her as she walked towards them.

"I have just met Tobias Matthay!" That was all Adelaide could say as her mouth broke into an enormous smile.

"Who? Rose replied. "Were you very nervous?"

"Yes, I was!" Adelaide replied, trying to release the tension that had enveloped her body.

Aunt Alice ushered both girls out of the foyer and into the fresh air. "I think you have earned a well-deserved cup of tea, so let's find a tearoom and make sure you get plenty of cake, too!"

"Thank you, Aunt Alice, that sounds perfect!"

The three of them strolled along the bustling street, Alice leading while Adelaide and Rose followed, their excited chatter weaving through the hum of city life. As they walked, their eyes caught sight of a small establishment tucked along Baker Street, a charming little place called the Dutch Oven. Curious, Adelaide followed her aunt and cousin down a short flight of stairs, eager to uncover what lay beyond. As she stepped inside, she felt as though she had stepped straight into a Dutch travel brochure. The long, spacious room was elegantly divided by pillars stretching from floor to ceiling, giving a sense of grandeur despite the cosy atmosphere. A large, inviting kitchen dresser stood proudly adorned with delicate blue and white Delft pottery, its intricate patterns adding a touch of tradition to the space. The walls were partially tiled in a soft, calming green, complementing the polished, inlaid wood flooring beneath their feet. Small tea tables, each set with delicate cups and saucers, were scattered along the walls and in the centre of the room, accompanied by sturdy wooden chairs that seemed to whisper of quiet, comforting afternoons. In the far corner, a small gas stove cast a gentle glow, filling the room with a warmth that was more than just physical. A waitress in a crisp white cap and apron arrived, moving with practised ease. Aunt Alice ordered a pot of tea, and without hesitation, they all agreed that the golden-brown scones resting on the counter looked far too inviting to resist.

"Well, my dear, tell us what it was like as you entered the Royal Academy of Music?" Aunt Alice asked her niece.

Adelaide thinks of her mother and her favourite line, "You went in and ..."

"Well, let me think. The entrance hall was full of students, some carrying music cases of all shapes and sizes."

"Thank goodness you didn't have to take in your piano!" Rose laughed.

Alice ignored her daughter's attempt at humour, but Adelaide grinned and raised her eyebrows, making Rose laugh again.

"The walls looked like they were made of marble, with an incredible stained-glass window at the foot of a staircase. It is a stunning building, and I look forward to exploring it properly. Then I had to find where I needed to register, and it was all very bewildering, but after asking a porter, I eventually found the correct room. I sat beside a nice lady called Sonia, so hopefully, I've already made one friend!"

On their return to Dorset Square, Rose asked if she could take Elise for another walk. Adelaide was beginning to realise that having Rose around to help with Elise would be a godsend when her studies began in earnest. Mrs Coates wouldn't even entertain Elise in the kitchen, so she had to stay in Adelaide's bedroom when she went out. After handing Elise over to Rose, she watched the pair hurry off towards the park, and Adelaide went to her room to read all the information Miss Lupen had given her. It had started to feel very real to her now, and she could not wait to begin. There were more books to buy, which only filled her with even more excitement, so she decided to buy all the suggested reading, too. She would have loved to take the list to Theodore's bookshop and ask him to order them for her. The thought of Eva suddenly intruded on her excitement. *Was it really Eva who had been involved in the break-in of her cabin and then the sinister note?* Pulling herself together, she refused to allow thoughts of Eva to spoil her time in England. Instead, she decided she must write some letters, and a letter to Valentine was at the top of her list. Adelaide hated how they had parted like strangers. Was he even aware of Eva's deceit, or had she betrayed him, too?

15 Dorset Square
London

September 1913

Dear Valentine

I hope you are well and enjoying your new role as a music professor.

I have recently enrolled at the Royal Academy of Music, and my lessons are set to commence soon. You can well imagine my excitement! I have already been introduced to two of my tutors, Mr Whitemore and Mr Matthay. I must confess that I was quite overcome upon being introduced to Mr Matthay. I know I have much to learn, and I hope they will be as encouraging as you always were. I miss our lessons together, and I hope I have not caused you any offence. You were so distant on the Ayrshire, and I felt saddened that we never had the opportunity to say farewell properly.

Are you well, Valentine? I do hope life in Leipzig is everything you had hoped for, and that Eva is enjoying her role as the wife of a successful musician. Perhaps, if time permits, I may have the pleasure of visiting. Your descriptions of the Conservatoire were always so vivid; I should very much like to see it for myself.

London is much busier, noisier, and dirtier than Wellington, but it is rich in history, and the parks are truly delightful.

With fondest regards,

Adelaide

Chapter 29

The Royal Academy of Music - Michaelmas Term

Life settled into an orderly rhythm as Adelaide slowly became accustomed to her new life in London. The Brokenshire household ran a 'tight ship,' to use one of her brother Joseph's idioms. During the week, Uncle Hugh left the house at precisely eight o'clock, and breakfast was served based on his routine; if you weren't up in time, you either finished the leftovers or did without. Mrs Coates was very firm about this. "I've better things to do with my time than wait around to clear up after dawdlers. It makes the rest of the day late, which won't do."

Adelaide had always been an early riser; she hated wasting the day, and today was no exception. It was her first morning as a student, and she wanted to arrive at the Academy in plenty of time. She had carefully packed Violet's music case the night before and chosen a smart but comfortable outfit to wear. On her walk to the Academy, she used the time to arrange her thoughts and mentally prepare herself for the lessons ahead. Mr Whitemore was waiting for her as she arrived. Checking her watch, she was relieved to note she was not late. "Good morning, Mr Whitemore."

"Good morning, Miss Ellwood. Are you ready for your first lesson?"

Mr Whitemore's teaching style differed from Valentine's, but how he explained complicated pieces of music reminded her of how Violet would talk to her. Her initial nervousness quickly vanished, and she thoroughly enjoyed her first lesson.

As she packed her case, Mr Whitemore said, "Miss Ellwood, we will have our first orchestra practice on Friday. After hearing you play, I feel you are more than ready to perform with a full orchestra. Do you think you are ready?"

"I would be delighted to perform with an orchestra. I must admit I have never had the opportunity, but it has long been a wish of mine to do so."

Excellent. The orchestra practises twice a week, and as the concert approaches, we begin rehearsals in earnest. The first concert will be held here in Queen's Hall. We encourage our students to invite family and friends, but I understand that might be a little difficult for you, as you are so far away from home.

"That is true, but I am lodging with my aunt and uncle, so I'm sure they would love to attend."

Adelaide walked home that afternoon with a spring in her step. She was looking forward to writing to her mother about Mr Whitemore and his invitation to join the orchestra. When she arrived at Dorset Square, three letters were waiting for her. Joan saw her walking up the steps and opened the door, pointing to the letters waiting for her on the side table. "Thank you, Joan. Is anyone home?"

"No, Miss, they are all out. Mrs Brokenshire said she would return around four, and I believe Rose is staying overnight with one of her friends."

"I think I'll go to my room, then, and read my letters."

Joan nodded as she took Adelaide's coat, brushing a stray leaf from the collar before hanging it neatly on the stand. "Rose asked me to take Elise out for a little walk, since she was going to be away. I hope that was all right?"

"That was very kind of you—thank you. I'm sure Elise was most grateful. I'm fortunate that Rose has taken such a liking to her; I hadn't expected to be away from her quite so often. At home, our housekeeper usually looked after her when I was out."

"That's quite all right, Miss. She's a lovely little dog. Both Rose and I are happy to look after her when you're busy with your studies."

Up in her room, after a warm and enthusiastic welcome from

Elise, Adelaide placed her bag on the chair and spread her letters across the bed. She hesitated, unsure which to read first. The handwriting revealed that one was from her brother and the other from Theodore. The third bore a German stamp, yet the script was unfamiliar and certainly not Valentine's. The envelope was marked with the crest of the Leipzig Conservatoire. Curious and still hopeful that it might somehow be from Valentine, she picked it up. Upon opening it, her heart sank as inside was the letter she had written to Valentine, along with another letter addressed to her, written in German. She could only decipher a few words and the sender's name: Gustav Lehman. Puzzled, she wondered if she could find someone to translate it for her. Setting it aside for now, she turned her attention to Joseph's letter.

Joseph's note brimmed with news of life aboard the *Mauretania*. As usual, he launched into intricate details about the ship's engines, most of which made little sense to Adelaide. He assured her that Kitty was well and that she was an angel, patiently enduring his frequent absences. Then, almost as an afterthought, he shared a significant piece of news.

I am so thrilled, Adelaide. We thought it was not meant to be, but the doctor has assured us that Kitty and the baby are doing well. If all goes as planned, our little one is expected to arrive just before Christmas. You must visit. Kitty made me promise to ask you. I'll be home for Christmas and New Year, so please say you'll come.

Smiling and holding the letter towards her heart, she felt so happy for them. So much had happened since Joseph had left to go to sea. Would they even recognise each other? Putting the letter on her desk, she decided that Liverpool couldn't be too far from London, so she would ask Aunt Alice to help her. Turning her attention to Theodore's letter, she was just about to open it when she was interrupted by a knock on her door. It was Joan. "Sorry to disturb you, but Mrs Brokenshire is home, and she wondered if you'd like to join her for tea in the drawing room?"

"Thank you, Joan, that would be lovely. I'll be right down." Adelaide placed the letter from Herr Lehman in her pocket, deciding to ask her aunt for some advice.

Aunt Alice was reading a book in front of a roaring fire. It was a picture of cosiness, and Adelaide was ready for a cup of tea and one of the delicious-looking scones on the tea tray. Pouring her niece a cup of tea, she asked about her first day as a student, and they chatted amiably about this and that. "Aunt Alice, I received this letter today." Adelaide placed the letter on her aunt's knee. "It is from someone called Gustav Lehman, but it is written in German."

Alice picked up the letter and tried to read it. "I see what you mean. I can only make out a few words, but not enough to make sense of them. Why don't you send it to the gentleman who looked after you on the ship?

"Why yes, I hadn't thought of William. I should tell him. If he doesn't understand German, I'm sure he'll know someone who does."

Three days later, William arrived at the house with the letter translated and many questions. Her aunt and uncle were home, and Adelaide was relieved to have them with her.

"Adelaide, how are you? I'm so pleased you wrote to me. It's good to see you again."

His smile was warm, and he was smartly dressed in a dark grey suit. His demeanour was confident, with an air of quiet efficiency.

"Hello, William. It's good to see you too. Did you have any luck with the letter?"

"I did indeed."

"Do sit down, Mr Armstrong," said Alice, gesturing to an empty chair near Adelaide.

"Thank you, Mrs Brokenshire. Please, call me William."

Alice smiled. "And you must call me Alice. Of course, you know my husband, Hugh."

Hugh shook William's hand. "So, what's this letter all about, then?"

"Yes—the letter. I had it translated. Shall I read it aloud, or give you the main points?"

"Read it, please," Adelaide replied, eager to hear everything.

"Of course." William began to read:

"My name is Gustav Lehmann, and I write from the Leipzig Conservatoire. As you will see, I am returning your letter addressed to Herr Spielmann, for, most unfortunately, Herr and Frau Spielmann never arrived here. We have had no communication from them since our correspondence with Herr Spielmann when we offered him the post of Professor of Music. Should you have any news of his whereabouts, I would be most grateful if you would inform me at your earliest convenience. Herr Spielmann was given an advance upon his salary to cover the expenses of his journey to Germany, and this sum must now be repaid."

Adelaide put her hand to her mouth in shock. "I don't understand. Where are they?"

"This is a bad business." Do you know where Mr and Mrs Spielmann went after leaving the ship?" Hugh asked William.

"I have made a few enquiries. They purchased tickets for Calais, but never boarded the train. It is as though they vanished into thin air. We have checked the ports, the border controls, and the hotels, but there has been no sign of them. It is possible, of course, that they changed their names, or even separated."

"No. That cannot be right," Adelaide replied. "I know Valentine, and he was so eager to return to the Conservatoire. I fear something dreadful must have happened."

"You know Valentine better than we do, but you must admit their behaviour on board ship was most suspicious. Do you think Eva could be behind his disappearance?" William asked.

" I-I am not sure. As I've mentioned before, Eva is the most complex person. It is almost as though she has two distinct characters. At times she could be perfectly friendly, and then, quite suddenly, she would become cruel. Oh, yes! I just remembered that I have a letter from Eva's father, Theodore, upstairs. I haven't had time to read it yet. Perhaps he has heard from them. I shall fetch it at once." With that, she rose swiftly, leaving three surprised faces behind her.

A few minutes later, Adelaide returned with the letter. Sitting down, she opened it and began to read. "No, nothing. Theodore has not heard anything from them, and neither has Valentine's family. He wondered if I had heard from them. He sounds very worried."

"Is there anyone else who may know of their whereabouts? Someone they would confide in?" William asked.

"I don't know. Perhaps Valentine's sister, Giselle? But she would have told her parents if she'd received any news from her brother, and I can't think of anyone else."

"Not to worry." William tried to reassure her. "I must be going now, but if you hear from anyone with news about Valentine and Eva, will you let me know?"

"Of course," Adelaide replied.

Hugh followed William out of the room and to the front door. Adelaide could hear them talking, so she strained to catch their conversation, but could only make out muffled responses. Aunt Alice looked at her niece. "This is all very mysterious, isn't it?"

"Oh, Aunt Alice, I'm so worried about Valentine, but I'm sure William, I mean Mr Armstrong, will do his best to find them!"

Aunt Alice smiled at her niece, "I think my niece has taken rather a fancy to the charming Mr Armstrong."

"I haven't! He's just been so helpful and kind, that's all." Adelaide felt her cheeks burn with embarrassment until she realised her aunt was teasing her, and they both started laughing.

Chapter 30

November 1913

Gusts of wind and torrential rain heralded the arrival of November. Adelaide did not relish her walk to Monday morning lessons, though she was grateful for her smart new winter coat and boots, which she had purchased from Selfridges at the insistence of her aunt and cousin. Wandering up and down Bond Street, Oxford Street, and Regent Street, she found shopping for clothes to be quite the experience. The latest fashions from Paris adorned the windows, and to her surprise, she found the outing far more enjoyable than she had anticipated. By lunchtime, she was the proud owner of a coat, hat, and boots — all suitable for a British winter. Rose had spied an elegant umbrella, which she promptly added to the growing bill, while Aunt Alice selected a beautiful dress for Adelaide's birthday.

"You can wear it to your first concert," she said. "It's a lovely colour and will make you look very elegant seated at the piano."

Mr Whitemore was waiting for her as she walked into his room. "Good morning, Mr Whitemore. Am I late? The weather is atrocious out there!"

"Good morning, Miss Ellwood. Indeed, it is. Do you need to dry out, or are you ready to begin?"

"No, I am ready." Adelaide sat down at the piano. She liked the fact that Mr Whitemore was very economical with his conversation. He said what was needed and nothing more.

Adelaide had been practising Beethoven's *Moonlight Sonata* in C-sharp minor for the concert. Mr Whitemore had explained that her performance would contribute to her end-of-term examinations, so Adelaide devoted all her spare time to perfecting it. When she finished the section, he asked her to play. He congratulated her but offered a few suggestions for improvement. Adelaide never took offence at his criticism; she knew that to excel and reach her full potential, she must always remain open to learning. Both Violet and Valentine had taught her that. A small bubble of concern threatened to distract her as she wondered where Valentine could be.

The main entrance hall of the Academy was crowded with students moving about, carrying their music cases on their way to lessons, making it hard for Adelaide to get out. Suddenly, she heard her name being called. "Adelaide, wait for me!" She stopped and looked around to find the source of the voice, but it was impossible to see. Adelaide decided to stand still and wait for the person to find her. It was Sonia, closely followed by a new friend, Evie. Sonia exclaimed, "Gosh, it's busy in here today. Are you going for some lunch? Would you like some company?"

"I am, and yes, I would!" Adelaide replied, happy to see her friends. "Although if it is still raining as hard as it was this morning, I don't want to go far!"

"It seems to have stopped, but it looks rather windy. I can see all the leaves twirling around the street," Evie said.

Sonia linked arms with each of her friends and pulled them towards the door. "Come on, ladies. I know a little tearoom just a few yards away. We'd better stick close together in case we all get blown away!"

They found a window seat and ordered tomato soup, as well as apple crumble and custard for dessert. "Perfect for a wintery day," announced Evie as she handed back her menu to the waitress. Evie Salisbury was the eldest of the three and an aspiring pianist, as well as a talented violinist. Adelaide would sometimes sneak into the studio where Evie was practising to listen, closing her eyes and allowing the music to take her to magical places. Evie was engaged to Edward Launchester, heir to the Launchester Estate in Dorset. Evie's only condition when agreeing to marry him was that she could finish her studies. It was non-negotiable, and, according to Evie, her parents had been annoyed with her for days. Teddy, as Evie called him, had taken Evie's side, and their parents reluctantly agreed to postpone the wedding until the following summer. After waving Evie off on her first day at the Academy, Teddy and his old university chums set off to Europe, travelling by train to wherever they fancied. He sent Evie an occasional letter containing hilarious details of their adventures and mishaps. Evie thought it was all a hoot and would read sections of his letters, making Adelaide and Sonia gasp with horror at some of the situations he had found himself in, even spending a night in a police cell in Sorrento after attending a champagne party at the villa of a Contessa overlooking the Mediterranean. He had managed to lose his friends and the hotel key and could not remember the hotel's name. The Carabinieri had found him fast asleep on a park bench and decided to put him in a cell to sleep it off and recover his memory.

"Your fiancé is totally irresponsible," Sonia told her friend. Adelaide would have loved to have had the courage to agree with Sonia, but instead nodded wide-eyed in shock at such goings-on.

Evie grew serious for a moment. "Marriage is for an awfully long time. If we're lucky enough, that is, so why not let him go wild and get it out of his system? His father is getting on in age, and one day soon, Teddy will have to grow up and take over the running of the Estate, and so will I, for that matter. I'll be Lady Evelyn Launchester, don't you know!" Lifting her nose in the air and waving her hand like royalty, but unfortunately, just as she did that, the waitress was about to serve their soup; if the poor woman had not been an expert at manoeuvring her tray, it could have all ended in a messy disaster. Their near mishap sobered them a little, and they quietly ate their soup while chatting about the upcoming concert. Adelaide faced the window, with her friends sitting on either side of her, neither wanting their backs to the window. As Sonia explained an interesting technique her tutor had shown her, Adelaide's attention was drawn to the passers-by struggling with their umbrellas against the wayward wind. Suddenly, her eyes met those of a woman standing still while the others moved around her. The woman was staring straight at Adelaide. "Eva!" Adelaide shouted, interrupting Sonia's flow.

"Are you all right, Adelaide? Who is Eva?"

Adelaide looked at Sonia and then back through the window, but the menacing figure she had thought was Eva had gone, or perhaps it was someone who resembled her.

"You look like you've seen a ghost," Evie added.

Not a ghost, just someone I thought ought to be elsewhere. I'm sorry; maybe it was someone who looked like her."

Walking home later that afternoon, Adelaide couldn't get the image of Eva's staring face out of her mind. *Was it her, or could I have just imagined it?* It had all happened so quickly, but she decided to send a message to William to let him know, hoping it would help in his search for Valentine.

Chapter 31

December 1913

The end-of-term concert was about to begin, and Adelaide stood backstage with her fellow students, anticipation thrumming in her chest. She was both excited and nervous, for seated among the audience were her aunt, uncle, Rose and, to her quiet delight, William Armstrong. A rush of happiness swept through her at the sight of him, though doubt was quick to follow. Surely, the only reason he had come was to catch a glimpse of Eva, should she be lurking nearby. It had been thoughtful of William to express his concern, confiding in Adelaide that he feared Eva might have unfinished business with her and that she could, perhaps, be in some danger. Adelaide, however, wished only to believe that Valentine and Eva were happily settled in Leipzig.

With Mr Henry Chase conducting, the orchestra entertained the audience with a lovely 'Music of the Mountains' repertoire, featuring renowned Austrian and Swiss composers. Adelaide could hear the thunderous applause and took it as her cue to be ready at the side of the stage. She had to squeeze through a narrow corridor, which felt even more claustrophobic when she was nervous. Finally, she was called to the piano to a warm round of applause. She bowed towards the conductor and the rest of the orchestra before sitting down at the piano. The conductor glanced at her sideways and nodded, and she nodded back to show she was ready. Adelaide felt the music, the smoothness of the piano keys, and as the audience faded away, all her senses sharpened as Adelaide placed her fingers on the keys for the final chord. A hush swept over the hall. Then came the applause, warm and persistent, prompting her to stand and take her bow. As she rose, her gaze swept towards the front row, and a thrill ran through her at the sight of William, smiling broadly and applauding with clear enthusiasm. Beside him, Rose clapped just as fervently, her eyes shining with pride.

Back at Dorset Square, the family had gathered in the drawing room to drink a toast to the 'star of the show.' Adelaide felt an unusual feeling of pure contentment from being surrounded by people who cared about her. She only wished her parents and brother were there too. She looked over to the fireplace where Uncle Hugh and William stood, deep in conversation. *I wonder what they are talking about*.

"Adelaide, come and sit over here. You must be exhausted after your performance." Her Aunt was patting the empty cushion next to her.

"It will be Christmas soon. It will feel quite different from what you are used to in New Zealand," Rose chatted excitedly.

"It certainly will be. It is summer in New Zealand now. We would be preparing to go and stay with Uncle Henry and Aunt Victoria at Woodlands. You should come and visit us one day and meet your New Zealand family."

"Oh yes, wouldn't that be wonderful? Could we go to New Zealand one day, Mother?"

Alice looked at her daughter, shaking her head in dismay. She conceded that it would be a marvellous idea, but only a pipe dream at the moment. Seeing her daughter's disappointment, she quickly added, "But never say never!"

Hugh and William, having finished their conversation, joined the others and took their seats in the two armchairs by the fireplace. Just then, a knock on the door announced the arrival of their coffee, which Joan brought in on a large silver tray. Placing it carefully on a side table, she made a discreet exit. William took the opportunity to speak to Adelaide as the conversation died down. "I thought your performance was wonderful."

"Thank you. It was my first performance with an orchestra, so

I was a little nervous, but I enjoyed every minute of it. Mr Chase is an excellent conductor. In fact, the whole orchestra were a joy to play with. So many talented individuals playing as one, which feels pretty special, don't you think?"

"I do indeed. I'm afraid music was not something my family showed any interest in. It wasn't until I joined the Army that I was introduced to music in the officers' mess. I was ribbed quite a bit for not knowing my Mozart from my Bach."

"Where does your family live?" Alice asked him. She had picked up her embroidery frame, and Adelaide was always amazed by how she could embroider and talk at the same time.

"My family are from a small village not far from Dorchester. My father is the local doctor, and my mother manages the surgery, including all his patients' medical records and other administrative tasks. He is a brilliant doctor, but very absent-minded!"

"Do you have any brothers or sisters?"

"Yes. There are five of us. I'm the eldest, followed by Victoria, then Beatrix, Ben, and John. We were quite a lively household growing up. Our parents were so busy with patients and home visits that we were often left to our own devices, and it was chaos! I try to visit when I can, but it's not always easy because of my work schedule. I've managed to get some leave over Christmas, so the whole family will all descend on my poor parents for a big, noisy reunion." He looked up at the ceiling and laughed as he described his large family, but Adelaide could sense he was close to them and was excited to see everyone. It made her think of Joseph and Kitty, and how eager she was to see them, but it had been so long since she last saw Joseph that she worried their once close relationship might feel different.

"What are you thinking about, Adelaide? You look miles away." Aunt Alice's voice interrupted Adelaide's thoughts.

"I was thinking about Joseph and Kitty and whether I could

visit over Christmas. It's been so long, and I would love to see them, especially now, as I'm to be an aunt!"

"It is up to you, of course, but I know your father is still very upset about Joseph's choices since leaving home," Hugh added, trying to be diplomatic.

Adelaide didn't know how to answer that, so she stayed quiet. William took this moment to take his leave, sensing Adelaide was upset by her uncle's comments.

"Well, I hope you get your wish, Adelaide. Now, I must say goodbye as I have work tomorrow, and it's getting quite late."

Desperately wishing to ask about Valentine, Adelaide spoke quickly. "Before you go, might I ask—have you any news of Valentine? I've felt rather unsettled since thinking I saw Eva, imagined or otherwise."

William shook his head. "I'm sorry. There's no news, and no sightings of Eva. But that doesn't mean she isn't about. Do stay vigilant, and if you see her again, let me know at once."

"I will. And thank you for coming to the concert."

"My pleasure."

They exchanged a quiet smile. William reached for his coat, then paused, his gaze lingering a moment longer than necessary, as though he wished to say more but thought better of it. From across the room, Rose giggled and nudged her mother, who promptly shushed her and turned her attention to seeing their guest out.

Up in her room, Adelaide lay wide awake and found sleep impossible. She lit a candle and sat at her desk to write in her journal. It helped her organise her thoughts and record wonderful events to reflect on when she needed something to smile about. *You are like that character, Anne of Green Gables, in that new book everyone is reading.* She could hear her mother's voice chastising her for not facing the sometimes-harsh realities of life. But *why*, she wondered, *would I want to dwell on bad things?*

Reflecting on William, she considered how different he was from Valentine. She felt secure with William and was eager to learn more about him. Valentine was so reserved and formal that their conversations only became lively when they discussed music. She missed their piano lessons, although she thought of him fondly despite what had happened since leaving Wellington. Bowing her head, she said a silent prayer to herself. *I hope he is all right.*

"It's snowing!" Joan exclaimed as she stepped into Adelaide's bedroom, balancing a small tray with a steaming cup of cocoa and a piece of shortbread—still warm from Mrs Coates's oven.

Adelaide looked up, startled. "It's what?"

It was December 14th, and she had just finished her first term. Lost in an essay titled The Colours of Music, she was determined to complete it before the Christmas festivities swept her away. The end of the Michaelmas term had brought a rush of examinations, and although the holidays had started, her mind remained focused on her studies and the essays still to be written before classes resumed in January. Joan gently placed the tray on the desk, then moved to the window and drew back the curtains. "Look, Miss," she said softly, her voice tinged with wonder. "It's snowing. Maybe we'll have a white Christmas after all."

Placing her pen carefully on the desk, Adelaide gazed out of her bedroom window to witness the silent snowflakes falling softly onto the rooftops of Dorset Square. It was only four o'clock, but it was dark already, and the blackness of the sky gave the white snow a truly magical effect. The pair stood together, mesmerised.

"It's just like the images you find on Christmas cards!" Adelaide exclaimed. "I have to go outside and see it properly."

"It's freezing out there; you'd better wrap up well!" Joan laughed, amused by Adelaide's childlike excitement over the snow.

"Come with me, Joan! Show me how to make a snow angel and a snowman. I want to throw snowballs too!"

That was the scene Alice came upon as she passed Adelaide's open bedroom door. The girls were doubled over with laughter, gazing out the window, completely unaware of her presence. Smiling to herself, Alice cleared her throat, then stepped in with mock sternness.

"It's only a dusting of snow and hardly enough for a snowman! If it keeps falling through the night, you can go out in the morning. No sense catching a cold over nothing." She turned to Joan. "Go help Mrs Coates, will you? I'm sure she'd appreciate an extra pair of hands."

"Yes, Mrs Brokenshire." Joan gave a quick curtsy, flashing Adelaide a mischievous grin as she slipped out of the room.

"It's not 'nothing,' Aunt Alice. It's snow!" I have never experienced snow at Christmas, but I can now understand why Christmas is always depicted as so magical here."

"Indeed. It must be strange for you to celebrate in the height of summer."

"It's all I've ever been used to. We usually go to Woodlands and have a picnic on the beach. However, Uncle Henry and Aunt Victoria insist on a huge festive feast in the evening. I imagine Mother and Father are there now, my first Christmas without them."

Suddenly, the mood changed, and Aunt Alice quickly distracted Adelaide before her melancholy got the better of her. "From the sighing and banging that is going on downstairs, the Christmas tree must have been delivered. Let's go downstairs and save your Uncle Hugh before he hurts his back, or worse, Mrs Coates scolds him for knocking into all her freshly polished furniture!"

They hurried down the stairs just in time to witness Uncle Hugh, Rose, and Joan wrestling the Christmas tree through the hallway towards the drawing room, while Mrs Coates tutted and sighed at the trail of pine needles and scuffed paintwork left in their wake.

"Goodness!" Alice gasped, casting a glance at her husband.

"Goodness indeed," Hugh muttered, huffing and puffing as he manoeuvred the tree through the doorway.

Eventually, the tree was settled into a corner of the drawing room, standing tall and ready to be decorated. Rose's excitement was infectious, and Adelaide soon found herself kneeling beside a box of shiny Christmas ornaments, eager to begin decorating.

Alice's voice was heard over the excited chatter. "Supper first! Mrs Coates will wait for no one, and then we will decorate the tree!" Turning to Adelaide, "Perhaps you could play a few Christmas carols to get us in the mood?"

"I would be delighted to. I have been working on 'In the Bleak Mid-Winter' with Mr Whitemore. It is a beautiful piece and means so much more to me now that I can appreciate the freezing British weather!"

They all laughed as they walked towards the dining room, and Mrs Coates, with Joan's help, served them a warming dish of beef stew and dumplings. Adelaide asked for a second helping because it was so delicious, immediately regretting her greed as she struggled to finish the apple pie Joan had served her for pudding.

The evening was indeed filled with Christmas cheer. Once the table had been cleared and she'd finished helping Mrs Coates, Joan was allowed to assist, and her wide-eyed pleasure made Adelaide's heart sing. Living away from her family and only seeing them once a month must be hard. Adelaide felt a connection with Joan, as she missed her parents terribly. Uncle Hugh made a show of unwrapping a few decorations and then announced he had work to do, disappearing into his study.

"Bah, humbug!" Rose whispered under her breath, causing

Joan to giggle.

Adelaide began to play a few Christmas carols on the piano, her fingers dancing lightly over the keys as familiar melodies filled the room. Aunt Alice sat by the fire, quietly working on her embroidery. From time to time, she glanced up to offer her opinion on the placement of an ornament upon the tree, but for the most part, she was content to observe as the fir was transformed into a glittering vision of Christmas cheer. As the final decoration was set in place, a beautiful Christmas angel dressed in white, adorned with a silver crown and feathered wings, the door suddenly flew open, and everyone turned in startled silence. Rose gave a delighted cry as her brothers, Lawrence and Michael, appeared in the doorway, calling out, "Surprise!" With a joyful laugh, she ran straight into their outstretched arms.

"My dear boys, you are home. What a wonderful surprise!" It was Alice's turn to welcome both her sons home. "Why didn't you let us know?"

"Well, if we had, it wouldn't have been a surprise!" Lawrence replied.

Adelaide suddenly felt shy. She was still sitting at the piano and wasn't sure what to do, so she remained where she was, not wanting to spoil the happy family reunion.

Michael suddenly spotted her and extended his hand to welcome her. "And you must be Cousin Adelaide, all the way from New Zealand?"

Standing up from her piano stool, she took Michael's outstretched hand. "Yes, I am, and it is so good to meet you. Rose has told me so much about you both."

"Oh, has she? I bet it wasn't all good!" Laughed Lawrence. "I'm Lawrence, obviously." Her older cousin grinned at her. She was taken aback at how much he looked like Joseph. Tall, sandy-coloured hair and a freckled complexion. He smiled with his eyes, too, just as Joseph did. Without thinking, she blurted out,

"You look just like Joseph. You could be brothers!"

"Well, they say that about cousins sometimes," Lawrence replied, his face lighting up when he smiled. His brother, Michael, was as tall as Lawrence, but his hair was jet-black like that of his father and younger sister.

Joan was dispatched to bring coffee, and Alice fussed around them, checking if they'd eaten and instructing them to remove their outerwear and sit down as they were making the room look untidy!

Upon hearing the commotion and recognising his sons' voices, Hugh entered the drawing room with a broad grin and welcoming handshakes. Adelaide observed the cheerful family scene, all talking at once, and she felt the joy in the room lifting her spirits. She missed her own family but smiled inwardly at the thought of her upcoming trip to Liverpool to visit Joseph, Kitty, and their new baby, who had arrived safely only three days earlier. A boy they had named Samuel after Kitty's father. Joseph was not due back on board the *Mauretania* until after Christmas and had sent a letter inviting Adelaide to come and stay for a few days. "Try and stop me!" She said aloud after reading the letter.

"Play some more Christmas carols, Adelaide!" Rose's voice interrupted Adelaide's thoughts, and laughing, she happily obliged.

Chapter 32

Liverpool - December 1913

Adelaide exhaled with relief as the train finally pulled into Lime Street Station. The journey had taken longer than expected, and she couldn't recall ever feeling so cold. As the train departed London, snowy landscapes unfurled outside the window—glittering fields and frost-laced rooftops drifting past as they wound through towns with unfamiliar names. Her only companion, an elderly man, had disappeared behind his newspaper, choosing silence over conversation. Fortunately, Adelaide had come prepared, and her book proved to be a welcome escape from the long hours and lingering chill.

As Adelaide stepped off the train, her eyes immediately found Joseph in the crowd. He stood waving eagerly. "At last, you're here!" he called.

"Joseph, it is so good to see you." She ran into his outstretched arms and let his familiar hug envelop her.

"Come on, let's get you home. Kitty is excited to meet you."

After two bus rides, Adelaide was so cold that she had lost all feeling in her hands and feet. They had so much to talk about, they didn't know what to say first. Adelaide took the easy option and asked about baby Samuel.

"He's bonny, that's for sure. Always hungry and looks like me, so everyone says. How you can tell when a baby is only a few days old, I'll never know!"

"Has Kitty recovered? I can only imagine how awful it is to give birth."

"Oh, not at all. Kitty was so brave. I, on the other hand, was a nervous wreck. Pacing back and forth downstairs for what seemed like hours!"

"If that is all you had to endure, I think you had the easier role!" Adelaide laughed.

Finally, they reached Victoria Avenue. Adelaide was surprised at how small the neat row of terraced houses appeared compared to their aunt and uncle's spacious home in Dorset Square. Joseph took her hat and coat and told her to leave her bag where it was; he would take it upstairs later.

"Joseph, is that you?" a woman's voice called from the sitting room.

"No, dearie, it's the milkman, and I've found someone loitering at the railway station."

"Oh, Joseph, you're not funny. Bring Adelaide to sit by the fire." Adelaide entered one of the cosiest sitting rooms she had ever seen. Two armchairs were placed on either side of the fireplace, where Kitty sat with Samuel in her arms. She tried to get up, but Adelaide stopped her. "Please don't get up, you both look so cosy sitting there by the fire. I'd hate to disturb you."

"It is so wonderful to meet you at last. You are just as your brother described you!"

"Really? I was fourteen when he left home." Adelaide laughed, looking fondly at her brother.

"You haven't changed a bit," Joseph replied.

"Put the kettle on, would you love? I'll put Samuel in his crib, then we can have a good talk."

The next day, Joseph took Adelaide to the docks to see his ship. As they approached, she halted, her eyes widening in awe. The *Mauretania* towered over everything, its sheer size leaving her breathless. Tilting her head back, she strained to take in the vast structure, feeling almost insignificant beside it. Compared to the *Ayrshire*, the modest vessel she had travelled on, this was a giant.

"We can carry up to 450 passengers. Can you imagine that?" Joseph said, with pride in his voice. "It's like a massive floating hotel, and my job, along with the other engineers, is to make sure we maintain top speed. We've won the Blue Riband several times, you know."

"Yes, I do know. You have mentioned it several times in your letters." Adelaide replied with a smile, which made Joseph laugh.

"Sorry, but I am rather proud of her!"

Afterwards, Adelaide enjoyed a lovely afternoon with Kitty and the baby while Joseph went out to find a small Christmas tree and run various other errands. Kitty told her all about her life before she met Joseph.

"I was born in Chester, about forty miles from here, and we lived in a large house with servants. I bet Joseph didn't share that with you. Trying to hide her surprise, Adelaide shook her head. "No, he didn't. He just told me about the day he first met you and decided to marry you there and then."

Raising her eyebrows, Kitty shook her head. "He tells everyone that story, and if it weren't for his friend, Jack Mason, I wouldn't have believed it except that he was with Joseph when he announced his intentions at that first meeting."

Adelaide laughed. "That sounds like my brother!"

"My father was a Colonel in the Cheshire Regiment but was unfortunately killed at the end of the Boer War in 1901."

"Oh, I am so sorry."

"I was only thirteen years old at the time, and my mother had to give up our home and sell most of our possessions as we just had a widow's pension to live off. Mother never really recovered and died when I was eighteen, so I had to find work, and that's why I ended up working in the café by the Liverpool Docks. Some things are just meant to happen the way they do, and I'm glad I was there that day when your brother walked in with his friend."

Samuel began to cry, and Kitty excused herself to go and feed him. Left alone, Adelaide explored the small but cosy room, filled with trinkets from Joseph and Kitty's life together. When Kitty still hadn't returned, Adelaide wandered into the room at the front of the house, which she had noticed as she had come in. As she opened the door, she was met with a much smarter room, featuring a bottle green settee and armchair. Photographs lined the mantel: one captured their wedding day, and another showed them standing on the seafront, looking windswept and happy. There was a photograph of an Army officer with an older version of Kitty standing beside him. *They must be Kitty's parents,* Adelaide thought to herself. Then there was one of their parents and one of her sitting at the piano, smiling at the camera.

Just then, Adelaide heard the front door open and Joseph step inside, clutching a small fir tree in one arm and a shopping bag in the other. Standing in the doorway of the front parlour, she greeted him warmly. "Goodness, you look quite chilled! Let me take that bag for you."

"It's like the Arctic Circle out there," Joseph said with a laugh, "though the winter sun does its best when it bothers to appear. Where's Kitty?"

"She's gone to feed Samuel. I've been admiring your parlour—it's so handsome. Why don't you use it more often? It's much roomier than the sitting room."

"Heavens, no," Joseph replied with a smile. "Kitty wouldn't hear of it. It's our best room, kept for Sundays and special occasions. And it's cheaper to keep just one room warm."

Adelaide's cheeks coloured. She hadn't meant to highlight her brother's modest means, but he seemed entirely untroubled. *There's so much I've yet to understand about real life,* she thought, reproaching herself.

Over supper that evening, Joseph and Kitty were eager to hear all about Adelaide's life since Joseph had left home. She spoke of her time at Mrs Easterwood's Academy, her music studies, and the sorrow of losing Violet. She also felt she ought to tell them about Valentine and Eva, and what had happened to her at sea.

"Why didn't you tell us any of this before?" Joseph asked, his brow furrowed with concern. "What a dreadful ordeal to bear alone."

Adelaide tried to reassure him, explaining how kind Uncle Hugh, Aunt Alice, and William Armstrong had been throughout it all.

"I don't like the thought of her still roaming the streets with such hatred in her heart," Joseph said, visibly troubled. "What are the police doing about it?"

"They're searching for her, and for Valentine, too. Perhaps by the time I return to London, they'll have been found."

All too soon, Adelaide's visit drew to a close. She hugged Kitty tightly, then gently stroked Samuel's soft little cheek. Whispering so as not to wake him, she said, "You have a beautiful little boy. I'm so happy for you both."

Reaching into her travel bag, she pulled out several small parcels and placed them beneath their modest Christmas tree.

"Just a few little gifts for Christmas Day—and to say thank you for your warm welcome and hospitality."

"Oh, Adelaide, you needn't have done that," Kitty said, her voice thick with emotion. "But thank you. That's so thoughtful of you."

Later, at the train station, Adelaide said her sad farewells to Joseph. He gave her a big, brotherly hug, almost lifting her off her feet, which made her laugh. Setting her down, he grew serious.

"Promise me you'll be careful and look after yourself. If my shifts work out and I get shore leave, I promise Kitty and I will visit in time for your graduation."

"That would be wonderful! And I promise I will be careful," she replied. "But please don't worry, I'm sure all will be well by the time I'm back in London."

As the train pulled away, Adelaide waved from the carriage window. Joseph's tall figure stood on the platform, briefly illuminated by the pale morning sun before being swallowed by a billow of steam from the engine. Tears threatened, but she swallowed hard and found her seat. The carriage rattled gently as it began to move, the rhythmic clatter of wheels on the track offering a kind of comfort. Reaching into her bag, she opened her book and began to read, more for distraction than interest. Unable to concentrate, she used it as a shield to avoid conversation with the other passengers; the sound of their muffled voices and rustling newspapers filled the compartment. Deep in thought, she was grateful to have seen her brother again after so many years had passed. She wasn't sure what her parents would make of Joseph's modest life, but to her, it was clear that he and Kitty were blissfully happy with their home and their newborn son. Surely that was all that mattered. Kitty had been so warm and welcoming that Adelaide felt as though she'd known her forever. Her only sadness was that she would return to Wellington in a few months, and Joseph would stay in England. Still, she hoped she might persuade her parents to visit when they came to take her home.

Chapter 33

Dorset Square – January 1914

Adelaide was staring out of her bedroom window, lost in thought. It was raining steadily, and she shivered. The snow that had fallen before Christmas didn't last long and was replaced by dark grey clouds filled with rain and an icy wind that, according to Mrs Coates, "Could cut you in half."

Sitting at her desk, she tried but failed to write in her journal. Pausing for a moment, she glanced at William's note that had sat on her desk waiting for her return from Liverpool. Putting her pen down, she picked up the handwritten note. William had wished her a Happy Christmas and wanted to let her know that he had visited Scotland Yard and spoken with an Inspector Perkins, who had agreed to post some of his men around Dorset Square and the Royal Academy of Music, just as a precaution in case it was Eva she had seen. Placing the note back on the desk, she wondered what William had done for Christmas and hoped he'd managed to visit his family in Dorchester.

Christmas had passed quickly after she returned from visiting her brother. There had been a small cocktail party, which Adelaide found awkward as she didn't know anyone. It was a relief when Aunt Alice asked her to play the piano, giving her a sense of purpose. She received much praise, and the conversation with her aunt and uncle's guests became much easier afterwards.

Christmas morning was a new experience for her. The sky remained dark, and the air carried a crisp chill as everyone gathered around the breakfast table. When asked about her usual Christmas morning routine, Adelaide's cousins cried out in mock jealousy upon hearing that she typically began the day with a swim in the sea. After breakfast, they moved to the drawing room, where presents peeked out from beneath the tree. Adelaide was touched by the thoughtful gifts from her aunt, uncle, and cousins. She received several books, a new journal to write in, and a set of delicately hand-embroidered handkerchiefs, each bearing her initials alongside a sprig of lavender, undoubtedly her aunt's handiwork.

She felt confident in her choices, reassured by the delighted expressions on Lawrence and Michael's faces as they unwrapped the leather notebooks she had hurriedly bought from Daunt's bookshop on Christmas Eve. For Rose, she had chosen The Secret Garden, a favourite of hers, which she hoped would also become a favourite read for Rose. Her aunt had been delighted to receive a pair of grey kid gloves, thoughtfully selected after Adelaide had overheard her lamenting the loss of hers following a recent trip to the theatre. Uncle Hugh was equally impressed with his silk tie.

When Adelaide presented Mrs Coates with a box of chocolates, beautifully wrapped with a red ribbon, Mrs Coates forgot her usual stern demeanour and was genuinely delighted to receive such a thoughtful gift. "Why, thank you, Miss Adelaide, how kind of you! I shall sit by the fire later with a good book, and I'll help myself to the first layer at least."

Joan was thrilled to receive a knitted hat that matched her coat perfectly, and equally delighted with the bag of pear drops Adelaide had tucked alongside it. "Oh, thank you, Miss—you are so kind. My favourite sweets and a beautiful hat, too!" Adelaide smiled fondly at Joan, pleased to have brought her such happiness.

A knock at the door pulled Adelaide from her thoughts. "Come in!" she called.

Joan entered, carrying a parcel and a letter. "A young gentleman has just delivered these—said he was from a firm of solicitors." She paused, trying to recall the name. "Sorry, Miss,

I can't remember their name, but both the parcel and the letter have your name on them," Joan said, handing over the brown paper parcel and the official-looking envelope.

"How mysterious," Adelaide murmured, taking them from her.

"Oh yes, and Mrs Brokenshire asked me to remind you that luncheon is early today, as Mrs Coates is taking the afternoon off."

Adelaide nodded absently, already focused on the envelope. Joan gave a polite dip of the head and withdrew.

She didn't recognise the handwriting, but gasped as soon as she opened the envelope and unfolded the letter. "Valentine," she whispered, hardly daring to breathe. With trembling fingers, Adelaide began to read.

December 1913
London

Dear Adelaide,

You might be wondering what has happened to me after all this time, and I must begin by offering my sincere apologies for the length of this letter and for not having had the chance to see you in person. Once you have read what I must now reveal, I trust you will understand why. I owe you an explanation, and it is time I shared my side of the story. I pray you may find it in your heart to forgive me.

First, I must tell you that the time I spent teaching you remains among the greatest joys of my life, and I do not say this lightly. You possess a rare and natural gift for music, one that cannot be taught. I would never presume to claim credit for your accomplishments, for by the time I came to you, your technical mastery was already well established. The credit, along with your diligence and determination, belongs to Miss Ivery. I merely offered a little polish, as it were. Believe in yourself, my dear Adelaide. Before you is the opportunity to work alongside some of the finest musicians of our time. Don't hide your talents - share them with the world!

Now, I must confess to you certain dreadful truths that I have long carried, and I am ashamed to admit that I lacked the courage to act honourably. I married Eva because I had no choice. It pains me to say that I was not strong enough to resist her. As I have since discovered, I was not her only victim. Eva moved stealthily within the shadows, undaunted. She honed her skills aboard the ship that brought her to Wellington. Torn from the place she called home and from her beloved grandmother, she harboured a deep resentment, which I believe she channelled into harming others. She kept a notebook always upon her person, and would listen at doors, in corridors, and from darkened corners. Unseen, she gathered secrets and preyed upon the sorrows of others, blackmailing them and demanding payment for her silence. She never asked for large sums, only what she deemed each person could afford.

I was, indeed, one of those victims. Eva's price for silence was marriage and a passage back to Germany. Somehow, she secured my appointment at the Leipzig Conservatoire. In other circumstances, I would have rejoiced at the opportunity. But accepting meant leaving behind the one person I loved with every fibre of my being, yet could never be with. Had we been discovered, we would have been arrested. I feel no shame in telling you this, though I fear it may cause you pain. You know little yet of the world's cruelties, Adelaide, but this kind of love is forbidden by law. I had no choice but to accept Eva's terms. I am grateful she did not recognise my beloved when she saw us in the woods that day. At least I can keep their name out of all this.

After our marriage, I noticed Eva was never without her notebook. One night, while she slept, I took the chance to read

312

it. What I found horrified me. So many people, just ordinary folk, who had been ensnared. They had not committed grave crimes; they had only faltered, often for love.

During our time aboard the Ayrshire, I lived in constant fear that my true nature would be exposed. Eva never let me forget what I had sacrificed for her silence. She was the one who ransacked your cabin, needing to retrieve certain items. If they appeared to have been stolen by another, she would seem innocent. I have no proof, but I believe Eva is a member of a secret German society known as Die Stille Hand—The Silent Hand. If possible, please share this with Armstrong. I long to be free of these secrets and lies.

After your cabin was broken into, Eva feigned concern and played the victim with remarkable conviction. But it was not long before I uncovered the truth. She had two accomplices aboard the ship, hired by The Silent Hand to protect her and assist in retrieving the music box she had hidden in plain sight in your cabin. The true treasure lay within its lining: a fortune in diamonds entrusted to her by Hermann Wagner, the leader of The Silent Hand. She was to deliver them to a contact in Calais. The diamonds were destined for the Kaiser's war chest—the Silent Hand's contribution to rebuilding a more formidable navy.

It was Eva who left the knife and the note in your cabin on the final evening. That was when I realised she was unhinged. She kept insisting that "He" had told her to do it and that it was not her fault. I confronted her after we left the ship. She laughed and said you deserved to suffer and that she had hated you since school. I believe her mind is deeply disturbed. Please, be cautious.

We continued our journey and booked into a hotel near the train station. While there, I took the music box and this letter to a solicitor, instructing him to keep them safe until I returned. If I had not contacted him by January 1st, he was to send both to you.

If you are reading this letter, my dear Adelaide, then something dreadful has happened to me, and I fear Eva is more dangerous than ever.

I beg you to take care. Speak to Armstrong. I hope the authorities may find her before she finds you.

Forgive me,
Valentine.

Adelaide let the letter fall back onto her desk. Her hands trembled as a wave of shock, betrayal, and fear surged through her, leaving her breathless. Had Eva somehow caused Violet's death? And what of her mother's accident—had Eva pushed her on purpose? Trying to steady herself, Adelaide turned her attention to the parcel. She carefully untied the string and peeled away the brown paper. Beneath it lay the silver music box. She ran her fingers over the intricate filigree birds. Placing it gently on the desk, she lifted the lid, and the delicate notes of Für Elise drifted into the room. But as the melody played, her heart sank—the box was empty. Confused and fearful, she decided she must speak to her uncle and ask him to contact William. She desperately needed to see William.

Chapter 34

Scotland Yard, London - December 1913

Inspector Philip Perkins of Scotland Yard was a man with vast experience. He made decisions quickly and with purpose. His thirty-year service record was exemplary, and retirement was almost within reach. He had promised Mrs Perkins only yesterday that he would consider putting in his papers, but had unfortunately added 'in the New Year' at the last minute, leading to an ominous silence from his wife for the rest of the day. He was, therefore, quite relieved the next morning when his Sergeant, Frank O'Grady, had called by to pick him up and drive him through the snow and ice towards Scotland Yard. It was only two days before Christmas Eve, and all was quiet on the murder and serious crime front. By nine o'clock, he was savouring his first cup of tea of the day and reading a few case files without much enthusiasm. That was until a knock at the door announced the arrival of Major William Armstrong.

"Enter!" Shouted Inspector Perkins as Sergeant O'Grady ushered William into the Inspector's office.

"This is Major William Armstrong, Sir, with British Intelligence, recently returned from an assignment in Wellington, New Zealand."

William shook the Inspector's hand and took the seat offered by Sergeant O'Grady, who sat in the other chair beside him, producing a notebook and pen from his pocket, ready for anything that might need to be 'taken down.' Sergeant O'Grady was a big, burly man in his early 30s with narrow eyes and a truculent jaw. Inspector Perkins would often forgive his roughness because he was a handy person to have by your side and had often saved him from a few dangerous encounters, and even though he was rough around the edges, he was eager to learn and do better. Inspector Perkins liked that in a man.

Turning his attention to his visitor, he said, "What can I do for you, Major Armstrong?"

Normally confident in his work, William hesitated. How could he begin to explain the tangled web of intrigue he'd been drawn into since his posting to Wellington twelve months earlier?

"Thank you for seeing me, Inspector Perkins. It's difficult to know quite where to begin."

"Well," the inspector replied, settling into his chair, "I always find it best to start at the beginning, don't you?"

William drew a steadying breath and began. He first spoke of Eva and her resentment at being forced to leave Germany when her family moved to New Zealand, and about her irrational jealousy of Adelaide, which had begun when they were at school together.

I spent the past year in Wellington, monitoring activity connected to Imperial Germany. One individual in particular, a businessman named Hermann Wagner, drew our attention. The intelligence we collected suggested he was encouraging local businessmen, many of whom were of German descent, to invest in German infrastructure. They were making substantial profits, but the concern went beyond mere commerce.

William paused, uncertain whether the inspector wanted to say something. Instead, Perkins rose and walked to the window, gazing out over the London skyline. Then, turning with his hands clasped behind his back, he said, "Interesting story—but what exactly do you expect Scotland Yard to do?"

William nodded and continued. "Eva Spielmann was seen visiting Wagner's home on several occasions, behaving suspiciously. Nothing conclusive enough to warrant arrest, but troubling, nonetheless. Around that time, Adelaide's father, Mr Ellwood, a senior legal advisor at Government House, approached me. He'd been assisting with intelligence on German operatives posing as immigrants and passing on sensitive information. Since I was returning to England, he asked me to keep an eye on his daughter, who was travelling to London to study at the Royal Academy of Music. He suspected Eva and felt awful for involving Adelaide without warning her. On board the Ayrshire, it became clear Adelaide was being used as a cover—allowing them to travel without suspicion, and then onward to Germany."

Realising how complex and detailed all the information he was trying to impart was, William summarised the rest: the silver music box Eva had asked Adelaide to safeguard, the break-in, and the knife left with a threatening note on the final night of the voyage.

"With the captain's help, I kept watch until Adelaide was safely with her aunt and uncle. I gave Mr Brokenshire my card and asked him to contact me if anything seemed amiss. Then, just a few days ago, Adelaide was certain she had seen Eva near the Royal Academy. It happened quickly, and she couldn't be sure— but it's troubling. The Spielmanns were meant to be in Leipzig. Valentine had accepted a post at the Conservatoire of Music, yet when Adelaide wrote to him there, the letter was returned with a note stating he'd never arrived."

Inspector Perkins listened intently. Beside him, Sergeant O'Grady recorded every word in his black notebook. At last, the inspector spoke.

This is certainly an intriguing case. I agree—this woman, Eva, must be located, especially if she poses any danger to Miss Ellwood. Do you have a photograph I can share with my men? I'll instruct them to keep watch around Dorset Square and the Academy.

William reached into his coat and handed over a small photograph. "I'm very grateful, Inspector. With Christmas approaching, I'm due to visit my family as I haven't been home in some time. It would ease my mind to know the police are keeping watch."

As they parted, Inspector Perkins added, "I think it would be wise for me to meet Miss Ellwood. But it can wait until after Christmas. Perhaps you could arrange a visit in the New Year?"

"Of course, I will be in touch after Christmas. Thank you again."

William left Scotland Yard feeling much happier. He had been worried about Adelaide ever since she mentioned seeing Eva again. As he walked back to his office in Whitehall, his mind briefly dared to think of Adelaide Ellwood and how intriguing she seemed. Her shyness, petite frame, and beautiful pale blue eyes made her look delicate, but that wasn't the full story. She was clever and intelligent, and when he heard her play the piano for the first time on the ship, he was smitten. It was wrong that she was being used in this way, and he wanted to protect her with all his heart. Shaking his head, he knew falling in love would be a mistake. In his line of work, it would be almost impossible to have a serious relationship. To make matters worse, the woman he was falling for lived on the other side of the world and had told him quite categorically that she planned to dedicate her life to teaching and playing the piano.

Chapter 35

Dorset Square – January 1914

Adelaide walked in a daze towards her uncle's study and gently tapped on the door. She didn't know what he would think of the letter, but she knew she had to show it to him and ask for his help. Letting herself in, she smiled awkwardly at her uncle. He was deeply engrossed in a book and was surprised to see her standing there when he looked up. "Adelaide, my dear. What brings you to my study? Noticing her pale face and trembling body, he rose and led her to the sofa. "Sit down and tell me what's wrong?"

She handed him Valentine's letter. "I think it would be easier if you just read the letter, Uncle Hugh."

Adelaide sat in agonising silence as Hugh read the letter, uttering a few exclamations as he read. Finally, he put it down, looked towards his niece, and didn't speak for a few seconds.

"This is an ugly business indeed, and right now I think you need some hot, sweet tea; you are in shock. I'll ring for Joan and see if she can find your aunt, too."

It wasn't long before Joan brought in the tea, followed by her aunt.

"Adelaide, my dear. What has happened?"

Alice sat beside her, placing an arm around her shoulders and drawing her closer. The warmth of her aunt and uncle's kindness caused an unrestrained sob to rise deep within her tiny frame. "I don't understand why Valentine has written this letter, and I find the contents utterly upsetting and confusing. What do you think it all means?"

Alice looked over Adelaide's head at her husband with a puzzled expression. He picked up the letter and shook it slightly to draw attention to the letter in question. Untangling herself from her niece, Alice reached her hand out for Hugh to pass her the letter. Hugh hesitated at first, not wishing to subject his wife to its disturbing contents. Sighing, he placed it in Alice's outstretched hand. As Alice began to read the letter, Adelaide sipped the strong, hot tea Joan had given her, which soothed her a little.

"I can't believe what I'm reading," Alice exclaimed.

Hugh stood and took back the letter from his appalled wife. "I have left a message for William as he was not at his desk, which is damned inconvenient as we need to find out what all this means as soon as possible!"

Just then, the front doorbell rang. Moments later, they heard Joan open the door, followed by the sound of several heavy footsteps echoing down the hallway. She soon appeared in the drawing room doorway, announcing, "Major Armstrong, Inspector Perkins, and Sergeant O'Grady from Scotland Yard."

Alice and Hugh swiftly composed themselves. Adelaide sat upright, hurriedly trying to gather herself, as William paused at the threshold, momentarily puzzled by the solemn atmosphere. *Had they already found out?*

"Mr and Mrs Brokenshire, Adelaide," he began. "I'm sorry to arrive unannounced, but this is Inspector Perkins and Sergeant O'Grady from Scotland Yard. I'm afraid we're here on official business. I hope this isn't a bad time?"

Hugh gestured toward the seating area. "On the contrary, your timing is perfect. I have been trying to contact you. Adelaide has received a disturbing letter; one I believe you need to see."

"A letter, you say?" Inspector Perkins stepped forward. "May I take a look?"

Hugh handed it over. The Inspector read in silence, his brow furrowing. When he finished, he passed the letter to William. "This certainly casts everything in a new light," he said gravely, meeting William's eyes.

Adelaide found it excruciatingly embarrassing to sit there watching everyone read such a personal letter from Valentine. She directed her question at no one in particular and asked, "Why are you here? You can't have received Uncle Hugh's message that quickly."

Inspector Perkins stood again, knowing what he had to say needed to be said standing up. "I'm afraid we have some news about your friend, Valentine, Miss Ellwood."

"Valentine! You know where he is. Is he all right? Where is he?" Adelaide had so many questions.

"I'm sorry to say that Valentine's body was discovered in the River Thames yesterday. We can't rule out foul play yet, and we are just waiting on a post-mortem to be carried out to make certain." Inspector Perkin's crisp, matter-of-fact words were like shards of glass hitting Adelaide's senses. She let out a cry and pressed her handkerchief to her mouth in an attempt to stop herself from any embarrassment.

"This is just too awful. I think my niece has had enough shocks for one day. Perhaps it would be better if I took her to her room, and you could talk to my husband." Alice's strained voice broke through the silence as the others watched Adelaide with concerned faces.

Adelaide shook her head, "No, please, I must know what happened. It is all right, Aunt Alice. I am all right, I promise."

Alice took hold of Adelaide's hand, squeezing it as if trying to give her courage, even though she was finding it difficult to take in the news herself.

Inspector Perkins took his cue to continue. "Valentine's death and the fact that you have received this letter from him indicate he took his own life, unable to live with what he and his wife have done. However, as I said, I will not rule out foul play yet as the doctor on the scene noticed bruising on each arm, as if he had been held or taken roughly by the arms and perhaps shoved into the Thames."

"What about Eva? Have you found her? She is the one who has caused all this." Adelaide had gone from shock, horror, and sorrow to anger.

"I take it you knew this German couple very well before coming to England?" Sergeant O'Grady had been silent until now and wanted to expedite the proceedings. He felt that Inspector Perkins was sometimes far too soft.

Adelaide looked at Sergeant O'Grady with utter distaste. "They are not German; they are citizens of New Zealand. I can't believe Valentine had anything to do with Eva's deception. It says so in his letter; his only crime was weakness in not standing up to Eva in the first place."

"Same thing, as they were born in Germany," O'Grady said smugly.

"That's enough, O'Grady." Inspector Perkins was beginning to be irritated by his Sergeant's interrogation skills. "Miss Ellwood has had a terrible shock, and we still need to find Eva. Now Valentine is dead, who knows what she may be capable of? Also, Adelaide now has the music box, which we need to check to see if it still contains the diamonds."

Realising he had overstepped the mark, O'Grady apologised and busied himself by taking notes. William and Hugh began to examine the music box, and nothing appeared out of the ordinary. Then, William noticed a small tear in the blue velvet lining, and he gently tugged at it. Eventually, the false bottom was revealed, and inside it glittered five large diamonds. William emptied them into his hand, and everyone gasped.

"Eva mustn't have had the chance to deliver them to her contact. Valentine at least put a stop to that, but unfortunately, it has cost him his life." Inspector Perkins said bluntly.

William was watching Adelaide and felt awful for causing her so much pain. "Adelaide, this means Eva will most definitely be in the area, waiting for an opportunity to steal back the diamonds. I will post two men outside the house to ensure she doesn't try to break in looking for them."

"I do not want two policemen standing outside our home!" Alice spoke sternly. "It is bad enough that my niece has somehow become involved. I don't know what I will tell her parents. I really don't." She sat down almost in a heap, and Hugh went to her, patting her hand and offering her words of comfort.

William felt he needed to speak up for Adelaide. "I believe Adelaide is innocent in all this and has been used most dreadfully, all to satisfy a disturbed woman's need to return to Germany. I am sure Eva Spielmann is unhinged." Adelaide looked up at William, her delicate blue eyes conveying gratitude; at that moment, he felt an overwhelming sense of protectiveness towards her.

Adelaide suddenly thought of Ernst, Marta and Giselle. "Has anyone told Valentine's family? They will be devastated. Do they need to know everything?"

Understanding what Adelaide was trying to say, William nodded and looked to Inspector Perkins for guidance. "I don't think we need to mention the letter unless further evidence comes to light, and I feel his family are involved as well."

"Thank you." Adelaide's voice was a mere whisper.

"I think we have everything we need for now." Inspector Perkins said. "May we take the letter as evidence?"

Adelaide nodded, grateful that the letter was being taken as far away from her as possible. There was so much she didn't understand and didn't want to. The letter and music box were placed in a paper bag and carried outside by Sergeant O'Grady. William turned to speak to Adelaide, "Are you continuing with your studies?"

"Of course. It's the reason why I am here. I won't let Eva ruin that for me. My parents are coming in time for my Graduation and the end-of-year concert, and I want to make them proud. Eva is not going to stop me!" Her voice was quivering, and William was impressed by her determination.

William lifted his hands in surrender. "Apologies, I was only thinking of your safety."

Softening her tone a little, Adelaide said, "I appreciate your concern. But I doubt Eva, even in her disturbed state, would think I'd be carrying the diamonds about my person, would she?"

"No, probably not, but please be careful. Don't walk anywhere alone, and you can contact me anytime, day or night, if you are worried."

"Thank you. Oh, and would it be possible for the music box to be returned to me when you have finished with it? Minus the diamonds, of course." Adelaide gave a weak smile.

"Of course, I don't see why not," William replied.

Chapter 36

The Royal Academy of Music, Lent Term - January 1914

A new term was beginning, and Lawrence insisted on accompanying Adelaide on her walk to the Royal Academy of Music. A frost had settled overnight, and the icy wind reddened their noses as their breath curled into the cold morning air while they strolled through Regent's Park. Uncle Hugh felt it necessary to explain to his sons what had happened to Adelaide and all about Eva Spielmann. Adelaide was mortified. She wished the whole affair could vanish as though it had never happened. But Uncle Hugh spoke gently, explaining that his only concern was her safety. Lawrence and Michael were both horrified and fascinated by the revelations, and they solemnly vowed to protect their cousin at any cost. Adelaide was visibly upset and embarrassed by the whole business and spoke in her defence.

"I am not a damsel in distress, and I'm sure Eva is long gone, especially now that poor Valentine is no longer with us." She couldn't quite bring herself to say the word dead. It was still too painful.

"Well, I need to go and purchase some supplies for my return to University next week, so I'm going that way anyway," Lawrence said nobly and grinned at her.

"I'm going to Scotland this term," Lawrence announced as they walked along Marylebone Road towards the Royal Academy of Music.

"Oh, really. What will you be doing there?" Adelaide asked, looking up at her huge cousin. They looked such an odd couple as they walked side by side—Lawrence's height at odds with Adelaide's tiny stature.

"I'm going on my first excavation of a Chieftain's village not far from Hadrian's Wall." I need to buy plenty of warm and waterproof clothing as I reckon it will be rather chilly up there, but I can't wait."

"It will be fascinating to discover and examine ancient artefacts to understand how we lived thousands of years ago," Adelaide replied, sharing her cousin's enthusiasm.

"Indeed. I will never tire of it, and if all goes well, I hope to join Professor Johnson on an excavation trip to Egypt next year. As long as I keep my nose clean and my grades up!"

"Keep your nose clean? What has that got to do with studying and going to Egypt?" Adelaide looked up at her cousin, a confused expression on her face.

Lawrence started laughing, "Oh, Adelaide, you really are the best! It's just a saying. It means to avoid trouble. Don't you use that phrase in New Zealand?"

"No, we don't. Well, I haven't heard anyone say it." Adelaide raised her eyes and laughed with him.

The entrance to the Royal Academy of Music was bustling with students. "Enjoy your first day back!" Lawrence shouted as he left Adelaide to navigate the steps leading up to the main entrance. She clutched her bag and made her way to Mr Whitemore's music studio. Despite the grief she had felt over Valentine's death, she had diligently practised throughout the Christmas holidays. It had been her solace, rekindling memories of their time together when they were teacher and student, before all the sadness. After her piano lesson, Mr Whitemore congratulated her on her improvement. They discussed the upcoming concert and whether she would like to accompany the orchestra again for some performances. Adelaide agreed without hesitation. Her next lesson was with Mr Macpherson, but not until two o'clock. Wondering what to do, she realised she was hungry. In the café, she spotted Sonia Kirkland sipping tea and reading a book. "Sonia! Happy New Year. Did you have a lovely Christmas?"

"Adelaide! I was hoping to see you today. Happy New Year to you, too. What did you think of your first wintery Christmas?"

"Cold! But I had a lovely time. My aunt, uncle, and cousins made my first English Christmas very special, and I got to see my brother, sister-in-law, and little nephew." Adelaide sat beside her friend, placing her lunch tray on the table. "It's good to be back, isn't it?"

Sonia groaned. "You speak for yourself. I'm so behind with my assignments. We went to stay with my grandparents over Christmas, and they don't have a piano, and it was so noisy I didn't have a chance to study."

"Oh, I'm sorry to hear that. Hopefully, you can catch up. Can I help you with anything?"

Just then, Evie arrived and greeted her friends. The three girls spent the next half hour talking about their Christmas celebrations, Adelaide being careful not to mention anything about Valentine or Eva.

At two o'clock precisely, she entered Mr MacPherson's classroom and began what was to be an enjoyable hour's lecture on Aural Harmony. Afterwards, she sat in the foyer, waiting for Lawrence to collect her, reading through her notes and thinking about the assignment Mr MacPherson had just set for the class. She checked the large ornate clock on the wall several times and began to worry. An hour had almost passed, and although it was only four o'clock, it was growing dark outside. Ignoring her promise to William, she packed her papers into her case and started walking back to Dorset Square. *Lawrence will catch me up, no doubt*. She assured herself and distracted herself by thinking about a complicated piece of music she was to play at the concert. Humming the music quietly to herself, she was unaware of a figure lurking just beyond the glow of the streetlights, matching her step for step.

Eva had been waiting for Adelaide most of the afternoon. Knowing she would have to leave the building soon, Eva paced up and down outside until her patience was rewarded. Valentine's death had unsettled her, but the men assigned to help retrieve the diamonds had told her it was necessary. "We had our orders. He knew too much and was surplus to requirements." Ralf had yelled at her. She couldn't watch when they had seized him. She had closed her eyes, trying to block out the sounds of a struggle, Valentine's cry of surprise, and the loud splash as he hit the icy river. He didn't stand a chance, and when it was over, Eva felt nothing except relief that she had obeyed the insistent voice in her head.

Christmas had been difficult. Ralf and Tobias, Her *Silent Hand* contacts kept threatening her, telling her to stay in London until the diamonds were recovered. Her lodgings were cold, dark, and damp, and there was no money left after her trunk was stolen within two days of arriving in London. She had been reduced to selling some of Valentine's clothes and pawning his watch so she could eat.

January brought Eva out of her dingy lodgings and into the bustling city. She had to pawn her wedding ring to buy smarter clothing that would help her blend in while keeping an eye on Adelaide. She knew it had been a close call when she spotted Adelaide sitting in a warm café, laughing with her friends. Her dirty old clothes and messy hair made her stand out, and Eva was sure Adelaide had seen her. *There must be no more mistakes*. The sinister voice warned her. Eva flinched. He was angry today, she thought, as she headed towards Marylebone.

The pavement and entrance to the Royal Academy of Music were a hive of activity that morning, and Eva tried to blend in with the eager students ready to begin the new term. Walking past the entrance was tricky as she tried to avoid the many students carrying their various instruments into the building. One young woman struggled with a large cello-shaped case until a porter came out to help. Eva chastised herself for not bringing a bag with her to blend in more. As she moved further away from the building, she soon spotted Adelaide walking with a tall man. That could be a problem. Watching them at a safe distance, she felt relieved as the man carried on walking, waving at Adelaide as she went inside.

After that, all Eva could do was wait. After a few hours, her associates, Ralf and Tobias, arrived, visibly angry and wanting to know what the hold-up was.

"She is bound to come out soon," Eva nodded towards the Royal Academy building. You go to the park; she always walks home that way. Keep out of sight but be ready." The two men nodded curtly and disappeared into the crowds.

The park was still pretty, even in the winter. The pond had frozen over, and grey squirrels were scampering up and down the trees, retrieving their hidden supplies and hoping for an offering of some food from a kind human. Adelaide loved their bushy tales and was smiling at one close to her. She bent down and held her hand out, apologising to the creature that she had nothing to offer. He began to move forward, but, realising there was no reward, he scampered up the nearest tree. Adelaide stood watching the creature, shouting her apologies as it ran up into the branches and out of sight.

From her hiding place, Eva seethed with rage. *How can you be so happy? This is all your fault.* She struck the tree beside her with a clenched fist, letting out a sharp cry of pain.

Adelaide paused and glanced around. In the dimming light, she saw only a few distant figures hurrying home against the cold. She lingered for a moment, then continued. The air was biting, her breath swirling in front of her. She tugged her collar higher around her neck and ears, grateful for the warmth of her thick winter coat.

Watching the squirrels had slowed her pace, and now a chill had crept into her bones. Spotting the park's exit ahead, she quickened her steps, the thought of a steaming mug of hot chocolate urging her forward. As she passed a small grove of trees near a dense shrub, a robin darted out and perched delicately on a low branch, singing a sweet, clear melody. Adelaide stopped, captivated. Robins, she decided, were the most enchanting birds she had ever seen. Suddenly, the quiet moment was shattered as she heard the sound of heavy footsteps coming up quickly behind her. Turning instinctively, she barely had time to react before strong arms grabbed her roughly and dragged her into the thicket. She was pulled out of sight, her back scraped by branches. An oily hand clamped over her mouth, the stench making her gag. Then, out of the shadows, Eva emerged—eyes wild, a knife glinting in her hand.

"Tell me where the diamonds are," she hissed, "and I'll let you live."

Adelaide tried to scream, but the owner of the oily and diesel-scented hand covered her mouth again.

"If you tell me where the diamonds are, the men will leave you alone."

The hand was released from her mouth. "I, I haven't got them. I gave them to Inspector Perkins of Scotland Yard. He is looking for you." Eva screamed something in German at her. Adelaide was starting to feel faint when, suddenly, Eva lurched forward. There was a flash of metal, and she felt a sharp pain in her side and then darkness.

"Adelaide, Adelaide, wake up, please, an ambulance is coming. You are safe. She opened her eyes to see William kneeling beside her; her coat had been opened, and he was pressing something soft onto her side. His face was full of anguish. "I'm so sorry I couldn't get to you in time. I am so sorry. You'll be all right, but we need to get you to the hospital."

"Eva, it was Eva … and two men. I think from the ship. They smelled like the ship. How did you know where to find me?"

"Lawrence had been delayed and was worried, so he got word to me. I must have just missed you. Don't worry about all that now. We have the men in custody, and Inspector Perkins is interrogating them now."

"And Eva, where is Eva?" Adelaide tried to focus on William's face, but everything went black again.

Chapter 37

It had been snowing again. Adelaide was reminded of the first time she watched the snow with Joan through her bedroom window, before Valentine's death, before being attacked. So much had happened. Dr Potts had just arrived to check on his patient. She was desperate to return to her studies but accepted she had to wait until she was well again and fully recovered. The doctor had entered, flustered and cold. His nose was bright red, and Aunt Alice quickly sent Joan to bring him some hot tea with a nip of brandy in it. "You are exceedingly kind, Mrs Brokenshire. It's wicked out there. Now then, how's my patient doing?"

The wound had healed well, and Dr Potts had already removed the stitches. When she was first taken to the hospital, the surgeon had told her how the angels must have been smiling down on her that day. Though the wound was deep, no vital organs had been damaged. At the time, she hadn't felt particularly lucky, but she had appreciated the sentiment. Now, Dr Potts was pleased with her recovery and assured her there was no need for further visits so long as she avoided anything too strenuous. Once he had gone, she turned to her aunt and pleaded to be allowed to return to her studies.

"Certainly not!" Her Aunt responded with alarm. "Firstly, it is snowing and freezing outside, and secondly, you are not to go out anywhere without a chaperone."

"But Aunt Alice, I need to finish my studies; otherwise, I will have wasted my time here, and Eva will have won."

"Nonsense. Your uncle has spoken to your tutors, and they have been very understanding. You are already up to standard, and over the next month, you will only need to pass two more examinations and complete your dissertation, which I know you have been working on since your arrival. Rose and I must go out tomorrow if the snow has abated, and it is only an if; we will accompany you to the Academy."

"Thank you, Aunt Alice. You have been so wonderful about all this, and Uncle Hugh. I am so sorry I brought all this trouble to your happy home."

"You have nothing to apologise for. Eva Spielmann is responsible for all this, and the sooner she is captured, the better. Are you still set on going to Valentine's funeral?"

"Yes. I must pay my respects and say goodbye properly."

"I think it will be very distressing for you. Will you not reconsider?"

"I know it will be very upsetting, but my mind is made up. Uncle Hugh and William will be there. I will be fine, I promise."

"Very well, as you know, the family does not usually encourage women to attend funerals, but I suppose these are different circumstances; however, I have my reservations about you going."

"I will be all right, I promise."

During her recovery, William visited frequently, and when she felt strong enough, they took short walks around the private gardens of Dorset Square. He was charming and funny, sharing many stories about his childhood in Dorchester and his service in the Army. Adelaide thought he had already experienced so much at such a young age. She had decided he must be around the same age as Joseph, and she was certain her brother had enjoyed many adventures in the Merchant Navy as well. When Adelaide told William this, he laughed and, shaking his head, said, "Not many people have experienced what you have and lived to tell the tale. You are a very strong and resilient young lady, and you've shown great courage."

Adelaide was touched by William's words and smiled fondly at him. At the same time, she wondered where this might lead. In a few months, she would return home to Wellington, while

William would stay in London, as the situation with Germany and the rest of Europe remained very unstable. She had plans to teach and perform, something she couldn't do if she were married. It wouldn't be fair, and when William kissed her one afternoon, she pulled back and tried to explain how she felt. He was a little hurt, but he understood. He had no idea where he would be stationed next, but he made her promise to always keep in touch. He gave her the address of his commanding officer in Whitehall so that wherever he was, her letters would find him.

On the day of Valentine's funeral, William arrived promptly to escort Adelaide and her uncle to the church. He had been granted the use of a car and driver, and was grateful to offer Adelaide and her family a comfortable journey to the cemetery. Arranging a proper burial service for Valentine had proved difficult, as it had never been proved conclusively that he had been murdered. In the end, Reverend Turner relented, and the funeral arrangements were made.

Valentine's uncle and aunt, Ewald and Minna Spielmann, were waiting in the car. Ernst had written to his brother, pleading with him to represent him at his son's funeral. Ewald duly obliged and was grateful to Major Armstrong for contacting them and organising all their travel arrangements, including securing a decent hotel at a reasonable price. His wife, Minna, was less understanding and had accompanied her husband under duress. She had never forgiven her brother-in-law for taking his family to the other side of the world. She believed he should have brought them to Amsterdam, as she and Ewald had done, where they had made a good life for themselves.

Hugh helped Adelaide into the car, and she smiled shyly at the elderly couple sitting opposite them. Hugh sat beside her, and William jumped into the passenger seat. Hugh made the introductions, and everything was civil, if not a little awkward. Ewald and Minna spoke little English, while Hugh and Adelaide had no grasp of Flemish or German. As they travelled towards the church, the language barrier loomed between them, a silent presence in the confined space of the vehicle, forcing communication into hesitant nods and fleeting smiles.

Reverend Turner stood outside the church waiting to greet them. He was a portly figure, and his robes did nothing to flatter his rotund belly and double chin. Yet his kind features softened the impression, and he welcomed each of them with quiet dignity. Inside, the coffin was already in place. Without any next of kin in the country, Valentine had been bound for a pauper's grave until Hugh and William stepped in, ensuring he was laid to rest in an oak coffin. Apart from the white lilies that lay on the coffin, which Alice had provided, Adelaide couldn't help but think about how lonely the coffin looked and how sad that made her feel.

The service was simple, stripped of personal tributes with no recollections of Valentine's life and his accomplishments. When the service had finished, the pallbearers carefully lifted the coffin and began the walk to Valentine's final resting place.

As Reverend Turner began the committal, Adelaide stood beside her uncle, drawing comfort from his steady presence. When she leaned into him, he gently took her hand. She held a single white rose in her free hand, and once the coffin had been lowered into the ground, she gently threw it on top of the coffin and whispered her farewells.

Since reading Valentine's letter, his confession and the startling revelation of his true nature, Adelaide's feelings towards him had shifted. A few days after Inspector Perkins had taken the letter away, her aunt sat her down and, in the gentlest terms she could manage, explained that it was not unheard of for two men to share "relations," as she phrased it. Yet, she added with quiet gravity, such bonds were considered unnatural by society and, if discovered, punishable by law.

Lawrence and Michael, with less restraint, had filled in the details more vividly, leaving Adelaide bewildered and struggling to grasp the possibility of such relationships. But after much reflection, she came to her own quiet conclusion: *perhaps one does not choose whom to love. Perhaps love chooses for you.* Rather than feel betrayed or angry, Adelaide resolved to remember Valentine not for the secrets he had kept, but for the gifted musician and devoted teacher he had been.

As the time came to leave, Hugh walked ahead with Reverend Turner, making sure to offer his thanks for giving Valentine a decent burial. Adelaide watched as Minna threw some soil onto the coffin and whispered a prayer, crossing herself as she did. Minna then joined her husband and walked towards the church. Turning to follow them, a cluster of ancient moss-covered gravestones caught her attention, and a shiver crept up her spine. Had she seen someone or something lurking in the shadows, watching? Then, before she could even cry out, Eva emerged like a spectre of fury. Wind tangled her wild hair, her eyes ablaze with unbridled hatred. The sheer force of Eva's charge sent Adelaide sprawling onto the muddy ground. The breath knocked from her lungs. In an instant, Eva was upon her, straddling her with terrifying speed, fists clenching around Adelaide's head. The first slam was jarring. Then another. And another. Her skull rattled against the damp earth as Eva shrieked, "Ich verfluche dich für immer!" *I curse you forever …*

Gasps of horror echoed through the graveyard as William fought to tear her away. It took everything he had to wrench her free, locking his arms around her in a vice-like grip as Eva fought with the ferocity of a cornered beast, her nails clawing, her fists pounding. She twisted, kicked, and screamed with rage, her teeth sinking into his hand in a savage attempt to break free. He gritted his teeth against the pain, refusing to relent. Chief Inspector Perkins and Sergeant O'Grady had been standing at a respectful distance, and the sheer speed of Eva's attack was like a lightning strike, unrelenting and utterly unexpected.

O'Grady, what are you doing? For God's sake, man, help Major Armstrong!" Perkins's shout jolted the Sergeant into motion. He surged forward, slamming into Eva and William, sending them crashing to the ground. She writhed beneath them, her cries shattering the stillness of the graveyard, but they held firm, wrestling her into submission, cold steel cuffs snapping shut around her wrists.

In the chaos, Hugh had managed to pull Adelaide up from the ground, carrying her toward the sanctuary of the church.

When William was certain Eva was contained, he raced to the church. The scene before him was a portrait of quiet devastation. Minna and Ewald sat in the pews, their faces pale, their hands clenched together in shared shock. Reverand Turner was handing Hugh a blanket to drape around Adelaide's trembling frame. Her clothes were soaked through and streaked with mud. Her hair hung in dishevelled strands around her pale face. Apart from a few scratches, she appeared unharmed, but the shaking in her limbs spoke volumes. William sank to his knees beside her, gathering her icy hands in his own. "Adelaide, I'm so sorry. She came out of nowhere. I wasn't fast enough."

She met his gaze, "I'm all right, really. Have you caught her?" Her teeth chattered as she spoke.

His jaw tightened. "Yes. Eva is in custody. She will never, ever, hurt you again. It's over."

The enormity of what had just happened crashed down on her, and a strangled sob tore through her as she flung her arms around him. William, momentarily stunned, wrapped her up in his embrace, holding her for as long as she needed.

Chapter 38

Royal Academy of Music, Graduation Concert – January 1914

Sir Alexander Mackenzie, Principal of the Royal Academy of Music, stepped onto the stage to a generous round of applause. He waited for the sound to settle before offering the audience a warm smile.

"Ladies, gentlemen, and students, both past and present, it is a great honour to welcome you this evening. Our students have rehearsed tirelessly this term to showcase their collective musical talents, and I am confident you will find tonight's programme exceptional. In addition to the assembled orchestra, three outstanding pianists will accompany them at various points throughout the performance. So, without further ado, please welcome our first pianist, Miss Adelaide Ellwood."

A fresh wave of applause filled the auditorium. Adelaide nodded politely to Sir Mackenzie, then took her seat at the piano, waiting for the room to fall silent.

The orchestra was poised and ready as Sir Mackenzie raised his baton, the motion deft and theatrical, as if conjuring music from thin air. Then the first notes rang out, bold and commanding. Adelaide's small, delicate hands flew across the keys with dramatic precision.

William sat transfixed, checking his programme and making a mental note that she was performing Liszt's *Piano Concerto No. 1*. He was eager to impress Adelaide after the concert with his newfound knowledge.

Seated beside Alice, Marie watched her daughter with a mixture of pride and relief, grateful for how well Adelaide had endured such a harrowing ordeal. She would never forget the day Robert had sat her down and told her everything of the horrors Adelaide had faced since leaving Wellington: Eva's unforgivable cruelty, Violet's tragic death, and her accident. Such dreadful things, she thought, had no place in the lives of people of their standing. Her initial shock soon gave way to a simmering anger not only at Robert for keeping it all from her but at Eva's parents as well. She had half a mind to march down to their bookshop, give them a piece of her mind, and see to it that none of her friends ever set foot in that establishment again.

Robert, ever the voice of reason, placed a steadying hand on hers. "It wasn't their fault," he insisted. "I have it on good authority that they were entirely innocent in all of this."

"Innocent!" Marie's voice rose, sharp and incredulous. "They are Eva's parents, Robert. How can they not be to blame?"

"Marie, dearest, please try to calm yourself," he said, his tone firm yet soothing. "I've booked an earlier passage to England, and I think you should focus on packing. It wouldn't be wise to interfere in an ongoing investigation. Promise me you won't visit Mr and Mrs Miller."

Marie's anger simmered beneath the surface, but the tasks ahead softened its edge. Reluctantly, she nodded. The demands of preparing for their journey to England left her little time to dwell on the injustices of the past.

Robert exhaled slowly, a quiet pride swelling in his chest as he watched Adelaide. Her resilience, her ability to rise above the cruelties she had endured and focus on her studies, filled him with both admiration and a sense of relief. Yet, a shadow of regret lingered. Beside him sat Joseph, who had arrived in London with Kitty and was warmly welcomed by the family, but the moment had not been as straightforward as he had hoped. When Joseph reached for his hand, the old disappointments flared up. Instead of embracing the reunion, Robert had offered little more than a stiff nod, an echo of past hopes that had gone unfulfilled. He told himself his standards were born out of love: Joseph was to follow in his footsteps as a successful lawyer, Adelaide to marry well and bring him grandchildren. But the choices of his children were theirs alone, and he had no right to demand otherwise. Even as the ache of lost dreams pressed against his chest, he forced himself to accept their lives as they were, though it pained him deeply to let go.

He suddenly realised that the music had stopped. Jolted from his thoughts, he joined the rest of the audience and clapped eagerly, shouting a few bravos for good measure.

As Adelaide took her bow with Sir Mackenzie, she looked out onto the smiling faces of her family. The only person who had been unable to attend was Lawrence, who, as he explained in his letter of apology, was still "Up to his neck in Scottish mud!"

Michael and Rose were clapping enthusiastically and cheering next to an equally excited Joan, who had been allowed to attend after Adelaide and Rose had insisted that she should be included. Joan stood clapping and grinning up at Adelaide. Dressed in her Sunday best, she was in awe of the beautiful and ornate concert hall and had even bought herself a programme as a keepsake of such a special evening, one she would never forget.

After the concert, everyone returned to Dorset Square, where drinks and a light supper were served. Adelaide stood by the window of her aunt and uncle's large drawing room and gazed happily at all the dear faces. Seeing her parents and brother in the same room again was the best gift of all. A wave of exhaustion engulfed her. The music she had been asked to play was strenuous and had taken a lot out of her. As soon as she was able, she escaped to her uncle's study, where she kicked off her shoes, sighed with relief, and sank into a chair. Tilting her head back, she closed her eyes, letting the quiet settle around her until a voice interrupted.

"There you are! I've been sent to find you."

Recognising William's voice, Adelaide groaned without opening her eyes. "I'm exhausted. Playing the piano takes so much out of you."

William leaned against the doorway, grinning. "Should I go back and tell them I couldn't find you?"

Her blue dress was gathered up, legs curled beneath her, and she suddenly became aware of how dishevelled she must look. Opening her eyes, she stretched her legs into a more dignified position.

"You were incredible tonight, Adelaide. I was quite mesmerised by your performance. I understand why the piano is your passion and why teaching and performing mean so much to you. Just don't forget me on your travels. And when you're invited to perform for the King, be sure to stop by and say hello."

Adelaide laughed, looking up at him. "Don't be silly. I doubt I'll ever perform for the King! But one day, if I can make a living from performing and teaching, it is a dream of mine to open a music academy. It's so difficult for students to reach all their grades on the other side of the world, and I want to change that if I can."

"If anyone can, Adelaide, you can."

"Thank you, William. I don't know how I would have survived all this without you. You are my knight in shining armour."
William was about to respond when Rose burst in, grabbing Adelaide's hand and pulling her to her feet.

"Adelaide, you can't hide away in here! You're the guest of honour. Everyone wants to talk to you."

Adelaide rolled her eyes at William, who matched the gesture before following her back into the drawing room, where Hugh was merrily serving cocktails while Joan, back in uniform, moved between guests with a tray of canapés.

Marie, seated next to Alice, was enjoying one of Hugh's famous cocktails. She felt exhausted. The journey by sea had been long, and it had been hard to relax as she was impatient to see her daughter after her awful ordeal. It had taken Marie a few days to start believing that Adelaide had emerged from the situation unscathed and with no hint of scandal.

"Good heavens, Marie," Alice exclaimed when she shared her worries with her sister-in-law.

"Adelaide has received nothing but sympathy and has been inundated with good wishes. Even the Royal Academy has been so understanding."

"That be as it may, I can't help worrying. Adelaide is such a sensitive soul. Will she ever be able to trust anyone ever again?"

"Oh, Marie dear, you need not worry too much about that. I have noticed quite a change in Adelaide during her time in London. I believe the awful events that have plagued her since Eva appeared in her life have only made her stronger and more resilient."

"I hope you are right, Alice, I really do."

Adelaide joined her mother and aunt, declining a cocktail, but instead, helped herself to some of the delicious-looking canapés served by Joan. Smiling at her, Adelaide asked. "Did you enjoy the concert, Joan?"

"I did, Miss. It was wonderful to hear such beautiful music. I have never been to a concert like that before. I will never forget it."

"Adelaide, you were wonderful, dear. I was so proud of you performing in an orchestra, and you did so well, too. Especially in front of someone so talented as Sir Alexander Mackenzie!" Marie enthused.

"Thank you. We had so many rehearsals; I thought my hands would stop working at one point. But it was so worth it. It has been a remarkable experience."

During a pause in the conversation, Adelaide noticed that Kitty was sitting on her own, looking a little lost. "Excuse me, I must check that Kitty is all right. It must be quite daunting meeting us all like this for the first time."

Marie lowered her voice and said, "If you must. It wouldn't have been a problem if Joseph had chosen someone a little more educated and used to society."

"Mother!" Adelaide whispered, her shock showing all over her face. "How can you say such an awful thing? If you just tried to get to know Kitty, you would see what a wonderful person she is, and you have a grandson, too!"

"Indeed. That's all well and good, but as I probably will never see him grow up, what's the point?"

Adelaide, already overtired and emotional from the concert, could find no suitable words to respond to her mother and felt a sadness creeping over her.

"Well, I am not going to ignore my nephew as he grows up, regardless of the distance."

As she walked away from her mother, she didn't notice Joseph standing behind her, unaware of the sadness etched on his face. He understood then that his parents would never accept his wife and the life that he chose, and he knew that this would be the last time he would ever see them. He would, however, never forget his sister's words and felt immense gratitude for the love his dear sister had shown to Kitty.

"Hello Kitty." Adelaide sat down beside her sister-in-law. "This is all a bit overwhelming, isn't it?"

Kitty smiled and tried her best not to look as uncomfortable as she was feeling right at this minute. "Congratulations, Adelaide. You are indeed as talented as your brother has always been telling me!"

Adelaide chuckled, "Oh, I'm sure he tells you all about my misdemeanours too. I bet I was such an annoying little sister."

"Maybe just one or two stories. But always told with love."

"I'm going to miss you all so much when I return home at the end of the month." A warm smile crossed her face. "However, I plan to return to England one day, though. Thanks to Mr Matthay, I already have invitations to perform and lecture."

"That's wonderful news." Kitty's face softened with pride. "I hope you'll write as often as you can. I want Samuel to grow up knowing he has a famous aunt and to understand that with enough effort, anything is possible."

"I promise to write often, as I'd love to hear all your news and how my nephew is getting on, of course. Joseph sends wonderful letters, but they're all about his ship, how fast it travels, and how incredible the engines are!"

Kitty laughed, well aware of how easily Joseph became animated when discussing the *Mauretania* and its powerful engines.

"What are you two laughing at?" Rose strolled over, curiosity flickering in her eyes.

Standing by the fireplace, Robert, Hugh, Joseph and Michael were deep in discussion with William, all eager to know what was happening to Eva now that she had been arrested. Eva had been in prison since her arrest in March, and a date had still not been set for her trial.

Overhearing the men talking, Alice declared, "That is not a subject for such an evening," making them apologise and stop their conversation immediately.

"No, please, I want to know. Has Eva been charged? What is going to happen to her?" Adelaide pleaded. "It's been such a long time since we've had any news."

William knew it was futile to keep anything from Adelaide, so he chose his words carefully and tried to answer her questions. "Inspector Perkins was about to charge her with blackmail, the attack on you and all her other crimes, too many to mention, when I was instructed to arrest her for treason. She has been taken to a military prison where she will be tried, and if found guilty, and I'm sure she will, it won't be a good outcome for Eva, I'm afraid."

"You mean she will be hanged?" Adelaide's voice was but a whisper.

Hugh said what everyone was probably thinking. "She has committed some terrible crimes and aided an organisation that was assisting another country to become more powerful than us, so the punishment must fit the crime, don't you think?"

Shaking her head, Adelaide replied, "I don't know. Even though it horrifies me to know that she deliberately killed an innocent woman just to hurt me and probably had some part to play in Valentine's death, too, I believe she has madness in her."

Her nerves already frayed, Marie stood up abruptly and said, "Let's have no more talk of this. This is supposed to be a celebration. I don't want to hear another word about that evil woman!"

"I'm sorry." Adelaide felt awful and could see how upset she was. "Why don't I entertain you one more time? I might have about one more tune left in me!"

Chapter 34

Woodlands, Dunedin – January 1919

Storm-laden skies menace and threaten, their granite shadows stretching over the turbulent sea below. A shard of gold appears momentarily, trying in vain to push its way through the clouds, but its efforts are swiftly smothered, swallowed by the storm's relentless grip. The heavy heat over the Christmas period had left behind its inevitable legacy of thunderstorms. Today was no exception.

As it had been for the past five years, Christmas at Woodlands had been a quiet, subdued holiday. The war was finally over, and after the excitement and relief of the end of hostilities, the reality of the consequences of war arrived home with the men, injured beyond imagination, some with mental scars which would stay with them long after their wounds healed.

Adelaide wrapped herself in a blanket and sat beside a small rocky outcrop, watching the dramatic scene play out before her. Her journal lay precariously in her lap. Holding it tightly with both hands, the strong wind was determined to rip the book from her and toss it without care onto the beach. Without thinking, she called out for Elise in case she had strayed too near the crashing waves, but the sadness in her heart reminded her that her little companion had died just before Christmas. They had been happily playing in the garden together when suddenly Elise lay down, panting. As Adelaide tried to help her, two brown eyes stared up at her, just as they had nine years earlier, and somehow Adelaide knew it was time to say goodbye. She had sat there in the garden, gently stroking Elise's head until her eyes closed one final time.

Shaking her sadness away, she tried to think instead of the

charity recital that had been organised for the 12th of January at the music salon of Josiah Westfield & Son, which, since her first performance there all those years ago, had been a popular venue for many more plays and concerts, and this one was no exception. She had been invited to perform alongside members of the Wellington Music Society, a thoughtful opportunity she gladly accepted. The concert, organised by Mrs Drumford and her ladies of the Women's Christian Group, was in aid of the Widows and Orphans charity. To anyone expressing interest in attending, Mrs Drumford explained warmly, "It's a small gesture to support families torn apart and left destitute after the war."

Adelaide held the blanket tighter around her and sighed sadly. The war had left an indelible mark on everyone, including her family. Within months of returning from London, the shadow of war spread its dark web across the world, and Adelaide knew nothing would ever be the same again.

Lawrence and Michael enlisted almost immediately after war was declared, marching proudly alongside their brothers-in-arms to fight for King and country. But when they returned to Dorset Square just before Christmas, they were barely recognisable as the men who had gone. Broken in both body and spirit, they bore the indelible scars of the battlefield.

Lawrence took a bullet to the shoulder in the early days of the Battle of the Somme in 1916. As soon as he was deemed fit to return, he was sent back to the front. In 1917, he earned the Military Cross for leading his men to safety. A heroic act that cost him the sight in one eye.

Michael fared well until April 1918, when a gas attack ended his war. He was shipped home and swiftly transferred to a sanatorium in Scotland, where it was hoped the crisp, clean Highland air would help his damaged lungs.

Rose, eager to contribute, joined the Voluntary Aid Detachment when she turned eighteen. Much to her mother's dismay, she was deployed to a field hospital in France to care for the wounded. She proved to be a skilled and compassionate nurse. In a recent letter, Aunt Alice told Adelaide that Rose had no intention of leaving her post just yet, as there were still many broken bodies that needed healing. "If only a nice young man would catch her eye and take her away from all this horror," Alice had added wistfully. Adelaide sighed when she read those words. *The war had taken nearly all the nice young men.*

Her thoughts then turned to William. It had been years since she had last heard from him. His final letter had arrived more than three years ago, just before he was deployed somewhere overseas. After that—nothing.

She could only assume the worst. Either he was dead or lying gravely wounded in some distant hospital. What other explanation could there be for his silence? Her father had tried everything to trace his whereabouts, but no one seemed to know where he had gone or if he was even still alive.

Her younger cousins, George and Douglas, had fought bravely, but only Douglas returned home. George was killed at the Battle of the Somme in 1916, and even though Douglas survived, without his twin, he was adrift. The horrors of war clung to him, manifesting in relentless night terrors. During his worst moments, Adelaide sat with him, reading aloud from the stories they had loved as children, her voice a tether to something familiar. Sometimes, he would sit downstairs, silent but listening, as she played the piano for him. And slowly, imperceptibly at first, some colour returned to his cheeks. He began to eat again, the weight of grief shifting, if only by degrees.

The war had left its mark on more than just soldiers. The Millers' bookshop had also suffered. Adelaide was deeply distressed to learn of the pain her dear friends, Theodore and Elisabeth, had endured. When war was declared, a wave of anti-German hysteria swept through the country, stoked by the newspapers. Neighbours who had once been friends were suddenly seen as enemies, eyed with suspicion and contempt. News of Eva's arrest and the downfall of The Silent Hand had made the front page of the Wellington Post. Several members were captured and tried for treason. One night, someone hurled a brick through the Millers' shop window. The word Traitor was scrawled on it.

None of it mattered to the mob that Hugo and Louis, the Millers' sons, had both enlisted. In 1915, they joined the Allied expedition at Gallipoli. Only Louis had come home. Hugo had given his life for a country that now despised his family. The bookshop closed for the remainder of the war, and due to his age, Theodore and Elisabeth were allowed to seek refuge with his brother's family on their farm as long as they did not return to Wellington.

Against her mother's wishes, Adelaide remained steadfast in her loyalty. She was determined to show support when Theodore, Elisabeth, and Louis were finally allowed to return home.

"Theodore and Elisabeth are my friends," Adelaide declared, her voice steady with conviction. "They are kind, decent people, and I won't be swayed by petty gossip." She had even set aside two cherished first editions that she had discovered in a quaint London bookshop just for Theodore.

As she stepped into the shop, the bell above the door rang out, and the familiar scent of beeswax and old pages wrapped around her like a memory. She was instantly transported to a time before her journey to England, before the war, when her greatest concern had been choosing a book, sipping tea, and talking with Theodore about "cabbages and kings," as he always used to say.

The shop looked the same, but it wasn't. There was no Eva. No Hugo. And behind the counter, in his usual place by the till, stood Theodore. He was thinner now, stooped and frail. His grey hair had turned completely white.

"Theodore," Adelaide said softly, not wanting to startle him.

He looked up, confusion flickering briefly in his eyes and then recognition. His face lit up with a smile that washed away the years. "Adelaide! It's you. What a wonderful surprise! Elisabeth! Elisabeth, where are you? It's Adelaide!"

Laughter and chatter filled the shop as the three reunited. Elisabeth bustled off to make tea while Theodore shuffled to the door and turned the sign to Closed. He gestured for Adelaide to sit. She handed him the two books she had carried with such care. "These are for you," she said with a smile. "First editions. I found them in London."

Theodore held the books, and tears travelled down his whiskery cheeks. "My dear, I don't deserve these. I don't deserve your kindness, yet here you are."

"Oh, Theodore, please don't think that. What Eva did to me was not your fault. She was deeply unwell. William told me so after they had transferred her to a military prison. Then, soon after, she was committed to a mental institution after being diagnosed with schizophrenia, which is a devastating illness. I read about it in several articles, and the ship's doctor during the voyage home helped me understand it better. He was incredibly insightful. And while I can't deny that what she did to me and others was beyond terrible, I can at least try to understand that she wasn't in her right mind."

Theodore had been gripping the books tightly as she spoke. He nodded, the emotion evident on his face. "You are the kindest soul I know, and I am grateful that you still wish to visit us. It has been hard these past years, losing Hugo and discovering all the wicked things Eva did."

Elisabeth entered, carrying a tray of tea and biscuits. It was clear she had been listening; her eyes were red and watery, and she regarded Theodore and Adelaide with gentle affection. She placed the tray on the small table before settling into the remaining chair. As she poured the tea and handed Adelaide a cup, she said softly, "Tell us all about your music and your plans. Let's talk only about pleasant things."

The wind changed direction, momentarily jolting her back to the present. Hugging the blanket tighter, she stubbornly remained seated and returned to her thoughts. She had purposely not spoken to the Millers about Valentine, and they hadn't pressed her for more information. Adelaide only wanted to remember Valentine as the talented musician he was, who taught her to play with greater depth and understanding than she had thought possible.

No one could tell her what had happened to Valentine's parents. The shop had been sold, and they just vanished, leaving no forwarding address. Giselle had written to her a few times, but after Valentine died, Adelaide's letters to Giselle had been returned to her unread. All she knew was that Giselle had gone to Paris, but the war had prevented letters from getting through. Guessing her question, Theodore explained that Ernst and Marta had disappeared one night without a trace, and no one had heard anything from them since.

"Adelaide, where are you? It's almost lunchtime – Mother is herding us all in!" Helena spotted her as she was packing up her things. "There you are."

"Here I am," Adelaide replied, smiling at her cousin.

Chapter 40

The music salon at Josiah Westfield & Son – 12th January 1919

The Music Salon had been transformed into an elegant drawing room, adorned with a profusion of summer blooms. Vases of alstroemeria, coreopsis, and montbretia, with delicate sprays of gypsophila, were arranged about the room. The Mayor, Mr John Luke, and his wife were the guests of honour, sending Mrs Drumford and her committee ladies into a frenzy of excitement as they fussed and checked every detail to ensure perfection.

Adelaide was already dressed for the concert. She had chosen a lilac silk gown, finished with the pearls Helena had given her. It was simple, one of her favourites, though much to her mother's annoyance, she continued to show little interest in the latest fashions. Comfort had always mattered more to her. At her mother's insistence, however, her long hair had been swept into a neat chignon with Peggy's assistance, secured by a pearl clasp. Violet's brooch, her lucky charm, was the final touch. With time to spare, she wandered into the garden and settled into a shady nook to review her music.

Peggy soon appeared, carrying a cup of chamomile tea. "To calm your nerves. Not that you need it, mind, but it'll do you good."

Adelaide sipped the tea, letting its warmth soothe her. She knew the piece so well that in her mind the notes unfolded effortlessly, melodies weaving themselves into the quiet afternoon air. Her eyes drifted shut just as a shadow crossed her face. At first, she thought it was merely a cloud passing over the sun, but when curiosity got the better of her, she opened her eyes and gasped.

"William!"

"Hello, Adelaide." He smiled down at her.

"Where have you been?"

"Fighting a war," he answered dryly.

Adelaide immediately regretted her words. "I'm sorry… it is such a shock to see you standing here. It has been so long. I wrote often, but my letters went unanswered. I feared the worst."

He stood before her in his uniform, as handsome as she remembered, though his once-black hair was now peppered with grey, lending him a distinguished air.

"Well, as you can see, I am very much alive. I ought to apologise for not writing or letting you know I was coming. That was inconsiderate of me. But I will explain tomorrow. Perhaps we could take a walk, and I will tell you everything."

Adelaide could only nod, torn between the urge to rush into his arms and the shock that kept her rooted in place. Then, the sudden realisation that she needed to leave, or she would be late, made her stand and say, "It's wonderful to see you, William, but I'm afraid I must go. I'm performing in a concert this afternoon."

"I know, and I have a ticket. May I offer you all a lift?"

Pulling herself together, she managed a steady reply. "That would be most kind. Thank you."

The orchestra was already assembled, tuning their instruments, as Adelaide watched from the sidelines. Seeing William again after so many years had unsettled her, and she struggled to remain focused. She was to perform halfway through the programme, allowing the orchestra a short interval. It was a mixed ensemble, comprising schoolboys and retired gentlemen. The war had claimed many of its finest performers. Even the conductor, James Turner, had been pressed out of retirement to teach at Wellington College for Boys when all the younger men went to fight. Adelaide had rehearsed with them only a handful of times, but as she was playing a solo, she was content to practise on her own.

Scanning the audience, she spotted the Mayor and his wife seated in the front row alongside Mrs Drumford and the other committee ladies. At the opposite end sat her parents, her father deep in conversation with William. When she glanced back again, William caught her eye and smiled. She returned the gesture, warmth flooding through her at the sight of him after so long—a feeling so overwhelming that she had to remind herself to concentrate.

Before she could be further distracted, Edwin Westfield, Josiah's son, stepped onto the stage to enthusiastic applause. He welcomed the audience and offered thanks, on behalf of the Women's Christian Group, for their generous support of the charity. His father had passed away two years earlier, leaving everything to Edwin, who had vowed to honour his legacy. Having survived the war himself, he had returned home determined to fulfil his father's wishes to the letter.

Under James Turner's steady guidance, the orchestra played splendidly, their efforts rewarded with ever-growing applause. At last, it was Adelaide's turn. Edwin returned to the stage to introduce her. Taking her seat at the piano, she waited for the applause to subside. Then, placing her dainty fingers upon the keys, she began to play *Clair de Lune* by Claude Debussy.

William closed his eyes, letting the music carry him back to the days when he had felt invincible. Adelaide's self-proclaimed "knight in shining armour." But much had changed since the voyage on the Ayrshire, and the terrible day Eva had attacked her in London. He had endured so much, as had they all. Tomorrow, he would tell Adelaide everything, praying she might understand.

After the concert, refreshments were served in the next room, where the many committee members, including Peggy, offered trays of tea and biscuits to those who had chosen to stay to socialise. Adelaide was standing next to her parents, who were the first to congratulate her. Suddenly, she heard a familiar voice shouting her name. "Addie, don't move. Let me catch up with you!"

Marie turned to see who was calling her daughter. "I do wish people wouldn't shorten your name; it is quite unnecessary."

Robert smiled conspiratorially at his daughter, who often called her Addie when Marie was out of earshot. Looking around to find where the voice came from, Adelaide gasped as she recognised her friend Charlotte. "Lottie, I can't believe it!"

"Addie darling, I had to come and watch you perform. We only arrived yesterday, but I had to see you. It's been too long!" Adelaide looked at her elegant friend. She was wrapped in wealth, and her husband, Matthew Hibbert, stood beside her with an air of sophistication and charm. "Did you bring the boys? I would love to meet them."

"Of course, we plan to show them the delights of New Zealand, an education in itself! It's impossible to speak here, darling. We must have tea together soon. I'll be in touch!"

And with that, she disappeared on her husband's arm, waving an elegant, bejewelled hand to familiar faces as she walked towards the exit.

The noise and crush of people talking together was getting too much, and Adelaide really wanted to find William.

"Where's William?" She asked her father, a frown appearing on her forehead. She was beginning to get a headache.

"William has left, and he asked me to let you know he would call on you tomorrow to go for that walk he had promised." Does that make any sense?

"It does. Can we go home now? I'm feeling very tired all of a sudden."

The next morning, Adelaide was awake early after a restless night. Wrapping herself in her dressing gown and putting on her slippers, she headed to the kitchen to find Peggy. Her dear 'Peg' was busy preparing breakfast for the family. She had aged considerably over the past five years, and her hair was now completely grey. Her movements were a little slower, but she was still just as devoted to caring for the Ellwood family.

"Good morning. You're awake with the larks this morning. Sit yourself down, and I'll get you some tea."

"Thank you. I'm in need of a good, strong cup this morning."

"Oh, and why is that then?" Peggy busied herself with the tea things, all while watching her like a hawk.

"I saw William at the concert. He just appeared out of the blue after all this time. I don't know what to think. He is coming to see me today to explain everything."

"Well, I'll be..." Peggy rubbed her chin. "That's a turn-up for the books, for sure."

"Drink your tea, then get yourself dressed. Moping about in your night clothes will not help, and there's no point in worrying about what he might say as there's nothing you can do until you see him, right?"

"Oh, Peg, always so wise. You are right, of course. I will start the day and keep busy!"

Peggy watched her go, her step a little lighter. Whatever that Armstrong fellow was going to tell her, she prayed it was kind. *That sweet girl has had enough shocks to last a lifetime.* Shaking her head, she carried on with preparing breakfast.

William rang the doorbell as the hall clock was chiming two. Peggy went to answer, pushing Adelaide into the drawing room. "Go in there to receive him. Take a deep breath and compose yourself."

Standing by herself in the drawing room, Adelaide felt anxious. She sat down, then stood up. How to greet him? Should I stand or sit? "Oh, help, I don't know!" She shouted at herself.

"Are you all right in there?" William was smiling at her as he entered the drawing room.

Adelaide couldn't help but laugh. "I'm absolutely fine, thank you."

"Shall we go for a walk first, or would you like some tea?" She desperately tried to keep things formal, but she wanted to shake him and beg him to tell her where he'd been all this time.

"Let's go for a walk, shall we? It's a beautiful day, and we can enjoy tea at a café. How does that sound?"

"Perfect. Let me get my hat, and then we can go."

They decided on a walk to the botanical gardens. As they entered the gardens, they were greeted with an array of colourful flowers that lifted Adelaide's spirits. William gestured for them to sit on a park bench. "I suppose I'd better start at the beginning." He looked at her so intensely that it made her feel concerned for him. "Only if you want to. I don't want to pry."

"I want to." He smiled at her.

"After you returned to New Zealand, I knew it was only a matter of time before I would be called back to my regiment. I was given a few months to find and arrest anyone associated with Eva and The Silent Hand and then pass on any intelligence I'd gathered to the top brass. Then, I was back in uniform and ready to join my regiment, but instead, I found myself being shipped off to Egypt to help train the newly formed Australian and New Zealand Army Corps – the Anzacs. We were in the middle of the desert surrounded by Pyramids, and some days, the heat was unbearable, but that didn't matter, not when we knew so many of our brothers in arms were being killed in France. It's difficult to put into words, and I lost so many friends."

William paused. Adelaide remained silent, acutely aware of his anguish. After a few seconds that felt like minutes, she gently placed her hand upon his, heedless of who might be watching.

"In April 1915, we landed at Gallipoli, charging up the shore under a hail of Turkish fire. We pushed forward as best we could, but their defence was unyielding. After that, everything grows indistinct, for I was struck down and sorely wounded." He absently rubbed the scar along the side of his forehead.

Adelaide reached out, her gloved fingers tracing it lightly. She had not noticed it the day before, concealed as it had been beneath his cap and hair.

"All I recall is waking in a field hospital at Alexandria, more than a fortnight later. Our losses had been dreadful, and retreat was inevitable. They told me I had been insensible for weeks, and when at last I came to myself, I had forgotten everything— even how to walk, to eat, or to speak. It was a bitter struggle to regain what I had lost.

"In time, when I could walk without support, they sent me back to England, and I spent several months in a convalescent home. And you will never guess where it was." He gave a mirthless smile, then answered his own question. "Launchester! The estate had been taken over by the Government and turned into a hospital for men like me."

"Evie and Teddy's place!" Adelaide exclaimed. "What a coincidence, and how fortunate. Did you see them? Evie and Teddy, I mean."

"No. I was told Teddy was in France, and Evie had joined the V.A.D.s, working in a hospital somewhere in Yorkshire. It took a year for me to recover, but I know I was one of the lucky ones."

"It was heartbreaking reading the newspapers every day— and then we heard the dreadful news of my cousin George, and also Theodore Miller's son, Hugo."

"I was sorry to hear about your cousin. Your father told me yesterday."

Wishing to change the subject quickly, Adelaide said, "Evie and Teddy—do you know if they are back home? I must write to them."

"I'm afraid I have no idea. I left Launchester in 1917. I stayed at my parents' home for a while, and after that, I was given a desk job at Whitehall. Everyone kept telling me how lucky I was, but I didn't feel it. I still don't." William looked straight at Adelaide and stopped speaking momentarily, and she wondered what he would say or do next. He was not the person she said goodbye to in 1914, but who was?

"Once I was working in London, I should have written to you, and I regret that now. Seeing you at the concert, I knew I was foolish to think you would not want to see me."

"Why did you think that?"

"I felt different. I jumped at the slightest noise and had terrible nightmares. I didn't want you to see me like that."

Adelaide shook her head gently. "For bravely running into the line of fire, for wanting to protect us. I only think of you and all the other men who fought so bravely with a sense of pride and admiration. The hardest thing was not knowing where you were and how you were faring. I did nothing to help the war effort apart from playing the piano to support my mother's various charities. We felt so far away from everything, but when the death notices started rolling in and all the young men, well, it was hard to bear. I opened a small music school for children who had lost their fathers, providing them with something to focus on, and my paying students helped support it. Nothing like Evie or Rose, bravely volunteering as nurses."

"Everyone has their particular strengths, and yours is music. Listening to you play yesterday was a true delight, and it soothed my soul. It was beautiful."

Tears welled in Adelaide's eyes, and she tried to dab them away surreptitiously; something was happening between them, and she never wanted to stop sitting with him on this wooden bench in the Botanical Gardens. He took hold of her hands as if he knew what she was thinking.

"I'm so glad you came to see me. How long will you be in Wellington?"

I've been assigned to the New Zealand Government for the next year at least, tying up loose ends and finishing my investigations with the German immigrants who had to endure being detained. A necessary evil, as you learned first-hand."

"Indeed," Adelaide answered.

"Adelaide, is there a chance we could be more than friends?" William's voice was gentle as he took her hand.

For once, her usual awkwardness didn't overtake her. Instead, she smiled, bright and certain. "I hope so. Let's take it one day at a time and see where it leads us."

William's grin widened, and without hesitation, he pulled her into his arms and kissed her. This time, Adelaide didn't pull away — she melted into him, letting the moment unfold.

When they finally broke apart, laughter bubbled up between them, their joy almost childlike in its simplicity.

"I've dreamed of doing that for years!" William admitted, his whole face alight with happiness.

Adelaide was suddenly aware of the vivid roses, the towering trees, and the deep blue sky. It was as if she had stepped into one of her own Sonatas — her life, at last, feeling as it should: beautiful, bright, and full of promise.

Chapter 41

Liverpool - 1960

It had been almost a month since her mother's funeral, and Grace had visited her father nearly every day, helping him with household tasks and ensuring he ate properly. The rest of the time, they sat together at the dining room table, drinking tea while he shared memories of his sister, Adelaide.

After Grace discovered the music box, Joseph retrieved an old suitcase from the cupboard beneath the stairs. Inside was a record of Adelaide's life: journals, letters she had written to Joseph, letters Joseph had written to her, and numerous others from cousins and friends. There were newspaper clippings and various photographs, including one of her being introduced to King George V.

Grace was impressed but also confused.

"I don't understand why you never talked about her. She had such an amazing life and career! I might have tried harder to stick with playing the piano if I'd known how talented she was." Grace laughed.

"Adelaide was far too busy travelling the world, lecturing and performing. Her life was so very different from ours." Joseph smiled at her. "I remember how she would often wax lyrical about the piano in the many letters I received from her, and she would say something like, "No other instrument mixes joy and sorrow as beautifully as the piano."

"That's very poetical," Grace answered.

"Perhaps if we'd pushed you a little more. It's never too late, though!"

Grace pulled a face, "I'm forty years old, Dad. I think my piano-playing days are over."

"Why are they over? Never say never!"

Grace laughed, "I think the piano is best left to other people. My life is already busy enough without adding piano lessons. And gosh, what would the neighbours think of me banging away at my scales? No, I don't think so."

Joseph shook his head and took hold of his daughter's hand. "Anyway, I hope you now have some insight into your Aunt's life, but …"

"What is it, Dad?" Grace's look of concern forced him to continue.

"There's one more bit of the story I need to tell you, but it won't be easy."

"Oh, right. Well, I'd better put the kettle on then." Grace stood and made her way to the kitchen.

As he watched Grace walk towards the kitchen, Joseph trembled slightly. He was dreading telling her the truth. How would she react? Was it worth causing her any more pain when he probably only had a few more years left in him? Maybe he should write her a letter to be read after his death instead. However, he knew what his dear Kitty would have said.

As Grace poured the tea, Joseph cleared his throat. "Dad, are you ok? You are starting to worry me now. What do you need to tell me?"

"Before I tell you the rest, I want you to know that your mum and I loved you very much, and we believed with all our hearts it was for the best."

"Dad … out with it."

"My darling girl, this is very hard for me to say, but we are not your real parents."

Back at their home, Daniel was waiting anxiously for Grace to return. She had been out longer than expected, and the dinner he'd been instructed to put in the oven at five o'clock was now solid and dried out in the casserole dish. In the end, he'd bought the children fish and chips to keep them happy. They had eaten without fuss and gone straight to bed.

At last, he heard the key in the door and let out a relieved sigh as Grace stepped inside.

"You're back late, love. Is your dad all right?"

Grace barely registered his words. The shock of her father's revelation had left her reeling—tears, disbelief, anger, more tears, and then a kind of stunned silence.

Seeing Daniel's worried expression, she collapsed into his arms, sobbing, trying to tell him what her father, who she now realised wasn't really her father, had just said.

Daniel guided her to the sofa, set a box of tissues on her lap, and held her until her sobs began to ease.

Blowing her nose, Grace drew a shaky breath and repeated the words she could scarcely believe.

"I thought I'd misheard him at first …"

"Dad, what did you just say?"

"Grace, love, this won't be easy, so please be patient and hear me out. I promise I'll answer any questions you have. But, yes, your mum and I adopted you, and we have loved you as our own."

Her face drained of colour. Tears welled in her eyes, the shock settling into something deeper, sharper. Then, the realisation hit.

"Is it Adelaide? Is she my real mother?"

Joseph's heart ached as he met his daughter's gaze. There was no need for words. He nodded, knowing there was no way to soften the truth, only to brace himself for the pain it would bring.

"Why didn't Adelaide want me? Why did she give me to you?"

"Hear me out, love." Joseph pleaded.

Grace looked at her Dad, utterly confused. "I'm listening."

"Well, where to start … It was June 1914, just before the outbreak of World War I. Your mum and I had left Sam in Spider and Mary's capable hands, as we had been invited to celebrate Adelaide's graduation from the Royal Academy of Music.

We spent a few wonderful days exploring the city and taking in the sights, but the highlight, by far, was seeing Adelaide perform on stage. My shy little sister, once so reserved, now commanded the stage with effortless grace, weaving music so beautifully it felt almost unreal.

Your grandparents were there too, and I realised then that they had never forgiven me and knew that I'd probably never see them again. However, it meant a lot to Adelaide that we were all together, so that more than made up for the lack of welcome from my parents.

I also met William Armstrong that evening. He had been a great support to Adelaide through all the Eva business, and I could tell instantly that they were smitten with each other. Of course, when I asked Adelaide about it, she flatly denied it!

Anyway. I went back to sea soon after, and that's when I had the accident that caused my wonky leg, as you used to call it." Joseph tapped his leg, attempting to smile to lighten the atmosphere, but staring at Grace's stricken expression, he thought better of it. Clearing his throat, he continued, "I was invalided out of the Merchant Navy and unable to work until my leg healed. With no money coming in, your mum was able to get her old job back at the café where we first met. Sam was only small then, so when I was discharged from the hospital, I watched him while your mum went to work."

"Your friend, Spider. He wasn't so lucky, was he?" Grace added gently.

"That's right, I lost my best friend that day. We were fixing a loose railing on a narrow walkway in the engine room. We could have delegated the job to some of the maintenance crew, but we knew it would be dangerous and felt it was best to attempt the repair ourselves. Unfortunately, and I never found out why, the ship suddenly dipped and rolled, catapulting us both off the walkway. Spider landed first and died instantly. I was luckier. He saved my life when I landed on him. I became very depressed because I had survived, and Spider hadn't. However, your mum would have none of it. She would often pull me up sharply and make me count my blessings, insisting I visit Spider's widow, Mary, and help her out, which gave me a sense of purpose. She was a clever one, your mum."

Joseph hesitated, aware that Grace was likely itching to protest, desperate to declare that Kitty wasn't her mother and was grateful when she remained silent.

"The war was brutal, and of course, I was of no use to the Navy. However, with my knowledge of ships and the docks, I was offered a desk job with the Mersey Docks and Harbour Board, and somehow, we managed. After the war, life gradually returned to a semblance of normalcy. I think it was around August 1920 when we had an unexpected visitor. I could scarcely believe my eyes when I opened the door to find Adelaide standing there, smiling up at me. I just stood, utterly stunned, until your mum took charge. We had no idea she was returning to England. And then, as she slipped off her coat, it became unmistakably clear that she was expecting a child. Your mum fussed over Adelaide at once, urging her to sit down. Only after pressing a cup of tea into her hands did she allow her to explain the reason for her sudden return.

Adelaide told us that William had asked her to marry him, and at first, she had been overjoyed to accept the proposal. But soon reality set in, and no matter how much she loved him, marriage would mean the end of her music career. She had received an invitation to perform and lecture in Canada, and almost simultaneously, William had received orders to return to Egypt."

"So, William is my real father?" Grace interrupted.

Her words stung, and he wasn't sure if he could go on. How he wished Kitty were there beside him.

"Yes," he said at last, "your real father was William Armstrong."

"Why didn't he insist she marry him? Did he run a mile when he found out she was pregnant? What a coward!" Grace's voice trembled with anger.

"No, no, it wasn't like that at all. When Adelaide met with him, determined to tell him the truth, she couldn't bring herself to do it. She wrote their conversation in her journal. I'll fetch it for you."

After rummaging for some time, he drew out a faded blue book. Turning to the right page, he handed it to Grace, who began to read the fragile handwriting.

Tonight was one of the hardest nights of my life. I broke my darling William's heart because, deep down, I knew it was the right thing to do. I had to set him free.

My reasons were selfish, perhaps, but music is like breathing to me. I yearned to travel, to perform, to share my passion and to speak about my craft. I wanted—no, I needed—my thoughts and practices to matter.

I will never forget the look in William's eyes as I spoke, the confusion etched across his face as he tried to understand why I could not do those things with him. But how can I be a wife, a mother, and a scholar? It is not possible.

William could not understand why I had to make a choice. Yet I knew, in the depths of my heart, that the choice was inevitable. To be a good wife, I would have to follow him, dutifully accepting each new posting and embracing the life expected of an officer's wife. And with that, my dreams would wither.

Once I admitted the truth, there was no taking it back. The weight of it hung between us, heavy and unyielding, until William finally walked away, hurt and angry.

"Is he still alive?" Grace asked softly, her eyes brimming with tears. She didn't look up; she just stared down at the journal.

"I'm sorry, but I don't know," Joseph answered gently. Grace's despair was breaking his heart.

"And you don't know if she ever told him about me?"

"She never told me she had."

"How could she be so heartless?" Grace burst out.

"Grace, love, please listen." His voice softened. "I know none of this can ease the hurt you're feeling. But to us, to your mum and me, you were a gift."

"I'm sorry—it's just such a shock." Grace's voice faltered.

"I understand, truly I do. Anyway, there we were, the three of us in this little sitting room, deciding what to do for the best. Your mum didn't hesitate, and she told Adelaide exactly what would happen. She arranged to take Adelaide to stay with Maude, who had married a farmer and was living in Coniston in the Lake District. It was the perfect place, secluded and out of sight. Sam went too, and had the time of his life riding the tractor with Maude's husband, Alfred, thoroughly enjoying life on the farm. I had to work, so I stayed here and got your nursery ready. I painted the box room, and Mary gave us a cot and everything we needed. She was a great help in those early days, as we had little time to prepare for a new baby. Sam adored having a little sister, and he never questioned how you came to us. He simply became your big brother.

Adelaide stayed at the farm for a while to recover, then sailed to Canada, where she began her tour. You've seen the clippings: New York, Toronto, London, Europe—she performed all over the world."

"Did she ever visit me? I don't remember ever seeing her."

"No, love. She chose not to. She feared that if she got to know you, she wouldn't be able to leave. And she truly believed you would be better off without her. Times were different then, and Adelaide had endured so much. Music was her life."

"What about your parents? Did they know? How could she have kept it from them?"

"Sadly, our parents both died not long after the war, of influenza, as if the war had not claimed enough lives. A few months later, Peggy passed away as well. Adelaide was heartbroken, but she poured her grief into her music. William, of course, was there for her."

"And your cousin Helena? Weren't they close?"

"They were, yes. But Adelaide never mentioned in her letters that she had said anything to her, so I cannot say whether Helena was aware. And I was not about to ask."

Grace sighed and finally looked up from the journal. "Gosh, I feel so confused. But I can't disregard forty years of living with two wonderful people who loved me unconditionally—and Sam, of course. Oh God, does he know?"

"No. The only people who knew the truth were Maude and Spider's wife, Mary. To us, you were our daughter, and that was the end of it."

"I have a lot to take in, and it's very late. I'd better get home; Daniel will be worried."

"Will I see you tomorrow?" Joseph asked quietly. She hesitated and was about to say she'd think about it, but she could never hurt him like that. He was her father, whatever else had come to light.

"Of course I'll see you tomorrow." She stood, kissed the top of his head, and left.

Daniel sat beside Grace, his mouth open in surprise at the revelation. "Are you angry, upset? How do you feel?"

"To be honest, I have no idea. I'm in shock, I suppose. But spending the past month with Dad, reading through all her journals and letters, I think I understand why she chose to give me away."

As she spoke, a sob came from nowhere, and Daniel held her close.

As she wiped her tears with a tissue, she almost felt sorry for Daniel. His face was full of concern.

"I'm okay. I had a wonderful childhood. Mum and Dad were the best parents anyone could have wished for. It's a shame I never got to know my birth parents, though. Even if it was just as "Aunt Adelaide and Uncle William." I find it hard to believe that she chose not to tell William. I'm sure she had her reasons, but it seems very selfish to me."

"His name was William?" Daniel's astonishment was unmistakable. Grace studied his face, confusion flickering across hers until realisation struck, stealing her breath. "William! Our son's name. What are the odds? I can't believe it." Her voice wavered. "What must Mum and Dad have thought when we named him? How did they manage to keep this secret for so long?" A swirl of emotions rose within her.

"It was a different time back then, wasn't it?" Daniel said, still hugging her tightly, searching for the right words to comfort her. "Women didn't have the choices they have now. From what you've told me, her music was her calling, and she couldn't give up the life she had worked so hard for. And to make things worse, the man she'd fallen in love with was a soldier who would have needed his wife to conform to the traditions and expectations of being the wife of an officer."

Grace sighed, sat back, and pulled a face. She realised Daniel's jumper was soaked through with her tears. "Look at me. I must look awful and look at your poor jumper."

"You're very welcome," Daniel said, smiling at her whilst handing her another tissue.

Chapter 42

Once Grace had gone, the weight of what he had just told her felt like a punch to the stomach. Joseph remained seated in his chair, gazing at the empty one opposite him. "Kitty, my love, did I do the right thing?" he murmured, though he already knew the answer. As much as it hurt him, Kitty would have wanted him to tell Grace in person so he could explain himself properly. *Had he, though, and would Grace ever forgive him?*

He had always believed Adelaide would have made a poor mother, not intentionally, but out of a kind of fragility. There was an innocence about her; she chose only to dwell on the happy and the beautiful. Their parents had sheltered her, and she had lived in that cocoon willingly. Her gentle ways and shyness often stirred jealousy in others. He thought especially of Eva, and the devastation that woman had left in her wake. Most people would have been traumatised, even embittered, but not Adelaide. She forgave, put Eva's cruelty down to illness, and never spoke of it again. Her journals overflowed with idyllic sketches and lyrical recollections, all delightful to read, but never the whole truth.

He remembered a newspaper review of one of her compositions: "Miss Adelaide Ellwood is too poetic for this everyday world ..."

A letter she had written to him in the spring of 1940 came vividly to mind. Grace, then grown, had joined the Women's Royal Naval Service. She had just completed her basic training and had sent Joseph several photographs of herself in uniform. His heart had swelled with pride, and he immediately thought of sending one to his sister. He had discovered that when war was declared in 1939, Adelaide had refused to return home. Instead, she had remained in London and joined the hundreds of musicians who, under the direction of the pianist Myra Hess, gave lunchtime concerts at the National Gallery — offering Londoners solace in the midst of the Blitz.

Parts of her letter remained etched in his memory:

Marylebone
1st September 1940

My Dear Joseph,

How wonderful to hear from you, and my goodness, Grace has grown into a beautiful young lady. You must be so proud of her.

I truly appreciate how you have tried to keep me connected to her life, but as far as I am concerned, she has always been, and will always be, your daughter. I feel no bond with her, and I hope that doesn't sound too heartless, but in my heart, I know it is the truth.

When Grace was born, I had two choices. I could have chosen the life of a wife and mother, following William from one posting to the next, and abandoned my dreams. But it would have destroyed me.

Instead, I chose a life of music, and it has given me everything I ever dreamed of. I have travelled the world, found success, and lived fully.

Sometimes I think my life could be told through music — a series of sonatas, each movement capturing a different moment. Gentle, loud, dramatic, peaceful. And I would not change a single note.

All my love,
Adelaide

A week later, on 7 September 1940, the first great air raid on London began. Three hundred German bombers pounded the city of London. Adelaide had been walking back to her flat and had been caught by flying debris from one of the bombed buildings, killing her instantly. Why she hadn't gone to an air raid shelter,

Joseph would never know.

The memory of his journey south was still fresh. The train was packed with soldiers, every seat filled. His old leg injury throbbed with each bump, but pride kept him quiet. As Adelaide's closest relative, it was his duty to identify her body. It was one of the worst days of his life. In a city being devastated by bombs daily, arranging her funeral was extremely difficult, and Joseph felt he had no one to turn to for help. The hospital morgue was too overwhelmed to assist, and as he left, trying to erase the image of his dear sister lying there in that cold, sterile room, he paused briefly at a row of empty chairs and sat down, resting his head and hands on his walking stick.

"Mr Ellwood?" a poised woman in a smart suit interrupted his thoughts.

"Yes," he replied, barely managing the words.

I'm Sonia Kirkland, a close friend of your sister. We studied together at the Royal Academy of Music, where I now lecture. I came to identify her body, not knowing you'd travelled from Liverpool. I'm so sorry for your loss; I can hardly believe she's gone." Her voice wavered slightly, and she tried to suppress her distress with a lace handkerchief pressed to her mouth.

"Miss Kirkland, of course, I remember Adelaide mentioning you often in her letters." Joseph tried to stand to greet her, but his legs failed him.

"Please don't trouble yourself," Sonia said gently. "May I sit with you?"

"Yes, of course. It's been a difficult day, and one I never expected." Joseph tried to explain.

"I can only imagine. I understand organising her funeral may be quite challenging for you, given the circumstances of this terrible war. Still, I'd be honoured to assist with the funeral arrangements — we have permission to bury her at Highgate Cemetery in recognition of her musical contributions. Of course, I defer to your wishes."

Joseph remained deeply grateful to Sonia and the community of musicians who had performed with Adelaide over the years and who gave Adelaide the farewell she truly deserved. When he returned a week later for the funeral, he was profoundly moved by the quiet dignity of the service and the many people who came to honour her life and music. Aside from himself, there were no other family members able to attend. Despite her protests, he did not want to subject Kitty to the strain of travelling to a city being bombed daily; it was already hard enough that their own city of Liverpool was suffering the same fate. The rest of the family was scattered across the globe, and the war prevented their presence. Nevertheless, the many letters he received, especially those from Helena, Lawrence, and Rose, which were tender and filled with memories, gave him comfort.

Adelaide was laid to rest beneath the yew trees of Highgate Cemetery, where ivy curled over timeworn stones and silence held its breath. Few remembered that Valentine had been buried there too, more than two decades earlier, in a shaded corner where the light filtered gently through the branches. Waiting patiently for kindness, perhaps from someone who understood him and would let him explain …

Chapter 43

Wellington - 1950

It wasn't until after the war that Joseph was able to take Kitty to New Zealand. He had received a letter from Adelaide's solicitors in Wellington, containing a cheque for £1000, more money than either of them had ever dreamed of. Their 'Overseas Adventure,' as they called it, was pleasant for the most part. It was their first proper holiday together. As they disembarked from the ship and went through customs, they spotted a well-dressed couple waving at them. They were about the same age as Joseph and Kitty, and Joseph suddenly realised who they were. "That must be Helena, and I am guessing her husband, Gabriel. Helena was in her twenties when I last saw her. I had forgotten we'd all grown a little older!"

"Helena, is that you?" Joseph shouted over the noise of the disembarking passengers.

"Joseph, just look at you, aren't we getting old?" Helena pulled them both into a warm embrace before turning to introduce Gabriel. He extended a hand toward Joseph with an easy smile.

"Hello, Kitty. I recognise you from your photograph and our many conversations with Adelaide. She was rather fond of you."

"I was very fond of her, too." Kitty smiled, searching for something more to say to these kind and welcoming people. But after the long voyage and the relentless noise of the port, exhaustion crept over her, leaving her feeling suddenly overwhelmed. Sensing her weariness, Joseph placed a protective arm around her and gently guided her through the throng of people. Gabriel quickly took charge, his tone reassuring.

"Let's get you out of here and back to the house where you can rest and recover from your long journey, and I'm sure we can rustle up some decent refreshments to revive you!"

On their first evening, after settling into a charming room with a view of the bay, Helena informed them that their daughters, Isabella and Florence, would be joining them for dinner.

"I hope you don't mind, but they were eager to meet Adelaide's brother and his wife, even though I suggested they wait a few days!" Helena said apologetically.

Joseph smiled, "We don't mind at all. We are looking forward to meeting them, too."

It was a warm, convivial evening. Isabella and Florence wanted to know about their mother when she was young, and Joseph enjoyed teasing Helena by telling them about all the high jinks they would get up to at Woodlands. Later, as they sat drinking a nightcap, Helena spoke of how Adelaide had at last realised her dream of opening her music academy in 1927.

"I wondered," she said with a gentle smile, "whether you might like to visit the Ellwood Music Academy tomorrow, provided you feel up to it, of course?"

Joseph inclined his head. "That would give me great pleasure. Adelaide wrote to me of it from time to time, but to see with my own eyes what she accomplished would be wonderful."

Kitty sat back, quietly observing the exchange, wondering how Joseph was truly feeling. Outwardly, he seemed to enjoy reminiscing, but she knew the fear gnawed at him. The possibility that Adelaide had confided in Helena about Grace, that the truth might yet emerge during their stay. A pang of sadness struck Kitty at the unfairness of Joseph's denied inheritance, as it was clear Adelaide had been able to fund the building of the academy with the inheritance she received from their parents. Yet as she watched him, her heart swelled with love and gratitude. None of it seemed to trouble him; it was one of the many reasons she adored him.

Their first night was a restless one. They lay side by side, wide awake, each absorbed in their own thoughts. Helena had given no hint of knowing Adelaide's secret. She had shown only a genuine interest in the lives of their children. Even so, Joseph could not shake the unease, the fear that everything he had worked so hard to build, everything he held most dear, might be at risk.

Kitty tried to soothe him. "You are overtired, and being back after all this time is bound to stir up memories. Adelaide, your parents, even Peg—all gone. It must feel strange."

"It does," Joseph admitted. "I am not the man I was when I left here all those years ago. And though I am glad I came, and I look forward to showing you the country of my birth, I must confess I shall be relieved to return home. Is that a dreadful thing to say?"

In the silence that followed, Kitty drew closer. Holding one another tightly in a strange bed, in an unfamiliar land, she could not help but agree.

The next morning, Joseph and Kitty could not conceal their delight at the resplendent sight before them: a table generously set with bacon, eggs, golden toast, and a bright array of fresh fruit. Kitty reached for an orange, holding it carefully in her hand before lifting it to her nose. She breathed in deeply, savouring the sharp citrus aroma. "Goodness," she murmured, her voice thick with memory. "I haven't seen one of these since before the war."

Gabriel, watching her with quiet amusement, smiled. "I believe rationing was a lot worse for you, wasn't it. Although we eventually had to endure rationing, I don't think we suffered quite as much."

"We still do," Joseph replied, half in jest, though his words carried a sober weight.

Kitty nodded, her eyes fixed on the orange. "During the war, fresh fruit like this was almost mythical." She placed it gently back on the table, as though it were something sacred. "You learn to cherish the ordinary when it has been beyond reach for so long."

"In that case," Gabriel said warmly, serving himself another slice of bacon, "you must take full pleasure in all that is before you. And should there be any delicacy you particularly long for, do not hesitate to say so! If it is within our power to procure it, we most certainly shall."

Joseph and Kitty both laughed at Gabriel's declaration. "Thank you, Gabriel, that is very kind of you," Joseph answered for both of them.

"I trust you both slept soundly?" Helena asked kindly. "If the journey has left you still fatigued, we can, of course, postpone today's visit."

"Nonsense. We slept well in our lovely bedroom and feel quite refreshed and very much looking forward to visiting the Ellwood Music Academy." Joseph answered as brightly as possible after their restless night, believing a small white lie would not harm.

Helena's expression softened. "Wonderful. As you know, Adelaide entrusted the academy to me in her will. At first, I was astonished, indeed rather overwhelmed by the responsibility, but in time it became a source of deep fulfilment. I count it a privilege to have had a hand in preserving her life's work. Today, Isabella and Florence oversee the daily affairs of the academy, while I devote myself to the small museum we have established in Adelaide's honour. It serves not only as a tribute to her but also to the many pupils who have passed through these doors. Some of whom have gone on to distinguished careers."

The Academy, as it turned out, occupied the very building that had once housed the Easterwood Academy. Joseph blinked in surprise as the realisation dawned, prompting a ripple of laughter from Helena.

"I had no idea! Adelaide never mentioned it was her old school, I'm sure of it. How serendipitous!"

Helena nodded, "Kathryn Easterwood was nearing retirement and struggling to find someone suitable to carry on the school's legacy. Adelaide believed it was fate, or divine intervention, depending on your leanings. It was the perfect solution. A portion of the museum is dedicated to Mrs Easterwood and her remarkable achievements. Sadly, she's no longer with us, but her memory is very much alive here at the Academy."

Joseph felt a quiet swell of pride rise within him. Through Adelaide's letters, he had come to know much of her journey, but standing here, surrounded by the tangible fruits of her vision, was profoundly moving. Her generosity struck him anew: scholarships were still awarded to gifted students of modest means, and the Saturday workshops she had begun in 1915 for children who had lost their fathers continued after yet another devastating war, when grief had once again settled over so many homes. This place was so much more than a place to learn. It was a living testament to compassion, resilience, and the enduring power of one woman's belief in the transformative potential of music as a force for healing.

After a very enjoyable few days exploring and enjoying Helena and Gabriel's company, it was time for them to travel to Dunedin to visit Douglas and his family. Helena warned Joseph that Douglas had never really recovered from losing his twin, and Woodlands would probably seem quite different to him. Even so, Joseph felt he should go, and anyway, he wanted to show Kitty some of the South Island before they travelled home.

The journey to Dunedin was an experience for Kitty, who had never travelled further than the Lake District to visit her friend, Maude. Joseph discovered the little guest house in Picton was still in business, and they enjoyed a few days exploring and taking in the beautiful scenery. When the train pulled into Dunedin station, there was no one to meet them, so taking a cab, they nervously made their way to the house, not knowing whether they would be welcome. With the care of his family, Douglas recovered from his traumatic experiences during the war. When he was ready to work, he secured a position under Simeon Hardwicke, a wealthy and influential businessman. Marrying Simeon's daughter, Prudence, two years later cemented his place as Hardwicke's Vice President. It was as if he had shed his past entirely. He was no longer the "twin that survived" but a hardened businessman moulded in his father-in-law's image. Together, he and Prudence had three sons, all of whom became deeply entrenched in the Hardwicke empire.

When Henry died in 1930, Douglas inherited Woodlands, and Victoria soon found herself evicted from the home she had cherished for nearly fifty years. Yet despite the upheaval, she found joy in her final years, cared for by Helena, Gabriel, and her granddaughters.

Joseph and Kitty's arrival at Woodlands was met with a chilly reception. Joseph saw no sign of the eleven-year-old boy he remembered so dearly. Instead of a quiet evening to allow Joseph to reconnect with his cousin and get to know his family, Prudence had arranged a grand dinner where Joseph and Kitty had to endure the company of strangers, and where Douglas and Prudence took great pleasure in flaunting their wealth and status.

Later, in the solitude of their room, Joseph kept apologising. "This is not the Woodlands I remember," he murmured. "Uncle Henry and Aunt Victoria will be turning in their graves."

The following morning, they departed before breakfast, unwilling to stay in the house any longer. As their taxi arrived at the entrance, Joseph saw Douglas standing in the doorway, arms crossed, a smirk playing at the corner of his mouth.

"Leaving so soon, cousin?" Douglas called, his tone laced with mockery. Joseph stopped abruptly, turning to face him. His voice was measured but firm as he delivered his final words—an unfiltered condemnation of the man Douglas had become. "You should be ashamed of yourself." He didn't wait for a response. Joseph then turned and strode away, stepping into the waiting car without a backwards glance.

Before they returned home, Joseph thought he should find out if Theodore Miller's bookshop was still in business, as it had meant so much to Adelaide. He knew Theodore would no longer be around, but perhaps his son, Louis, had carried on the family business. Helena wasn't sure, but she recalled Adelaide frequently visiting the bookshop.

Finding his way through the streets of Wellington felt strange to him. Much of it was unrecognisable, with new buildings and busier roads. After what seemed a long and painful walk, he spotted the shop. It was still called Miller & Sons, but the frontage had been newly painted and was bright and welcoming. One side of the shop was a small café; the other was still filled from ceiling to floor with books of every shape and size. It looked like it was thriving, and as Joseph entered the shop, he thought the ambience of the café and the bookshop together was wonderful.

"Good morning. How can I help you today?" A middle-aged woman with a cheerful smile greeted him.

Resting on his cane, he smiled and said, "I'm looking for Louis Miller. Is he still the owner of this establishment?"

"Why, yes, he is my husband. I am Mrs Francesca Miller. Do we know you?"

Joseph began to explain who he was and why he had come. Francesca raised her hand to interrupt him, a broad smile on her face and asked if he wouldn't mind waiting a moment while she went to get her husband. A few minutes later, Louis entered the shop and greeted Joseph warmly.

"Mr Ellwood, what a pleasure to meet you. I recall Adelaide frequently mentioning you. She used to give me piano lessons. I was so saddened to hear about her death during the Blitz; it was just awful, and her musical talent is sadly missed."

"Thank you, that's very kind of you to say. I felt I should come to see for myself. Obviously, the shop has changed somewhat since your father's time, but it is lovely to be here. This shop and your parents meant a lot to Adelaide."

Louis nodded in agreement. "As Adelaide did to my father. They remained great friends until he died in 1935. She would often bring him books to sell from her travels around the world. Even after everything with my sister, Adelaide remained a true friend, and my parents were very fond of her.

"May I enquire what happened to your sister? I have all Adelaide's journals and letters, but she never wrote about Eva after she was arrested."

"I don't blame her. It was a difficult time for all of us. Even after losing my brother, who fought so bravely for this country, we were ostracised, and I didn't think my parents would survive. I came home after the first war to a very different home, and it took a long time for people to accept us again, even though I was born here. Anyway, you wanted to know about Eva. She was supposed to be tried for treason. However, her insanity was evident by the time her trial began, and so instead she was locked away in a lunatic asylum somewhere in England, where she lived for a further ten years. Then, one day, she somehow managed to escape the nurses and climbed up onto the roof. As they started chasing her, in a moment of madness, she believed she could fly and sadly jumped off the roof. Well, that's the story we were told anyway, and after that, my sister's name was never mentioned again."

"I'm sorry; that must have been very hard on you all," Joseph said, unsure of what to say under the circumstances.

"It was a long time ago, and that part of my life is firmly locked away. The future is where we should look to!"

After a pleasant hour with Louis and Francesca, reminiscing, he returned to Helena's house feeling satisfied that he had solved another piece of the puzzle of his sister's life. The only part of her life he didn't know much about, and probably never would, was her relationship with William Armstrong. He would have liked to know more about him, especially if or when they finally tell Grace the truth.

Helena hugged her cousin tightly as they were about to board the boat to take them home. "It has been so wonderful to see you again, Joseph. Keep in touch, won't you?"
Hugging her back, he promised to write and looked forward to hearing all her news as well.

Sitting on the deck one morning, Joseph was staring out to sea as his wife occupied herself with knitting a jumper for one of their grandchildren.

"A penny for them," Kitty said.

Smiling, Joseph replied, "I was just thinking about how I have enjoyed visiting the place of my birth and seeing Helena again. Not so much, Douglas, but it was an enjoyable visit despite that. However, I can say without hesitation that Wellington no longer feels like home. My heart belongs to Liverpool, and more importantly, you and our children."

Epilogue

The day after Joseph revealed the truth about her real parents, Grace found herself aching to see him. Exhausted and raw, she stood at his front door, the weight of the last twenty-four hours pressing down like a storm cloud. When Joseph opened it, she stepped forward without a word and wrapped her arms tightly around him.

"Hello, Dad," she whispered.

He held her just as tightly. "My darling girl… That's what I needed to hear this morning. I haven't slept a wink—I've been so worried."

"Neither have I," Grace murmured, pulling back slightly. "Daniel and I talked most of the night. Poor thing had to drag himself to work this morning, but he helped me make sense of it all. It's still hard to grasp how a mother could walk away from her child like that… but I'm not angry. Not anymore."

She paused, her voice catching. "I've been blessed. Loved by two incredible people I'm proud to call Mum and Dad. And I'm lucky to have a wonderful brother—even if I wanted to throttle him sometimes when we were growing up."

Joseph smiled through tears that fell freely down his whiskery cheeks, listening to his daughter speak with such clarity.

Grace reached for his hand, her own tears matching his. "I'll miss Mum for the rest of my life. That sadness will always be with me—but that's okay. Isn't grief the proof of a life well spent? Not a reminder of absence, but of the richness and joy of having had her in our lives."

Joseph brushed a strand of hair from her cheek and smiled through the tears. "She'd be proud of you," he said softly.

Grace nodded, her hand still in his. "Of us."

And in that moment, surrounded by memory and love, they could move forward—not away from sorrow, but with it, folded gently into the shape of their lives.

Author's Note

Adelaide's Gift is a work of fiction, though true historical events are woven throughout as the story unfolds. I take full responsibility for any inaccuracies and hope, dear reader, you'll allow me a little artistic licence in the service of the tale.

The inspiration for this novel comes from my great-aunt, Valerie Claire Corliss—a woman born in Dunedin, New Zealand, in 1892, whose life I knew little about. During the quiet days of lockdown, with travel out of reach, I turned to the wonders of the internet and began my research. The turning point came thanks to my daughter, Christina, who contacted the National Library of New Zealand. I am deeply grateful to Dr Aleisha Ward, research librarian at the Alexander Turnbull Library, whose generous offer of a few hours' research opened the door to Valerie's remarkable legacy.

Valerie was a gifted lecturer and teacher, devoted to the art of musical interpretation and the works of the great composers. She played a pivotal role in organising the British Music Society throughout New Zealand and pioneered several initiatives that shaped the country's musical education, including summer schools for music teachers and widely sought advice on modern teaching methods. She represented the Tobias Matthay Pianoforte School in London and visited England on three occasions, exchanging ideas with some of the world's most celebrated artists: Tobias Matthay, Dr John McEwen, Sergei Rachmaninoff, Frederic Lamond, Sir Henry Wood, and Dame Myra Hess. Valerie also wrote extensively in the 1930s, contributing thoughtful articles such as The Orchestra in Relation to Pianoforte Teaching, The Art of Listening to Music, Music and Psychology, and Colour in Music and the Related Arts.

My great-grandfather, Cyril Esmond Corliss, affectionately

known as 'Ping,' captured my imagination from the start. He served as an engineer aboard RMS *Mauretania* between 1909 and 1911, before settling in Liverpool with his wife, Constance Winifred Roberts. I was ten when he died, and though my memories of him are few, they remain vivid. The most enduring is of him gently holding a small black-and-white photograph of his beloved wife, who had passed away in 1967. Even at that young age, I could sense the depth of his loss. I would sit quietly at his feet, transfixed, as he spoke of happier times—his voice soft, his gaze distant, as if reaching back through the years to touch what once was.

This story is my way of honouring them both and of breathing life into the fragments I uncovered and imagining the spaces in between. It is a tribute to resilience, creativity, and the quiet legacies that shape us across generations.

The idea that ordinary lives, especially those of women in history, can leave extraordinary imprints.

This work of fiction is a quiet tribute to those whose influence endures not through fame but through grace, creativity, and the lives they touched.

Anne Valerie Wilson
October 2025

Acknowledgements

This book is dedicated to everyone who walked beside me on my very first writing journey. Your support and encouragement throughout the process have meant a great deal, and I genuinely believe I wouldn't have finished the book without you. I hope you all recognise who you are, and I will be eternally grateful for your kindness and support.

In particular, I want to thank my dear mum, **Jill Wilson**, who fostered in me a love for the English language and a lifelong passion for reading. You never doubted my ability to write this book—even when I expressed my own doubts to you.

To my remarkable daughters, **Christina Burgess** and **Liane Orgill**, for their unconditional love and unwavering faith in my ability to complete this project. Thank you both for your patience with my endless ramblings and for your encouragement whenever I needed it, day or night!

To my wonderful grandchildren—**Hannah**, **Olivia**, **Harvey**, **Alex**, and **Sophie-Lee**. Your enthusiasm, delightful ideas, and unwavering faith in me inspire me greatly. Your encouragement was humbling and joyful in equal measure.

My twin brother, **Graham Wilson**, thank you for making the publication of this book possible and for your unlimited positivity and "just do it" attitude, which kept me motivated every step of the way.

Nicola Huelin, thank you for reading my tentative first draft and offering such enthusiastic and encouraging feedback.

Amanda Benton, I am deeply grateful for your wise advice and for guiding me around the streets of London, so I could imagine walking in Adelaide's footsteps.

Denise Gardner, my best friend—thank you simply for being you, and for believing in me.

Sonja Morrey, **Louise Cowell**, **Carolyn Hammond**, **Helen Pleece**—we met at school over fifty years ago, and when I finally found the courage to share with you that I had written a book, your excitement and encouragement meant the world to me.

Last, but certainly not least, my dear dad, **Peter Wilson**, whom we lost three years ago. I know he would have been proud, as he always was. I miss you, Dad.